THE FACELESS THING WE ADORE

HESTER STEEL

page

PAGE STREET HORROR

pAgE
PAGE STREET HORROR

Distributed by Macmillan, sales in Canada by The Canadian Manda
Group.

29   28   27   26   25   1   2   3   4   5

ISBN-13: 979-8-89003-289-8

Library of Congress Control Number: 2024946004

Edited by Alexandra Murphy
Cover and book design by Rosie Stewart for Page Street Publishing Co.
Cover illustration © Peter Strain

Printed and bound in China

To Jennifer & Cemil—middle finger up, and thank you x3
And to Megan, who I accidentally wrote this book for

"I have spent an all but sleepless night, I have told lies and made a fool of myself, and the very air tastes like wine. I have been frightened half out of my foolish wits, but I have somehow earned this joy; I have been waiting for it for so long."
—Shirley Jackson, *The Haunting of Hill House*

PART ONE

ADORE

CHAPTER ONE

INTO THIN AIR

I CUT OFF MY HAIR AT 3:00 A.M. IN AN AIRPORT BATHROOM.

I find the scissors in my bag; I must have slipped them in during the fight. So here I am, alone in a bathroom, with scissors I'll have to chuck out at security anyway, another scrap of my life I can't keep.

They gleam.

They say, *you've lost almost everything. Give a bit more.*

My hair hangs down my spine when it's loose. Every morning, I sit on the bed, wrapped in the duvet because the heat's always out, and weave my hair into an intricate plait while Craig plucks at his guitar and traffic grinds by.

I mean, I used to. Past tense.

So many memories are woven into that hair. I imagine them cut away, leaving me light like a bubble in a wide sky. Iridescent, insubstantial, pop.

I could go home. I could beg and be forgiven.

I eye myself: pale, skinny, with flower tattoos spilling over my shoulders.

My eyes are red from crying. I don't look like someone who hesitates.

Fluorescent light flickers off the blades. I snip off my plait.

It coils into the sink and sits there, hairs unspooling like worms. I examine my new self, head cocked. Messy. I keep chopping; every time I look up, I expect to have this badass pixie cut, but I just look alien and disheveled. So messy. I keep cutting. My jaw's tense.

"You all right, love?"

The woman behind me in the mirror wears a cleaning uniform, too much mascara, and a look of concern. Fair. Bits of hair cling to my neck, itching, and to my cheeks where I tried to wipe my tears and rubbed my skin raw.

"I'm fine." I give her a big, bright grin. "I just . . . need to change my identity. Um. For a job. I'm a spy?" My laugh comes out all frayed and untethered.

The cleaner reaches for her walkie-talkie, face flat. That familiar *Aoife, you're screwing up* look. I don't think the joke hit.

I look hideous.

"I, um, have to go." I push past her, only to hesitate in the doorway; the airport exit's there, the way back to my life. I can't do this. Look at me: My hair's a mess.

I imagine lemons, sun-warmed bark, the slippery skin of olives. So vivid they fill my senses. I *can* do this.

I walk toward the departure gates.

As the door swings shut, I glimpse the cleaner, sighing, preparing to sweep away the remnants of me.

Thirty-six hours ago, I stole something from my boss.

In fairness, you take what fun you can in Tallerton. Picture it: a town all faded under shop signs. All the gray anonymity of a city, none of the thrill, a dormitory town of accountants and consultants under a flight path. The best you can hope for there is a job in a chain pub where the customers' imaginations never go any further than what's under your shirt. Dreams die under concrete in that place.

That was me a day or so ago, dying under concrete, at my job at a chain pub, pouring drinks, ignoring my aching feet. Carpet patterns swirled, bleach and cider reeked, cheesy pop jangled, the TV scrolled local news, and I was being shouted at.

Being shouted at is quite normal for me, and there's a reason for that: I'm useless. Which is exactly what I was being informed of by a burly man in a farmer cap and suspenders. He thinks those give him personality, but I know his imagination, too, doesn't go much further than what's under my shirt. I learned that quickly when I first worked a late shift with him, and since I'd informed him that I had a boyfriend, my share of the tips had mysteriously shrunk and my workload had mysteriously doubled. Mind you, that might also be because I was useless.

"What the fuck is this? Don't try and answer, I know you'll struggle, I'll help you. This is a pile of post. Delivered this morning. Sitting here behind the bar. Let me guess, postman came and dropped it off and you . . . forgot what post was? Didn't know what post was in the first place? It goes. In. The. Back. Office." He enunciates slowly, like I'm a toddler. "On. The. Desk. Big wooden thing, four legs. Go! Go and do it before you get distracted by a pretty bit of fluff or something." The fluff in here was never pretty, only ever concerning. I nodded, hoping my blush wasn't too obvious, and slipped into the back office while my manager tutted and apologized to two pinstriped women waiting to order.

I was used to this. Some people bring out the rage in others, and it's a way to be noticed, at least. So I don't think it was any kind of resentment that drove me to flick through the letters and packages before putting them on the big wooden thing with four legs. Definitely not an urge to throw away something important just to make his life difficult. I wasn't even really aware what I was doing until my hand hesitated on a thicker brown paper envelope with a weight inside.

The handwriting on the address was bouncy and curly, little circles for the "I"s in my boss's name and a full-on smiley face scrawled in the corner. This was definitely personal, not work, and I was definitely meant to pass this on to him; the weight and shape of the object inside felt very much like a biscuit.

I peered through the door; he was deep in conversation with one of the regulars, ignoring a growing queue. I slipped a fingernail under the flap of the envelope.

Inside: a postcard, text side up; I didn't flip it yet, like the picture would be a fun surprise. I get so few fun surprises these days. Alongside it: a sandwich bag containing, yes indeed, a biscuit, flaky and flecked with poppy seeds.

Hi! Just wanted to wish you well and let you know no hard feelings about the whole firing thing. Including a biscuit so you'll know what lovely food I'm eating every day, and a picture so you'll see what a lovely place I'm living in now. Truly, thank you! Enjoy life in Tallerton! Elise xxx

I covered a snort. I vaguely remembered hearing about an Elise who worked here before me, but although our town's small, it's not the sort of place where you *know* people. Still, just from that, I liked her. What a deliciously petty thing to do. Imagine the courage and vividness a person must have to do something like that.

Perhaps that playful pettiness was contagious, because without really thinking, I unwrapped the biscuit and placed it on my tongue, flipping the postcard for my surprise.

The world flickered, like the connection was bad.

Crumbling on my tongue: honey-sugar, lemon, poppy seeds, spices I'd never known the name of; a little stale, must have been weeks in the mail, but still rich and sweet.

In my hands, images: ocean; cliffs; coves with twisty pines; a whitewashed village; spilling pink flowers; a vivid, cerulean sky—

Dizziness. The rush of blood in my ears echoed the pounding of waves.

My hand holding the postcard felt alien; the idea that it was a post-card—four photographs printed on cheap cardboard and already fraying at the edges—felt alien; the dank, beer-scented storeroom felt alien. Reality was there. Here, this me, was a shadow. My senses were with wind and chattering insects, warm earth, the taste of lemon. My skin blossomed with the touch of a sun I couldn't be feeling.

A logical part of me wondered if the biscuit was drugged somehow. I strangled the thought and stared down at the pictures of that place, at the name of the country scrawled in a corner, as though I could fall into them.

Time was off; how long had that biscuit been crumbling on my tongue? I swallowed, and in its place my mouth filled with an unaccountable laugh, which felt like relief. Something like bubbles and light condensed in my belly, like I was holding that place inside now, pine trees pressing against my stomach walls, flowers twining through my lungs, saltwater crashing inside my bones—

"Aoife, are you going to be in there all day? We have *customers*!"

I jolted, and reality fell back together, small and cold. "Coming!" I slipped the postcard into my back pocket, slapped the crumbs away from my fingers, and hurried back out to the bar.

I stumbled through my shift, muddling orders, jumbling numbers, baffling customers. All the while, something sang in me. I walked home like the pavements were clouds and dreamed of tumbling through saltwater, of a cave in a cliff. I woke restless and crushed my life between my fingers.

CHAPTER TWO

BIRD OF PARADISE

AND NOW I'M OUTSIDE AN AIRPORT IN A CITY I'D ONLY HEARD OF A FEW DAYS ago, watching dried flowers swept up in hot wind and traffic. The sky is pastel-pink at the edges, the mountains are craggy, sleeping beasts. I'm gripped with panic: *What have I done?* I'm glowing: *I did it.*

I hunt for a taxi rank, adjusting the straps on the little canvas backpack that contains my whole world now. I packed it in a tearful rush, Craig yelling. I wonder what he'll do with the stuff I left. Burn it? Keep it, in case I come home—

My eyes burn. It's not home, just a place where I was waiting for my real life to start. I always thought there was a door in it somewhere, and me and Craig would step through into something better. If there was, it's slammed shut for me now. But that's the universe, right? It's *full* of doors. There's one here somewhere, creaking open for me; I'm going to find it.

Instagram and Pinterest and travel blogs promised pastel architecture and fruit pastries, gorges and forests, a sliver of coast giving way to a clutch of islands. Feels far away from the glass and cement and tarmac, the peeling signs for resorts and car-hire firms, the corrugated-plastic taxi stand—*there it is*. But the windblown palms and pink-soaked hills hint that those promises weren't a lie.

A wild to vanish into, and something out there, *calling*.

I jump into a battered taxi with a dashboard plastered with stickers of saints and footballers. The driver's got a farmer cap. It smells of must and dirt in here. Must and dirt smell like adventure.

"Hotel?"

I'm buzzing; no way I could sleep. "Take me somewhere interesting?" I feel like a pinball pinging, trusting spin and gravity. Something's tugging me but won't give me a direction yet; it doesn't compel me, just tempts me to follow and find out. "City center, I guess."

We roll onto the highway, following signs toward the city. Billboards I can't read flash by; trees I can't name bask under the sun. Travel-bleary and overexcited, I let it all blur into colors and try to listen to that tug, like it's the universe talking, guiding me toward that open door, rather than just a fragment of fantasy. If I listen really carefully, it sounds like waves whispering, wind in lemon trees, laughter, rhythmic song—

And there it is, as my eye catches a signpost: a mad sense that I've seen it before, been here before. The rushing in my ears redoubles; can I taste lemon?

"Here," I say, before I can second-guess it. "There. That one. The archaeological site."

The driver looks at me sidelong but turns onto the dusty side road, pulling up into a car park under regimented trees. We're still far from any sign of a city, but this can't be too weird, right? I'm a tourist, here's a tourist attraction. Though by the looks of it, not one that many people bother to come to.

I fumble for my wallet; my stomach plummets. Fuck. I forgot to get cash.

How are you even alive? Craig would laugh, when I had what he called my "Aoife moments." And I'd say, *You,* and he'd grin and say, *Bloody right, you wouldn't last a day without me.*

And now I am. Without him.

The driver gives this exhausted sigh. The kind of thing I usually inspire.

I end up doing some probably illegal money exchange with an equally exasperated ticket seller, but pretty soon the driver's grumbling and my excitement's slumped into nausea. I collapse onto a bench, head in hands, sun starting to burn. What am I doing?

I look up. A path between trees. Olive, I think. Those little pale leaves.

I'm meant to be here. I waited my whole life for the universe to direct me to the path it was opening for me. I think I finally heard it speak. Refusing to prepare or plan can be freeing, if I don't look down.

The path's dappled. My steps stir dust; crickets chirp.

I don't read the information signs, just step through the tree line. The shame and sickness evaporate.

A cluster of monoliths stand sentinel before a panorama of trees, cliff, and ocean. I've never seen a sea like that: royal-blue, edged with jade and lacy foam. The stones loom, shadows sharp.

Nobody's here. I'm alone with something ancient and a sky a thousand miles too wide.

My breath's shallow. This is more than excitement. The word might be *holy.*

The breeze breathes in the treetops, but all else is quiet, even the insects and birds muffled. My heartbeat reverberates as I approach the stones. So ancient that the fingers that carved those images must be dust now. Simple shapes: a closed circle inside an open circle, bisected by a single line.

Is it the sun that's making me dizzy? I rest my fingers against the stone.

The cave yawns. It's dark out here, stars and branches, but in there the blackness is complete, drawing me in—

A laugh echoes, startling in the stillness.

I blink; I can't remember what had me so absorbed. I look around, like I've been caught doing something, but nobody's there. The sound came from further on.

Past the fence hung with signs saying Dig Site, No Entry, and Danger. The fence with a hole in it.

What's the worst that could happen? Booby traps. Gateways between worlds. Monsters. Quicksand?

The tugging inside my skin whispers, *Yes.*

I peel back the wire and slip through.

Among the trees, the crickets are even louder. Leaves rustle, shivering shadows. Two bags are propped against a tree, a rainbow tote bag and a practical leather rucksack; a sketchbook sits on top, creamy pages open.

My fingers itch with jealousy at the drawings, of spindly trees and clustered rocks. I forgot my sketchbook, didn't I? It's in my underwear drawer. Craig will—

No. I slip off my bag and lay it next to the others. Look, they're together. I'm part of something.

Hidden among the trees, I peer out.

A patch of dry grass edges a plunging cliff. There's another standing stone, bigger. At its foot are two women: early twenties, around my age.

One's cross-legged, khaki dress spread around her, hands in her lap. She's small and snub-nosed, mousy-brown hair in a bun, smile clear and pure. I sometimes spotted people at home and felt this kind of immediate liking, twisted into yearning this way, imagining them as my friends.

Never spoke to them. What would I say?

It's the other girl who captivates me, though.

She's colors. Her plump chest swells under a mustard-yellow vest, her wide hips and belly curve inside blue trousers, a hot-pink scarf binds her curls. She's expansive in a way that fills the world, mouth lipsticked and laughing.

I think of bright-colored coral reef fish. I don't know what a *bird of paradise* is, but that's what enters my head.

What turn did the world take that she gets to be so vivid, and I'm stuck as me?

"Go on, then," her friend says. Softly accented English. "If you *dare*."

"Of course I dare," the bird-of-paradise girl says, her accent American, words caught in the eddy of a laugh.

She wriggles out of her vest and trousers, snatches off her scarf, and stands naked.

I should, um. Walk away. This is evidently not archaeology going on here.

The girl inhales. It's not her body that's captivating me—that's just making me go red—it's her expression, like she feels the sun in every cell. Like she feels something else.

Something else. Something more. I don't know what it is she's soaking in, but it's something I've craved throughout a quiet, ordinary lifetime. Something childhood stories and commute fantasies promised and never delivered.

She kneels in front of the other girl. I hadn't noticed the wreath of flowers on the rock beside her, but the seated girl places it on the bird-of-paradise girl's brow, reverent: brilliant pink blooms, a froth of grape leaves, and pine sprays.

They begin to chant, softly. My chest tightens. There's a familiarity to its rhythm; I've never heard it, but it's like it's been echoing in my breath and heartbeat since I was born. I strain to make out the words. Something about surrendering?

The naked girl's hands come together, fingers twisting, eyes closing, face transcendent; she stretches toward the sky and begins to dance.

The air grows thin. Everything's oversaturated, lines sharp, colors dazzling. I taste ozone, my skin prickling like lightning's about to strike.

She's lost in something ecstatic, aglow with it; no colors are naturally that bright. The light seems to split into rainbows around her, and she smiles so impossibly wide, like she sees it even through her closed eyelids.

Adore. That's one of the words of the chant. *Adore*, something, *surrender*—

Existence flickers like a signal lost in a storm. My senses overflow with lemon and salt and sweetness, the rhythm of waves in my ears.

And then she laughs, and something breaks, and she flops back onto the rock beside her friend. And I have no idea what I just saw or felt, but my heart is jackrabbit-fast and my mouth is dry as all this dusty earth, and the tugging in my skin has become a happy thrumming.

Craig sneers in my head. *You bloody perv. See one girl naked and you think you're having a religious experience or something.*

I was meant to be here. I know it suddenly. I was meant to see that.

I can't exactly step out and say, "Hi, naked lady I've just been spying on," can I?

I know what I can do, though.

When I was little, my mother had a vase. I thought it was the prettiest thing in the world with its roses and gilded mouth. And there was a day, one of many days when I wanted my mother to play with me and she didn't even have time for a "Not now, Aoife."

So I dropped the vase and watched the pieces scatter across the kitchen tiles.

I stared. I did that. I made the world different.

I liked when mum was angry. She noticed me. But I got scared, too; I cried and said it was an accident. When she'd finished shouting, we tried to fix it. And after it was full of cracks, but it had a story, and I'd had *hours* with my mum, all to myself.

That was when I learned that sometimes you have to make the world different, even if things end up broken. To show people that you exist, and that existence has consequences.

When I was fifteen, there was a boy, my friend's older brother. He was beautiful, with messy hair and playful eyes. He played guitar; his songs sounded like something outside our narrow town.

So I snuck into his bedroom and stole one of his books of chords.

I scrawled all over it, drawing his face, his hands plucking strings, illustrations of the lyrics. I slipped back into his room and left it there.

Later, he cornered me and asked if I'd done it. I blushed, but he said, "You're a good artist." The world swirled; doors opened; he forgave me. He wrote a song: "Aoife Made a World on Paper." Two weeks later, he kissed me. Two years later, we ran away. And then I never needed to show the world that I existed. My world was Craig. He knew.

But I remember that instinct.

I don't know how to approach these impossible girls. So I just go back to the bags, snatch the sketchbook, and take off.

CHAPTER THREE
BEAUTIFUL SECRETS

My mind's turning circles. As I mangle attempts to ask directions, I replay memories of the girls, of the uncanny sensations that filled my body. As I walk through the growing heat to the bus stop, I feel the enticing weight of the sketchbook. As I sit on the bus and watch the hills thicken into a chaotic urban stew, I'm remembering the bliss on her face. Was it longing for that bliss that captured me, or was it something *more*? Anything feels possible.

Why else this pull, that taste of lemon? Something is here for me, and I'm twitching in the bus seat, every instant drawing me closer.

The city punches into my awareness, cement suburbs giving way to alleyways, shutters, palm trees. I join the crush of bodies spilling off the bus and walk for hours, passing souvenir shops, pigeons, streetside cafés.

I slip into one and order a coffee. Even something so mundane feels adventurous in this newly shaped world. The coffee's thick and zinging. I breathe the scent of jasmine sprawling across a whitewashed wall. Sun on my face. Free.

I take out the sketchbook, another wrapped gift to tear into. The hand-writing's squirmy, Spanish or Italian. Little symbols: a closed circle inside an open circle, closed eyes above an open mouth. Sketches: faces, flowers, a house overgrown with vines, a beach—

A cave, stretching open—

I blink away vertigo. These little coffees are strong.

I flick through further, new pages, new vistas; new handwriting, which I'm pretty sure is English, just illegible. A rough scrawl, like the person couldn't contain their excitement. Lists bullet-pointed with stars, occa-sional words in all caps: TEMPLE, BRONZE AGE, BREAKAWAY CULT, ORIGINS. There are far more exclamation marks than is normal or acceptable.

I flip back and my chest seizes with relief: There's a note in English inside the cover. IF FOUND, PLEASE CONTACT GIULIA ROSSI. A smiley face and an email address.

Giulia. Is she the bird-of-paradise girl, or her friend with that sweet, inscrutable smile? I whisper the name like an incantation, then attempt to tap out an email on my phone:

Hi, I'm Aoife—Delete.

You don't know me, but—Delete.

I saw you chanting and dancing naked and the whole universe went swirly. I'm not sorry that I stole from you so I could see you again. Definitely delete.

Hi, I found your notebook in the car park at the standing stones?

A flimsy lie, but safest. I look up at shop windows glittering and pas-tel paint peeling and tourists posing. I'm newborn into a new world. I shouldn't be afraid of anything.

I hover my finger over the SEND icon, but find myself paralyzed with nerves. I blink before the nerves do, and pocket my phone. Later. I'll be brave later.

It's hours before I find a hostel because I'm busy wrapping myself up in the chaotic streets. The hostel has wrought-iron balconies and a terrace draped with vines. I adore it. The receptionist, a young local, grins sidelong at me like we're old friends; a couple of travelers playing backgammon wave.

Am I made to be in this world? This feels right.

I ask for two nights and hand over my card, then watch a tabby cat licking its paws until the receptionist says, "Sorry, that's been declined."

That can't be right. I just got paid, I'd worked extra shifts; we had *savings*. *We.*

Reality pops and drenches me in cold.

I make him try it again, and again, and then drop into an armchair and shake as I open my banking app. The brightness is falling away, and I'm tumbling into this horrible pit of suspicion that's widening in my belly.

We share the account. We agreed. We're a unit. And there it is: Three days ago, my pay; then yesterday evening, Craig Bauer transferred the entire contents of this account into the private one he uses for his band.

I know he was scared for me, going off alone. He'd have emptied the account to stop me from getting on the plane, to protect me from myself, not realizing I'd be too silly to check my balance. Desperate measures, except he forgot what a mess I am.

The pixels blur and wobble. It's Saturday night, his band has a gig, he'll be drunk; if I message him, he won't see it even if he hasn't blocked me and why would he reply after how I treated him and oh god what have I done—

Fucked it up, haven't you? Aoife's fairy-tale fantasies, meet the real world.

The receptionist brings me tea when he sees I'm crying, which makes me cry more, and oh god, I'm a wreck. I must be having a breakdown. I was spying on a naked person. I've barely slept. I cut off my *hair*.

I wipe my eyes and try. "Do you have any jobs going?"

The guy's sympathetic look is almost believable. "In this economy?"

I try to imagine my parents' reaction if I called them for the first time in five years, asking for a loan. "Thank you. All right. Thanks."

I try to think. There aren't options. *Help.* A few minutes ago, I was blessed and called and drunk on it. Now—

Now I have to be brave.

I open my email again, open the draft message to Giulia Rossi, and without taking a second to think about it, press SEND.

The reply is almost instantaneous.

I arrive at the restaurant early; I don't have anywhere else to go. I have ten pounds left. I turn two into a lemonade. Everything's hopeless anyway.

I threw my life away for this: a harbor lined with terracotta-roofed buildings, an orange sunset soaking yachts and spindly palms. A lemonade. A sketchbook.

Still, when I touch the pages, my heartbeat ratchets up. It's like the universe is whispering: *Just trust. I'm keeping my promise.* I still feel that. I *won't* let it slip away.

But if this doesn't lead to anything—and what could it?—where will I go?

I squeeze my eyes shut. I won't cry again. I'm on an adventure.

When I open my eyes, I see them.

They're laughing, lit up by strung-up café bulbs. The bird-of-paradise girl touches her friend's wrist, a gesture so intimate that my breath catches. There's the closeness there of two souls that have happily swallowed parts of each other. A little gesture that just says *love*.

I feel hollow. Did I ever have friends like that? It's been so long; I've been busy.

The bird-of-paradise girl strides toward me like she knows me. She's read my awkwardness, or she spotted me this morning. An image of her naked body flashes behind my eyes, and I think I turn a bit purple.

"Yes, you're here!" She claps, making her bangles ring. "It's Aiofe, right?"

"Ee-fa," I correct her, then I feel stupid. What am I doing, the first thing I say being to tell her she's wrong? Now I'm stuck. "Like *if* in a really bad fake accent."

She actually laughs, but my blush deepens anyway, like by giving her my name I've exposed myself, messed up somehow.

"Aoife, sweet." The bird-of-paradise girl sits down, right there, opposite me. "I'm Larissa, this one's Giulia."

Larissa. A new invocation. I nearly say, "I'm Aoife" again, but I swallow it just in time. "Hi."

"You rescued my book!" Giulia focuses that warm beam of a smile on me. "Thank you! If I don't bring the sketches from the temple, Kiera will kill me."

Larissa's laugh is bubbly. "Behead you with a ballpoint pen."

I smile. I have no idea who they're talking about, although I want to, desperately, wishing suddenly that I'd read the signs at the site, that I could tie it to all the hints in the sketchbook, draw a clear map to find my way. *Temple.*

My fingers tighten on the sketchbook, the fierceness of my grip surprising me. I surprise myself again by blurting, "What were you doing there?"

Larissa narrows her eyes, glances around, then leans forward. "*Sneaky stuff.*"

"Sneaking badly," Giulia sighs.

"Well"—Larissa's lip tweaks—"if someone saw us, we were sneaking *terribly.*"

Our eyes meet; hers are amused, mine must be horrified. She *knows* I saw her, and she's probably added it up about the notebook and sure, if I leave I have nowhere to go, but I'm considering walking off into the wilderness until I become a tree or something.

Giulia meets my eyes. Hers resonate with a curiosity about me that matches mine about her; there's sympathy, too. "Are you hungry? You look hungry."

I stammer. "H-how can I look hungry? I'm not, like, coming across as a starving orphan or something, am I?"

My god. Literally everything I say is wrong.

Giulia rattles off a list to the waiter, then turns back to me. The amusement in her smile is conspiratorial. "You've been staring at everyone else's food since we got here."

My own laugh is brighter and higher than I'm used to. "You got me."

"It's on us." Larissa must have noticed the tension in my shoulders; it starts to ease.

Giulia nods. "We owe you a thank-you for our book." She holds out a hand.

I grip the sketchbook. I'll give it to them, we'll eat, then they'll take it away and this door will close like all the others.

My hand won't open.

"What is all this? In the sketchbook. At the temple. I want . . ." *I want to know what I felt, when the colors got bright and the air hummed and I tasted lemon like I do in my dreams.* "I want to know, if I'm going to give this back."

I wait for fallout.

"Why do you care why two weirdos are getting naked in an archaeological site?" Larissa's tone's casual, but alertness glints. I try not to quail.

Giulia pours wine from the zigzag-painted jug deposited on our table. Through the golden liquid, the tables mutate, and the boats and buildings twist into new shapes.

"It sounds like a cool story?" Okay, good. That was a good thing to say.

"Legitimate reason to hold something hostage." Larissa raises her glass. Chunky turquoise and coral rings clink. "But you go first. Pray tell, why were *you* stumbling across us in the first place?"

We touch glasses. I shouldn't drink alone in a strange city with no idea where I'm sleeping. The wine is sweet and crisp. I like it. I will have more.

"I broke up with my boyfriend." The words squeeze my throat. It's the first time I've said them. "We were having problems, and I saw a postcard from this country, and—"

And I felt this call, but I can't say that. I'll go with the easier story, the one I was telling myself. That Craig had fallen for this impulsive, free spirit that had guttered out once we hit the reality of a cold home and bills and late shifts. And I tried to be that girl again, so he'd remember why he wanted me.

I can't lie to those eyes, those playful dark ones, those warm hazel ones. I'm going to hold out the truth like a hand they might take.

"So I bought tickets. For the next day. So we could have an adventure. Anyway, he . . ." This isn't coming out flippant. Try harder. "He wasn't happy about me spending our rent and risking my job. Fair play. He said some things that I guess needed to be said, and—" *He kicked me out, he kicked me out, don't cry, don't cry.* "I didn't have anywhere to go, but I had this ticket, so I . . . went."

Larissa mouths, "Hell yes." Giulia touches my hand, surprising me.

I shouldn't still be talking, so I talk fast. "I'm on my own and I'm excited and scared and I have no money and I don't know what to do."

This is going so wrong. At least I didn't say the thing that will tip me over from pathetic to deranged. About the *pull*. The pull that—I see it now—intensified when I saw them.

"You're brave." Giulia squeezes my hand.

"What's your plan?" Larissa asks.

I shrug. I try to remember what I was imagining. I wasn't. It was all light, unformed.

The immediate future is that food appears, and we forget everything because *food*. Shrimps, cheeses, crispy leaves in tangy sauces. Sharpness and richness and chili burn. My throat's too busy gulping food to choke on tears. Sometimes it's worth throwing away your life for a mouthful of spiced soup in a fairy-lit café. Sometimes there's just now.

Larissa says something about "food silence" and how this food is nearly as good as at *home*. I nibble cheese and walnuts and wonder where their home is. They seem happy. Bold, wrapped up in life, relaxed together. There are things I miss; I can't place what they are.

Giulia stands, gesturing at the bathroom. Larissa continues mopping up sauce. "I'm *saying*. The food's even better on the islands. Wait until you get there, you'll see."

I put down my fork and sigh, looking up into the fairy lights. "I don't think I'm going to get to see them."

"Of course you are!" Larissa finishes her bread, a big bite; she eats with so much relish, lives with so much relish. I wish I had her optimism. "You're coming with us, right?"

The lights go swimmy. I'm blindsided, giddy, fireworks. "I—"

"Listen." She leans forward over the table, like she's going to reach for my hand, but she doesn't, just looks in my eyes, intent. "There's an island. A half day from here by ferry. It's where we live now, and it's . . ." A flash of that transcendence she showed this morning. "It's not like anywhere else in the world. Not like all *this*. It's pure and it's strange and it's gorgeous, and there's secrets there." Her eyes narrow, just slightly, like she's reading me. Or like she already recognizes the pull in me, the mystic madness that would allow me to tear apart my life and run off into the unknown. "Beautiful secrets."

My breath's half-held. I nod, although there wasn't a question. The taste of oil and lemon, the harbor lights, they're backdrop; it's all her, the whole world is those sparking, dark eyes.

She breaks her gaze away and begins to eat again. "And like I said. Food's like this, but like times fifty. We're heading back tomorrow, and I cannot *wait*."

"And you're inviting me?" I misunderstood. I misunderstood, of course I did, people don't make offers like that. I brace for the embarrassment.

"I'm *asking* you to come, actually. I'd like you to be there with us."

I can't think of any time ever that someone told me that.

There's a quiet while it becomes real.

"What do you think?" Curls spill around big eyes. I'd follow her anywhere; it's like she's that voice of the universe. Like the call is coming from those lips. "Fancy another impulsive adventure?"

What other option do I have? If I did, would I take it? Of course not. I came to find this. It found me.

"I'd love to," I whisper.

CHAPTER FOUR

MISSING

I CRASH IN THEIR HOTEL ROOM; THEY GIVE ME AN ENTIRE BED, CURL UP together in the other. Giulia warns that where we're going is remote: patchy internet and phone reception on the way, none once we reach our destination. I don't bother to message anyone. I'm ready to vanish.

I lie awake listening to their breathing, to the breeze tapping vines against the window, until exhaustion takes me. My dreams are indistinct shafts of light and shadow, and smell of earth and lemon, saltwater and honey.

I'm still half in dreams as we make our way to the port and the ferry powers through fog, muffled islets drifting by.

We chat over polystyrene coffee cups. It's easy, being around them; they work to make it that way. We compare my Tallerton to Larissa's Denver and Giulia's Milan, discuss bands, pizza toppings, travel destinations. Safe routes for me to slide into their world.

They've both been away from *home*, the mysterious home we're heading toward, for several weeks, Giulia doing something with family property in Italy and Larissa doing a permaculture course in Greece. The excitement of return bubbles. Larissa's twisting her rings, whooping into the wind that flutters her rainbow dress. Giulia closes her eyes, savoring the pitch and plunge of the boat, face suffused with joy.

I don't ask what's ahead; why spoil the surprise?

I scan the horizon instead, eager to see it. I feel like it's eager to see me, too.

I blink away the image; a fragment of a dream, my vision clears and—

That hazy shape emerging from the mist: I know. Something thrums, everything thin and bright, a now-familiar feeling. Something resonates, my body answering. Like I've been here.

Dark. Cold rock at my fingers, cold water around my ankles—

The image is gone, forgotten too fast to grasp.

The water fades to turquoise, flashing with fish. Shapes form on the shore: whitewashed buildings, beaches. Olive terraces, fishing boats, slender trees.

It doesn't surprise me, really, that the scents, the colors, the breeze, are exactly what those half-real sensations promised. A shiver runs through me, and I can almost translate it. If it had words, they would be: *Yes, you are so close now.*

———⊖———

The island envelops us in quiet like nothing I've ever heard.

We follow a dirt road between lapping sea and pines. The scent of salt and herbs is sharp after a lifetime of diesel fumes and rainy pavements. I'm childlike, bouncing, *pointing* at everything. Red flowers! A lizard!

A painted fishing boat! With every step I spot something new and with every step I am closer to something, and I can't gauge the distance but it's shrinking moment by moment. And moment by moment, I swear that attraction is getting stronger, the subtle tug becoming a magnetic pull.

Giulia and Larissa put up with my overexcitement. Their eyes are shiny, too.

A village appears as we round a headland, and it's not the source of that tug of temptation, I know, but I still stop short and stare. It's gold stone and white paint, a scattering of vine-crawled houses around a narrow harbor. A pocket of life miles from anywhere, bathed in white sunlight, spiked with palms.

This *place*. I want to drink it. I want it to drink me.

Giulia and Larissa have stopped, too, wrapped up in a kiss, slow and soft, Larissa's hand sliding along Giulia's hip. They haven't been couple-y around me before, and a twinge needles through me. Maybe it's Craig's absence that makes me wish it was me shivering under Larissa's lips.

They break apart and look at me, matching smiles, matching blushes, matching curiosity at my reaction to the village.

My mouth is dry. "Is *this* where you live?"

Larissa grins, indulgent, like I'm a toddler who's asked if a puddle is the sea. "Nah. Our place is further. This is *nothing* next to it, trust me."

I trust her.

Giulia checks the time. "Best not try and make the hike today, unless we camp out. I don't think Aoife wants to sleep on a rock somewhere?"

I absolutely want to sleep on a rock somewhere. But Larissa's already sweeping us toward a pastel-pink café with a hand-painted sign saying, Rooms to Rent.

I linger outside the wooden door, like the harbor, the impossibly blue sea, might vanish. All this beauty feels like a rice paper skin that could be torn away, and I don't want to look away from it, so I don't, flopping down onto a bench for a moment and turning my face up to the sun. Pink flowers dance in the corners of my vision.

I wait until enough time has passed that I feel mildly neglected, then gather up my bag and step inside the café. The cool of thick stone walls washes over me first, then the enticing smell of food, then the sound of a muffled sob.

Giulia's elbows are propped on the bar top, and her head's in her hands. I know the sound of someone hiding tears through gritted teeth. I got good at that.

Larissa's arm is around her, and she's glaring at the barman, who has a face like a slammed door and is glaring back. I rush over, then hesitate before placing an awkward hand on Giulia's back. I look to them both for an explanation, but get nothing.

"I thought she'd be back," Giulia's saying. "She . . . I thought she'd come back by now. I thought—" She looks up at Larissa, maybe not seeing me, maybe not caring. Her words are a cautious step. "He was angry with her, wasn't he?"

Larissa ignores me too. "Lia. *No.* He loves her. He loves us all. Please don't think like that."

My stomach clenches. *He loves us all.* Imagine being part of an *all*, and *loved*.

Larissa gives me a subtle nod, a gesture toward the door. I know she means, *I've got this.* It shouldn't feel like a slap.

Outside the light smarts my eyes, but I relish the pain; who knew sunshine could be this bright? It flutters on the water, catches in the palms. I slide into a plastic chair and scuff my toe against a cobblestone, frustrated even among all the beauty. I shouldn't want so hard for it to be my business, whatever they've got going on here, whoever *she* is. Whoever they meant by *he*, who loves them all. Larissa's voice had been warning and reverent all at once.

"What can I get you?" A shadow cuts across the paper tablecloth. The waitress's English is polished, her hair is dyed maroon, and her smile is forced. I know; I smiled that smile for years.

"Um. Lemonade?"

She doesn't move. The mask slips; behind it there's hostility, but curiosity, too. "You're going with those girls? Across the island?"

"I am." Things feel weird, off. But that fact is still a bright ray across everything.

Her eyes dart to the door, then settle on me, appraising. "You know what's up there?"

I shake my head. I *like* not knowing.

"I wouldn't go," she says. "I don't know much about that place, but it's nothing good. That poor girl . . . ." She looks at me expectantly, like she's daring me to ask, and when I don't, stubbornness outweighing curiosity, she folds her arms. "I don't want to have to give your family bad news if they come looking for you."

As if my family would care.

Our eyes lock, sympathy and sternness meeting nerves and defiance. Turning back feels impossible. *Is* impossible. I don't even have money for the ferry, and that fact is a relief, keeping me bound to the only path I want to be on. I'll ask about *that poor girl*, in a moment, of course I will. But I'm bound into this now.

She relents first, pulls out a notebook and begins to sketch. "At least let me help. There's no phone signal up there; you can't call for help. I'll draw a map. If you have to run, best you don't get lost."

This feels absurd, paranoid; it doesn't inspire fear, only curiosity about how somewhere gets a reputation like that. I unfold the paper. An island, marked with a triangle mountain, a dotted line path, a few landmarks, and two crosses: *village* and *farmstead*.

She's looking at me weirdly. Like I'm already gone.

I imagine trusting her and telling her everything. I imagine her having a spare bedroom full of flowers, space for an easel, a job going in the café. She'd teach me to cook local food. I'd get a tan, never venture out of the village, and never go home.

Something kicks out against the fantasy. I didn't come all this way to feel *safe*.

I say, "Thanks," then, "Lemonade?"

Her face goes flat.

It's my turn to relent; I feel like I'm doing her a favor by even asking. "What did you mean by *that poor girl*? Did something happen?"

She jerks a thumb at a poster in the café window. "I'll get your lemonade." And she's gone.

I look around; no sign of Giulia and Larissa. Just an old man strolling along the harborside, a few fishermen mending nets in a boat. I get up and peer at the poster.

It looks fresh; a printed sheet, nothing official. In the photo, the girl looks happy. Her eyes are crinkled above cheeks ruddy with cold, wind splaying strands from her ponytail around the hood of her jumper, a can of beer in her hand. And I've seen her before, a background face, on buses, behind a bar. You don't know people in Tallerton, exactly, but there's a familiarity.

Below are the words MISSING PERSON and a name: Elise Calloway.

The girl who sent the postcard.

CHAPTER FIVE
NOBODY WILL MISS YOU

I SPEND THE AFTERNOON ALONE. LARISSA AND GIULIA HAVE RETREATED TO A room above the café, according to the waitress; they didn't tell me. I drag a sick weight of embarrassment and loneliness and confusion as I wander the village.

Still, I lose myself in the streets, in radios playing songs in unfamiliar chords, in the wind rippling through laundry. I'm really here, and it dazzles.

I dip my toes at a scrappy beach, watching threads of light netting my bare feet. The waves sound like the island breathing. What's it inhaling? Me, I hope.

I try to worry; I feel like I should worry. The poster said that Elise was last seen on this island a few weeks ago, probably not long after she sent that postcard. I wish I'd remembered to pack it, to check the date. There's been no news broadcasts; the island isn't crawling with police. Someone's looking for her, someone cares. But a cheap printed poster feels so vague, like she stepped out somewhere and was just gone.

And now here I am, finding her postcard then accidentally following her to the very place where she was last seen.

That should be scary. But it feels like a confirmation, like fate dancing a path for me. The *yes* in me resounds even louder. Like I've almost got it.

Elise. Whatever happened to her brought this island to me.

I find Larissa and Giulia on the café terrace when I return. Larissa jumps up to hug me; her grip's fierce and releases relief. It feels good. I could melt into her colors.

Giulia's smile is wan. She says, "I'm sorry, hey?" and passes me a glass of wine. "We . . . had bad news."

I think *Elise*, but just squeeze her hand, like she did for me last night.

That look, it's like she's sizing me up from a new angle. I try a hopeful smile, but something turns stony on her face. My hand sits on hers, awkward, until I pull it away.

Larissa raises her glass; I clink mine against it and sip. This wine is sharper. There's pine resin, in the wine or the breeze.

We're quiet for a while, subdued. Elise lingers between us. Missing. *Gone somewhere.* I can't place why that feels good.

When Giulia heads inside to order dinner, Larissa brightens and turns to me. "I hope you like hiking. It's a hell of a journey. You'll be *aching*." I imagine she relishes that ache like she relishes everything. Her tongue snakes out, licking a droplet of wine off her thumbnail.

I toy with the saltshaker. Mentioning Elise feels like an invasion, so I say the other dangerous thing. "The waitress said . . . it isn't safe."

Larissa huffs, then smiles. Both are reassuring. "Of course. The villagers put up with us because we spend money, but they say *all sorts of things* behind our backs."

I look at the wine, like they might have drugged it, and Larissa laughs, so I laugh too.

"Point is . . ." She shakes back her hair, watching the sunset like it's a gift specifically for her. "There are . . . secrets, up there. But you didn't ask for an easy ride, did you? And like I said. They're beautiful."

The happiness spills out of her eyes and into me. Beautiful secrets. That's what I came here for. And she's a beautiful secret, and I'm in on it. I'm about to plunge into something, and it feels like that something is Larissa, a girl as wide as the world, spilling her colors into the uncanny blue-pink sky.

A shadow crosses the table; Giulia coughs. I pull back, heartbeat spiking, realizing how deeply I'd been gazing into Larissa's eyes.

The tension relaxes after a while, and we drink late into the evening, as the lights come on, bobbing in reflections. The stars transfix me: so *many*. Larissa giggles, sharing in my delight; Giulia smiles thinly, eyeing me like she's trying to solve a riddle. It's me and Larissa talking, really. Giulia just watches, inscrutable.

At last, Larissa stretches. "I need *sleep*. Bedtime for me, darlings."

Giulia pauses, swirling her wine. "I'd like to talk to Aoife. Can we walk?"

Larissa nods like the question was for her. "Sure. See you upstairs."

"A walk sounds good," I say, like I'm reclaiming the question, although my chest tightens.

As we stroll along the harborside, Giulia slips her arm through mine, startling me. Where do these two get the audacity to share touches so confidently?

The road skirts a farm wall, the stone storing a trace of the day's heat; we rest against it, staring at an expanse of dark sea. Look: The sea's clear enough to see stones in the shallow water, even by night.

"Aoife," Giulia says. Foreboding sinks through me. "I like you, okay?"

Over the wall, trees stand in rows, their arms twisty. The village lights glow. Above, the stars; ahead along the path, the dark.

"But?" I guess.

"But," Giulia swallows. "I don't think you should come with us."

That hit you like a truck, didn't it, love? Why are you surprised? Just because people are nice to you doesn't mean they want you around.

"I—I . . . why?"

Giulia squeezes her lips together. "Where we're going is . . . it's not safe. I . . . ." Is she going to cry again? "If something can happen to *her,* she was so happy, so close to . . . . What could happen to you?"

"Giulia, I'm sorry—" *about Elise.* "But I'm . . . not scared, okay?" I understand why. "I have nothing to lose. I'm ready to take a risk."

"She was too," Giulia snaps, startling me with her sudden fierceness.

Her name hangs, unspoken. A warning.

Giulia softens. "If you need money, I have money. Sleep here, take the ferry back, have a holiday, go home. Now that I know she's actually gone, it's . . . different. I imagine you gone. Don't get sucked in. What we have may be wonderful, but it's terrible, too."

"And I can't have it?" Resistance flares.

"No." In the darkness, her tight jaw looks like it's not made for her face, like she's trying on someone else's expression. "I won't bring you there."

She walks a few paces then looks back. I think she sees the miserable hunch of my shoulders and gets that I need to be alone. She murmurs, "Don't be long," before vanishing.

I sink onto a rock and press my knuckles into my forehead.

Who wants you around? Who ever has?

A laugh echoes in my head. Look at me. Forcing myself into someone else's adventure, when I'm not wanted. When there's only one place I've ever been wanted.

I look up and the ocean is slick and the stars are endless and I miss *Craig*. I miss knowing that however much I messed up, he'd be there, arms open. He knew I was a fuck-up. He was okay with that.

I can't believe I pushed past the edge of his patience. For what?

The trees rustle. A seed of a thought cracks open.

If I did vanish, like Elise, who'd know? My colleagues wouldn't notice. My parents would . . . not be surprised. Who, except for Craig, gives a damn about me? And I've lost him.

That's right, love. If you disappeared tonight, who'd miss you? Nobody.

I crane my neck back. The stars teem.

Nobody would miss me. It doesn't sound sad. It sounds like freedom.

A poster, a brilliant smile, a face made for adventure. Sometimes people vanish because something takes them. But maybe sometimes people vanish because they find somewhere *better*, somewhere meant for them.

My mouth floods with the taste of honey. *Yes. So nearly there.*

The idea roots and blooms. I have my backpack. And folded in my pocket, the map the waitress sketched for me.

The way back is also the way *there*.

As the thought spreads its canopy over me, I panic, its absurdity blotting out the light. Am I really thinking about following a rough map into the dark, alone, in a place where a girl vanished? Because pain makes me reckless? Because I can't hear *no* again when it's all the world ever told me and I felt so close to a *yes*? Because of dreams, a tugging at my bones?

Those aren't *reasons*.

But I taste lemon, feel sun; my body knew this place already.

I am near the edge of something uncanny. Even if I had anything to lose, I'd still follow this. When you feel so close to something beyond what we *know*—and I feel it more and more—there's no resisting. You have to let the unknown take you.

There's something else, too, something I can't name. Something harsh and hot gathering inside.

I'm not asking *anyone's* permission.

I walk into the dark.

CHAPTER SIX

RUN

I'VE WALKED ABOUT TWENTY MINUTES WHEN I REALIZE HOW STUPID THIS IS. The road's petered out into a path disappearing into the pines. Cold sets in at night. And it's so dark ahead.

What's telling me to keep going? A feeling that a promise is about to be kept.

Icy water churns around my calves. I am starting to understand what waits inside the cave, and what it will do with me. But I'm drawn on—

I blink. I don't remember.

I loop my hands through my bag straps and turn onto the path.

It's steep and rocky, and I stumble. Bells jingle far off; I can't place what they could be. Sometimes forest opens into fields, vineyards, but they're vague. My phone light barely picks out the path, and after a few meters, the light is devoured and dissipated.

The island shivers around me, alive. The same life pumps through me. A delirious, terrified joy. I—

Something shuffles between the trees.

Primal instincts tickle the back of my neck. I think of eyes in the dark, teeth, and hungry bellies. I try not to breathe or twitch.

Was Elise here, frozen in a predator's gaze? Is this one of the last things she felt?

I raise my phone light—

Nothing. The branches shift, the leaves ripple.

I walk on, heart thudding, feeling like every step is impossibly, explosively loud. Do they have bears out here? Wolves? That feeling you get, when *someone's* watching you, and you know it without even looking. There's something following me, even if I don't see it.

Terror takes control.

My fingers slip. I drop my phone and pelt up the path, white-hot panic whipping. Don't look back don't imagine teeth clamping down—

I stumble.

Slam into the ground, winded.

I scramble up and press against a tree. The darkness is total, except for a slash of sky between the branches. My breath's shallow. I brace.

Nothing.

I wait for long moments. Perhaps not the longest of my life—I've been braced like this before—but time ticks by in heartbeats, and every one feels like the last. But nothing comes.

Imagining things. Of course I'm filling this dark with monsters. I try to ground myself, run my hand over the mossy tree trunk. Strange, this moss; soft, slippery with some wetness that feels alien in this place of dry leaves and dusty soil.

I breathe in deep and gag; a heavy stink of rot, like a vegetable bin on a hot summer day, fills my nostrils and throat. There's slickness on my hands, on my bare shoulders where they press against the tree.

That buzzing: It can't be flies? Do flies come out at night?

Something squirms against my skin, a flick of a worm wriggling or an insect opening its wings; I flinch into another wave of nausea and push up to my feet, slapping and clawing at my skin in disgust.

When I catch my breath, the stench of rot is suddenly gone. I run a finger along my arm; hard to tell in this dark, but it feels clean. The droning buzz of insects has dissolved, absorbed into the song of crickets in the night.

Must have stumbled into some trash dumped out here, or something; I don't really care enough to investigate any further, just hope there's no maggots in my vest. I have bigger problems. Stupid, stupid—my phone's gone, no way I'll find it in this dark.

It's like the island has swallowed me. I walk slowly, hands raised, the starlight just strong enough to illuminate the path. I don't feel like I'm being watched anymore, but I imagine things ahead; my mind gives them no shape.

I step out onto a plateau.

A rising slice of moon reflects in streaks on distant water. Silhouettes of cypresses drip down a gorge ripped into the landscape. Stars, *all the stars*. More than there even *are*.

I stretch, wriggling my fingers toward the sky. I imagine being struck by lightning, a buzz through my body leaving me livid with energy. I'm alone and free and terrified and drunk on beauty.

I slug water and curl up, head on my bag. I'm keyed up and chilly, but Larissa was right, I'm aching; I should rest.

The solidity of the rock whispers, *Be safe, go back.*

I stare up into the dark places between the stars and whisper back, *No.*

I dream of a cove under cliffs, a narrow cave passageway, and whispered temptations. I wake sweating in a blare of sun, and it takes a second to remember.

I . . . did that. I ran out here alone.

Well done. Another genius Aoife move.

I stretch. No regrets. When Larissa and Giulia arrive home, I'll be waiting there, my past ripped out at the roots.

I walk for hours, following the map, winding along cliffs, crinkly sea below. The heat intensifies, blazing the last chill out of me. Actual bliss. I find a spring bubbling up and drink deep from my hands. On a sweeping beach that burns white in the sun, I wade into the cool water, letting it churn against my calves. A cargo ship rusts offshore.

Salt-sticky and sweating, I follow the path uphill. *Homecoming*, something in my step says. The trees thicken; the grass grows greener, the earth darker. Shadows dance, light filtered through lemon trees. A staticky quality to everything, suddenly.

I've been here.

I slip off my sandals, sink my toes into warm earth. Familiar and unfamiliar.

This place where the wind rustles, that smells of pine and lemon and soil. I know it.

It knows me.

I don't need to check the map. I'm here.

There's nothing. No ruins. No animal guides or chainsaw-wielding maniacs or doors in the air. Just a twist in my gut that says I made it.

Everything's watching, isn't it? Trees, sky, insects. Like the island's curious what I'll do.

My neck prickles. It's not my imagination this time. Someone's watching. I hear breathing, half lost in the movements of leaves.

I turn in a circle, but there's nobody. My mind's starting to zoom into panic again when I spot a pair of legs through one of the trees.

I make out his face among the branches. He can't be much older than me, but looks a lot more, I don't know, adult. His red-brown hair and beard are cropped, and he's looking at me like I'm an onrushing disaster.

Our eyes meet. *I see you.*

I try a smile. "Hi?"

He lands on his feet with perfect balance. His shirt's tartan, jeans mud-stained, and movements calm and workmanlike as he snatches the shotgun I hadn't noticed propped against the tree and levels it at my chest.

His eyes judge me. They aren't merciful. Scratches mark his cheek. Violence?

"This is private land." There's a hint of Yorkshire in his voice, which seems wildly out of place, softened by an accent I've only ever heard in this country. "You're going to leave now."

I eye the gun. It's old-fashioned, like a prop. I've never had a gun pointed at me; if I take it in, I might realize this should be terrifying.

"I'm sorry"—I don't know what to say, this wasn't meant to happen—"but I'm not."

The guy snarls professionally, which is impressive. He seems to have a whole library of snarls and glares. "We're not a shelter for lost children. Would you kindly piss off?"

I stand my ground, trying to work out what to say. A postcard! Yearning! A bad breakup? I don't think those would pass. His jaw's twitching.

"I . . . my name's Aoife, and—"

The words falter. Everything's still. I sense the presence behind me even before the beardy gun guy looks over my shoulder.

Pine needles crack as a man steps into view. He must have been there the whole time, watching; it's like these people emanated from the island itself.

This guy looks more like a tech bro than a farmer, with glasses and geometric tattoos. He's too young to be that bald, and his flower-print shirt is too jaunty for the massive knife in his hand.

"Who's this?" His eyes don't judge, but the glint on his blade definitely isn't friendly.

"Trespasser." Gun Guy glares at me. "Looks like a lost tourist; she's making these goldfish faces."

"Larissa and Giulia," I yelp, remembering the obvious. Maybe having a gun pointed at you gets in the way of logic. "They invited me, so I came, because—" Stop talking, Aoife. "Even before, I felt like . . . like this place was calling me."

Their eyes narrow. It's not a *what nonsense is she spouting* look; it's a *what kind of trouble is she dragging in* look. Trust me, I know the difference.

Gun Guy presses the barrel against my chest. The metal's warm. I didn't expect that. I wonder if it's from the sun. Or from shooting the last intruder.

I remember Craig yelling as I walked out, and the way Larissa touched Giulia's wrist. My eyes settle on Gun Guy's.

Something nasty twitches in his lip. "Nobody knows you're here, do they? Which means no laws apply here, not to me with you. So. There are some nice beaches on other islands; you'll have a lovely time if you turn around, now, and leave."

His tongue turns *leave* into *live.*

Tech Bro watches silently, amused, like whatever happens to me will unfold on a screen, light entertainment that isn't his business.

"Aoife, holy fuck!"

Larissa barrels between the trees, a knight in shining tie-dye. She pulls up sharply; her eyes fix on the gun and widen. Behind her, Giulia clasps her hands to her mouth. I resist an urge to wave.

"What"—Larissa's voice shakes with building rage—"the actual *fuck*, Sage?"

Tech Bro chuckles. "Well, this *is* a morning. Good to see you two."

Heat wavers. Something's being communicated in glares, a power play I can't read.

"Please," Giulia says. "We invited her. It was our mistake."

Mistake. The word's a kick to the chest.

"It wasn't your place to invite her," Sage snaps, lowering the gun reluctantly.

Larissa cocks her head. Her eyes are gorgeously dangerous. "And yet! I did. Isn't it funny how these things happen?"

Tech Bro laughs. "Missed you every day. Let's take a look at this friend of yours."

He actually steps closer and examines me, and I meet his eyes. I can only hope the bold tilt of my chin offsets the desperation pulsing in my chest: *please, please, please.*

His eyebrows draw down. "Have we met?"

We haven't. But. Like the scents of lemon and soil, like the play of sun and earth here, there's some familiarity. I risk a smile.

Tech Bro grins broadly, like something's decided. He shoves the knife into his belt. "Well! Welcome. Aoife, was it?"

I can't speak. This turned around so fast, it's too fragile to trust.

A breeze shifts shafts of sunlight, shuffling the leaves.

"Aoife." He reads my silence as a nod. "I'm Oscar. This is Sage, and he will give you a lovely apology, won't he?"

Sage glowers. I don't think he'll be apologizing.

"Nice to meet you." My voice is a dry whisper.

Oscar clasps my hands. The map's in my palm, sweat-sodden beyond repair.

"Welcome to the Farmstead," Oscar says.

CHAPTER SEVEN

FARMSTEAD

WE WALK UNDER THE TREES, SILENT. THE GUN SWINGS WITH SAGE'S STEPS. Larissa tries to link her arm through Giulia's, but Giulia tugs away, staring at the ground; Larissa pouts. Oscar's grinning at me sidelong.

The trees open onto a perfect cove. Cliffs tower, jagged-toothed; sea lolls onto sand like a tongue, foaming white. It's a mouth I'd happily jump into.

A farmhouse nestles among groves. Golden stone, shutters, vines. Solar panels and rigged-up windmills harvest the sky. Huts and tents scatter through the greenery along a pebbly beach.

People work in the groves and vegetable patches. Soft electronic music pumps from somewhere. Smoke. Chickens pecking. Someone splayed on the sand, soaking in the sun.

"Welcome to the Farmstead," Oscar repeats. "It's been waiting for you."

My eyes say, *Me?* He nods. I can't speak; I'm bursting with certainty. This is what I've been waiting for. Something is here, it *wants* me.

The cave, enfolding me in dark—

The image dissipates.

"What is this place?"

Oscar shoots me another grin. "A surprise."

We pass more people as we make our way down into the groves. A sunburned couple, Scandi-blond, sawing a plank; a stocky woman working on an earthen hut with a gangly guy in a straw trilby and eyeliner; an older woman in a flowered dress and apron carrying a basket of fruit. Eyes settle on me among the rustle and buzz, curious. Where suspicion flares, Oscar gives nods and gestures, and it recedes and turns to smiles.

"Where shall we put her?" Larissa beams at me. "We've got a spare hut, right?"

Sage clicks his tongue. "We're not a holiday camp."

Oscar tuts right back. "Be nice, Sage. The hut by the fig tree's empty now—"

Giulia chokes, a sound of sharp pain. She shies away from Larissa's hand and stalks off; before I can follow, Oscar takes my arm. His hand's warm, and he's ignoring whatever Sage is hissing about, something like *too close to . . . .*

"It'll be fine." Oscar slaps his shoulder, getting much the response he would from a statue. "Come and see, surprise guest."

That should be blaring alarms, but I don't want to stir myself into paranoia and ruin the glow of arrival. There's vivid blue ocean hanging out past those trees, and over there I think there's beehives.

And the hut, my god. Adobe walls, shuttered windows. Grape vines cast dappled shade; there's the fig tree, and those are actual figs on the branches, aren't they? I swell. I now understand what *home* feels like.

I can't even form the words to thank him; my mouth opens, then stays that way.

"You're welcome." Oscar reads me and pats my arm. "Go relax. There's clothes in there, should be about your size."

I smile; another perfect coincidence, another sign.

His eyes settle, judging; for once I don't feel like I'm coming up short. "Don't worry about the others. We're cautious of outsiders. And people are shaken up about . . . well. A loss is hard. But Larissa knew you belonged here. If you've been feeling something like a pull, a call . . . you have, haven't you? There's a reason."

Sunlight hangs in curtains in the dusty air. I could cry at the rightness of this. "I hope so."

I watch him leave, then gaze at my new surroundings. It's trees and sandy soil, opening onto the beach; the nearest building is a wooden cabin a little way off into the foliage, painted shutters and a heavy iron door closed up.

I enter *my* hut and collapse onto *my* bed—bouncy mattress, woven blankets, soft pillows. Simple, rough, honest, *mine*. What if there's no time limit? What if nobody's going to destroy it because I dared to love it?

While I'm washing off the dust and sweat in a rigged-up shower around the back, someone leaves a tray of food: yogurt and honey in a ceramic bowl, sun-warmed peaches.

I eat wrapped in my towel, listening to the sea. Its whispers hiss a rhythm, everything resonating with delight that I've found my way into its arms.

It's the sea that lures me out, clear as vodka and twice as dizzying. In my bag, like a promise from the old me, I find my bikini. I slip out barefoot. The horizon's all shades of blue, white-gold cliffs folding in. I pick up a pebble: a tiny misshapen planet.

I approach the water. Close my eyes, feel sun on my eyelids.

A heartbeat thunders through rock as the walls close in—

"Careful!"

I open my eyes, inches from the waterline. The girl racing down the beach has punkish short hair and a look of panic. She stumbles trying to run on sand with an armful of books, which she's cuddling like a brood of babies.

She's looking at me like I'm juggling dynamite.

"Hi," I say, coherent. "Swimming—"

"No!" She tries to hold up her hands and almost drops the books, ratcheting up her panic. Her face has that reddish-gold glow of a faded sunburn. Whole nebulae of freckles, and these vivid golden-brown eyes.

I remember all the reasons there have ever been to be shy. Oh god. She's in a cotton shirt and shorts; I'm in a bikini. She's shorter than me, and I feel like some half-naked giraffe. "It's dangerous?"

The girl looks toward the tree line, actual fear on her face. I follow her gaze but can't see anything.

"It's . . . not safe. It's also very forbidden, and I really don't recommend it for a *lot* of reasons." She swallows. South African accent, I think?

I blink. The waves gently tumble pebbles, playing with light. "Is there something in the water?"

Her voice drops to a whisper. "Not just in the water." Jerky movements of golden irises and bushy eyebrows, directing my gaze back to the trees, warning.

Defiance whispers that I could just leap in anyway, but I surprise myself by doing what I'm told. I'm *not* screwing this up. I'm here for a reason. Oscar said so.

I step away from the water, aware of the knobbly skinniness of my exposed body, all the wrong angles. I try to distract myself by peering at the books. Hardbacks, antique-shop dusty. I glimpse the words OLD FAITHS and LEGENDS OF THE——, the rest buried by those freckled arms. "You're, um, reading."

"You're, um, new." The girl has a sideways smile that I think might be painfully cute. "I'm researching local mythology, you would not *believe* the resources here, it's wild, and you don't care about this. I'm Keira."

"Oh!" I click. "You're the biro beheader."

Keira blinks.

"Larissa said . . ." I half-remember. "Keira. Dangerous. Ballpoint pen."

"That's me. Yep. Inky serial killer." Kiera's fake snarl almost works. Pieces fall together: the handwriting in Giulia's sketchbook, the exclamation marks. It tracks. This girl is a human exclamation mark. "You're Aoife, right? Sage mentioned you. Welcome to the Farmstead, just . . . take care. Don't leap into too many things you don't understand."

I think that smile is approving? "How else do you learn?"

Kiera laughs. There's brightness on her face, and I think I put that there. She attempts finger guns, fails because of the books, and heads toward the farmhouse, leaving me with this grin I know must be goofy.

It falls away.

A man's under the trees, watching.

He's angular, with wispy silver hair, silver in his thick red beard. Neatly ironed trousers, strands of shells around his neck. A CEO gone feral or a pinstriped wilderness prophet. But that's background; everything is that *face*. Chiseled out of something ancient.

Our eyes meet.

The sharpness, the weight of that gaze. I have never felt so naked; it strips me away.

Those eyes have seen great and terrible things. They've learned to judge the world with harsh wisdom. How do I know? Have we met before, somewhere? They're judging me, and I need desperately to see approval in them.

He turns away. Disgusted, or indifferent. Which would be worse?

Laughter echoes in the empty spaces. *Fucked it up already, haven't you.*

I run back to the hut, sand burning my feet. I want to strip off not just my bikini, but my skin, my face. Shed myself like a snake.

I find clothes in a wooden chest: hipster-retro stuff, very '80s. Made for someone shorter and broader than me, but I try some belted shorts and a t-shirt, and they hang comfortably.

In the driftwood-framed mirror, I look transformed. Hair shorn and wild, face sun-kissed, clothes unfamiliar.

I focus on those things. I can bury the old Aoife under them, until she breaks down into mulch for the fresh thing that will grow from her. The girl who made a stranger laugh has to subsume the one who made that strange, captivating man turn his back.

I focus on that burying for a long time, until I barely recognize myself, then wind my way barefoot through the groves to the farmhouse.

The farmhouse door stands open. I expect it to be full of people, hopefully with tea and explanations, but silence hangs heavy over the terracotta tiles and golden stone walls.

Everything's expensive, rustic-chic. There's electricity here, I haven't seen much in the rest of the commune. I *have* to bounce on the leather sofa, rub my toes against the woven rugs. I expect someone to appear and tell me off, but nobody does.

I trail my hand along the wall, like I'm claiming it, hesitating at a carving: a closed circle inside an open circle, bisected by a line. I've seen that before.

At the back of the house is a vast kitchen full of herbs, rough wood, colorful tiles, opening onto a garden. There's a pot of coffee, and a woman with twirly graying hair, who greets me with a smile so warm that something curls up happily inside me.

She presses a hand to her chest and says, "Teresa," and I do the same and say, "Aoife," and she squeezes my hand before gesturing to a rolling pin and a bowl of dough.

Afternoon sun streams through the windows, there's flour in the air, warm dough stuck to my palms. Teresa sings keening songs. I think at first she doesn't know English, but when she does speak, it's clearly her first language, accented like Sage's with a local lilt and a Yorkshire twang. She's just letting me be quiet and relax.

When the dough's rolled, she guides me out to an herb garden, buzzing with bees and heady with scents. I recognize basil, rosemary, mint, oregano, marijuana.

Teresa points out a couple of unfamiliar plants and gives me a warning look. "Never touch those. That's belladonna, and that's hemlock. Deadly poisonous, and we're hours from any hospitals." She strokes another and chuckles. "Careful with these, too. Fun, but dangerous if you don't know what you're doing."

"Why would you grow poisons?" I swallow hard and regret that second cup of coffee.

Teresa's eyes crinkle. She probably didn't put belladonna in my coffee. "When you ask *why* around here, the answer's most likely to be *why not*."

I can't feel a breeze, but the leaves nod and shiver.

We return inside with handfuls of mint and parsley. Thinking of toxins sprouting next to them thrills me; I want to go back and touch them. I think I get why Teresa grows them.

The kitchen's full of enticing scents by the time Larissa appears. She shoots me a smile like I'm in on something. "Teresa, that smells amazing. Can I snatch Aoife?"

Teresa nods and pats the pastries: *Good job.*

I follow Larissa. The light's low, adding a glow to the edges of leaves. Dust and insects dance. We pass Giulia hanging out bedsheets, and I wave. She looks away pointedly and slips behind one of the sheets like a veil. Sickness swells in my stomach.

Once we're out of earshot, Larissa pauses, closes her eyes, and inhales; the tension on her face eases. The leaves quiver, the air tightening almost imperceptibly. "Ignore her," she says finally. "She's embarrassed because we know she got scared. We don't have much time for fear. Except as, y'know. Extra flavor."

"Why did she get scared?"

Larissa pauses at the door of her hut. It's vivid orange and splashed with abstract spirals. Wind chimes tinkle, dripping shells and sea-glass.

"Because you ran away." Larissa's gaze wanders, refusing to settle on me, deepening my shame. "You never came back to the room. We fully freaked out. We debated reporting you missing but decided we should check here first. But we thought something horrible had happened. Giulia was already going off after this thing with our friend who left, and she would not stop *blaming* herself."

"Oh." My shoulders droop. "I'm sorry. I . . . didn't think."

I wait for Larissa to sneer. *You never do, do you?*

She doesn't. She grins. "It was badass. Walk here alone at night? I could never. Can't tell if you're brave or deranged, but I love that energy."

My heart surges. She's this overwhelming, dazzling force, and *I* impressed *her*. Then I have no idea what to say except to mutter, "Thanks," which probably undermines it.

"Giulia will be okay, is what I'm saying." She rests her hand on the door handle. "And don't worry about the friend she's upset about. It's safe here, really. She'll have left in a huff and show up again in a few weeks. People worry too much, because people here love each other too much. You'll love her too when you meet her."

Larissa opens the door and there's more colors: rich blue, terracotta orange, hot pink. Hanging glass bottles twist the light. Houseplants sprout, erasing the line between grove and room. It's perfect. It's her.

Could I make a place that was *me*? I'd have to become something first.

"Let's get you ready for the feast!" Some disorientated part of my brain takes that as *marinate and cook you*, and I flinch. Larissa giggles, then bares her teeth like she is going to nibble a morsel off me. "*Shhh.* I'd only eat you up if I was *really* hungry. It's a celebration for me and Giulia. It's really an excuse to dress up, although 'we're all beautiful' is a good excuse too. We made a special trip to the mainland last year to get formal clothes; that was fun. This one's . . . spare. Think it'll fit?"

It's a full-on evening dress, short and silky rose gold. I stare. I've never had anything pretty like this.

Larissa says, "Try it on," and I go pink. She expects me to just . . . strip? Her grin goes wicked, and she adds, "You're so cute," and covers her eyes like a child hiding from a monster. I wriggle through a quick change. She whistles and reaches out to help with the zip.

When her fingers brush my skin, I shiver; I wonder with this lightning blast if I have a crush on her. I've never felt like this about a girl, but I never did about a guy other than Craig, either. Is it a crush to feel like someone's a door I want to step through? To want someone to chew me up and spit me out as something new?

There's a gorgeous lack of self-consciousness in her as she tears off her own clothes. I can't help gazing at her curves, a plump bounty of flesh that must be so soft to touch. She finds my stare adorable. Her dress is reds and oranges, beads and embroidery.

"I still don't understand," I admit, as she hunts through her makeup bag. "Why there's poisons in the garden and mythology books. What this place *is*." *Why someone vanished, or left so mysteriously. Why I can't go into the sea.*

"That's part of the fun," Larissa assures me. "Close your eyes." Her fingertip smooths glitter across my eyelids. An impossibly intimate touch. "Your mind's very open. That's good. You'll need that." The slick of lipstick against my mouth startles me. "There! Cute."

Did I ever have a friend who'd lend me clothes or do my makeup? I never had time for the girls at home; Craig reminded me I didn't need them, that he got me in a way they never would. I didn't realize I'd missed this.

We pose in the mirror. The sunset light's sepia and fire, and with my hair spiked and tattoos against the lace, I look like this burning punk princess, completely unfamiliar.

Larissa beside me is an underworld queen, red lipstick and turquoise beads, plastic flowers in her hair, mystery wafting from every pore. She blows me a kiss and sprays me with oil that smells like jasmine and lemongrass. "Ready to fall in love with everybody?"

Nerves clench; I don't know how to handle people. But maybe the girl in the silk dress does. I blow Larissa a kiss back. She links her arm through mine and leads me out.

CHAPTER EIGHT

WORTH GIVING EVERYTHING FOR

It's full of lights. Solar-powered fairy lights and paper lanterns drip from branches, and beeswax candles glimmer, reflecting on silk and sequins and glowing faces.

For the first time, I see how many people are here. Fifty or sixty, clustered around tables on the farmhouse terrace. Most are young, but not all; an elderly lady with a sharp, vivacious face is telling a story to a girl with a creatively ripped dress and a bob, who's laughing deliriously. Most seem Western European or American, but I catch snatches of a wider world. A girl with fire tattoos and the straw-trilby guy toast each other in clashing languages I can't place; two boys walk by with unfamiliar wooden drums under their arms; the guy arm-wrestling with Oscar wears a green-yellow flag as a turban; a cacophony of tongues mash together.

It's probably like the scene at a tourist hostel, except for the feathers, beads, and sequins, and the rapturous happiness. The excitement. Something exciting is happening.

Maybe it's just the food. Because oh my god, the food. Stews, still-warm bread, tart and spicy sauces, fruits and vegetables that crunch in my teeth. I smile when I spot the pastries I made with Teresa. I love watching people eat things I've cooked, seeing my work disappearing into people's bodies, like I'm becoming part of them.

The wine's chilled, air perfumed with jasmine and rosemary. It's all so beautiful.

But mostly, it's *them*. The way they look at me, curious and open. They slip morsels onto my plate, *Try this*, run their fingers along my arms like I'm a work of art, bombard me with names, *Don't worry, you'll get used to us*, compliment my pastries, admire my haircut, *Did you really hike here alone?*

Teresa points at the pastries and gives me a double thumbs-up. Kiera, the biro killer, meets my eye, ridiculously handsome in a white suit and watercolor silk cravat, although our gazes sputter, and she looks away. Oscar toasts me and winks.

I can't shake this feeling like they know me. Like I know them. Like we've all been together, somewhere, and this is a reunion. I'm struggling to grasp it but there it is: They seem to *like* me.

Maybe the exciting thing is *me*.

Larissa elbows me in the ribs. "Have you tried the shrimp thing? It's Pietro's secret sauce. Pietro's Giulia's husband, have you met yet?"

Larissa waves at another table, where Giulia's beside a skinny guy in suspenders. There's tiredness behind his smile, like he's just emerged blinking into light. I'm also blinking, trying to get my head around Giulia being married.

"It's sweet," Larissa says. "They came here together. Got married on the beach."

"I thought you and Giulia were . . . ." I wave a shrimp on a fork in a way that probably doesn't have the implications I'm going for.

"Oh, we are." Larissa snaps up my shrimp in one gulp. "People don't own each other like that here. Or we all do. We're all a bit in love, and those boundaries between together and not together get . . . messy. Which is part of the fun."

She finds it cute all over again that this information makes me dizzy, just so alien from my and Craig's tiny world. And it's terrifying, because maybe the way she makes my stomach swoop isn't forbidden.

She says, "You're missing a shrimp," spears another, and lifts it to my lips. It bursts in my mouth, flesh and spices; her eyes glow at the pleasure on my face.

Stillness sweeps the tables. I almost choke: *I did something wrong.*

But all eyes are on the figure emerging from the farmhouse.

The man from the beach.

He wears a cream suit and a driftwood-and-hibiscus garland, colors of bones and blood. The light makes his wispy hair a halo, but if that face is angelic, we're talking old-style angels, all wrath and destruction.

Quiet follows him, like he casts a pall.

I expect everyone to bow or something—maybe he'll make a speech— but he just settles beside Teresa and Sage, sitting back as Oscar pours him a glass of wine. The chatter picks up again, less raucous.

Before he arrived, weird as it was, I felt all attention on me. Now it's divided, eyes flickering from him to me. Two black holes orbiting each other.

His gaze meets mine again, imbibing me slowly, every inch. I stare back, all questions, all hope, until he looks away and murmurs to Teresa.

"Who's that?" I don't know why I whisper. He knows I'm talking about him.

"Jonah." There's reverence in Larissa's voice. "He, Teresa, and Oscar are the founders; they're married, him and Teresa, and Sage is their son. Jonah's . . . well . . . ."

"Intense?" I hazard. People around him are laughing louder, smiling wider. Like proximity to him is intoxicating.

Larissa skewers a piece of cheese. Is there something nervous in her laugh? Her eyes are shiny when she looks at him. "You wouldn't *believe.*"

"We should all be intense, shouldn't we?" It's the Norwegian woman who greeted me with cheek kisses and called me *sister,* making me unsteady with her grin. "We should all be intense for . . . ." She falls quiet, giving me a look that says, *Don't ask.*

I give her a half-smile; she returns it in full. What to do when you don't know what are secrets and what are surprises to be revealed? You gulp wine and let it pull you along.

Dizzy heat rushes through me; how many glasses have I had? Lights shudder, it all swims deliciously—

※

I don't remember how I got here. We're on the lawn between herbs and hanging lights. The straw-trilby guy strums a guitar, several people pound hand drums, the elderly woman plays flute, Larissa adds a deep bluesy voice. Others play bottles and forks and tabletops, and it weaves together with beats from the speakers. An improvised techno-folk-rock mashup.

The dance is chaos: jumping and flailing, circling with linked arms. Images come like camera clicks, slow then fast. Oscar and Sage are doing a tango, Giulia and Pietro sway in each other's arms.

Jonah's leaning back in his chair, watching through half-lidded eyes.

I try to pull back against the hands drawing me in, I don't *dance*, but apparently nobody cares if you just convulse instead. I'm thrown from arms to arms, carousel-spinning, and I'm at peak dizzy when I overhear "... a copy, which might have details of a rite—" and collapse into Kiera, who wasn't dancing.

I'm clinging to her neck. Oops. I interrupted her mid-conversation, but now she's alone, who was that? "Hi?"

She helps me upright, talking loud and mile-a-minute. "Hi. *Thank* you for rescuing that notebook. Giulia's notes from the temple were *super* useful, it's the only site outside this island with evidence of . . . ." She trails off, maybe noticing that her hand's still on my arm, and mine's on the back of her neck. You're meant to move those, right?

Why is this confusing? "I . . . yeah, I found it. But I need to thank *you* because I had no money and no plan and it brought me here so,"—*shut up, Aoife*—"it was"—*don't say fate*—"good coincidence." *Good save.*

"Good for both of us," Kiera agrees. What is that in her eyes; just a warping of the lights? It looks like recognition. "What would you have done?"

I shrug. The dizziness is good, Kiera a steady point to focus on. "Work at a hostel or farm, I guess. Wrangle goats or something."

"Wrangle?" Kiera snorts in a way that shouldn't be so cute. "Is that what people do with goats?"

"People do all sorts of things with goats." I didn't think it was funny, but Kiera cackles.

Am I flirting again? I feel her breath, and it's scary, and I want to keep being scared. Why is my hand still on her neck?

The heartbreak and fury that would crack across Craig's face, if he saw this.

I pull away. "It's nice to meet you," I garble, which I think isn't even the correct thing to say here, we've met already, never mind; I stagger into the melting lights and noise. I glimpse her face, baffled—hurt? I think I need to go? I'm messing up badly.

I'm halfway into the dance, halfway out. My head spins, but it's not just the wine. This . . . I've never been anywhere like this. This joy isn't posturing. Look at those faces.

They like me, maybe, but they adore each other, and I'm a stranger. What will it take, to be part of that *us*?

Someone's in front of me, and time's glitchy, I don't know how she got here, and it's Giulia. Her hair's wild, her chiffony brown dress askew, her face blurry.

I try not to mangle words. "I'm sorry I . . ." What did I do? "Upset you, ran away."

Her eyes narrow. "No. You're not."

I'll remember jokes we laughed at on the journey, and it'll always hurt. The fury's wrong on her, like ill-fitting clothes. "I didn't . . . ."

"You didn't think at *all*. Larissa can say whatever, you weren't invited. Nobody *here* asked you. They're being nice, because they're nice, but you're *not wanted here*."

Nausea washes through me. She's talking out of the chilly depths of my own mind. I look around for reassurance, but there's none, I'm flushed, ashamed, oh god, I'm—

"Hello, you two!" Oscar appears, breathless. "Enjoying the party?"

Giulia's mouth opens and closes, like a beached fish, and that's hilarious for some reason. Feels like the world's going to pop. I was upset about something a second ago. "Yes!" Giulia's voice is far away, but does it sound off? "It's good to be home."

I'm reading her face wrong; why would she look scared?

She gives me a fake smile and vanishes into the dance. I sway and try to make my mouth work.

"Too much wine?" Oscar chuckles. "Teresa's stuff is dangerous. You should get some sleep."

My gaze slides to the grass. I'm making a fool of myself, huh. "Okay," I murmur. "I'll . . . yeah."

I turn away from the lights and laughter and only turn back when Oscar says, "Aoife, wait."

I brace for a cruel joke.

"You'll be happy here," Oscar says. "You have that look I had. That *seeking*. Before here my whole world was strategizing, profit, but I knew there was *more*. I was right. When you really find what's here . . . it's bigger, better than you ever imagined. Worth giving everything for."

The warmth drains from my cheeks and curls in my chest. "Promise?"

Oscar nods. "You won't mess this up. Just let us guide you and be brave and trust."

I watch the flicker of the party reflected in his glasses, and I trust him. I trust this.

I'm not sure how I stumble back to my hut. But that warmth still nestles inside me as I curl up, too exhausted to even change, and drift off.

A crawling, slick wetness. A subtle brush of antennae strokes my ear; there's a greasy popping as I roll over, the larvae and fungi in the sheets bursting under my weight. My face sinks into the pillow, and putrefaction fills my mouth, nose, eyes—

I jolt upright.

Breath shallow, I fumble for a light switch, but there's no electricity in the huts, is there? I find a lighter by the bed; the tiny flame traps the dark in flickering shadows.

My bed is not, in fact, full of rot and hungry insects. A fragment of a nightmare. Drunk weirdness. Disorientation. An unfamiliar ceiling, unfamiliar sheets, the unfamiliar murmur of waves outside.

As the panic dies down, my body starts complaining. Pain stabs my impossibly heavy head. My tongue's thick and dry.

How much wine . . . heavy, heady stuff, knocked me out, although I usually have a good head for drink. Oh god, I made an idiot of myself. They must think—what people usually think about me.

I'm tempted to slump back and try to sleep it off, but the fear has alchemized into excitement. I put aside the shame. I smell salt, pine, earth, a night I could breathe in.

Distant music fades in and out. Drumming, some eerie whining string instrument. It's more primal than the music from the party. Sounds like masked dances in the moonlight, beach raves.

I stumble outside to the sink and splash water onto my face. It's chilly, and starts to pull me back together. I take in stars and insect chirps; the night's thrumming. The earth holds the day's heat like a living thing. Jasmine blooms in the dark.

The wind shifts the music, teasing directions. Beach, farmhouse, cliffs? I step onto the path, then my heartbeat hitches.

A snuffling, whining sound. Close. Someone crying.

Coming from the cabin. What was it Sage said about my hut? *Too close to*—

I sneak closer. It's a log cabin, bigger than our huts; fancier, carved with patterns—I know that closed circle–open circle symbol, don't I—the door steel, the windows shuttered. I'd thought it was abandoned, or a storage shed, but there's someone in there for sure.

I'm still in my party dress, punk princess disheveled, wine on the lace, soil on my skin. The music, there and not there.

The sobs heave, interrupted by sniffles.

Shyness grips me. I remember crying uncontrollably among the bins behind the pub; the shame of being seen like that was brutal. Of course this person's hiding in an isolated cabin. They don't want to be bothered. Especially by me, klutzing in, less than coherent.

The sobs hitch; it hurts secondhand. "Hey. I'm . . . in the next hut. If you want to talk."

The crying stops. The quiet congeals.

"I'm okay." A girl's voice, startlingly young, shaky. "Please go."

I don't want to, but what, am I just going to stand around like a weirdo? "I'm here," I repeat stupidly. "If you need me."

"Okay." The voice is strained. "Thank you."

I'm blushing as I retreat, the thrill dampened down. Exhaustion drags me back to my pillows, and uneasy dreams follow of something lovingly enfolding me into its core.

CHAPTER NINE

THE CAVE AND
THE CABIN

I WAKE SLOWLY, JOY RISING AS MY EYES OPEN. LIGHT DAZZLES THROUGH leaves, a whole shadow-puppet show. I hear waves, wilder today, a papery whisper. I'm here. And someone's knocking on my door.

"Aoife, hello!" Alarmingly practical overalls, blonde hair in a long plait. It's the Norwegian woman. Red cheeks, silver rings—Frida. "Please come for breakfast! You're on the chore rota with me and Aksel; you should get some good food first!"

She's beaming, and I match her smile. Included on the rota; *included.* My hands will help shape this place; I'll be knitted into it.

Fresh fruit, goat's milk, eggs cooked in tomato and spices, a sunny kitchen full of chatter. People make space for me, pour me coffee, compliment my outfit. I'm falling into rhythm with them, sliding down into their world and settling there. Kiera meets my eye over a book, and I nearly drop the orange I'm peeling; we grin.

Aksel and Frida are building a shed in the groves, where yellow flowers flare underfoot. A plump chicken scratches; I kneel to thank it for this morning's eggs. It looks at me with beady eyes and makes a burbling noise like it's saying I'm welcome.

Aksel's blond hair stands out against his suntan, and Frida's plait swings like a metronome as they saw, bickering cheerfully in Norwegian. I get my hands sticky while varnishing planks. My skin sprouts sweat and sunburn, but the heat burrows into my bones and fills me with life. There's something refreshing in the ache.

Imagine endless days like this.

After an hour or two, I realize I've barely thought of Craig. The shock's heavy, relief and loss. I picture his face until it hurts again; I owe him that.

We break under a peach tree with iced tea. They can't grow tea here, can they? This place seems way more prosperous than a remote commune should be. The tea's tart and sweet; I taste lemon and remember how my body dreamed of this place.

Aksel notices me brooding, and grins. "I've seen that look before."

"I had that look all the time." Frida smiles over her cup. "When I first came. *This is too good to be true.* Like it's wrong that people could make a place and be happy there."

The lemon tastes fresh. "Is that what this place is?"

Aksel winks. "A little secret: You won't get anywhere by asking obvious questions."

Frida pours another glass; the sun flashes off her ring. It's embossed with a symbol, a closed circle inside an open circle, a single bisecting line.

This might not be an obvious question. "What does that mean?"

Frida looks at her hand. When she says, "Nothing," her lips and eyes screw up slightly, like the lie is painful.

I remember. "I saw that at the temple. On one of the standing stones."

I'm not sure if I'm after information or a reaction. Sometimes it isn't just material things you have to break, to remind the world that you're there. Having Frida and Aksel, so self-contained and happy, see that I exist? That feels good.

Frida flounders. Aksel replies instead. "Interesting. We bought it at a souvenir shop. I guess it's inspired by prehistoric art."

Frida grits her teeth. Whatever it means, it cuts so deep that denying it physically hurts.

"Can I look?" The frustration of having answers so close is making me playfully reckless, another new pleasure. If she's going to lie, why shouldn't she hurt for it, a little?

Frida's mouth is a thin line, but she drops the ring into my palm. It's warm with echoes of the sun and her flesh. I feel an urge to hurl it away, or swallow it, to see what she'd do. I trace the symbol.

The blue sky, the cool tea glass, waver like a signal's been lost.

This moment exists already somewhere. Is this me? I stand engulfed in darkness, frigid turbulent water now up to my waist, tracing the symbol on the wall. Who carved this, so deep into this cave, and how, in this dank blackness where no light shines? This dark takes everything that enters it. It's taken me. I hear a heartbeat, heavy with satisfaction, drawing me forward. I say, "No," and the dark smiles because it knows better.

A hand on my forehead. Cold water at my lips. "Too much sun," Aksel tuts. "Take it slow, city girl."

That felt so real. I've seen it before, haven't I? That damp, cavernous darkness. Was it a recent nightmare, or a bad trip years ago?

It lingers now. Just like my skin knew the warmth of this sun, it knows the cold of a rocky passageway. My fingers know the carved stone, my legs the tug of freezing water. I can't call these visions: They're playing out in my flesh. My lungs are still tight from the suffocating air, rot and salt filling my nose.

I shiver. That one was not tantalizing. I felt like I'd never see light again; I felt *taken*, swallowed.

But it was compelling, too. The sick fascination of broken taboos and violent temptations.

The visions of sunlight and lemons came true—

"Is there a cave here?" I blurt.

Aksel looks at me sidelong. "No. Just a crevasse in the cliff." He wipes his hands together, although they were clean. "Right. Let's get this section done."

I return Frida's ring; she takes my hand, folding my flesh and bone between hers like they could meld together. "Oh, Aoife, you do belong here. I see it in your questions. Thank you for coming to us." She tightens her grip, and I tighten mine, glowing: *She wants me here.* "Don't be afraid, okay? It's going to be beautiful."

And I'm alone, skin cold from a dark place it's never felt, lemon lingering on my tongue.

✦

By evening, I'm exhausted and tempted to slink to bed, but Teresa corners me, a chicken tucked under each arm. I recognize my bird friend from this morning.

Soon I'm back in that heaven of spices and sun, chopping onions. Teresa sings to the chickens, stroking their feathers, and the sound is so soothing that I settle, too; it's a jolt when she snaps their necks. But I stay in that calm, sleepy state as I watch them flutter and fall still. She plucks and guts them, still singing to the stripped carcasses, the movements of her fingers and knife lovingly focused.

The stew is rich and spicy, the meat tender and somehow more delicious for being a gift from my chicken friend. I fill my belly to bursting, then hand bowls around as people appear. I hum Teresa's song. What is this peace this place gives me?

Eventually Kai, the straw-trilby guitarist, swoops in and demands that Teresa gives me a break. She winks and produces a bottle of dark liquid and a plastic-wrapped joint from her apron.

Kai claps his hands. "All praise you, mother of—" Someone elbows him, and he coughs. Weird. Teresa being Sage's mother doesn't seem like a secret, just wildly unlikely given the people they are. "Cheers, Teresa. Come on, new girl."

He links his arm through mine, and I'm swept along, praying I won't say something wrong. Kai chats about how confusing it is being new here, he's only been here a few months himself, he's from Kyoto via Melbourne, he met Darya, the tattooed Russian, in the capital when his band had just broken up and here he is, and *look* at it.

I look at it. The beach, spangled with lights and stars. "It's unbelievable."

Kai's grin widens. "Wait until you *do* believe." He plops onto a beach blanket with Darya and Pietro. I shuffle in, hoping my smile isn't too awkward.

They don't give me time for awkwardness. Pietro shakes my hand solemnly and apologizes for Giulia; Kai wants to know about the music scene in London, and I get away with pretending I know. Darya spins poi, colored ribbons whirling in the twilight. She lets me try; I get tied up in knots, and they laugh, but without a shred of cruelty. When I say or do silly things, they seem to like me more.

Is this what having friends is? I've never been enfolded like this. Only by Craig. I'd never known how good it could feel.

Darya switches to spinning fire. I'm so mesmerized by the twirling flame that I don't notice the presence beside me until I look around into a pair of golden-brown eyes and a hesitant, "Hi." My chest splutters.

"Kiera!" Kai elbows her and says something about plucking up courage. She makes an angry noise; I'm not sure I get the joke, but that was sweet.

I can half-accept that I feel something about Larissa, but this is baffling. Being around Larissa is like drowning in honey. Being around Kiera's like cautiously handling something that might come apart. How can those be textures of the same thing?

We slot back into the conversation, and the night spins on in fire and stargazing. However exhausted I am, I can't leave.

"I can't believe it won't all go pop if I turn my back," I tell Kiera.

She raises an eyebrow. "Historically, that's rarely happened."

I snort, and she looks startled, like she's surprised she can make me laugh. "It's too much to be real." I breathe the salt air. I dreamed this; it became real. A shiver I know should be fear rises as I remember the other vision. "There's more, isn't there?"

She looks at me levelly. "Like what?"

Darker things, my eyes say, I think. *Weirder things.*

She gives me the slightest, slowest nod. The firelight muddies some struggle on her face, shadows flickering on her lips and eyes, rewriting them incomprehensible. She's different tonight; still twitchy, but at a different pitch.

When she speaks, it's rushed. "Be careful, okay? Keep alert. There's a lot here you don't know yet." She swallows. "And like I said, best not to jump too deep into things you don't understand."

I make a shocked face and say, "But that's my brand!" and she brightens. That daring, that tempted curiosity, rises again. "What about Elise? Did she . . . jump into things?"

Kiera's eyes widen.

Pietro shoves the bottle into my hand, face in mine, beaming. "Drinking game time!"

And there's no time for more questions, just a cluster of friends drinking and laughing under the stars until sun-drunk sleepiness overtakes us.

I'm not quite ready to sleep, though, hesitating at the door of my hut after we've said goodnight. Kiera's comments stick in my head. Keep alert, right?

I remember Aksel mentioning a crevasse. It would be at the end of the cove, where the cliffs rear up, right? I'll just look. It's not like there's *danger* here; Kiera didn't mean that. Just things to investigate. I'll investigate. Yes.

It's a short walk, the moon bright on the sand. The cliffs tower, making me feel so tiny that there's a reverence to it. But when I arrive, there's nothing like a cave there, just jagged rock; I can't even find what crevasse Aksel was talking about.

I brush the stone, like a portal might open at my touch. It's warm from the sun, a fleshy heat; should it still be so warm, so late into the night? Either way, there's no magical revelation. The cliff stays a cliff.

A familiar laugh resonates. Aoife and her fantasies.

Relief should dog my steps back to the hut. I just feel unsettled, like something was offered then pulled away.

In the groves, quiet and dark fold around me. Shadows take human forms, light hints at something inhuman. Bells ring softly from somewhere.

Another sound comes clear: footsteps creaking.

The cabin. It's coming from there.

Keep alert. The steps move backward and forward, someone pacing, restless. Foreboding rises in my throat as I approach.

And then, suddenly, a blast of song, such a shift from the uneasiness of the moment before that I almost laugh: a young girl's voice, the same from last night, bursting into an anthem from a musical.

It rings out through the clearing, deliciously alien to this quiet night, to the moonlight on the bulbous melted-wax olive tree trunks. It's a kid's voice, a teenager; I haven't seen any kids here, have I?

She reaches the crescendo, and I can't resist joining in; in case she can see me through those closed-up shutters, whoever she is, I dramatically sink to my knees and fling my arms to the sky.

I laugh into the melody, and I wait for her laugh to respond.

She falls quiet. There's a scrambling from inside.

"Hello?" I cringe at my own voice. God, imagine being interrupted singing like that. The awkwardness stings.

I wait to see if the shutters will open and if the mysterious girl will reveal herself, but there's only silence, and I slink away, even more uneasy.

CHAPTER TEN
PEACHES

MORNING. SUN ON LAVENDER. I SIT ON THE GARDEN STEP WITH TEA, AND swirl honey into yogurt, watching how they soften and meld. Sharp and sweet as the warmth of my mouth binds them. Listen to birdsong.

So much peace and beauty in this morning. Is it *too* perfect? I think of Elise, hungry tunnels, eager whispers, Teresa singing as she works a knife through flesh. Imagine if the villager's warning was right; imagine if this is not safe, but a lure, a place of ravenous appetite closing around me. I think of flies, gorging themselves on the bait inside a carnivorous plant, unable to lift off as the petals fold in.

No. You don't stumble across monsters on sunbaked beaches; places where people laugh and lick food from each other's fingers don't have ghosts. The sun sanitizes them. Girls do not vanish in paradise.

I jerk at a hand on my shoulder. Larissa's face is so close that my heart turns cartwheels. "Got you on the rota with me. Do you like goats?"

"I like wrangling them. I think?"

I am not great at wrangling goats. I'm muddy and bruised as we hurry back from the goat pen with buckets of milk under building thunderheads. I'd be sick with shame, but I'm laughing and Larissa's approving.

I wish Craig could see this. Aoife, wrangling goats. Making friends. Being the impulsive dream girl he always wanted.

In the kitchen, Maisie, the old Irish woman, teaches me and Larissa to make goat's cheese and jams, regaling us with stories as the wind gets up and the sky darkens to pewter. I lose myself in it, stirring the water and sugar and fruit, steam redoubling the thundery heat. I might be boiling too, growing tender, leeching my color and flavor into the sweetness.

The thought makes me dizzy; I look up. The air's thick with sugar, the first drops of rain slapping the windows, curtains moving in a breeze I can't feel.

Maisie's gone. It's just Larissa, leaning against the table, watching me. Her grin's playful, all teeth. Something about it makes me aware, with a thud, that we're alone. Everything's still, the rain thickening outside, cocooning us. Lightning flickers; I wait for thunder.

A peach sits in Larissa's palm, ready to be sliced for the pot. All that soft, sun-freckled skin. It's so fragile, isn't it? It could come apart in her hand.

It's so quiet; I'd have expected everyone to be piling into the farmhouse to escape the rain, dripping and whooping, but nothing moves. It's just us in the steam and rattle of the rain.

She says, "Hey, Aoife," and steps up close to me. "Do you want to know a cool thing I learned once?"

I nod. There's the thunder, a warm rumble that just thickens the close air around us. Back home, thunder booms once. Here, it begins and doesn't end, resonating. Makes it feel like time's gone wonky.

If that carnivorous flower closed up around me right now, I might let it, for another few instants of standing here beside her.

"There's this idea," Larissa says, soft. "That time's just something we perceive. To string everything together. That actually, all moments exist all at once, bunched up and forever. Your brain tells you that you're moving forward through time, but really, it's all simultaneous and eternal. Which means even if we don't know it, we are always going to be standing here in this kitchen listening to the thunder and making jam; this moment cannot be destroyed, and I really, really like that, don't you?"

A shudder and a grin all at once, rippling through me. "I was just thinking something like that. Only, way less coherent and philosophical, and it involved carnivorous flowers."

She laughs. "I don't actually even want the context for that." She examines me as the laugh dies down, something growing soft in her gaze. "Hey. I want to show you something, okay? No questions, because this is going to be weird, so you just have to go with it and trust me. All right?" She's standing so close. "About time you got a beautiful secret to play with."

I hadn't thought my chest could get any tighter, but apparently it can. I nod. No questions.

"What you do," she whispers, voice half lost in the thunder, "is let go. Feel the sensation, breathe out, and let it go. It's easier than it sounds. Something's there to take it."

"Something—something is *what*?" I had not had a single expectation; I had not in any way been prepared for her to say that. A shudder rises, remembering those cold passageways, the hunger in them.

"What did I say?" She raises an eyebrow, eyes glittering playfully.

"No questions?"

"No questions. Just trust. Like this." She raises the peach to my lips.

I bite down. Sweetness bursts on my tongue—

"Give up the taste, let it go—"

She's right, it's easy. My mouth and mind were holding that flavor only lightly.

Something else is there, around me, inside me, to accept that offering.

The taste is gone from my mouth, there only in echo; the air, the steam, the swimmy light, and the storm, all shiver and flicker as they accept what I've given. It's like my body belongs to something else, is an organ through which something can taste the world. I feel its appreciation, its pleasure, redoubled in me, sweeter than any mouthful.

I feel the edge of something, so close. My senses are jumbled; it's like it's speaking to me through the thunder.

My thoughts tumble. There were so many hints and promises that the universe was stranger and more magical and dangerous than life so far had promised. This is not a hint; this is as good as a confirmation, and it leaves me giddy with belief and disbelief and terror.

"You feel it?" Larissa breathes. "That's how it starts. Does it want more?"

I can't say what *it* is. I can't separate it from the thundering of my heart or the smell of sugar or the patter of rain. But I know. It wants more; it always wants more.

Larissa's hand finds my wrist, my pulse. Her fingers move there; I shiver.

The shiver continues, out through me, into whatever's around me. I offer the sensation, of Larissa's touch, of what that *does* to me, and it's no longer mine, and the fabric of everything sucks it up greedily. *More.*

"Are you scared?" Larissa asks.

I nod. I don't say, *I don't know if I'm scared of this presence, of what it's doing, or that you're going to kiss me.*

"Give up the fear."

I feel my shallow breath, the ache of the uncanny behind my breastbone, the dark places in my mind stirring with panic at her closeness. I find fear in every cell. I say to the presence, *This is yours.*

I'm not afraid now. The stone walls and cool flagstones and colored shutters flutter like firelight, a shudder of satisfaction. Is that just lightning?

Thunder murmurs. I don't understand its language; I don't care. Larissa's hand finds my waist. If I look up, that'll be a *yes*, and something will happen.

You think she *wants* you? *Bless your silly little heart.*

I feel her breath. She does.

She steps away, leaving me blinking, peach juice sticky on my lips. She's laughing. "Good! It likes you, I can tell, it likes you so much."

I open my mouth, but she puts her finger to her lips. It's a secret and I'm in on it and I'm not. Thunder echoes, and it's just thunder; there's footsteps, whoops, doors slamming. Sage passes the kitchen with his usual glare. The rain's soaked a pattern onto his t-shirt; it looks like a map.

Larissa whistles ostentatiously and returns to slicing peaches. My mind's too giddy to form questions. I pick up the half-devoured peach and eat it down to the last shreds as rain streams down the steamed-up window. Some bites, I let myself taste and relish. Some, I offer the taste up and feel that delighted ripple.

I savor this fearlessness; I imagine something unearthly coiling in my stomach and spreading. It feels right, holding something like that inside my body. Like it belongs there.

This evening is quieter, a bonfire in the garden, Kiera reading local fairy tales from a book, Kai and Larissa contributing dramatic voices. Kiera's face enthralls as much as the story, but I'm yawning, overwhelmed by the day's strangeness. When my eyes drift closed one too many times, I follow the general drift back to the huts and tents in the grove.

Not straight to sleep, though. The thought of the girl singing in the cabin has been nagging at me all day; I'd been looking out for a teenager around the farm, but there's been no sign of her; is it concern or nosiness that make me want to check on her? But she's made it clear she doesn't want me around. She's trying to keep to herself, and I've stumbled in on her privacy twice.

That's why I'm quiet as I slip through the trees to the cabin, and that's why I'm surprised when she calls out, "Hey!"

I freeze. "Um—hey?"

I wait for a window or something to open, but nothing. Still, she speaks again. "Who are you?"

What a question. I have only the bones of it now. "I'm Aoife. I just got here."

"Aoife," she says. "I'm Myri. Short for Myristica, if you can believe that."

I snort. The words come out automatically. "Wow. Your parents must be brutal."

I wince. *Can you get* anything *right?*

"My parents love me very much, actually!" Myri says. "Thank you."

The quiet pulses, insects, wind-whispers, distant guitar strumming echoing from some group down on the beach. I'd like to ask, *Why don't you come out?* I'd like to ask, *Are you all right in there?* I'm scared I've invaded too much already with her; I have no idea how to interact with a girl behind closed shutters, face unseen, just a voice crying and singing in the night.

"Where are you from, Aoife?"

"England. Tallerton, you wouldn't know it." I grin. "You definitely don't want to."

"Try me," Myri says. "I have heard of it. You have black swans, right?"

"Yeah. That's probably the most exciting thing we have." I grin and sit on the cabin steps. There's movement behind the door, like she's sliding down to sit back-to-back with me. "Think I like it better here."

She snorts, though I'm not sure if it's a snort of agreement.

"Have you been living here long?" I ask. Seems safe.

She's quiet, for long enough that I think she's going to ask me to leave again. "I'd like to go to Tallerton," she says suddenly. "I'd like to see the black swans and buy cheap jewelry and eat fast food. Right now, that sounds really, really great."

"I'll take you someday, then." I have no intention of ever taking her or anyone there. I could float into the sky and pop at the thought: Maybe I never have to go home. "I know a really crap burger place, you'd love it."

She laughs. "This is going to be weird. Can I ask you something? Aoife who's new?"

I don't say that it's already weird, talking to her through a closed door, unable to picture her face, getting the sense that asking questions will get me nowhere. I don't say anything except, "Sure."

"Can you tell me a bit about your town?" There's a shift, like she's stretching. "I'm having a day where I . . . miss the world. Can you tell me about the swans and the shopping center and the crap burger places?"

For a second, yeah, that's *weird*, and then it isn't. It's a disorientating flip: This place is the pinnacle of adventure to me, promises of something beyond the canny, friendships and freedom and secrets. But imagine being a teenager here, cliffs and hills and horizon pressing in, dreaming of a wider world. No wonder she sulks alone in a cabin.

That's probably why the story that stirs in my mind is an old one. "When I was thirteen," I say slowly, "I just got on a bus. To see where it was going."

I don't say that it was the day that I'd done well in my exams and come home expecting a family party, like my brothers had had; that I'd arrived to an empty house, nobody caring; that I'd decided in that instant to run away.

"What was the bus like?" Myri asks.

I blink. "Bus-y? It had patterned chairs and schoolkids and old ladies?"

"Did you have a window seat?"

"Yeah." I focus the story on every tiny detail I can: the rows of flats, the arcades and rail yards and half-built office blocks, the fading historical buildings and the kids who smoked on their steps, the mums with pushchairs by the weed-clogged river. How I'd found a park holding an open-air cinema night, with deck chairs and fairy lights—a rare, actual *event*.

I don't tell her how I couldn't get in, too young and no money, and how I slunk home, dejected to learn that I couldn't even get into a film showing; I wasn't going to make it anywhere alone. I don't tell her how nobody had even noticed I was gone. I don't tell her how that bright-lit place lodged in my mind, a splinter, a promise that there would be somewhere like that for me someday.

I peer up at the stars. Even then, I was listening for something, wasn't I?

For some call. And now I've heard it. And it's lulling me, tangling me up, and I don't want it to stop.

"Thanks," Myri says after a long while. "I . . . this is weird, too, but can you not tell anyone you talked to me? I'm . . . it's complicated, but I don't want to get anyone in trouble."

A vice closes around my ribs. I'd settled down to the idea of her being reclusive, sulky, but my mind zooms off in terrifying directions: I imagine cruel punishments, a cabin where people are isolated for weeks for stepping out of line.

Which is *silly*; that doesn't fit at *all* with this place. I'm being over-dramatic. I am overdramatic; Craig always reminded me.

I settle on: "Are you okay? Is something going on?"

She sighs. "There's a hell of a lot going on you don't know about yet, new girl. Can you just . . . keep it private? We can be friends, but just for us to know about?"

I can choose, I realize. I can push, ask why she doesn't show her face, why nobody's mentioned her, why I could get into trouble; I can choose to follow my instincts, the nosiness forever tugging at me. Or I can choose to trust that, despite the secrets, this place is still that splinter of bright light and laughter I've waited for.

I felt something today, something undeniable, something *beyond*, with peach in my mouth and my breath mingling with Larissa's. I want to trust it and let understanding unfurl. I have to trust it, because if I don't, the sheer terror of it will be more than I can handle.

Besides. Everyone here seems to be bursting with secrets. Maybe I get one that's for me.

"Okay," I say. "If you like."

"Thanks," she says again, and yawns, and it's contagious, and I yawn too, and we both laugh. "Goodnight, Aoife who's new."

"Goodnight, Myri who I'm not supposed to talk to." I'm a few steps out onto the crunching olive leaves when she calls out.

"Have you been dreaming?"

". . . How do you mean?" A breeze ripples across my skin, too warm to raise gooseflesh.

"Dreaming. Or seeing glimpses, visions. Of the cave." There's a sudden tremble in her voice. "It opens, and you go inside, and . . . and it's just dark in there, complete dark, and the dark is smiling, all sleepy and well-fed—"

Terror grips me by the scruff of the neck, and the grove whirls around me.

"There's no cave," I manage. "I searched the whole cove. There's nothing there."

"You *are* dreaming," she says grimly, then: "I'm sorry."

"What—"

Her footsteps recede. Nothing but insect-spangled silence.

Maybe I'm dreaming. Maybe I'm not. Maybe I'm awake, fear rendering everything unreal; maybe I'm wrapped in sheets, dreaming uneasy of walking in the cove.

My toes sink into the pebbles and sand, cooled by the night air. I keep my eyes on the tree line, on the ocean, on the sand; I look up at the cliffs only when I'm halfway across the beach, like I might surprise the cave into existing.

Nothing.

Nothing, but even as the mingled relief and disappointment and embarrassment descend, something else does, too. That now-familiar thinning of the air, that sensation like approaching thunder, that new vividness to every color and sharpness to every shadow.

New instincts stir in me. I find all my fear, my worries about what's going on with Myri, my nerves that my new friendships will crumble, my terror at tumbling into the unknown. Like Larissa taught me earlier, I close my eyes, and I offer it all up.

And just like before, the tension unspools, loosening, no longer mine. Like something is, so tenderly, easing the doubt out of me. Like sucking the juice from a ripe fruit. I savor it for a moment, the new calm, the intimacy, the communion with something vast and delighted. Then I open my eyes.

The sickle moon turns the cliffs to jagged pearl, so I see it clearly, where it evidently was not just a few moments ago.

The gash of dark. The mouth of a cave.

I flinch; horror and fascination and temptation swoop down; like a frightened child, I squeeze my eyes closed again.

When I open them, the cave is gone, like a wound healed over.

CHAPTER ELEVEN

A COLLECTION

ANOTHER MORNING. THIRD, OR FOURTH? I SHOULD BE COUNTING. I SHOULD care, about things like time, or the world outside. This morning, I am not going to care.

Later, I'll let myself be fearful, curious, return to wondering about Elise, the mysterious Myri, visions that might not be dreams, about a presence that takes my feelings when I offer them. But this morning, Oscar's handing me coffee and ruffling my hair, and I'm scraping butter onto still-warm bread and the sky's alarmingly blue, washed clean. Some of the calm that came across me in my dream last night—or on the beach, if that really happened—lingers, cool and soothing.

A warm breeze sends puffs of flour and spices through the air, and disrupts Kiera, who's hesitating in the doorway, eyeing the kitchen with what can't be nervousness. She makes a beeline for me, and something that is definitely nervousness stirs in my sternum.

She pulls up short in front of me, and we both open our mouths to say something like, *Good morning*, or *Nice bread isn't it*, or *I like your hair today*, or one of a million normal things that normal people say to greet each other in the morning. I cannot remember a single word in the English language.

Kiera's mouth opens and closes, and she finds something to say, or rather, to blurt. "Do you know what was on this land before the farmhouse?"

Okay, I'll admit, this is more fun than "good morning." "Ooh, no, what?"

We made those grins on each other's faces, didn't we? That was us. She takes my enthusiasm and redoubles it, apparently relieved. "A burned-out monastery! Completely destroyed!"

She could tell me anything, and I'd feel just as thrilled as this. "Really? That's cool!"

"Yeah! Let me show you my collection!" There's a momentum, like she didn't plan any of this but she's in it now. She grabs my hand in this unthinking touch that I decide not to panic about. Her hand's marked with illegible scribbles.

I look down at the hand and panic about it, and she pulls away so I panic about that, too, but it all leaves me so breathless that I follow her. Feels like she's some fairy-tale imp sent to show me more hidden doorways; feels so good I don't bother to question who or what might have sent her.

The library's upstairs, behind richly colored stained-glass doors. Inside, it's wood and glass and iron, splashed with carpets in vivid blues and starry white, a vaulted whitewashed ceiling painted with black stars. I turn in a circle, caught up in wonder.

The bookshelves are stacked high. I've never read much; Craig scoffed when he found me with a novel and quizzed me to trip me up when I tried nonfiction. But I could sit here for hours, read every word, letting them change me.

Kiera's eyeing me like I might vanish. I don't think anything could make me do that. I want the carpets and books to absorb me. I want to be the words she sits at that desk reading.

She pulls me to a glass cabinet. The objects are laid on strips of linen, dried mud adhering to some, spiderwebs to others. An old coin, a broken tile, a silver icon, a knife, a terracotta jar, a rusted brass bell. That can't be a human bone, can it?

"They're all things we've found on the land." Kiera rests her fingers against the glass. "Incredible stuff. We've been naughty and not reported it. Jonah . . . wants these things to stay at home."

Her grin's slightly rictus. I compare the textures of the name *Jonah* in Larissa's and Kiera's voices; Larissa's resonant with awe and love, Kiera's shakier. I remember Giulia crying, Larissa assuring her "he loves us," and my nerves prickle with a sudden dread. He's already judged me and found me wanting, hasn't he?

"They're all from the monastery?"

Kiera shakes her head. "From what I've pieced together, and the records are *patchy* and what we've found sometimes contradicts them, but there's been something on this cove for millennia, farmsteads like this or religious establishments. There's evidence of Bronze Age temples, even earlier. Layers of isolated bubbles of civilization, and you want to know what's really interesting?"

"I definitely want to know what's really interesting." God, the way her eyes gleam. She's wound so tight with energy, fear and excitement interchangeable, alertness sparking, my skin tingling when that alertness is focused on me.

"They *all* ended in some kind of cataclysm."

I blink. That is interesting. Unnervingly.

"The monastery was shut down by the church, the monks got executed, some kind of accusations of heresy. There's records of battles, social implosions, disasters. If I hadn't, uh, dropped out of my master's course, there's a whole thesis there, why such an isolated place has seen so much violence, although I'd have to leave out"—she catches herself—"stuff."

"Stuff, huh." I raise an eyebrow. My mouth fills with the taste of peach, sun-warmed and sticky.

"Stuff." Kiera's smile twitches like something trying to escape.

"You don't worry? About . . . the history?"

Kiera considers, angling her head so her messy fringe flops. "I worry about a lot of things all the time, actually! Hey, want to touch something that's hundreds of years old?"

"*Absolutely.*"

Kiera hands me the bell from the cabinet. Her hand, my hand, and something ancient and fragile. Hoping I look impish and not obnoxious, I try ringing it.

Did it sound like that to the monks? I imagine them, moving like shadowy crows through cloisters, among rosebushes and wine. Did they feel the same uncanny presence?

The light through the shutters flickers with the breeze.

Do you know about the girl in the cabin? Do you know where Elise went? The questions form but won't emerge. That's how you break a moment.

The moment breaks anyway. Oscar's in the doorway, waving, vest printed with cheerful cartoon pineapples. Kiera jumps at him for a good-morning squeeze, and I stand there awkward. I bet Oscar gives great hugs.

"Village?" Oscar asks. Kiera gives jazz hands. I'm not sure what he means, so I jazz hands too, then shove my hands in my pockets when I realize they're not looking at me.

Kiera hurries back over, grabbing her laptop from the desk. "Aoife, I'm hitching on Oscar's supply trip. Café in the village is the only place I can get internet, and I've got, like, ten thousand billion things I need to look up. Chill in here if you want. Don't break anything please and don't touch anything that looks like it might crumble and no coffee in here even . . . ." She's still talking as Oscar winks and strong-arms her out.

It's quiet in their aftermath, the books drinking every scrap of sound. I return the bell to the cabinet gently, like the softest click will wake something.

Kiera said I could stay. Which sounds like a chance to *snoop*.

I explore the bookshelves, like I might stumble across books on visions, caves, disappearances, cabins. Or a secret door? All the best libraries have secret doors, right?

Nothing. Most of it's history, mythology. There's some new age spiritual stuff, psychology, farming, a selection of novels. This is silly. Oscar was right; I should trust and let it unfold. The beautiful secrets are for me, Larissa said.

I glance at Kiera's desk, scattered with Kiera's notes. It's not wrong, right? To be curious about what's waiting for me? She left me alone in here for a reason; she must have.

The notes are like the sketchbook, mostly illegible. I pick up random phrases in excited capitals: SUSTAINED BY EMOTION, CONSCIOUSNESS??? WHY THE OCEAN? PAGAN BELIEFS TO MONASTIC HERESY—TRANSMITTED HOW? I can't parse anything, but I pick up her tone in the press of the pen, the blotches of ink. Where she's written WHAT WERE THEY TRYING TO DO??? underlined three times, that looks like frustration. I touch it, like I could soothe her.

I move on. The cabinet's unlocked. *Here we go.*

These books are ancient, yellowing, bound in leather and odder things. Full wizard's tower aesthetic. I handle them carefully, like they might set off some curse, but the library's still, sun moving across the white walls and dark carpets.

I pick the most ominous-looking, cover unmarked except for—the familiarity sparks a smile—a closed circle inside an open circle, one bisecting line. I crack it open.

It's incomprehensible, intricate calligraphy in a language I don't know—Latin, maybe. But it's like the notebook, redoubled, richer; my mind doesn't understand, but my body responds, heart battering my ribs, nerves singing.

Secrets, in my hands, just beyond my understanding. Craig's laughing in my memory, *You never could understand things even when they were under your nose, eh love?* But Larissa's eyes shine in my mind, drawing me on.

A good half of the book is destroyed. Pages ripped out, scorched, covered with spilled ink. Behind the desecration, I glimpse illustrations, but details are lost. I look up, head spinning, and my eyes catch Jonah's.

He's right there.

A long, strange man in the doorway, in his suit and necklaces, sharp eyes slicing me open and spilling me out into that clean white room. How long has he been watching?

I can't speak. That gaze pins me.

"Aoife." My name, in his voice. It's like the sound of me has been stolen and reshaped.

My hand's on the book. I should be racing for an excuse, but my thoughts are frozen.

"You'll put that away," Jonah says, voice light, but not light enough to hide the sheer size of the consequences coming for me. "And I'd rather you left the library. Make yourself useful downstairs for now."

"I'm sorry!" I blurt. Panic rises, nausea, fingers gripping my neck, constriction, apologizing isn't enough but there's always hope hidden in it, begging for reprieve—

Jonah turns away.

I put the book away, carefully, and leave the library.

He's gone, but I know better than to be relieved.

—⊙—

I spend the day tight-wound, ready for disaster. I can't imagine what form it'll take, but I saw it on Jonah's face, looming.

Do they all know? There's coolness to Kai as I help him harvest lemons, suspicion on Aksel's face when I bring him tea. They let me sit with them at dinner, Kiera sneaks me a chocolate bar from the village, Oscar invites me into a card game, but eyes are narrow over their usual smiles.

I know this feeling, thick and heavy, the window of time between fucking up and paying for it. Craig would draw those times out, for days. He thought it would fix me. It didn't; I haven't learned.

I was stupid, nosy, paranoid. Missing girls, cabins, caves, strange lore, all those things crumble, smashed by solid reality: being unwanted. Messing up. Again.

When they kick me out, where will I go? There's nowhere.

I go to bed early because it's unbearable, trying to tell if the smiles are faked, if the whispers are about me. I can't sleep, listening to the waves and rustling trees. Will I still be here to hear those tomorrow?

I slip out to Myri's cabin, but there's no answer to my knock on the window.

So I end up wandering the groves, restless, too sick with dread and shame to take in the bright sweep of stars or the moths among the strung-up lights. The breeze is full of trickery, teasing at sounds in one direction and another, which is why I don't hear them until I've almost stumbled out of the trees into their circle.

Scattered cushions and candles on the beach. Jonah sits on a wave-softened tree branch at the epicenter, hands folded on his lap. Among the figures cross-legged around him I spot Kiera, hunched nervously; Larissa, managing to lounge even in a meditation pose; Sage, stony-faced; and Giulia, who's talking, twisting her skirt between her fingers.

I don't think they've seen me. I withdraw into the trees, and I should walk away, I know, I learned my lesson about snooping, but I can't resist.

". . . understand, that it's cruel." Giulia looks up at Jonah. "It's a betrayal of everything this place is and everything it made me."

Jonah nods. Flickery candlelight makes his features ragged, unreadable.

"But you know why." Giulia's voice cracks. "Please don't make me say it."

"It's not wrong to miss your friend," Darya says, and there's nods around the circle.

What is this? Some kind of group therapy? Imagine having a place where you can just talk, where others take your pain into their hands.

Giulia sighs a long, defeated sigh. "I'm just scared, all right? I see her walking around, wearing *Elise's clothes*, and I'm scared."

Candlelight moves shadows around the sand. They're talking about me, aren't they?

I wrap my fingers around my shirt sleeve. Of course these clothes are hers. Another gift from a friend I never knew.

"Stand up, Giulia." Jonah's expressionless.

Giulia stands. Shifting light etches fear on her face.

"The ocean," Jonah orders.

Giulia looks resigned. Her hands hesitate, but she unties her dress; it pools around her feet, leaving her exposed in her underwear. My face flares with secondhand shame.

She could just say no, right?

Face blank, Giulia walks to the sea.

I hold my breath; something dangerous, didn't Kiera say? But nobody's speaking. Giulia pauses at the lip of the water, then walks forward, moonlit water flaring around her, until she's waist-deep.

I hear sobs over the waves.

The moment shivers, until Jonah calls, "You can return now."

Giulia pads dripping across the sand, still sobbing. Pain or relief, or both? She slips her dress back on and stands before Jonah, not bothering to hide the tears.

Jonah stands and places a hand on her shoulder. The light hits his face again, and I see a compassion as deep and broad as the sky.

"Oh, Giulia," he says. "We're all afraid. We must be bigger than the fear. You see that now, don't you? You remember the scale of what we face. You'll be strong."

Giulia nods, and he gathers her into his arms.

He rocks her, strokes her hair, lets her stifle her weeping in his shoulder. He's so proud of her that it outweighs any anger. I see it on that strange, rugged face. Pride. Love.

I imagine being held, forgiven, like that. *Shh, Aoife. You know what you did, but it's all right.* It rips through me.

I might have had that. If I'd played it right, I might have been soothed by those hands, whispered to, forgiven and enfolded.

Craig would hold and soothe me, eventually, when I made mistakes. But when Giulia sobs in Jonah's arms, it's like watching the island, the universe, forgive her.

It won't forgive me. For intruding. Flinging myself into things I don't understand.

I walk away.

CHAPTER TWELVE
SALT, DISTORTIONS

I DON'T SLEEP, REALLY. I DRIFT AND I ACHE. I FEEL PARADISE DRIFTING AWAY from my grasp, inch by cruel inch, until sun creeps through the vines.

I choose a loose cotton dress and run my finger along the fabric in the fluttering light. *Elise, where are you now?* She had paradise. She belonged. What took her from this place? What took it from her?

I try to imagine a future without the Farmstead and see a void that will suck me in and make me nothing. When you've *had* the uncanny, when the universe has opened your mouth and placed everything it promised on your tongue, and that's gone, what do you become?

I walk slowly to the farmhouse, soil already warm under my bare feet though soft, gray clouds hang above.

The kitchen's empty. Have people started the day earlier, or later? Maybe it's because of me. I threw something beautiful on those terracotta tiles and smashed it.

My name's not on the rota, which intensifies the sickness in my chest;

I flounder, wondering if they're hoping I'll just *leave*. Recklessness and desperation stir in me, a *screw it* and a yearning for someone who, at least, seems not to hate me.

I find Kiera in the library and pause to drink her in. Sun outlines stray threads of hair; her undercut's growing out messy, her nose rings glittering. Forgotten pens behind her ears.

Something catches in my chest. She's perfectly placed in a world made for her. When do I get that?

She's examining an old pottery cup. I imagine her focusing on me that way, eyebrows drawn, lips twisted. Picking me apart, making me tremble.

I cough.

She fumbles, startled, and the cup slips from her fingers.

I expect it to break. How many thousands of years did that cup survive, how many hands did it pass through, just to become shards because of us? In my mind I see rose-painted, gilded shards of a vase scatter, and remember just how much I existed in that moment. The thought makes my heart pound, even though the cup rolls, unharmed.

We stare at it, then at each other, wordlessly excited by our little disaster and miracle.

"What's up," I say lightly, my belly twisting. The rugs and paper absorb my voice, but I feel like it's echoing, like I've been caught somewhere I'm not meant to be. Which, probably, after yesterday, I'm not.

Kiera kneels to retrieve the cup. "Books. Old stuff. Not anything close to enough sleep, actually! What about you?"

I think I've lost everything. "Nothing much. What are you working on?"

"Cross-referencing some symbols from the diary of a traveler from the 1800s." Kiera holds up a book, and there it goes, the enthusiasm flooding her, washing away my anxiety. "He was shipwrecked here, taken in by farmers, maybe even in this house. They had . . . beliefs. I'm trying to put it together with some older mythology."

"Cool myths?" The words feel silly, shaped wrong.

Kiera nods, face brilliant. "The continuity from Bronze Age beliefs, older, is incredible. It's like . . . primordial. Same symbols and legends, millennia old . . . ."

"That is very cool." I peer at the screen. Already weird looking at a screen again; the farmhouse is the only part of the commune with reliable electricity, and pixels feel like part of a forgotten outside world now. "That's . . . ."

"The standing stones, yeah. Giulia's photos. This one's my favorite." Kiera clicks.

I stare. A carving: a figure, a cave, something inside, rendered in curls, reaching—

Cold grasping my skin, jagged rocks. Irretrievable in the core of something . . . .

"What did they believe?" My head spins. I can't trust the matter around me; it's this veneer over . . . over what?

"Elements vary," Kiera says, teacher mode, eyes shining, "but the basic story is about a god of secrets and forbidden things. The other gods feared its influence over humans because any who saw it would be caught up in terror and ecstasy, with knowledge they were incapable of holding. So they trapped it in a cave."

The dizziness redoubles. The world would crumble if I touched it.

"Still, it was said that if someone was in need, they could find its cave and be rewarded with a miracle, at a terrible cost." There's something toothy in that grin, eager and fearful. "But the myths get vague. They're never clear what it actually wants."

A confused shudder rolls through me. I feel wanted. Desired by something vast, something I've felt the touch of. Something took part of me, the taste from my mouth and pleasure from my skin, and whispered, *More*.

Will I even be here long enough to understand?

"That's what you're trying to find out?" I say, voice thin.

"That," Kiera says drily, "is one of about ten thousand things I'm trying to find out. I've been bouncing around all day between *this* and trying to translate this other book from a weird Latin that isn't really even proper Latin and . . . ." She rubs her temples. "I feel like I'm really close to something."

"'All day?' It's not even ten o'clock." She looks blank at this information. Maybe she, too, thinks that all times exist at once. Whatever; at least this gives me an idea of what to do while I wait for the blade to fall. "I'm getting you tea, and *breakfast*. You need a break."

"Break," she says doubtfully, like she's not sure what that is.

The kitchen's still eerily quiet; a few more people are milling around outside and wave at me through the window. I can't read those waves, if they're covering disdain. As I boil the kettle and gather fruit and bread, I find myself thinking of Craig. There are whole hours here when I don't think of him, and oh god, how can I do that? It's like I forget he's out there, how angry and hurt he'll be. Does he miss me? Or is my absence a relief, release from my constant mistakes?

I try to picture where he is now. The world outside the island feels unreal, like it could dissolve. But when I think of his face, it's this place that becomes unreal: How can it exist, somewhere where anyone else wanted me? From all the angles, the picture looks wrong. Maybe it all feels so illusory because I'm about to have lost both, cast adrift from them completely.

I look for Larissa among the people in the garden, but there's no sign of her. It's starting to rain, heavy drops plopping in the dust and shaking the lavender. I ascend the stairs again, balancing the plate and the cup as I ease open the stained-glass library door. "I thought chamomile would be—"

I freeze as I take in the empty desk, and the books scattered, and Kiera, face down on the midnight-blue rug.

For a second, it's a nightmare, the worst thoughts rising—a seizure, poison—but she's breathing rapidly, chest rising and falling jerkily in her creamy white sweater.

"Fuck, what's wrong? Are you hurt?"

She sits up; her eyes have flared so wide I see the veins interlaced at their edges. "I. Am not! I can't!"

Is this a panic attack? I have no idea how you handle those. I search for a spot on the desk to put down the tea and food, but its's piled with notes. How long as she been here?

A book lies open, gilded illustrations and thick black script. An image of a robed monk on a slab, others circling him, dark swirls around their hoods. His face is marked with dark symbols, hands bound, hands straining—

The prickling on my skin matches the rhythm of the rain.

"Kiera?" I kneel, leaving the plate and mug on the carpet, and take her hand. There's something precipitous, terrifying, about dealing with her like this. Something I could smash if my hand slipped. Something unknowable behind it.

She grips my arm like she's holding back from tumbling off an edge. Even with the muscles spring-tight, her hand is shaking.

"I can't," she says again, softer, panic yielding to something deeper. That's a tear on her cheek, isn't it?

And I can't, either. I don't *know* people, I don't know how to handle them.

Still, I clumsily draw her into a hug. I try not to notice that this is the first time I've held her. That I can feel her heartbeat, like a frightened animal's. That my lips are millimeters from her sun-brightened skin.

A rush of recklessness: My lips find her cheek, a friend kiss, a reassurance, kissing away her tear—

I taste salt. I think of a photo I saw of the intricate salt-crystal structures in a tear; all that complexity is coming apart on my tongue and dissolving into me. Part of me wants to part her lips and taste not just her tear, taste *her*—

I pull away. I remember Craig. I don't deserve this.

"Can you tell me about it?" I ask, hoping I can pretend that that didn't just happen.

Kiera shakes her head. She didn't respond to the kiss, still curled around herself. "It's too big, I can't explain." Her eyes are huge, but she manages a strangled laugh. "You ever understand how far, far out of your depths you are? Like you were paddling and suddenly you're sinking into the goddamn Mariana Trench?"

"And there's weird fish down there?"

That was the right thing to say; her smile is curdled, but it's a smile. "The weirdest fish. Let me . . ." She stands, braced against the desk. "Sorry. I'll just . . . I'll tidy up. I made *such* a mess; it's a mess—" She looks down at a page like she can't understand language.

I don't know how to snatch her out of this spiral. "I'll—look, I'll be back."

Is that confusion in her? Hurt? I'm lost in an unfamiliar place. I grab her hand and squeeze, and dart out of the library and downstairs.

Someone, someone who knows people—Oscar's in the kitchen, tapping his foot to music, inhaling coffee. Relief soaks me to the bone. Perfect. "It's Kiera, she's having a crisis, I don't think she's slept—"

Oscar fixes me with a curious stare, an unfamiliar coolness. "Any idea what brought this on?"

I shrug. "There was a book? Something with monks—"

Coffee forgotten, he's striding toward the stairs with such intensity that I step back. He looks back at me like an afterthought, says, "Don't you worry, I've got this," and is gone.

The sound of rain closes back over, intensifying the silence. I stand nonplussed and absently swig his coffee. I should walk away, find something to do, hope that whatever's going on with Kiera draws attention away from my own stupid misstep yesterday. I helped. But this isn't my business.

The taste of coffee has washed away any salt from my tongue.

As stealthily as I can, I follow him.

The library door is deceptive. Those stained-glass swirls warp light, telling half a story.

To me, it's a story of two figures, one pacing—bald head, colorful shirt, there then lost to the distortions—and the other leaning against a desk. Is her head in her hands, or is she holding something up?

To them, it might be a story of a girl pressed against a wall, peering, trying to catch voices. But they don't look.

Spying, are you, love? You mess up everything so you go around snooping? Didn't you learn your lesson on this one already?

"... already know what you have to do," Oscar says.

"I don't." Kiera's voice cracks. "They failed, and how can we know *why*, or that others didn't bring disaster on themselves trying? You *know* the history of this place. I can't imagine where this ends—"

"None of us can." One shadow moves toward the other. The story is incomplete, I can't tell if it's protective or threatening.

"I know." The Kiera shadow straightens then slumps. "All this is meant to be *beyond imagining*, but—"

"But you won't share what you've found"—Oscar's voice is soft— "because you don't know what the consequences would be. Is that it?"

Kiera's quiet. Rich reds and greens reshape the shadows into something incomprehensible. Was that a gasp?

"Kiera," Oscar sighs. "It's been a struggle, giving up control. It's all I knew. Handing yourself over to the unknown is *hard*. We've talked about this."

"And I've told you I *know* that," Kiera snaps. I couldn't imagine her snapping. It makes everything even more alien. "I know a thousand times better than you that when you let go, you do not always end up in some fluffy utopia, all right? It wasn't like that for me!"

"You found your way here," Oscar says.

Kiera's quiet, then says, "So did Elise."

The shadows move. The silence stretches.

Kiera whimpers softly, and something in me cracks.

There's a visible shudder, a flicker, one I felt in the kitchen with a mouthful of peach. Then, it was subtle and sensuous, gentle.

This is different. This feels violent. This is a devouring.

Matter quivers, the aftermath of a wrenching and swallowing.

Before I can move, Oscar's striding out of the door, shaking his head. I freeze, incredibly busted.

He doesn't notice me. He pushes past and strides up another set of stairs. That's the book in his hands, isn't it?

My head's spinning, heart hammering. I can't understand what I half-saw, what I just *felt*. I don't want to *see*.

I open the door anyway.

Kiera's at her desk, typing, smiling placidly.

"Hey!" Nothing warped, nothing gone from her, Kiera's grin. It's like nothing happened. "Sorry for that, I got a bit overwrought."

"What happened—"

"It's all good. Want to join me on the balcony for that breakfast you brought me?"

I stare at her; she stares back, bright-eyed and relaxed.

The rain outside hisses steadily, like radio static.

CHAPTER THIRTEEN
NEARLY TIME

NORMALITY CLOSES BACK OVER; THE SUN COMES OUT, I'M CALLED TO HELP FISH off the rocks, Ana's made me a sandwich. People are still distant, but it feels like a reprieve, like my mistake yesterday's been offset. A few hours ago, I would have sobbed with relief.

And I am relieved, agonizingly. But the *wrongness* of what I felt in the library lingers, and the relief feels like it's closing around me, desperate hope clamping itself around my limbs. I understand now that I cannot lose this place, and that seeds panic.

I spend the evening on the beach with Larissa and Kiera and Kai, inventing legends about the constellations between the scudding clouds, Kiera rewarding the ones that are closest to existing myths with a fresh strawberry. I sink into bone-tired sleep and uneasy dreams, haunted by my own hunger and something else's.

Until I'm woken by screams.

I jerk upright, heartbeat skipping, tangled in sweaty sheets. I know that voice.

Myri's screaming like something's ripping her apart. Raw, brutal howls.

I stumble out of bed. Fuck, what's *happening* to her? Too disorientated for fear, I rush toward the cabin.

The air's perfumed with petrichor from the day's rain. When turbulent shreds of cloud swallow the moon, the darkness is almost complete. When it peers out, dappled silver turns the knots of the trees into globular faces. It must shine on me, too.

Still, I don't think Oscar's seen me.

Moonlight moves across him. He's outside the cabin, arms folded.

Which, well, that just looks so strange. If she's having a nightmare, if she's hurt herself, why would he just be standing outside like that? He looks like he's on guard. My sleepy brain won't put the pieces together. That blank-faced sentinel can't be the cheerful traveler who's been teaching me backgammon.

I should just approach him, right? It's Oscar. But I hesitate at a sound.

The swish of a skirt, the tread of heavy boots. For a second, I'm relieved; Teresa will help. But Teresa is not smiling. Teresa has that eerie calm that comes over her when she snaps chickens' necks.

I hear shredded words from inside the cabin: "I don't want to, I don't want to do it, *I want to stay me*—it hurts it hurts it *hurts*—"

Teresa's face doesn't even twitch. She exchanges a few quiet words with Oscar, and I shift backward into the foliage, a weird admission that I'm not here to offer help anymore, that I'm spying, that whatever's happening is not something I'm meant to be witnessing.

Myri's sick. She's hurt. She's having a nightmare. They're here to help. If I keep repeating it, maybe I'll accept it.

The cabin door opens, and I'm instantly glad I'm better concealed. Seeing Jonah makes my heart leap, like encountering a wild animal. Calm and inscrutable as ever.

Beside him, Sage. And on Sage's cheek—

A long scratch. The trace of a fingernail.

And maybe a kid in a fever dream lashes out, maybe she's having a fit, maybe the scratch is from earlier; there are so many sweet, reassuring explanations to wrap me up safe. But what I see is this: a girl screaming in a cabin, guarded, fighting like hell against whatever's being done to her in the most secretive hours of the night.

The four of them are talking; their voices are lost under shrieks, but I catch phrases: "struggling," "nearly time." I hear my name, redoubling the sickness that paralyzes me.

Myri starts yelling for her mother.

This isn't real. I fucking refuse to accept that this is real.

I squeeze my eyes shut. When I open them, Jonah and Teresa are disappearing into the cabin. The screams grow louder, interwoven with the soft sound of Teresa singing, the same lullaby she crooned to the chickens as she plucked and gutted them.

Sage rubs his cheek, face unreadable in the shadow. I watch him and Oscar and imagine rushing out, bursting between them, smashing through the door, and—what?

The screams ring, agonized, tinged now with an exhausted surrender.

Three Aoifes crouch in the bushes, breaths shallow, and one of them is screaming *save her* and one is pleading, *she can't need saving, trust, they're helping her*, and one is paralyzed by fear and the cruel truth that I can't do anything. I'm not enough.

Do something, fuck you. Just do *something*.

I do nothing. Myri's screams crescendo and subside into the cruelest silence.

Insects sing into the empty dark. My ears ring.

When the door opens, I half expect them to be carrying a limp body. But they carry nothing. Jonah reaches for his wife's hand. Their expressions are lost in shadow as clouds gulp the moonlight, but I feel that shudder as the matter of the world imbibes something intangible.

Emerging behind them, Giulia. Moonlight glances across her face, and it's turned away from Jonah's and Teresa's, and it's pale and troubled. I see nothing there to reassure me. I see the girl who told me not to come here, because she was afraid for me, because it was wonderful, but terrible too.

Jonah pulls a set of keys from his pocket. He twists a key, locking the cabin from the outside. Has it always been locked?

Something overbalances. The heady bliss of these past days falls away like a curtain.

My new home is lost to me, irredeemable. And I'm lost to myself. I listened, and I did nothing.

I stay frozen, breath held. They'll spot me. Giulia will smile that half-smile; Jonah's eyes will scour my pathetic soul. But they just disappear up the path. Somehow that's worse.

I still wait a long time before daring to dart to the cabin. Shutters hide whatever horrors wait inside. When I knock, I know there will be no answer.

A quiet long enough to confirm my fears, then they're proved wrong: three quick, soft taps.

"Myri!" I press against the door like I can force my way through. "Are you okay?"

"Aoife who's new." There's relief in her voice; my throat closes up.

"I'm sorry," I manage, "I didn't help you."

Her voice is raw from screams, but calm. "You have to go. Leave the island. Tonight, or tomorrow, just go. You shouldn't be here for what happens next." The calm leaves her voice. "I don't know you, but I don't want you in this. You've been dreaming too. Go!"

"No." The heat in my voice hurts. Determination's meaningless. She screamed, and I did nothing.

"Thanks for talking to me. You helped, okay? Talking to you helped. Remembering the world." A floorboard creaks.

I hammer on the door, but I hear nothing more.

The quiet buckles under a weight and crushes me. Everything is cold and stark now. There's no more waiting for explanations, no more hope of sweet secrets unfolding. Everything's flipped over and all that's left is this: I have to find a way to save her.

CHAPTER FOURTEEN
PINNED INSECT

I LIE AWAKE STARING AT THE WOODEN CEILING. I RELAX WHEN I THINK OF giving up, and my eyes slide closed, then I jolt awake: I can't. She needs me.

Practical thoughts. I couldn't break down that door. I fantasize about burning the cabin, darting through the smoke and pulling her out, the catharsis of watching it blaze. That would draw attention, though, even if it wasn't absurdly dangerous.

Who even *has* thoughts like that? Someone giddy on fiction, a paranoid fantasist. I am a silly girl lost far from home, tricked into a trap. Even trying to think of doing anything, of the scale of this, makes me want to curl up and screech into my pillow. I am too small. I am not meant for something like this.

But who would I be if I didn't try?

I need the keys. Last seen slipped into Jonah's pocket last night.

The idea of trying to pick his pocket gives me simultaneous palpitations and giggle fits. I'll need to search the house, hope he doesn't always carry them—

Somehow, it's dawn already. And it's not so hard to slip into the kitchen earlier than usual and find the name chalked under "house cleaning." Zina, the Czech artist with the perfect bobbed hair and sharp eyeliner-flicked glare. Nobody's here; I rub it out, replace it on a more appealing-sounding cooking shift, and scrawl "Aoife" in its place. If anyone asks, I'll say I like cleaning.

Not even a lie. So often I'd stagger home from the bar, then jump up a few hours later for a cleaning shift. I enjoy it, weirdly—another way of making the world different. Although the familiar smell of cleaning chemicals will press on the bruise of Craig's absence.

Except it doesn't; the herbal concoctions Teresa offers me smell strong and earthly. The smells of this place. Of what I'll lose if this works. That thought isn't a bruise; it's a gut-deep wound. I inhale, and I understand that once I do this, I won't exist. I'm a girl who found home, and I'll throw it away, and there will be nothing left of me.

The scratch on Sage's cheek, from Myri's struggle. You don't exist after ignoring something like that, either.

I eye Teresa for suspicion, but she just pats my hand, that shadowy side of her buried again in warm flesh and sugar. Maybe it was all just a nightmare: I see nothing of that person in her now. Teresa loves us.

Thanks for talking to me, Myri's voice echoes, soft and defeated.

The corridors swallow me whole in their warm light and patterned carpets.

None of the doors in the farmhouse are locked; there's that trust. The broom and duster have me covered. Keys, answers: Surely I'll unearth *something*.

I'm not *supposed* to do the bedrooms, but I can claim I'm being over-zealous. Sage's is a mess of shirts and artsy posters and philosophy books. Oscar's is clean bright lines, monochrome. I expect Jonah and Teresa's to be locked, but it stands open: chintzy wallpaper, flowers, butterflies in a cabinet. Exactly what you'd expect of an aging farming couple.

I get to work, dusting shelves, digging through drawers, plumping pillows, checking pockets. I'm on my fifteenth round of telling myself how stupid this is when I knock one of the butterfly cabinets.

Clink.

My heart thuds.

I look over my shoulder. Silence; I think the house is empty.

It wouldn't be so easy, would it? I touch the cabinet. No dust. The butterflies' wings show delicate patterns; each has a pin neatly through its heart. I imagine Jonah with a killing jar, wings fluttering against glass, slowing.

Behind the cabinet, there they are: keys. The same brassy metal as the cabin lock.

Reality swims in and out, distorted birdsong booming, herbal scents overwhelming.

Please. You think something that important would be so badly hidden that even someone as empty-headed as you could find it?

Or. They underestimated me. Saw a desperate girl who wouldn't question anything. The perfect next victim.

I slip the keys into my pocket.

They jingle when I move, and my confidence dissolves. People don't *do* things like this in the real world.

But none of this *feels* real. None of this can be real, but it is. I went out past the edge long ago.

The smart thing would be to hurry to my hut and hide the keys, but I hesitate outside the library. Kiera will be scribbling away, headphones in. I imagine her, me, Myri, a boat, an open sky. I wouldn't be so hollow, would I, with her there?

I close my eyes and feel how close that hollowness is. How it will feel to be nothing again, after being so close to being everything.

I can't name what surges at that thought. It's hot and tingles at the back of my neck, and it makes my fingers want to snap something fragile.

I jolt back into reality, and my chest seizes at the clinking from my pocket and the sound of footsteps.

Don't. Move. Aoife, do not *jingle*. I smother a completely inappropriate giggle.

"Nice dress," Sage says drily, emerging from an opening door.

If Jonah's glare is a polished pin, Sage's is a rust-flecked blade. I try to glare back, like I'm not standing there like a lemon, exposed in ways I don't even know yet.

I have no idea what to say. *Thanks, I borrowed it from a missing girl?* He knows. Look at him.

He doesn't care if I reply, anyway. "I was looking for you. Dad wants to speak to you."

Oh shit. Oh, shit. "Jonah—*me?*"

"Yeah. Hey—" He steps up close, and I step back, pinned against the wall as he leans in. His whisper is quick and urgent, so quick that his accent blurs the words. Did he say, "Leave here" or "Leave *her*"?

Shock seizes me. I want to ask who—Myri? Kiera?—but his look silences me.

"Office is in there," he continues blandly. "He's waiting for you. See you later."

And he's gone. I slip my hands into my pockets; I look like a sulky kid, but I have to hold those stupid jangling keys, keep a shred of me from the gaze that awaits me in there. All else is unknown. I can do nothing else; I walk into it.

I had imagined Jonah's office would be, you know, an office. But the door opens to a staircase, spiral like the whorl of a shell. I ascend through creamy light, breath shallow.

I emerge, and gasp.

How did they hide this? A dome, glass and iron: stained-glass symbols in rich blue, carmine, bottle green. The dyed light spills onto tropical leaves luxuriating in humid air.

And—I blink—flitting among the foliage, sunning their wings, are countless butterflies. Electric turquoise, black and red. Twitching, mouths unfurling to feed.

I turn in a circle, stunned, forgetting everything.

"You like it." I hadn't seen Jonah, seated at an incongruous desk, his necklace today all shells and white flowers over a pale gray suit. He rises. "Our solarium. We try to keep a few surprises tucked away. So there's always something to discover."

Leaves press against condensation, and the sun gets caught in droplets. This beauty disarms me. "I . . . how?"

Jonah's laugh is disarming, too. I couldn't have imagined it, but it feels utterly natural. It matches the flashes of wings. A light, boyish laugh, from an imposing, forbidding man. It throws me even more off balance. "Look at this."

Jade-green and milky, a chrysalis hangs from a strip of bamboo. It's so fragile and beautiful that I have an animal urge to crush it.

"Do you know what happens to an insect when it pupates?"

I'm too flustered, full of wonder, to think. "Not really?"

Jonah's lips twitch. "It dissolves. Releases juices that break its body down into a nice, nutrient-rich soup. That liquid reforms into something new, iridescent, and wonderful. It has to be unmade to remake itself."

My breath catches. I remember when he first saw me, how I longed to melt myself down and have the new me feed on the remains. I could believe, in this dizzy second, that he read my mind.

I try to grip the memory of Jonah's emotionless face as Myri screamed. The pieces are hard to hold under the full beam of his attention.

"The astonishing thing is, the butterfly retains the caterpillar's memories. It always carried what it would be, encoded into itself. It just had to be destroyed to find it. Wonderful, isn't it?"

I nod, not trusting my own voice. I remember what Larissa said about all moments existing at once. The butterfly already exists; the caterpillar persists. My head's spinning.

"Sit." Jonah gestures to two wicker chairs. On the desk between them sits a pendulum gadget, silver balls on strings knocking each other. Jonah sets it swinging.

His eyes are a rich hazel. The look in them stuns me: kindness, and fascination.

"Aoife. Why did you come here?"

My brain's frazzled, waiting for this coin to flip. I watch the pendulum. One sphere rises and hovers longer than it should, like gravity abandoning the rules. The colored light reflected on it flickers.

The wonder, the weirdness, awakens recklessness. There won't be another chance, and the thought of leaving here without *understanding* is agonizing. I feel like throwing a rock into water and seeing what it wakes up.

"Elise," I say.

"Elise." Jonah folds his hands. I fight an urge to giggle, imagining myself in a bizarre therapy session. "Are you a friend of hers? Family? Press?"

I swallow. "No, I—"

"Because if you are," Jonah interrupts, then pauses before continuing, "I would happily help. I hope someone can find the truth. We've tried contacting the police, asked the villagers to spread the word, but nothing's come of it. It's baffling. She left her clothes; her passport's gone, but nobody saw her getting on the ferry. And she seemed *happy* here."

There's consternation. And love. Despite myself, I have no doubt, suddenly, that he loved her. Loves her.

"She was—I hope she *is*—one of the kindest people I ever met," he continues. "I'd come to expect that she would be my daughter-in-law. I would like to know what happened. I would like to be sure it had nothing to do with any of our family here."

My face must be as full of consternation as his, mostly because I actually believe him. Even after last night. His sincerity is heavy, a blanket draped over us.

I want to keep throwing rocks. *What's in the cave? Why did I know this place before I came? What are you doing to Myri? What ... takes tastes from my mouth when I offer them?*

I don't. I'm mesmerized, but the keys prod at my thigh, a reminder. If

I give too much of myself away—and it feels so easy to take myself in my hands and give myself up to this man, even after everything—I might waste my only chance to save her.

Still, I meet his honesty with my own. "I'm not investigating. I found a postcard from her, and she seemed so happy here, you're right, and . . . even after I knew she'd vanished, it was like"—as the words form, a thought crystallizes—"maybe it wasn't a . . . bad disappearance. Maybe she found something better. I guess I was looking for that."

It hurts to understand what I'm here looking for, now I can't have it.

Jonah's eyebrows draw down, then he breaks into that beaming smile, transformed from stern to delighted. Caterpillar to butterfly, opening its wings. "What a beautiful thought. I hope so. What an unusual and brave reason to go anywhere."

It's easy to forget, under the radiance of that smile, that I'm about to run. To what?

"I didn't have anywhere else to go," I admit.

Jonah's lips purse. "No family? Partner?"

The thought of Craig is a shard twisted, spilling blood somewhere hidden. "Nobody."

"I'm truly sorry." That sincerity again.

Quiet settles. The pendulum swings. A butterfly alights on Jonah's chair.

"I won't keep you," Jonah says at last. "One thing, though. Tonight is a special occasion for us. Please don't take this personally, but it would be better if you didn't attend. It's sensitive in a way that might not mean much to you as a new arrival."

Pain spikes, a natural reflex. Unwanted guest. Awkward problem. The Aoife story.

But the pain slips away, something gleaming in its place. Everyone will be busy with this event. Nobody will notice me and another small figure slipping away along the cliffs.

I swallow a smile and a stab of pain as it grows ever more real. "Don't worry. It would be good to have some time to myself."

"Then." Jonah nods, message clear: We're done.

I stand, disturbing the butterfly on Jonah's chair, sending it fluttering toward a patch of glass the same orange as its wings. Like a child, instinctively, I reach up, as if I could catch it on my fingertip.

The keys clink.

"Aoife."

I stop dead among the leaves and butterflies, yellow and green light falling on my trembling hands, panic opening wide.

He shakes his head, as if observing a work of art or a scientific oddity. There's sympathy, too. "I do wonder what the world did to make you so angry."

Relief. But of all the things he might have said. "I'm not angry. Do I seem angry?"

Jonah's gaze is needle-sharp again. I remember the butterflies in his bedroom, pins through their hearts, corpses on display. "Not at all. But hidden things are always the most potent." The smile, curious and crooked this time. "I will see you soon."

I hide the keys in my hut and return to cleaning in a quiet frenzy, head ducked. Am I acting odd? Do I laugh too loudly when Larissa sprawls on the sofa, presenting herself to be dusted? Am I distracted playing backgammon with Oscar, his pieces gobbling up mine? Am I rushing the food that Teresa gives me, avoiding her eyes?

Can they tell I'm sick with dread, expecting a hand on my shoulder, an accusing shout? I'm far from shore, the future rising invisible through murky water to snatch me into itself. But it's easier to focus on the fear than the ache. When I think of *home* being so close and snatched away, I feel weird and spiky, and my fingers twitch.

How will I tear myself out of the grip of this place? It's wound around me, cherishing me like nowhere ever has. I just want to stay and trust and submit to whatever it does to me.

I return to my hut in the early evening, wound tight. There's tension around me, too, a stillness like something's waiting to stir. Like the island's holding its breath. Like tonight is a wrapped gift that the matter of things can't wait to tear into.

It's the hut that breaks me, the vines and fig leaves, the uneven floorboards I'd loved immediately because that little imperfection was *mine*. Home.

I slump on the bed, dig my hands into the rough sheets and cling, gritting my teeth. It's not fucking *fair*.

I know what to do, and it hurts, it fucking hurts. But I open myself, listen to the wind and leaves, the hiss of waves, and I whisper, *This is yours*. I take the feeling of *home* and belonging, the things I longed for, and wait as something intangible drinks it away.

It's gone. Emptiness in its place.

My grip on the sheets loosens. The call's eased. Now it says, *Go on, leave. See if you can*. I feel that hunger sniffing around me, *more*, but without immediacy. I was called, something wanted me. And I will never understand what I was so close to, if it was ascent or descent, bliss or obliteration.

I don't pack, but I take a shell from the shore. Retrieve the keys under my pillow, breathe deep to quiet the fear, and slip out.

I'm coming, Myri.

And then? Got a plan, have you? At least if there isn't one you can't fuck it up.

I shake it off. Sometimes you have to act and adapt as the consequences slam into you.

I pause outside the cabin. Nobody's here. It's working. I'm here for a reason, and it's not for the soil and softening lavender sky whispering that there's something bigger. It's for her.

I fumble with the keys. Part of me hopes they won't work; if they do, I'll be flinging myself into something irretrievably.

The lock twists open. Reality clinks shut.

There's elation in this fear: I am saving someone. I am throwing away everything, condemning myself to a hollow lifetime, a lifetime unwanted, just to be *for* something, *for* someone.

I swing open the door.

Strings and ribbons; it's all strings and ribbons, a cacophony of colors. Light swims through a seaweed forest hanging from the ceiling; threads trail from nails hammered into the wooden walls. Tied at the end of each is a charm, carved from wood or shaped from clay: a closed circle inside an open circle, one bisecting line.

There's a bed, a rocking chair, and nobody.

"Myri?" My voice is a whisper. "Myri, are you hiding?" Not that there's anywhere much to hide in here. "It's me. It's Aoife. Who's new. I'm here to help."

No reply.

I turn around in the stillness and silence, dread widening, wondering if I should start digging around for some sign of where she might be. Then, a crack from outside, a stick snapping.

I rush to the door, back out into the lavender evening light and around the back of the cabin, panicked hope making my voice maybe a little louder than it should be—"Myri?"

"She's not here anymore."

I freeze.

I barely recognize Larissa. She's half-naked, breasts and belly swirled with black and gold body paint, hips and legs wrapped in colorful cloth, feathers woven into her hair. Larissa gone feral, bird of paradise turned predatory.

Her look of apology chills the hell out of me.

"Where is she?" I grip hope. Larissa brought me here. She stroked my jaw as she spread glitter on my eyelids. She'll—

"Somewhere wonderful." She's all reverence. "She's so, so lucky, Aoife. She's lucky like you're lucky."

I open my mouth, lost. The girl in the cabin, the face I never saw; now I never will. Everything's falling away. Larissa was a door to something brilliant; now she's an abyss I'm tumbling into.

"I'm genuinely fucking sorry," she says. "But you made this way too easy."

I step back.

Arms close around me from behind.

I scream.

"Who do you think is going to hear that?" Oscar says, amused.

More figures appear between the trees, like actors coming onto stage, shadowy in the purple twilight.

Teresa. Sage. Kai and Darya and Frida and Zina, and all the others who lured and lulled me, lurking among the olive and fig trees, their welcoming smiles darkened into something ominous and hungry.

They could have snatched me any time; instead they watched, laughing, as I convinced myself I could escape. Now the trap's snapping shut.

Kiera's there, earthen cup in her hands, eyes downcast. Pain and shame bite deep. I nearly asked her to come with us.

"Just so you know," Oscar says, almost comforting, "you couldn't have done anything different. This was always coming." I hear the smile in his voice. "It's going to be glorious."

I struggle, but he grips me; Aksel joins him, pinning my arms. The hurt recedes as dread of something unformed and onrushing soaks my limbs. My kicks go limp.

Kiera looks wretched as she lifts the cup to my lips. She shakes her head, helpless.

It's sour and sweet. Herbs and honey. Lemon. I try to resist, but Larissa holds my mouth open, massages my throat like coaxing an animal to take medicine, and I swallow instinctively.

Uncanny warmth rolls down my throat and settles in my stomach, tingling and cramping. I think of thyme and parsley next to salvia and belladonna.

Look at you, love. Always knew you'd die from one of your fuck-ups, didn't we? Who do we blame, hmm?

The grove blurs and spins. Pins and needles sweep over me, then a chill. My legs—

I—

I hit the ground with a thud, winded. Olive leaves press against my cheek, feet move around me. A void opens inside me and starts to ease me in. I twitch my feet, seeking the comfort of blankets, confused by the dry earth against my toes—drifting—

No. Not after all this. Not without answers.

I force my eyes open.

Ribbons and threads, charms swaying in a breeze. Splintery wood against my cheek. I'm alone.

I'm inside the cabin.

Seconds ago, it felt like, I was outside in the grove, surrounded by people, in the purple-gold of sunset. Now I'm slumped on the cabin floor-boards. Through the shutters, outside is fully dark. Nobody is here.

How much time did I lose, in those instants of half-consciousness?

I get to my feet but know already what I'll find: the shutters and door locked tight.

And around me, inside me, that presence lingers, eager.

CHAPTER FIFTEEN

PERFECT PREY

Fucked it up, didn't you?

My head's clearing, and as it does, despair lurches.

A hollow laugh. *Got worked up in fantasies again, eh? You mess up going to buy milk half the time, and you expected to rescue a kidnapped kid?*

Terror for myself and terror for Myri jostle. I remember Elise's face, her eyes brilliant with excitement. She must have been locked in here, too, on the same path I'm on. And nobody's looking for her, really, just a poster in a café window that'll fade until her face is unrecognizable; she must have had no family interested in finding her, either. The world closed up over her so fast. Just gone.

A wave of nausea washes up the memory of Jonah, pitying, asking me if I had anybody. I told him I didn't. Perfect prey.

Here for a reason. Ha. I'm sure they've got wonderful plans for you.

They made me feel wanted. They knew how badly I needed that and used it to lure me.

You really fell for that. You really thought people actually wanted you.

I will not *accept* that.

I look at the window. Closed shutters. Locked, but maybe fragile.

I can sit here and wait for whatever's coming. I can cry in the night, sing songs to try to hold my sanity together; perhaps someone will visit me, and I'll ask them to remind me about the world. And then I will go where Elise went, where Myri must have gone, and the world will know me only as an afterthought, a *whatever happened to her?* and a shrug.

Or I can *try*, at least.

I strain against the shutters. Myri must have tried this, too. But Myri didn't have muscles from years of bartending, cleaning, shelf-stacking. I push, I *puuusssh*—

Nothing.

Nothing but a sudden, thick stench. I choke on it, I choke on its familiarity: the smell that hit me in the woods the night I ran, that I woke to find suffusing my pillows and wrote off as a nightmare. Rot, damp, decay. There's some slippery substance on my arm where I shoved against the window; it's light enough to see the riffles and lips of fungi sprouting from the wood, the lacy lichen crawling across the beams, a spittle-thick bubbling of slime.

I don't waste time wondering if the drugs are messing with my mind. This is real. The rules had been creaking; now they snap. The uncanny things I was promised were out there, after all, but they're not here to liberate me. They're here to consume me.

But: Rotted wood is weaker.

I push again, and push, and this time, the window flies open.

I scramble onto the chair. It's a goddamn rocking chair and nearly catapults me back down, a precarious scrabble. I grab the window frame, splinters of soggy wood and fungi adhering to my skin, and lever myself halfway out—

I tumble out and land tangled in a rosebush, bruised and scratched, but *out.*

I struggle free, thorns scratching my arms. I've crushed a rose, and my brain, too slow and too fast, registers the sadness and satisfaction of destroying something beautiful. Leaving my mark. Reminding them that I exist, and I won't vanish so easily.

It really is dark out here, like hours have passed, those long slow twilights condensed into seconds as I lay drugged. I need to run. But my breath and heartbeat choose this moment to go into overdrive, a delayed adrenaline kick. I'm panting, hands shaking, nauseous. *This is real*, I was kidnapped, I—

I got out. They underestimated me. Maybe that's something people do?

My gasps slow. I think I like that? I like that.

They underestimated me. Now I have a chance. I made it across the island once. I can do it again—

Unbidden, cruel, my mind offers me a memory, a snippet of a show tune sung desperately into the dark.

She never told me. Never asked me to save her. She knew what was coming and just sang alone to hold back the fear, trying to remember a world outside this grove.

It's too late. I *know* it's too late. Who knows how long I was out? Images flash, horror-thriller pictures, too realistic for this strange, monstrous night.

I can't go my whole life knowing I left a kid in danger. But I don't know where she is. *I'm just me, I was never meant for something, I was never enough I was never wanted—*

I jerk out of my spiral. *It opens*, she'd said. It opens, and you go inside, and . . . and it's just dark in there—

I know where she is.

I stare at the stars. That's something. I escaped a gray place and saw real stars before I got killed doing something stupid.

I run toward the cave.

⊖

Sand slips under my feet, stars scattered above, sea and trees blurred.

What are you going to do, hmm?

Reflected fire flares against the cliffs. A huge bonfire sends sparks spiraling.

Go in guns blazing and rescue her?

A rip in the cliffside, stretched open. *Mouth* is the right word.

Everyone's in a half-circle around the cave. I approach in shadow. Frida's plaits swing; Oscar's glasses flash reflected firelight; Giulia's and Pietro's hands are joined.

Some wear masks, some skulls, some wooden constructions, or craft feathers and paint, or carnival extravaganzas. Kiera's in her ivory suit and a goat-horned headdress. Larissa spins, wearing nothing but body paint and strings of fairy lights.

Jonah and Teresa stand with arms raised, robes flame-scorched, unmasked. The firelight flares his feathery hair and dances shadows across her face. The people I met were the chrysalises; these are the butterflies. His real form: priest, wilderness prophet. Hers: shadow queen, fairy-tale witch luring lost children to be devoured.

The *sounds* they're making. That barking, keening, unearthly chant; a mutated version of the soft syllables Giulia and Larissa chanted at the temple.

No sign of Myri.

I creep close enough to see the tears on Giulia's cheeks. To see Sage's eyes squeezed closed, zealous joy. To see the rapture on all their faces.

The cave looms, ominous darkness inside. *Something* inside, reaching.

However wild and strange they've become, they're nothing next to whatever lurks in there. Insects, adoring at the feet of something vast as galaxies.

Whatever's in there, whatever called me here, they're one and the same.

The thing I've glimpsed reaching from the cave, the thing that engulfed me in my dreams, was the same thing that seeded images of rugged coast in my mind, placed lemon on my tongue and sun on my skin. The thing I offered my feelings to, that stole peach from my mouth and Larissa's touch from my wrist and the sense of belonging from every cell of me. All one being.

It wrapped itself around me long ago. Invisibly, inexorably, it's been reeling me in.

I won't. *No—*

But it has Myri inside that slice of dark. They took that sweet, odd, brave girl, and gave her over to it, and they're *celebrating.*

My visions showed me the finality in that place; she's gone. But she sang when she was scared, she loved even the grayest parts of life with startling fierceness, she called for her mother. I can't let her be over.

More than that. Before, I was bored and small; now something incomprehensible has found me. It chose *me.* It hungers for me, and I hunger back.

I run forward. I elbow through the circle, the firelight, the wild chant.

Before the ritual-giddy dancers can grab me, before fear can close in, I dive into the cave.

CHAPTER SIXTEEN

THE FACELESS THING
WE ADORE

I EXPECT THEM TO CHASE ME. BUT NOTHING FOLLOWS ME, NOT EVEN THE light. I'm smothered in darkness and silence, firelight and chanting snuffed out.

The cave's taken what it wanted and snapped shut.

They didn't follow you because they knew you weren't coming out. Get it? It's got you, snatched inside itself. Game over.

I feel wet rock to either side, emptiness ahead: a tunnel. Total darkness. But my body knows this place, a terrible promise kept. All moments exist at once, right? This one was always there, and I felt it. I have always been here.

Reality shudders into place: This is happening. The warnings written in my nerves came true.

I'll never find Myri; I'll never be found.

But the fear and despair are numbed. There's a warmth, a thrill. I'm past the edges, and my end's waiting here, but something is breathing *Not far now,* and I'm creeping forward, icy water sloshing around my ankles.

A heartbeat, real and not real, thunders through the rock.

The water deepens, churning over my calves, my thighs, cold enough to bite my bones. Hidden things brush my skin; salt smarts in my cuts.

Come now. You've always been on this path. You're so close to its end.

When the water reaches my chest, I kick off my sandals; I can't imagine any world where I'd need them again. I let the current carry me, deeper into the passageways. I feel the island's weight, the claustrophobic awareness that I am under hills, soil, miles and tons of it, burying me alive.

My head scrapes the ceiling. The air's thin, dank.

Something in me is screaming that there's nothing mystical happening here; I drank drugged tea and wandered into a cave system, and I will drown. The cave fish will strip me down, dissipate my body.

But that's far away.

I inhale and plunge.

Cold water tumbles my limbs, disorientating. I regret my choice and kick up, seeking air, but my head hits rock. I try to feel my way back, but there's just stone and water—

My lungs cramp, desperate. Black and red flash behind my eyelids. They say drowning is an easy death. They don't tell you about the panic. I can't get out I can't, *air*—

It's right there it must be—something's fading, spiking, my legs are kicking, but they're far away and softness is seeping in, warm and relaxing—

A flush of images sweeps me away.

It's too fast to grip, familiar faces and objects misshapen, colors vivid, light blurry. A sick wrongness next to a fascination, the thrill of a scientist peering at a deadly virus or an astronaut gazing at an alien landscape as her air supply gutters out.

I am a million places. I'm an old man watching something emerge from the ocean. I'm a young woman dancing on the beach, howling that chant. I'm an artist carving images in a standing stone. I'm praying, running, in terror, in ecstasy, the languages and sensations of a thousand ages in my mouth and nerves—

All moments exist all at once, bunched up and forever—

The flicker eases. I settle into a moment. But it's not mine.

I'm sneaking through the groves. The path's familiar; this body isn't. I am in Elise's skin, and it's a warm, hopeful place, all open. There's purpose and home and excitement and something I think might be love. But there's something cooler and sharper, too. Determination and fear.

Spring flowers are shriveling in growing heat. This must be weeks ago, just before she disappeared.

Will the next missing girl glimpse echoes of me as she's eased into her own ending?

Elise, where are you now? All I can do is watch through her eyes.

I feel her fear spike from dread into something closer to panic, but she whispers, "I can do this," and approaches the cabin.

And I'm somewhere else.

I'm Teresa. My surroundings fracture through tears; the only sound is my own screams. The only solid thing lies in my arms: a child, skin cold, head lolling.

And then I'm Sage; a young Sage, a child, soaked shorts, too-big trainers. His arms are wrapped around the dead child, straining to carry her toward the cave. Tiny in its shadow, quailing, but moving forward.

The rush of moments stops; I break the surface back into myself.

I come up choking on saltwater.

My lungs find air. My feet find rock. This is me, my body, my now.

I'm shoulder-deep in freezing water, in suffocating darkness.

Vastness echoes, every splash and ripple reverberating. I'm in a cavern, I think, deep in the island's core. An invisible rocky cathedral. The darkness is disorientating; I sense only how tiny I am. A flicker easily extinguished.

Something's here.

Is it here with me, or am I *inside* it? Both; the edges blur. It's like something vast is towering over me, but also like I've slid into the chambers of its heart, the hungry hollows of its belly.

Terror lurches, then passes. My own heartbeat slows. Fear is too small for this; a heady awe builds in its place.

This is where I was called to. This is what called me. It has me, staring down at me and palpitating around me, and it's so, so much more than I can comprehend.

A voice startles me, distorted by echoes.

"Aoife?"

"Myri!"

Relief sings—*I wasn't too late*—but panic spikes. It has her, too; that frightened, quirky girl is in its grip.

"Can you find me? I'm—so scared—"

I swim to her; somehow, I know the way. A small hand reaches down and finds mine. I clamber onto a rock, limbs numb and clumsy from the cold, clothes waterlogged. I pull myself onto my knees but don't have the strength to stand.

So dark. I know her by shallow breath, a cold hand, strands of wet hair trailing on my skin. The presence shifts, unimaginable. We are utterly at its mercy, laid out before it, clasped inside it.

I'll wrap around her, protect her perhaps for a few seconds. All I have to give.

But no arms close back around me. The skin I find isn't trembling.

She speaks, sonorous and strange. "Thing of all shadows, here is your gift. Aoife delivers you her flesh and mind, human wonder in her skin, and all for you."

I freeze. That voice doesn't belong to the girl who asked about swans and tried to sound strong.

She's gone.

But she was never there, was she? She was a trick. A light tempting me into waiting jaws. I know it without knowing how.

There's no pain at that; the realization tips me into an odd peace.

I'm beyond mourning now, or fear. I'm gone, too. In the shadow and core of that presence, there's only space for quiet wonder in my last moments.

"I tried to save you." The echoes change my voice, too; it sounds like it's coming out of the past.

"You tried. You were seven years too late." She eases me onto my back.

"What's happening?" I'm talking out of a distant delirium, compliant, heavy.

"We give you with love, to the faceless thing we adore."

The water laps. The heartbeat booms. The dark smiles.

"Feel it enfolding us." She strokes the wet spikes of my hair. "You will be fully gone into it soon. It's easiest if you let go."

"What . . . ?" I don't feel sleepy; it's more like being dragged down, somewhere deeper. A slow, hazy dissolution. I end, and something else begins. I can't see the edges.

So dark. Tendrils are wrapped around me, intangible. Soaking me in, relishing the shivers in my flesh and the depth of my amazement. I don't know how, but I feel how they reach out, span the island, the world, beyond.

"*Shhh.* Give yourself to the Unseen."

I think of a girl with tired feet, in a flat that wasn't home. Listening for a call in her boyfriend's music, but never hearing it, because the real call was coming later, just for her.

Those tendrils reached from here, stroking me, filling my mouth with lemon and my head with dreams. Luring me. And now it has me.

I gave it so much already, offered up fear and belonging, the fruits of my senses. It's so easy to let it take the rest, every thought and every cell. It says *more.* It will take it all. I just have to relax and let it.

It's gentle. It takes the fear and sadness first, leaves me hollow and ready, leaves only the wonder.

I let go of Aoife. The thing Myri called the *Unseen* engulfs her, and she is gone.

CHAPTER SEVENTEEN

IMPRISONED

I AM GONE. I'M NOT GONE.

I am something and nothing. I'm Aoife and something else.

I feel cold sand under my limbs and breeze on my skin. I have limbs and skin, I am hot, scared flesh fascinated by its existence, meat animated by more than thoughts. Childlike, all sensation, newborn, all wrong.

Opening my eyes feels like stepping into a new universe.

Stars wheel. The many stars of the familiar sky above the Farmstead, only *others, more*. Like some veil's lifted, like new expanses of the cosmos are open to me.

Am I Aoife? She seems distant. A shadow that vanished when a light came on.

Cautiously, every feeling magnified beyond comprehension, I sit up.

I'm outside the cave, splayed. Does it matter how I emerged through those closed-up, drowning passages?

I'm naked, completely exposed, but awkwardness and shame are incomprehensible, irrelevant. Look at that skin. It's part of the same thing as the sand and air, and it isn't. Those freckles, those scratches, fascinating as galaxies.

Everyone from the Farmstead is gathered around me in a wide circle. Their eyes are closed, hands on their laps, firelight flickering on their faces. To a lingering human fragment of me, it would look like a promotional shot from a yoga-meditation retreat, if it wasn't for the masks and body paint. They're chanting. I don't need to know that language. It speaks to something that shifts in and out through my skin and bone.

I move my hand against the backdrop of serene faces. It flickers, the tiniest glitch as it comes up against a reality that isn't meant to hold it. That should distress me. I giggle.

Something tugs at my limbs, pulling me up.

You know where to go.

I'm guided. I'm music played by something. People stand, urgent, but it doesn't matter because I am music, I am waves, moving across the sand toward the water.

I hear someone shouting, "Stop her;" and that glorious sound rippling from my open throat, that's laughter, isn't it?

"No." It's Jonah. "Let her. She is guided."

I spin, dancing, giddy—isn't dizziness *fascinating*? The world brightens and swirls. I brighten and swirl with it, and stumble onto a rock protruding into the water. The forbidden water. There was a girl called Aoife; a girl called Kiera stopped her at the lip of that water. I look for Kiera. She's standing, stricken. I smile at her; I think that's a smile.

I spin and fall. The water parts for me.

And I learn what's in that water, what I was warned away from, what made Giulia sob into Jonah's shoulder.

THE FACELESS THING WE ADORE

What is in the ocean is agony.

⊙

The relieving cool, the burn of swallowed seawater, the firelight blurred through droplets in my eyelashes, are far away.

Everything else is a maelstrom of pain.

Every flavor of suffering is here. Stinging cuts, the bone-deep ache of old injury, the scream of smashed bones, fever, exhaustion. New kinds of pain: What does a tree feel when a chainsaw slices? What does a virus feel enveloped by antibodies? What makes a worm twist in the belly of a bird? I learn it all. And the agony reaches my soul, crushing me under humiliation, grief, terror, half-forgotten traumas.

I glimpse the places it springs from: bodies splayed in hospitals, laboring past any limits, straight-backed at funerals, hiding from ringing laughter in school corridors, hungry on potholed roads. Prey emptied out by predators' greedy mouths, fish gasping in airless ponds, seedlings dying under merciless sun.

What fragments of Aoife remain can't understand the sheer breadth of this. They shift to something closer, something they can hold.

The panic and wonder and horror that seize the bodies on the shore as Jonah cries, "It is time! It leads us! We follow!" The newly formed knowledge that until today the sea was a threat and bitter lesson, but now it's become a test and a promise.

The screams of those who dare to leap and are enveloped by nightmares.

I feel Pietro grasp his courage and fling himself in. I feel others follow, *I don't want to* but *just trust.* I feel others freeze, paralyzed by the shouts of people thrashing in the water.

I feel Jonah's sickness at what he needs to do. "We must all be brave!"

I feel the shame Larissa crushes as she approaches the jump, *I can't fear, trust trust trust.* I feel Teresa's remorse as she moves through the crowd, drawing people to the edge.

I feel Oscar hesitate.

I feel the thorns in Kai's and Darya's feet as they run, and the guilt that makes them turn back.

I feel shock rip through Kiera as Oscar shoves her off the rock.

As more and more people enter the water, a richer, stranger, deeper pain rises.

A pain woven through matter and spirit, felt in something other than nerves; the pain of atoms and energy, the fabric of the universe reeling and screeching.

What is in the ocean is nightmares. The concentrated pain of a reality.

Something is dreaming these dreams. That something is in me, and I am in it. And as the last people tumble into the water, the nightmares surge and our senses crumble—

The nightmares fall quiet. I am somewhere else.

They say that to look on a god is to plunge headfirst into madness.

But even madness is a *response.* There are things minds *can't* respond to.

The last scrap of my consciousness remembers: We face incomprehensible things all the time. The scale of the universe, the endlessness of death. We boil them down to things we can hold, write them in numbers and stories, because understanding them would break us.

I comprehend this being less than a bacteria comprehends the body it blooms in. Understanding it cannot break me, because I cannot start to understand.

There is no point trying to name sensations that weren't made for human senses. I just float in awe in an expanse that echoes with screams. It's pumps and pulses; light and dark that mutate; tastes I hear and chimes I feel and colors that wriggle under skin; it's galaxies in cells and momentum with no direction and so much desperate energy trapped in a dormant, dreaming state.

I understand one thing, though. The being I encountered is caged. Trapped in the cave, snared in the nightmares it seeps out into the world.

It asks me, in more and less than words, *What would you do?*

I am not me; I am just a snap in its intangible nerves, but there's something of Aoife in the answer, and it shocks me with its vehemence.

Tear my way out.

And it shows me how beautiful it will be when the nightmares end.

PART TWO

UNSEEN

CHAPTER EIGHTEEN

UNSEEN

I WAKE TO A HAND RUNNING THROUGH MY CROPPED HAIR. A SOFT VOICE SINGS in an unknown language. The light's pale and strange.

I'm Aoife. This mind is mine. This body is mine. I can't remember what was real and what I dreamed.

I'm on a sofa in the farmhouse, dawn filtering through the curtains, and I'm shaking and shaking and grinning like a child.

"*Shhh*," Teresa coos. "Be still."

I *can't* know what I've seen. It's like describing a new color. Memory quits, leaving me with echoing terror and euphoria.

It's part of me now. I'm part of it. I know that much.

The word *gift* resounds, translating into the word that was never spoken: *sacrifice*. I don't understand how I'm still here.

I don't understand how to sit up, either. Teresa's hands are soothing, her lap soft, easing the panic. My voice is slow. "What did you do to me?"

"Feel the sun," Teresa whispers. "Feel your body. What comes next will be hard. Take this moment."

The leather of the sofa is strange under my fingers, the realest thing I've ever felt. Teresa sings, holding me somewhere warm and quiet where I don't need to be afraid.

I force myself up. I won't be lulled. Whatever's coming, I won't go into it numb.

Teresa strokes my cheek. "You're ready, aren't you? Come."

Stumbling, I follow. It's tough, remembering how to tug the puppet strings of my body. I'm blinking like a newborn, learning everything all over again. I can't run, but it doesn't matter; whatever's happening is too far along to stop.

I don't know if that fills me with fear or joy.

The garden buzzes with bees, poisons and drugs nodding with the breeze. Lavender and rosemary perfume the air; the sky's golden. I sink onto the swing hanging from the apple tree. It bounces. The beauty tips the balance, and terror overtakes bliss.

This is too much. My breath goes rapid. *I want Craig.*

I need Craig. Then I'd relax. His arms, when he was sleepy and happy, were the only place I could. Sacrifice, next missing girl, lost to something uncanny; I could be it all, unbowed, if he could tell me I'd been brave.

"Aoife?"

My toes curl into the grass. Jonah emerges from the house, bathed in golden light, gaze softened but still captivating. Teresa stands by, hands clasped.

"Hi," I say stupidly. I stand, like I'm standing to attention. I try to feel ready. I'm not.

Jonah follows the path between flower beds, stirring up dust and tiny insects. "Aoife, I understand you're confused, and afraid. Last night—"

I didn't think I could speak, let alone interrupt Jonah. I surprise myself. "I died, didn't I?"

I felt it. I felt my heart seize, my organs and bones melt, my cells unravel, my soul or self crumble, I stopped *being*—

I'd been trying to write it off as a dream. But I died and I'm back and my body feels transitory as smoke.

I must be shaking, maybe my eyes are wild, because Jonah draws me to his chest, surprisingly tender and tentative. It startles me, the intimacy of being in the arms of the man who tugged at my strings as I walked to my death.

I should be angry. I should fight. Nothing in me wants to. I just want to understand.

"You died." Jonah strokes my shoulder. "And here you are. Every second you walk in the world now will be a miracle of miracles."

His heartbeat's steady; his shirt smells like lavender, saltwater, incense; he's warm. It feels nice. My muscles loosen, and I begin to cry. Dying was strange and lonely and the hideous scale of that presence makes me sickly with my smallness. I walked too far into the dark and the things there found me. I am theirs now.

Jonah rocks me gently as I sob into his shirt. I *can* cry in front of him. He will comfort me. At least I get to know what that feels like.

"I don't understand," I whisper.

"Then let us explain." I look up. Teresa's smile makes me cozy, even now. "You were a sacrifice. You know. But we can explain what comes next—"

"Because," Jonah picks her thread up with the confidence of a decades-long double act, eyes actually twinkling as I pull back and look at him. "We were sacrifices, too."

Jonah and Teresa wait until my sobs simmer down. I try to make that quick; I need answers, and I'm aware how embarrassing my snivels are.

"I died in that place, too," Jonah says, when I'm quiet. "We all did."

I stare. Is that what placed that clashing solemnity and glitter in his eyes?

"Seven years ago," Jonah locks his hands behind his back, "my family was here, visiting Teresa's family's land. There was a tragedy, and a miracle. The being we call *the Unseen* revealed itself.

"We did not know what it was, but we understood the depth of our debt. I offered myself. It dissolved me in its hidden heart, then returned me to the world, and took me into its service."

Its service. It occurs to me, with a tingling rush, that I might live.

"We're a community of offerings," Teresa concludes. "We give our flesh and souls to the Unseen, and it preserves us to do its work and find and offer others. Those who"—she beams at me, and I blink—"have shown courage and curiosity."

Pieces spin and rattle; something falls into place. "Everything was—"

"A test," Jonah confirms. "You passed. You entered the cave when you could have run. You showed yourself more than worthy."

His approving glow empties my mind. I bask, until my brain catches up. A voice from behind a door, a clink of keys behind a cabinet of butterflies, a sliver of cave in pearly cliffs, a trail of breadcrumbs scattered, spiraling me closer to the figure it always circled around.

"Myri—"

"Myri was never in danger," Teresa confirms. "She's extraordinary, and extraordinarily loved. She became what you needed, to guide you to your union with the Unseen."

"Stand up," Jonah instructs.

He takes my hand. Softness from someone so alien disorients me even more.

"It's in you now. In all of us. We're siblings carrying something unknowable in our marrow." His fingers move on my skin. "Breathe. Can you feel it?"

I feel my heartbeat. I feel another heartbeat, pulsing through the cool morning air, the herbs, the glitter of the sun. Already there in the passageways and caverns of my body. The same presence, a call and a hunger, so much more palpable now.

It suffuses me, and everything, and connects me to Jonah, the garden, the mountain and the sky and the beating hearts of my new family. It's wider than I ever imagined, wider than the world. It says, *Anything is possible*, and once again, that's freedom.

I let out a slow breath that shudders with wonder.

Teresa takes my other hand, runs her fingers over it lovingly, tracing my bones and tendons, exploring the uncanny new pulse. "There it is. You'll feel it more and more."

"What is it? Kiera said . . ." It's fuzzy. ". . . a god?"

The light in Jonah's eyes moves, the facets of his hazel irises shifting. "The truth is, none of us know."

I sit abruptly, the motion of the swing redoubling my dizziness. My mouth is dry; the words come out thick. "You . . . offered me, and yourselves, to it, and you . . ."

"Don't have the slightest idea what it is?" Jonah chuckles. "As if you're a stranger to flinging yourself into the unknown."

He has a point. I'm no less stunned.

"After offering myself." Jonah's hand comes to my shoulder, soothing, appraising the presence in me. Like he might read it through my skin.

"I set out to offer others, and to learn its nature and intentions. Until last night, I had succeeded in only one of those tasks."

The power and brilliance swirls. It's sickly, honey clotted in my throat. So unknowable I choke on it.

"We've been working on it," Teresa adds drily. "Kiera's researching the prehistory and mythology of this area. Myri, our oracle, spends much time in communion. All we knew was that it was an entity or phenomenon, filled with desire. That it called to us. And that if we gave ourselves, we were richly rewarded. That was all we had."

I twist my fingers around the ropes of the swing. The fear's ebbing and flowing; below it, elation thrums.

"The closest I have to a definition," Jonah says, "comes from our butterfly friends. You remember, I said that a caterpillar contains the design for what it will grow into?"

I nod, remembering that jade-green chrysalis. In my memory, it's between my fingers, and I squeeze. I know that didn't happen.

"Imagine our reality is a grub, nosing through the void, carrying the blueprint for what it can become. That is the Unseen. That is what we give ourselves to."

This tingling isn't fear, it's excitement. I kick off and swing, and the rush of rising and falling joins the rush of adrenaline.

Jonah and Teresa give me that moment, swinging under a sky I feel I could fling myself into. Why not? If everything evolves, perhaps I will leap into the clouds. The strange energy chimes, ripples like harp strings at that thought, that existence hangs at the edge of a vast transformation.

I slow, digging my toes into the earth. Jonah's smile doesn't match mine. Teresa's is strained. She's stepped back, giving me and Jonah space to shoulder this together.

Jonah lowers himself onto a rock. His amusement has dropped as suddenly as the passing of a storm, a new weight to him. "You've heard of the biblical Jonah?"

"Swallowed by a whale, right?" I make what might be an attempt at a cute shrug. The rest of me watches, nonplussed. What is he bringing out in me?

"A large fish, actually." Jonah scratches his neck, his shoulders hunched. "As a test, or punishment, because he fled instead of sharing the prophecy he was given. Perhaps it was too much for him. But what *he* saw was bathed in light. I walk in darkness." Dry amusement flashes. "Trapped in my own whale belly."

"Fish," I correct, then stare at myself internally because why would I say that.

Jonah surprises me with a rueful laugh. "I see, Myri has seen . . . something seismic coming. And last night, I understood what that is. What we are here for. And that . . ." He straightens and reaches for me, then falls back, an awkward gesture that stuns me almost as much as what he says next. ". . . is because of you, my dear."

The harp-string ripples redouble. I'm gawping; my brain's soup. Even if my mind can't grasp this, my bones do.

"Two days ago," Jonah says, "Kiera discovered a rite in a book from the monastery that stood here. We knew it was crucial, but we did not understand fully what the rite aimed to *achieve*. It was only when you walked into the ocean—the first initiate to do so on waking—and we followed you, that the Unseen showed us the final piece."

I try to fit this into my mind. Like what I saw last night, I cannot—I can't hold it.

"It's trapped." I manage. "Dreaming—"

"And we understand now"—Jonah's voice trembles with reverence

—"that we are here to wake it. Free it. Return it to the world. Midwives of a cosmic birth. That is what the rite will do. That is our great task."

What is it that's so overwhelming? The possibilities of a world infused with something awake, divine, and strange? Or that I played a part in this, that it's *because of me?*

I have to realize it again, over and over.

I try to remember what I glimpsed in the ocean, what it promised would follow its waking. I can grasp nothing but a heady rush of release.

Teresa steps up, running her hands down my arms and squeezing my hands like the proud mother of a bride. "Look at you. Our precious gift. Do you feel how delighted with you it is?" She pinches my cheek; the pain is sharp and sweet.

"Are you willing?" Jonah asks. "You've been the spark. Will you join our work?"

I pause. It's *too* beautiful to trust, isn't it? Maybe they tell everybody things like this, tell them they're special. I don't dare to take this into my hands. It'll shatter in my grip.

But I remember. A late night, a drunk guy whose grabby hands left me sick and shaky. Texting Craig to say I'd forgotten my keys, and getting a laughing emoji, *classic Aoife.* Waiting for hours on the doorstep in the autumn chill, watching rain, watching traffic, watching an advertising billboard. A big fake smile shining down, all teeth. A delirious feeling that the world was eating me, bite by bite.

I deserve more. I deserve a new world to bloom in.

Last night, I thought these people were my kidnappers. Now I understand: They're my liberators.

When I say, "Yes," the herbs and clouds breathe my answer and pulse with joy.

CHAPTER NINETEEN
NOT ALONE

EVERYTHING'S BIGGER. THE SKY'S WIDER, HONEY SWEETER. SOMETHING pulses erratically in me. I want to cry with emotions I can't pin down.

Still, breakfast's reassuring; the urge to stuff myself with pancakes suggests that this is still my body, all misshapen angles and colorful tattoos and sugar cravings, all new tan and hair starting to grow out spiky.

Everyone's gathered in the garden and kitchen, still smeared with body paint or clay, hair stiff with sea salt, wrapped in blankets, tired, wild-eyed, feral. They hug me, ruffle my hair, kiss my cheeks, pull my reborn body into theirs, making me part of it, my limbs their limbs, fingers lifting food to my mouth.

They look at me with wonder. Something of—I don't dare trust it, but I see it—how they look at Jonah.

The thrill isn't just about me, though. Everyone's eager to share their visions from the ocean. I hear Pietro insisting that after the nightmares ended, everything became doors, possibilities open and waiting. Giulia's leaning on his shoulder, trying to explain to Ana what she saw, endless adventures without fear, constant change without pain. Kiera's got both hands on Kai's shoulders and is yelling something about neutrons being totally different. Teresa's serving cocoa and keeps saying, "No death, there was no death."

Impossible realities echo half-overheard around the kitchen. The nightmare ended, and you could remake events, play with history. Matter became music. You could jump between universes like stepping through a curtain.

I try to remember what I saw, but the memories dissolve at a touch. They leave me with an ache I can't place, an aftertaste of a beautiful cataclysm or an incredible violence.

Larissa slides up beside me at the table, in a neon pashmina in the still-chilly morning, and delivers me a coffee. She knows I take three sugars. I beam at her.

"Hey." Is that *nerves*? "I should . . . apologize for kidnapping you, huh." She laughs when I laugh.

"I'm glad it was you," I admit, then laugh again; that's a really weird thing to say. "If I'm going to be kidnapped by anyone."

Larissa cannot be blushing. "It sucked, doing that, but it was the best way to see how far you'd go. Still, we thought it would be more work to get you to go inside the cave. We had plans to help you break out and lay a trail in there. Didn't expect you to kick your way out and run straight in. *That* was badass."

My beam goes less crooked. *I* impressed *her*.

"And yeah"—she shuffles her feet—"that thing about you making it easy. I was trying to scare you, but . . . I meant it. You did everything right. I never brought any offerings before, and I was scared I'd fuck it up, but I should have known you were born for this. The moment I saw you spying on us at the temple, I felt . . . ." Her voice falters. Unimaginable. "And now we know what we're here for. Because of *you*."

I sip my coffee, the taste of it so *loud*, and dare to slip my hand into hers. I have a thousand questions, but they're not the right size for words.

"You know none of that would have hurt you, right?" She's eyeing me, seeking the anger I should feel.

"Apart from the bit where a god ate me?" I ask drily.

She grins. "Nobody goes into the cave without coming out. It loves us. So much. It only wants to liberate us."

"What about the rot?" At least I can just about find words for this. "There was rot in the cabin. In my bedroom, too, and the woods. It was there, and then it wasn't . . ."

Larissa stares. "That doesn't . . . I don't know what that was." She's unsettled, then relaxes. "Don't worry. Weird shit happens around here, that's part of the fun." She breathes into my ear like it's a revelation just for me. "Just flow with it." Her fingers slide along my wrist, finding my pulse. "We're inside the Unseen now and it's inside us. And soon we'll release it, and ascend in it, together. And before that, we will kiss and taste a god in each other's mouths."

Her lips brush my ear and I think I might just die again, but then she's gone with a sidelong smile. These pounding heartbeats are offerings, aren't they? I feel the Unseen take them in. My body is altar and sacrifice all at once, and all I can think is that I want to give more, everything.

The day's a golden summer one, and most work's suspended today. Clouds scud and swirl. This is what it feels like, being reborn.

When the energy's bubbled down, it's just me and Kiera, in hammocks under vines. The breeze dances shadows on our skin. I'm quiet. Even now, it's scary talking to Kiera; I might drop my guard and fuck up. With Larissa, it's like she's guiding me to somewhere enticing. With Kiera, I'm running on uneasy ground, waiting for something to give way.

Finally, she props herself up on her elbows, setting her hammock swinging; she makes a little "eek" face, which is offensively cute. "So. Mindfuck, huh?"

I pause, then say, "Yeah. Mindfuck," and we giggle, and neither of us wants to stop so we keep going long after we've forgotten what started it.

Maybe those worries about messing up belong to the old Aoife. Not the Aoife who was reborn from a god and led its followers into a revelation. "I can't figure out if I'm terrified or deliriously happy or both."

"Ah!" The shadow is Oscar's; he carries three earthen mugs. "The Farmstead mood."

Kiera shuffles up. Oscar puts the teas down then tickles her, almost overturning the hammock. She shrieks, a happily fragmenting scream.

Oscar hands me a mug. "Teresa special. Mellows you out."

I pause. I hate taking anything wilder than a few beers; I'd only do it to avoid looking pathetic around Craig's friends. But this is new Aoife. I swig; lazy warmth floods me.

We lie there for minutes or hours. Oscar's full of stories. He talks about how they all plotted to lure Zina into the cave with poetry, how Maisie tried to run during her initiation then begged to be allowed back in. When he tells us about Larissa kicking Sage in the balls when she woke after dying in the cave, we cackle. In every telling, he underlines the layers of force and trickery it took to get people into the cave, promises that there's something uniquely brave in how boldly I ran inside.

Oscar moves on to his own story, how he and Jonah were friends and business partners in the outside world, what he calls *the dying world*. How Jonah invited him here for a holiday, tricked him into the cave with a story about treasure. How, as he dissolved, he'd understood that all the profit and strategizing and prestige had been a profound waste of his existence. How he'd woken, sold his company, and invested his wealth in building the commune.

"That's what all that money-chasing was for. To do its work." He barely pauses before saying, "Kiera, you have to share yours."

"Oh god," Kiera moans. "She doesn't want to hear this."

"I absolutely want to hear this."

Kiera looks shaky and it hits me. I make her nervous. I'm the intriguing stranger she wants to impress. Yesterday I could never have conceived of that possibility, or how good it would feel.

She pushes back her hair and lets it out in a babble. An archaeology degree she was failing, an unsettling dream, a summer school dig in the city that she scraped funding for.

"Except I wasn't . . . much use." Kiera makes a face. "Kept passing out on-site. Doing weird stuff, causing scenes. And there was this wicked hot day, and I didn't go to the site, downed half a bottle of whisky, wandered into an antique shop, and saw this old bronze knife and . . . pocketed it. Real *going back to your bad old days* stuff. Staggered to the beach and hid in some rocks and passed out or something, all just white heat in my memory."

"And then?" Oscar waves, and she grins. I flash back to Oscar shoving her into the water, her surge of betrayal. It's nice to see that forgiven. Makes me think whatever I saw through the colored glass was an illusion. Oscar loves Kiera, Kiera loves Oscar.

"I woke up and this weird fucker in a Hawaiian shirt was offering me an ice cream," Kiera concludes, "asking me why I'd nicked that knife with that *particular* symbol and telling me where I might find answers."

"And like an idiot"—Oscar gives Kiera the finger affectionately—"she followed that weird fucker home."

"Didn't bother to tell anyone. Left that night." Kiera's grin goes unhinged, and she makes jazz hands. "I'm a missing person!"

I laugh and raise my teacup. I'm missing, too. I was right, it feels like freedom. The thought overwhelms me, and I get happy teary and it's probably a good thing I'm interrupted.

"It was Pietro for me."

Giulia emerges between the trees. Soft steps, bare feet, breeze on her cotton dress.

I stiffen. She hasn't spoken to me aside from occasional hostile whispers. But now her lips, her snub nose, are crumpled in obvious apology.

"Hi," she says.

I say, "Hi." It's like we've tested waters and have no idea what to do next.

"Join us." Oscar shunts up, and Giulia sits, eyes shifting between me and Oscar like she's not sure whose permission she needs. "Giulia's story's beautiful, Aoife."

I say, "I'd like to hear it," cautious. Mistrust tingles, like Giulia's going to hiss an insult, but there's only softness there. This is the Giulia who took my hand in the café.

Oscar yawns and leans against the tree, eyes closing. Kiera sinks deeper into the hammock, snuggled around a sun-bleached pillow. "Pietro was sick," Giulia says. "*Months left, not years* sick." She eyes me, probably knowing this isn't the story I was expecting. "He wanted to travel while he still could.

He was drawn to these islands; maybe he felt the call. When we got to this island the visions started, saying *you can save him.* Then, in the harbor café, I saw Sage. It was like lightning out of a sunny sky. I knew he was the answer."

"Like I felt about you and Larissa," I say carefully. She smiles.

"Like something was saying, *This person will change everything.* He waved like he knew me, and I was . . . terrified. Like something terrible and lovely was coming, you know? We took the boat back with him that night.

"After we arrived, they tricked Pietro into the cave for his test, and made me think they'd sacrificed him in there, and I ran in, and we dissolved in each other's arms. When we woke up, he was healed. This place saved him, and it saved me too. I never knew . . . ."

"I know." I sigh out the joy.

"None of us could be the same, after this." Giulia's smile is another peace offering. I take it, and it seems to make her a little bolder. She still glances around. Oscar's slumped; Kiera's snoring softly, face screwed up in worry, adorably vulnerable. Still, Giulia keeps her voice low as she speaks the name, the one people pause before speaking. "Elise came here a little after us. I invited her after I met her on a supply run to the mainland. She was . . . adrift, like you. In a much worse way, actually." She makes a little face I can't quite read. "I was so happy that I'd managed to find her somewhere she could settle."

"I can't wait to meet her," I say. "When she comes back."

"When she comes back." Giulia's quiet for a second, then stands up. "Come with me? I want to show you something."

Everything unfolds; every discovery widens the world. I jump down, noticing how stiff my salty clothes are; I never bothered changing, too wrapped up in everything.

I follow her.

We walk in silence. It's that time of evening when the groves turn peachy pink. I try to concentrate on the beauty, and not my uneasiness around Giulia.

She's the first to speak. "I'm sorry I was cruel."

"Part of the test?" My tongue trips over itself.

Giulia looks at the ground, picking over a stony patch, or refusing to meet my eye. "Yes. If you'd stay if someone didn't want you."

"You"—second attempt at a sentence—"um. Convincing. Good job."

Her smile's crooked. "Yes. I did my absolute best."

There's layers here I can't read. "But are we . . . okay now?"

Giulia wraps her arms around my shoulders. Her sun-warmed skin against mine, more of the intimacy that suffuses this place. I relax into her.

"Come on." She leads me past the solar panels and beehives, toward the fields. It's where the goats live when they're not wandering the mountainside, bells on their collars ringing eerie messages.

The field's empty, wildflowers blowing in the wind. I look at Giulia sideways for an explanation, just before Sage steps out from the trees.

Accusing fury grips my gut; I believe Giulia was faking it, but Sage's hate was real. I start to say *what*, but Sage staggers back, screeching, as a jet of water hits his face.

"Aargh," Sage yells, fake-angry, "that's it. I am *coming for you*!"

He darts between the trees then bursts back out, chasing a smaller figure, her red hair flaring in the low sunlight like a flag.

The girl's laughing wildly, gripping a hose. She screeches as Sage chucks a water balloon, soaking her jeans and t-shirt. She spins, spreading droplets like a dog shaking itself. "You are the *worst*!"

I see it instantly: Myri looks just like the rest of her family.

She has Jonah's pale skin and cheekbones, Teresa's full lips and sharp chin, Sage's red hair. Higher and younger, her laugh has the cadence of Teresa's dry chuckle. And even playing with her brother, she carries the same weight Jonah buckles under.

I stare. I can't get my head around her. She's too slippery, too many facets.

"Not many of us see her like this," Giulia says quietly. "Jonah likes to keep her a mystery. And it's not safe for her to be out of the cabin for long; she has too much of the Unseen in her. She killed one of the goats once, with her bare hands. Another time they found her dancing on the edge of the cliff, with her eyes closed."

I wince, picturing it. "When she was screaming—"

Giulia nods. "She sees things. Glimpses. It's more than her human self can handle. Whatever's in the ocean, it's in her too. We try to help, but . . . ."

Those screams. Like she was being torn apart. Like the world was. I can't square that with this bright day, the enfolding wonder of the Unseen. But there's terror in the depths of what I've seen, for sure; I understand why a girl drowning in it might scream into the night.

"But she's still just a kid," Giulia continues. "Some of us get to know her that way. Me, Sage. She was close to Elise." Her face tightens a little. "Maybe you, too. She told me she trusts you."

Something cracks inside me. The relief that she wasn't fully a mirage redoubles the relief of seeing her laugh. She didn't need saving. I didn't fail her.

"Did Jonah tell you what the miracle was? What the Unseen did?"

Teresa clutching a corpse. *We understood the depth of our debt.* "I have an idea."

"I'm showing you this so you'll remember. Nothing here is ever what you think. Okay? There's always another layer." She seems hesitant, like she wants to say something more, turn it into a warning, but it slips away.

I nod. As soon as I have a grip on something, it transforms. I felt it in the cavern, how the heart of everything can mutate that way. It gives me vertigo, like the soil under my feet might send me tumbling into a clear sky.

"So, what are you?"

Giulia's laugh is shy and surprised. "Your friend. I hope."

"Sounds good."

I thread my arm through Giulia's, and she hugs it. The confusion turns exhilarating again. Perhaps that's what Larissa meant: The only way to survive this uncertainty is to fall into it. I close my eyes and enjoy the rush of tumbling.

CHAPTER TWENTY
WHERE I LIVE NOW

THE DAYS THAT FOLLOW ARE HEADY, A SPIRAL OF WORK AND LAUGHTER AND parties and food and sun, full of tiny wonders. The warmth of eggs collected fresh. Light on the ocean. The width of the sky. Fire spinning.

There's work, of course. My name's always scrawled beside a new one, a new person to sweep me up to collect firewood or to fish off the rocks. Never alone; no time to think. They share food, rub sunscreen into my skin, teach me card games, sing me their favorite songs. Friendships are weird. I don't know how to hold them or make them grow, but these people seem to understand. Ana helps me plant seedlings, cradling her hands around mine, fragile roots in my palms. It feels like that.

I learn everyone gradually, half from gossip. I only discover after my day in the fields with Ana that she was an environmental activist and has a past full of jail terms. I slice vegetables with Frida, dancing and bumping hips, and hear afterward that she was a drug addict living on the street, and also that she was a wealthy architect. I help João carry his drums, then hear a debate about whether he's really an army deserter.

Did Kai's band break up after he had visions of the cave onstage? Was Maisie *really* acquitted of poisoning her husband? Did Darya actually learn to fire-spin when she ran away with a circus?

"That's the cool thing," Larissa says. Sunset, lying on cushions. She's asked me to plait her hair, and under my fingers it's the silkiest thing. "You dump your past when you arrive. Let everyone reinvent you."

"What do they say about you?" The buzz of insects is soporific.

Her body softens. "I was a criminal boss, or a street artist, or an oil heiress. Or I was raised in another cult and rescued when the FBI raided their compound and discovered a plot to poison Denver."

I part her hair again. I can't get it right; her scent is intoxicating. Warm grass, sweat, herbs. "How did you get the coolest rumors?"

Her grin widens. "Spread them myself."

I let my fingertip linger on her skin, then panic and look for a safe subject. As usual, I find a dangerous one. "*Another* cult?"

"Oh, sure, this must be a cult. Look at us, living in isolation with our secretive ways, doing our eldritch rites for our eldritch-er god." She wiggles her fingers. She's drawn spirals under her eyes in blue eyeliner because she can. "Brainwashed zombies."

I make a zombie face, say, "Braaaiiins," and we giggle and go off on one another about whether zombies prefer brainwashed people or not—do they prefer their food clean?

"Brainwashed, whatever," Larissa says. "They can call us what they like. I'm an astrophysics graduate, did I mention that?"

"Is that a rumor you want me to spread?"

Larissa sticks her tongue out, then turns serious. "As if anything's better out there. Where you're just expected to keep taking, and needing people is weak but being alone is shameful, because people are accessories, or tools, and nothing's deeper than the skin. I choose to know there's something better. I don't *believe*. I *know*."

I know, too. It thrums under everything.

A sensation of reality bubbling softly, coming to a boil, is woven through our everyday life. A life that sweeps me up with ease.

Larissa joked, but I can't call this a cult. I always thought cults were all scriptures and strictures, rules and rites without gods. We have a god, but only two rules: Never swim in the sea. And never disturb the oracle.

Beyond that, it's all rigged together. We make decisions in messy meetings, although Teresa has the final call. She cradles her authority in her arms, gentle. Jonah is distant, wrapped in murkier questions, wearing authority not like a crown but like a yoke.

Dawns are smeared in pinks and blues; we meet them with meditation on the beach, then busy, clattering breakfasts. And then there's work.

The power here seeps into the soil; fruits grow abundant, crops sprout out of season. Plants luxuriate in an alien climate: mangoes, avocados. Teresa asks me to grind her home-grown nutmeg, a twist of sadness in her smile as she says its Latin name, *Myristica*. The land's eager to feed us, to make us strong.

"Fatten us up," Larissa jokes, and snaps at my finger. "Mm. Nearly ripe."

Because *something's coming*, and it wants us ready.

More and more, instead of farming or cooking and cleaning, I find myself assigned to help Kiera in the library. After a few days (or weeks?

Time's swimmy), Jonah calls me up to the solarium, officially declares me Kiera's assistant and asks me to keep him posted on how her work is going. I babble, thanking him for trusting me; he presses my hand to his chest, our touches automatic because we're extensions of the same thing, and tells me that he wishes more people had. I glow.

Kiera panics when I tell her I've been assigned to help her, going raspberry-red and mumbling something about disappointing Jonah. But she brightens quickly when she realizes she gets to teach me her *filing systems*.

When the day cools, there's dinner, music, storytelling, parties. Our friendship is automatic; we've been somewhere nobody else has. And *something's coming*, and we're approaching it together, blindfolded, hand in hand.

And we worship.

There's grand, planned rituals outside the cave, offerings of fruit and flowers, guided by Myri speaking in riddles. We dress extravagantly for those. Larissa and Zina have fun making me a costume: baggy black dress, golden body paint, a crown of fig leaves and jasmine. I look transformed, otherworldly.

Mostly, though, rites come on unexpectedly, the offerings less tangible.

Aksel places berries on our lips. There's something in them, and we spiral into the arms of the Unseen. I lie on the sand and ride the starlight on the ocean's skin, explore the bloody chambers of my own body. We offer our wonder.

There's drumming, and João leads us to a spring; we douse candle flames and gulp the cool water. We see the threads of energy connecting tree roots and fungi, watch light dissolve into leaves, the electricity in our nerves glimmering. The Unseen accepts our fascination, a sacrifice on its altar.

Zina announces we have to make a bonfire. Something uncanny flares, and our flesh takes on that flickering quality. The dance turns sensual, lips meeting lips, hands sliding across skin. Sighs and gasps are gifts, and the Unseen shudders as it accepts them.

I slip out of that one, awkward, but nobody minds. Just being here, that's worship. How can you not worship a god that's in your veins?

Even if I just stroke my skin, that's an offering; my body isn't mine, it's an instrument that lets something unknowable taste the world. The sweetest purpose I could give it.

Sometimes, when the noon sun bleaches everything rose-white and heat haze wavers like ghosts, we feel it close enough to touch. Sometimes, in the richest hours of the night when everything's shadow and sea whispers, it's closer. Moving between the stars, shivering with anticipation.

And then we sink into exquisite, exhausted sleep.

Time expands and contracts like lungs, breathing us. Because *something's coming*, we feel it closer every day, and we're here to make it real, our gift to the universe.

Even our dreams are gifts from and to the Unseen. They're uncanny, full of formless promises, their textures rich and eerie. The Unseen absorbs my sweat and sleeping breaths. So I'm disorientated when I wake to something outside my window.

It's been weeks, months, who knows, since my initiation. Time and this life have drunk me into their rhythms. My hair's grown out a little, turned to a mussed-up halo, and the hut has felt like home since the first day anyway. Still, in the tumult of waking it feels alien, an unfamiliar place where I'm defenseless.

Something scrapes down the window.

I force myself up. Every step is trembling, my fingers at the rough curtain—

"Boo!"

The face outside is ghostly, and cackling wildly.

"Holy shit, Myri." Should I be swearing around a kid? That's what she is right now, no oracle in her, just a teenager laughing. I slide the window open. "You scared me."

"Yes." Her voice is playfully serious. "Fear the oracle that comes in the night."

I rub my temples, trying to massage my brain back into place. "What's happening?"

"I wanted to hang out. Sage got me the cabin keys because I threatened to make him sing in the next ritual." Myri pouts. "I had fun that night, when you came and told me about the swans." She twists her hair into a ponytail with a hair elastic. Such a normal motion. Her grin is impish. "Walk? Promise I won't kill a goat. That was like *one time,* and I wasn't even myself."

A sweet ache rises. The girl in the cabin is real; I wasn't talking to a mirage. "Okay! Walk! Yeah, that sounds good!" I'm being too enthusiastic again.

"Don't worry," she adds. "If anyone finds us, I'll tell them I was sharing unspeakable secrets of the beyond with you. I brought biscuits."

With no idea how to respond, I head out in my pajamas for a walk with the oracle. Cool wind and curiosity perk me up. Something untamed and thrilling in the air.

She strides through the grove, between ripples of light and dark that flicker on her like strobe lights. Moonlight, or something else, something

Myri? "Thanks for coming. Most of the others see me as the scary hermit prophetess. It's nice to be human. It reminds me what things could be like if I didn't have this . . . hole in me. This thing in me, twisting up my dreams and making everything all . . . spiky and unexpected."

I shiver, wrenched by the sadness of that and touched by pride: I'm being honored with a chance to actually see her. How often have people given me that? Only ever Craig. "I'm . . . I don't understand, but I'm sorry it's happening to you?"

Myri looks back. "Sorry. I'm being weird. I *am* usually pretty creepy."

That makes me smile. We pick our way up the hill, a walk that winded me just a few weeks ago. This place is making me stronger, isn't it? Preparing me.

We settle on the clifftop, groves and ocean silvery below us. Myri pulls a tissue-wrapped package from her pocket. "Biscuit? Ma baked them. They're really good."

They are good. Shortbread bliss. Echoes of the mouthful of biscuit that first brought this place into my body, my mind, my life. "That thing in you . . . ? The Unseen?"

She nods, wiping crumbs off her chin. "Yeah. Seven years ago, something happened, and I've . . . got holes in me, and it's filled them in different. Being me is like, skating along feeling normal and then you plunge into a galaxy. It's confusing, actually!"

Seven years. I try to gulp it back, but it comes out. "I think I saw. You were . . . ."

"Dead." She turns toward me, freckles and dark pupils stark in the moonlight. "Yeah. I was."

My mouth goes dry, biscuit clogging on my tongue.

"It brought me back," she continues. "Kinda like you, but . . . I was *dead*. You were gone into the Unseen, and that's a death too, but I was *gone* gone. Then I woke up. But parts of me never came back, and it's like I'm held together with glue and string, and the glue and string are full of dreams and *want* something." She surprises me by resting her head on my shoulder. "It sucks. I don't get to be me. Just this . . . container."

I put my arm around her. I feel the sharpness of her shoulders, the fragility of her. I missed this feeling of being needed. But I'm astounded, too. That she'd tell me this, based on what? A short talk in the night, a moment when we sang together through a closed window? And she talks like it's a burden. How can it be a burden, to share your tiny body with something that could span a universe, to be infused with glory?

"I know what we're doing is right. It needs to be released, the world's all warped as long as it's trapped; it's bleeding out so much pain from its nightmares. But . . . when I try to see where it's all going, I . . ." A soft snort that isn't really a laugh. "You heard me scream. It all comes apart, and it's scary."

I remember. Those screams are scored through the core of me. "What do you see?"

She shuffles away slightly. "It's not anyone's *fault*, okay, just . . . so much brightness, everything warping, and . . . I don't know how it can be changed. Maybe, but . . . I don't want to do that. No. I don't want to talk about it."

I shake off the urge to push further. I feel the Unseen, its subtle heartbeat in the grass and moonlight. I feel how it loves us.

"Why are you telling me this?" I ask. This vulnerability, this surprising gift from a girl who's supposed to be hidden, is unnerving.

"Maybe . . . I don't know. Maybe it . . ." She shakes her head as if shaking off a thought. "Sometimes I feel like I know you, like I met you before, like I already knew you for a long time, and you helped me. Maybe it's stupid. Tell me more about where you're from?"

I stare at the ragged reflection of the moon and search out stories. A fight at our pub. Sneaking off from cross-country running and walking in the woods, not sure what I was looking for. My brother's wedding, the last time I saw my family.

Mostly I talk about Craig, dancing in the front row at his gigs and running backstage to kiss him, swimmy with weed and cider.

Talking about him is salve and salt in a wound I've been trying to ignore. Sometimes I daydream about bringing him here. I imagine him strumming his guitar on the beach, meditating beside me in a turbulent dawn. Home and adventure folding together.

Myri yawns. "I want to go somewhere like that."

"It's hideous," I assure her.

She shakes her head. "Only 'cause it's what you know." She shifts under my arm, snuggling closer again. "Elise used to talk about that town. Tallerton, right? She lived there too. She said you had to dig deep to find the good bits."

Elise. I forget so often. Nobody talks about her, which is odd. We care about each other so deeply here. But there's no hopes held out, no memorial candle, no talk of searching for her, just a name nobody speaks. Like she's resented for leaving, or like it's dangerous speculating what fate might have found her. Like something tossed into deep water, leaving no trace once the ripples dissipate.

"What was Elise like?"

Myri chews her biscuit, thoughtful. "Kind. Reckless. Brave. Kind of like you."

I can't help smiling. *Kind and brave, like you.*

"She and Sage were . . . ." Myri shrugs. "That's why he's weird about you. Wearing her clothes, living in her hut. He doesn't talk about her. But he thinks about her all the time."

The thought sinks in. Sage stares at me sometimes like I'm a puzzle, when he's not glaring outright. That makes sense now. Elise vanished like a stone in water, and the ripples of my arrival swelled over the ripples of her absence. Of course he hates me.

As if the mention of his name had summoned him, the wind shifts, delivering the sound of Sage's voice. "Myri? Are you up here?"

Two figures outlined in the moonlight, making their way up the hill toward us, two ink-dark streaks. Giulia, hair and clothes whipping in the wind. Sage, in a jumper too thick for this warm night. Myri jumps up and waves.

I fight off an old-world instinct to be embarrassed about being out in my pajamas.

"Time to get back to bed, little chaos demon." Sage approaches his sister with a grin, ignoring me. I wonder, as I always wonder when I see him, whether his whispered warning the day of my initiation had been part of the test, or a genuine attempt to get rid of me. At least I understand why, now. *Nice dress.* "*I* want to sleep, so I have to drag *you* back to your cabin so I don't have to stay up worrying about you."

Myri sticks her tongue out. "It's okay! You can worry about me *wherever* I am."

"Thank you. I will." Sage holds out a hand and pulls her to her feet; I climb up to my own, catching Giulia's eye. Her smile's amused and apologetic, and contagious. I take a quick look back up at the lemon trees, at the rising hills behind the cove, before we set off back down the path.

A few minutes picking our way down the rocky pathways, dust on our toes and moonlight in our eyes, and then Sage stops abruptly. "Do you see it? Another one. Again."

The stench hits my nose before I can reply: decay. The damp, mulchy smell of rotting matter. From that little outcropping by the path, a pile of rocks and a precarious pine tree that spreads its branches over the long drop back down to the groves.

Except the tree is dripping with rot now, fungi in great chunky shelves, flecked and powdery-white, the wood itself mulching into its own powder. Around it, the grass and rocks are smeared with sticky putrescence. Somewhere among the roots a small creature—too decomposed to be identifiable as a rat or bird, just something little and alive once—is a feast for larvae.

In everything, I'd forgotten that strange moment in the cabin when the wooden slats rotted before my eyes, weakening enough to break when I pushed. I hadn't thought to ask Myri if that damage was still there, if there were still mushrooms sprouting from her window. Hadn't wondered about how it echoed the rot patch I'd stumbled into on that mad late-night run, how I'd dreamed of decay thick and slick between my own sheets.

"This has happened before?" I ask Sage.

He looks directly at me for once, holds my gaze for a few seconds before peering closer to examine the tree. "It's been happening more and more."

"Especially around you," Giulia says quietly, "hasn't it?"

Sage doesn't reply, leaning forward in a way that makes me dizzy; beyond the tree is just the plunging drop. I look to Myri, like she might have some occult wisdom to offer, but she's just leaning against a rock, hands in pockets, all girl tonight and no god.

"Some kind of virus? Mold?" I feel stupid. Sage knows the land, I don't.

"You'd think," Sage says, actually reaching out to the decaying wood and letting an insect crawl onto his fingertip. He examines it critically. "Except it doesn't last. We come back up here in an hour or two, you can bet that tree will be right back to normal. Some chunks missing, perhaps, but not a mushroom or maggot to be seen." He looks back to me, raises an eyebrow, like he thinks I'm hiding an answer about it.

"I, um." I shrug.

"Not an expert on fungi, huh." He seems to forgive me for that, at least, and squeezes Myri. "Come on, you. Bed. Dad'll want you to dream some cool dreams, right?"

"I don't like my dreams right now." Myri turns to me and Giulia like we can do something about it. "They're full of bad promises, and they keep unraveling."

Sage and Giulia exchange a troubled look that locks me out. Giulia rubs Myri's shoulder. "Just trust, right?"

She glances at me, as if to check that I clocked her saying that, and I nod and say, "Just trust."

I hang back a little before following them, and dare to trail a fingernail down the damp, decomposing bark, leaving a residue between keratin and skin. There's the briefest flash of something as I touch it, a late-night unexplained thought, an awareness of a contained suffering, which is silly: Decay is a process; decay itself doesn't *suffer*.

I yawn and follow the others, and by the time I get back to my hut, any remaining traces of mold are gone from under my nail. I slip back into my dreams of shifting light and color, and anticipation of nights of long talks with my little neighbor, the glow of being trusted.

Nobody talks about the ritual Kiera found, that morning I stumbled across her panicking. Nobody talks about *what* is coming.

Even when it's just us, the sunlit library and a million things to do, somehow my curiosity and Kiera's overenthusiasm fall under a pall. I don't ask why she's making a list concerningly titled "alternatives to blood," or what the words mean that she intones as she paces, like she's rehearsing, or why the windows rattle eagerly in time with their rhythm. I don't even flip open the old leather book just printed with the word *embodiment*. I don't need to know, because when the time comes, I will. I trust.

When the dark circles under her eyes get too pronounced, I pull her out to the balcony, and she smiles gratefully. I report to Jonah every night, just for the glow when he touches my hand and assures me I'm doing well, I'm helping her, and she'll get us where we're going.

The anticipation's constant, life on the whirligig brink of a roller-coaster drop. But it's always unspoken. Perhaps because for all we yearn for what comes next, there is something in these days that we never want to end.

CHAPTER TWENTY-ONE

DECOMPOSITION

ONE SMALL SHARD SITS UNCOMFORTABLE IN THOSE DAYS: THE THOUGHT OF Craig. His absence doesn't overwhelm, but awareness of it surges up at strange moments. I expect him to be there, around any corner. Arms out for me, *There you are, love,* eyes snapping, *Why the fuck did you say that, trying to embarrass me?* Then he isn't there, and there's nowhere to put the love and shame except to exhale them and feel what inhales them.

I'm doing that one muggy morning on my way from the farmhouse, yawning, trying to unruffle my unruly mop of hair, eyes on the swirling, expanding clouds above the trees. I'm on the rota to work with Ana, collecting cherries and peaches at the edge of the groves. It looks like rain, and I hope it's coming; there's something glorious and refreshing about rain here, racing back along the paths with a basket of peaches, droplets bursting against my skin, laughing. I take the emptiness that Craig left me, give it to what roils in the air and clouds, and maybe it will fall back on me later, transformed.

I'm late, and I expect Ana to already have the ladder up, but I spot her from a distance, standing, hands on hips. Sage is crouched under one of the trees, head bowed.

I spot that, then the smell hits me; I take in what I'm seeing and choke on it. Like the tree on the cliff the other night (how long ago was that? Two days? A week?), the peach and cherry trees are black and gravid with rot.

The closer I get, the clearer the devastation: Fruits wither in puffs of mold, or lie blackened and swollen on the earth, and that earth boils with bugs, soft with damp. The leaves are graying and smeared, the bark chewed away and replaced with thick chunks of mushroom.

"Never seen anything like it," Ana's confirming. "It was *fine* yesterday. It was *fine*."

Sage straightens up, brushing black decay off his jeans. "This is the worst I've seen it." He raises his hand to examine whatever's smeared there. "It'll be gone in a few hours if it's like all the other times, but whatever it is, if it's getting into our food supply, that is *not* good. And those mushrooms? Not any species I've ever seen."

"This is not natural," Ana says softly. "It doesn't come and go like this." She gives me a sidelong look as I approach and speaks maybe a little too quickly. "Full of strange miracles, isn't it? Rot's there for something new to grow from, right?"

Usually when I'm with her in the groves and fields, she's the teacher and I'm the clumsy student. Now, though, she looks at me nervously, like I'm the authority here. A delighted shiver runs through me. "Let me look."

"The fungi expert," Sage says drily, and I can't tell what warmth there is in that teasing. Ana shoots him a glare and steps aside for me.

I regret my lack of shoes as my toes squelch in the soup of soil and rotten fruit. Never mind, the rain will wash it away. I kneel where Sage knelt, and—*maybe there is something special in you, they said you were a sign*—breathe in deeply, open myself to the Unseen.

A shard, a splinter. No, something softer than that. Something dissolvable, absorbable, but for now lodged inside, nestled, wrong under the skin, not belonging, not absorbed, not what it is meant to become, wrong and rotting, writhing still in some misguided attempt to still be itself as it comes apart so slowly now—

I don't know when I reached forward and snapped a chunk from one of the mushrooms, but it's in my hand, my fingers smeared with its secretions. On the outside, it was a slice of orange-amber fungus, freckled brown and white. But inside it's a richer, rawer red-pink, veined with white, so horribly like raw meat that I drop it with a jolt. Iron scent in my nose—

I'm kneeling on dry earth, staring at the striated bark of the cherry tree. Green leaves sway, ripening cherries hang in clusters, the breeze smells of dry grass and salt. Not so much as a freckle of mold.

Sage is kneeling beside me, hands pressed into the bark of the tree. Our eyes meet, a silent, *Did one of us do that?* A silent, *I don't know.*

Ana watches us, inscrutable.

"Weird," I say, my smile misshapen as I stand. I'm caught between confusion, fear, and a cocky wonder. That baffling glimpse left a sour taste in my mouth, half washed away by the sweetness of the shock that followed. *Be normal.* "Maybe there's something in the library that can help? I bet Kiera would be up for some research."

It's an obvious suggestion, and I'm sure he's thought about it before; still, he examines me like he's intrigued. It's not a friendly look, but his voice is even as he says, "Don't know if anyone's asked her to look into it. Not a bad idea."

"We probably shouldn't eat those," I add, looking up at the cherries.

Sage shrugs, plucks one, and tosses it into his mouth. Red-purple stains on his teeth. "If it's coming and going like this, it'll have touched everything by now, right?" He considers. "No different. Maybe a bit sweeter."

I'm not sure why a shudder moves through me, but I take a cherry too, and bite. It's perfect, smooth, ripe, swollen with juice. I can't place something in the taste—almost like it's not a taste at all; almost like I'm holding a deep sadness and frustration in my mouth. I swallow it down.

Sage and I spit out our cherry pips at the same moment, which sparks an awkward shared grin, and Ana starts setting up the ladder, still eyeing us both doubtfully.

The library becomes a lot more chaotic in the following days.

Sage's off on an obsessive research jag about what he's started calling the "blight," hunting through agricultural and occult texts. Research jags are Kiera catnip. And he's got Giulia on board, and Giulia inevitably comes with an attached Larissa or Pietro.

I struggle upstairs, thanking years of waitressing as I balance a tray. I pause at the door, listening to the voices inside—Kiera's off on something arcane as usual. "If we were to consider it an *entity*, rather than a physical phenomenon, something that could be summoned and presumably also *banished*—"

"Are you actually suggesting we use ancient occult magics for farming problems?"

"We do it every day. If we take a look in the *Ars Veneficii*—shut up, Larissa, you are not twelve—there's a section on—"

I grin. I could listen to her do this for hours, but my arms are starting to ache, so I push my way in to deliver the drinks. Black tea for Sage, who's reading on the balcony. Herbal tea for Giulia, who's lying on the rug with a book stack. Sugary black coffee for Larissa, who's cross-legged with Giulia's head in her lap, ignoring the books. Water for Kiera, who groans.

"Books. Drinks." She throws her arms open. "Some of these are *centuries old.*"

"Danger's part of the fun." Larissa waves her coffee threateningly, spilling drops on Giulia. She hisses; Larissa kisses her head. The ensuing play-wrestling almost doesn't cause any coffee damage to the rug.

Kiera covers her eyes. "Don't *any* of you have work?"

I can't stifle my grin. In my nightly reports, I just tell Jonah that Kiera's caught up in an interesting thread of research, imagining his delight when we reveal that we've found a solution to this. It makes me uneasy holding back; I don't know how long I can. But uneasiness recedes around them.

"I'm cooking," says Giulia, "Larissa's cleaning—"

"Which I'm doing right now." Larissa's splayed, Giulia on her chest.

"Behold," Kiera says drily. "The inner workings of a secretive cult, where—"

She stops. Oscar's in the doorway, eyebrow raised.

He's smiling, but the air cools. "Well, hello. I've not seen this room this busy before."

Guilty glances fly; Giulia and Larissa scramble to their feet. My cheeks turn pink, even though I'm meant to be here. Part of me shudders, a loopy paranoia, the suffocation of being watched.

I lock that away, gift-wrapped and waiting. When I commune later, it'll be fine fodder for the Unseen.

"They're just helping me." Sage appears from the balcony, hands open.

"Oh?" Oscar's voice is light, but he's laser-focused on Sage. A few days ago, I would have enjoyed the hell out of this. "With what?"

I've never seen Sage awkward. He's grumpily defiant, like a kid caught with someone else's toys. "The . . . rot. You've seen it? It comes and goes in a way that is *not* natural—"

Oscar's face is bland as ever. His hand, though, is trembling, and it's hard to tell if it's nerves or if it's going to curl into a fist. "Did your father tell you to do this?"

Sage opens and closes his mouth. We watch, nobody daring to speak.

"Thought not. I can't imagine Jonah approving using our limited time and resources to research movements of shadows when we stand in inconceivable light. Can you?"

Sage swallows. Something unreadable vibrates between him and Oscar. If I didn't know Sage, I'd swear his gaze was tearful. "It could be important. It could be a sign of something that could seriously damage the land. Or it might lead us to something—"

"*Might*'s a heavy word." Oscar pats Sage's shoulder. "It's quite simply explained. A mold or disease of some sort that emerges then is cleansed by the might of the Unseen. Focus, all right? Don't be distracted by questions that don't need asking."

"Why?" Giulia says.

The question ripples. Sage tenses. Larissa's mouth opens.

"Why shouldn't we ask about it? When it could be a real problem?" Giulia leans against the desk, eyebrow raised almost in mockery of Oscar's.

This tension's bubbled up so suddenly it feels like fear. Sometimes things feel perfect, then break.

Something trembles on her lips. She says it. "You don't like us asking questions, do you, Oscar? You don't like us talking about Elise either."

The name drops like a detonation.

"Giulia," Sage says. "Don't."

Oscar holds the moment, then his smile returns. "I'm glad you still think of your friend, Giulia, and our safety. Would it make you happy if I took this up with Jonah?"

Giulia cocks her head, not returning his smile.

Sage abruptly strides out. A door slams somewhere, or a fist hits a wall. That wasn't a sob, was it? Giulia glances back at Oscar, then pelts after Sage.

In their wake, we can breathe.

Oscar looks around. "The rest of you. Teresa will have tasks for you if you're not on the rota. A word of advice: This place feels like a holiday, sometimes, doesn't it? It isn't. You offered yourself up to do the work of the most precious unknown. These phenomena are not fun puzzles or toys."

I almost smile, despite my shame; I can imagine him berating a bright-lit office full of interns. It's fun when those glimpses of the people we were before shine through.

But the smile falters as his tone changes. "We need to be careful. It won't be gentle if we fuck up."

Kiera's pale. Larissa's teeth grit. My stomach knots.

"Don't squander your time," Oscar says.

When the door closes behind him, our eyes avoid each other. We file out and go and make ourselves useful.

CHAPTER TWENTY-TWO
OTHER GIFTS

I TRY, OVER THE NEXT DAYS, TO DO AS OSCAR SAYS. IT'S SIMPLE, AND SIMPLER still to raise a warning eyebrow when I catch Kiera cross-referencing a book on demon summoning with a field guide to mushrooms or notice Giulia and Sage whispering together. I eat cherries fresh from the once-blighted branches. We have bigger, brighter things to think about.

Besides. There's been an undeniable shift since that morning under those cherry trees. Ana's level-headed, devoted to the Unseen but more to the community and the land, but whispers have swollen her account of what happened in that grove, and the whispers are about me. *She touched the mold, and it vanished.* Hands and gazes linger on me longer.

And maybe it's that that stirs something in me a few nights later. A hot night, simmering with storms that won't break, lightning flickering on distant horizons, but the sky above us cloudless.

There's a bunch of us on the beach, sharing a bottle of whisky. There was a rush earlier, something eerie and holy stirring, but the energy shifted, and we ended up curled together, tangled in a way that's feral and intimate, like we're one creature.

I don't know how we invented this game. It's part of that spontaneity here, our minds tangling up just like our bodies do. People yell words: "brother," "instrument," "vegetable," a challenge to tell our most embarrassing or wildest stories about those things. No story, you drink. Best story, you drink.

I have no truly wild stories. I have a lot of embarrassing stories. The bottle keeps returning to me. The stars are spinning wrong, and the horizon's wonky. I'll be hungover for breakfast duty tomorrow. I don't care.

Kai drinks with a flourish, finishing a story about a fight with a semifamous footballer on a plane. We're laughing, because the story's funny or because it's Kai or because everything's deliciously silly. I'm flopped over, but straighten up as Aksel declares, "Languages!"

Yes, I have a story, an embarrassing one. When I thought I could learn French, linked up with a language exchange and headed out all giddy with a shiny new notebook. How the girl was sweet and so pretty, laughed like I didn't think I could make people laugh, how I lost track of time until I spotted three missed calls from Craig. How stupid I looked when I scrambled up to run to him. How she never answered my texts. How it became a running joke with Craig, the time Aoife tried to make a friend.

I can't tell that story.

I lie back instead and listen to Maisie's story about mistranslating a word and accidentally trying to order illegal drugs in a restaurant. But my mind keeps slipping back to the hurt look on the French girl's face as I pelted out of the café. I'm not that Aoife anymore, am I? I'm something else, loved, important. Larissa's fingers are looped around my ankle, I'm wearing a crown of yellow flowers that Frida made. I'm drunk and stupid, but they turn to me sometimes, seeking *my* approval.

An idea takes root. Oscar told us to leave the blight alone. But even Oscar wouldn't complain, would he, if we were moved by the Unseen? And if I really quiet my mind, follow that delicious loopy drunkenness into something higher, maybe it is pulling me. I can feel it, if I try to.

I breathe. The whisky-drunk wheeling stars and distant lightning breathe me.

I stand up and announce, "We should swim."

Quiet. Heads turn, Maisie's story crumbling. A thrill seizes me, redoubled by the drunkenness and the heady presence in the air.

I did that. I made them see me.

I fear the pain in the ocean, of course I do, but the fear's dulled by booze and the rush of their attention. Besides, I want to *understand* it. I want to glimpse again what I glimpsed beyond it, the promise of some gorgeous cataclysm. I want to see more clearly what I felt in the grove, that sense of something intrusive, breaking down but persisting. If the answer to the blight is anywhere, won't it be among those nightmares that seethe in the water?

Larissa stands first, no questions, tossing back her hair and throwing her dress onto the sand. Then there's a flurry of movement, discarded clothes and reverent excitement, an answering breeze fluttering the candles like a *yes.*

I hesitate. The clothes scattering the sand fling me back to Craig's friends' parties, where drinking games would often end with the girls stripping, and nobody wanted to be the prudish one. I'd sit hunched, trying to hide the gawky angles of my body. Craig would reassure me. *Don't be uptight. You're beautiful to me, and that's what matters, right?*

That world is not this world.

I throw aside my own dress, trying to forget I have a body and lose myself in the cool wind and the enticing murmur of the waves. Listen. That could be a call, couldn't it?

I close my eyes and walk forward—right into rough hands that shove me back.

Jonah's eyes are blades.

I stumble back, stunned with panic. Kiera grabs and steadies me. The thrilling silence has turned dangerous.

I don't know where he came from—I—I look back, but the shadows and the blur of my own eyes hide the others' faces from me. I can't find anything to hold. I'm *naked*, and that gaze strips away even more layers, flaying me, breaking me down.

I look down at the sand.

"Bed," Jonah says. Calm and impassive, but his voice slices through us. "All of you. You are drunk and treating our holy work like a children's prank. There are consequences for that."

And nobody says, *Sorry*—he knows we are—and nobody says anything; imagine saying something, imagine what would happen. Nobody knows what happens if you let Jonah down. But his forgiveness can't be infinite, can it?

He knows when our impulses are holy and when they're silly fantasies. He knows better than we ever can.

We gather up our clothes and walk away. Lightning shivers along the horizon, but if he's still there, it's not strong enough to outline him.

My head's pounding queasily when I arrive at the farmhouse the next morning. I can't tell what's a hangover and what's shame, like my body's inflicting punishment on the awkward, stupid thing inside it.

The awkward stupid thing is awkward and stupid through breakfast, avoiding eyes and whispers. I'm learning to read the language of this collective being. These are the kind of whispers that fade in a day or so, a temporary punishment. Still, they smart.

I clean the dishes until they're spotless and wipe down the kitchen five times, and then there's nothing to do except what I have to.

The solarium's thick with humidity, beading the windows and dripping from the leaves, the air hard to breathe. No Jonah. Even his desk's empty; the pendulum contraption's missing. Just a crumpled piece of paper lying in its place.

I resist; it was always the deal with Craig, some things I don't touch. Nobody likes me when I'm nosy.

Then I'm unfolding it, despite myself.

It's blank but bears the impression of a word written a few pages above it, in pen strokes so desperate they've nearly torn through, left an echo. It simply says, VESSEL.

I close my eyes, *just trust*, and breathe out my confusion. Butterflies take off in an iridescent burst. The Unseen soothes me, *Shhh, yes, more.*

Footsteps shake me out of the calm daze that follows; I drop the paper, making my best attempt at an innocent face.

Jonah looks exhausted, sparking an automatic *hangover solidarity* reaction that I thankfully strangle before it reaches my voice box. He's even more haggard than usual.

He waits for me to speak.

"I'm sorry," I say, but I am so tired of *always* having to be *sorry*, "I . . . overstepped last night. I thought maybe . . . I felt the Unseen calling me into the water, like it might have something to tell me, about the blight?"

I wait for judgment. He watches. The light is vivid and the shadows too deep, stirred by butterfly wings.

"I won't do it again." This is a stupid apology, all wrong in my mouth.

"Things could be very different," Jonah remarks. "The fun and pleasure are not for our sake. They are gifts to the Unseen through your minds and bodies. It takes other gifts, too."

He smiles, a flicker of almost beatific joy through the exhaustion, plucks a thorn, and pushes it into the meat of his thumb. I wince as the presence around us drinks in his pain.

"Not everyone," Jonah says softly, "can give the gifts it asks. Not everyone should have to. I bear them so you won't need to."

Maybe it's watching him hurt, maybe it's the bright blood droplet adhering to his skin, maybe it's my shame, but a wave of sympathy takes me. He looks old.

"You don't have to," I say. "We're here. I'd like to help."

I reach for him, eager for his hand cradling my head, for the way my name sounds in his voice, reborn, embraced in the movements of his lips. But he doesn't reach back.

Instead, he's there, face too close to mine, expressionless. "If you truly believe you could carry a fraction of the weight I do, you're nothing short of delusional."

There's quiet.

I know this quiet. It's a place, and I've spent many hours in it. It's where you go to change, to shape yourself around what was said or done to you. You become better there. I asked Jonah to change me, didn't I?

"I'm sorry," I say. "I'll go and do my work."

"No." Jonah's eyes fall on the crumpled paper, and he softens, the anger dissolving into something gentler and sadder. "No, actually, Aoife, I'd rather you remain here. There is a conversation that needs to be had, a conversation I have been putting off for too long, and I would like you to be here for it. Whatever mistakes you have made"—he places a hand on my shoulder, gazes deep into me, those bright, pale eyes, not forgiveness but a promise that I can earn it—"do not diminish your importance. Wait here, please, and think on things while I gather the others."

As he walks away, his shadow passes over the remains of the missing pendulum contraption. It lies on the floor, in pieces, stamped on over and over.

⊖

I wait in the thick, damp heat, sitting quietly, letting the shame do its work. I fix my eyes on a slab of glass, pomegranate-red; I run my fingers over the chrysalises hanging from their bamboo strip; I am changing. I am changing into the important thing I need to be. I listen to the quiet and feel a shifting, like a storm about to break: a wildness to the wind outside, a glimmer inside my skin, stirring in my belly. Thrilling and ominous, like the beauty of one of Teresa's poison berries on my palm.

Within an hour or so, people have drifted in, and the solarium is thrumming with that same energy. Jonah's pacing between shafts of colored light—newly energized, fingers clicking, smile flashing then fading, erratic and tight-strung. Larissa and Frida rest on cushions at his feet; Sage's examining the chrysalises. Pietro leans against the sofa where Oscar's sprawled.

Myri's in a ball on the other sofa, watching something on a tablet. She looks surprisingly human, considering how many people here know the prophetess, not the normal girl. Teresa sinks beside her, and they curl together; it's the first time I've seen them like that, mother and daughter. That's when I know this is real. Something's happening. Something important.

Kiera pelts up the stairs behind me, papers under her arm, breathless. That's all of us. A core group. Even after my disrespect last night, they invited *me* here, to join the trusted ones, the most devoted. Even Giulia isn't here, but I *am*.

Jonah doesn't bother with greetings. "I have something to ask."

I prop myself against a table of plants, like I could melt into the leaves to protect myself from the interrogation in that glare.

"I need to know that you are ready and willing to be part of this."

He doesn't need to say what *this* is.

The quiet hangs in the air. The butterflies move through it.

"Yes." Frida's eyes shine. "Absolutely."

The chorus echoes, Oscar's "Of course," Sage's surly nod and Teresa's calm one, Larissa's "Hell *yeah*," Myri's whisper. Kiera's rapid "Okay."

My own joins them, slipping out like I've released something. I haven't questioned it. All shame falls away in the face of *this*. If the void's yawning ahead, I'm leaping in, with a *purpose* for the first time.

"Good." Jonah runs a hand through his beard. "We will do the ritual tonight."

This quiet is lightning.

The papers slip from Kiera's hands. She scrambles to pick them up, yelling, "Fuck, fuck." Myri looks at *me* like I have an answer, and Sage says, "Dad, no," and we're relieved at that because we didn't have to say it.

Jonah waits. An unfamiliar smile moves across his face: twisted, amused, bitter as peel.

"Liars," he says. "My most trusted. You all lied to me." His gaze moves around the room, hunting. "You are not ready."

His eyes settle on me. Sickness churns.

"But I understand." There's this collective breath out as we recognize the softness in him. "I am also not ready. We do not know what it will look like. We do not know what will happen to any of us. I *believe* we will be rewarded in ways we cannot conceive of. But I do not *know* it, and what I do not know is suffocating me. I'm terrified, too."

The sickness in me shifts. A moment ago, I was afraid *of* Jonah, a little. Now we share the fear. Kiera's still crouched, gathering her papers, and she looks up at me like she's checking I heard it, too.

This is easier: We look at each other, instead of the question looming over us.

Jonah sinks back against the desk, bringing a hand to his brow.

"It doesn't matter." Teresa effortlessly picks up her husband's thread, arm still around Myri's shoulder. "This isn't a choice. We don't belong to ourselves. We're living sacrifices. We gave our bodies to do its will, and its will is to wake. We've all seen the blight: It's an omen, a warning of time running short. It needs us to do what we promised." Her voice softens. "There is no discussion."

Something unwinds. It's startling how much that relaxes me. How easy it is to stop being Aoife and become the hand of something too vast to question, moved by glory. My calm is a beautiful thing I can only watch in awe: I *am* ready.

Thinking of Craig is a twinge. When a living, present god enters this world, will he know that this was a gift I gave him?

"Three nights from now." Jonah lifts his head. "If you have doubts, make your peace with them. Kiera, tell us what you have."

Kiera almost drops her papers again. I shift to touch her shoulder; it's warm; my skin tingles. What happens to these bodies that hold us, in a world infused with the living Unseen? We'll know. Three nights from now.

Kiera gives me a nervous, grateful glance, and gathers herself. "It's a simple ritual. Cobbled together from folk beliefs and occult traditions. Local languages and herbal lore, structures from medieval heresies, some more modern, esoteric stuff, wouldn't normally make any sense, but if it draws on the energy in the cave, it'll work. We have what we need." She bites her lip. "Except. It requires, um, a . . . ."

"If you say human sacrifice." Larissa doesn't need to finish; the nervous giggles do it for her, release rippling around the room.

Kiera doesn't giggle. She screws up her mouth. "Not *exactly*. It asks for a vessel to contain the Unseen in this . . . plane, I guess. A human body and mind."

Immediately, before there's a chance for a giddying and sacrilegious longing to fully awaken in me, Sage says, "I'll do it."

He crosses his arms. His face is set.

"It's not clear." Kiera looks miserable. "If you'd . . . survive. Stay yourself."

I wait for shock and fear at that. I'm pleased to find none; if anything, there's a vague envy. What a gorgeous wave to be swept away by.

Sage shrugs. "I'll do it. If you know why, you know. If you don't, it's not your business."

Myri wriggles out of Teresa's arms and pads across the tiles. Her hooded jumper hides her eyes, colored beams catching her set mouth, her tilted chin. She lifts a finger to Sage's lips.

"Myri is still a child, really," she says, toneless. "She's already borne more than anyone should. We don't want her to suffer. Sometimes she's almost like a person.

"But didn't her life already end? Wasn't that shadow existence it gave her enough of a gift? She was never meant for anything except this. She should have had a normal life, seen cities, done badly at uni, drunk coffee with too much syrup. But that's not what she was for, and it's not our choice. The Unseen chose her. It might not work with anyone else. She's already infused with it. Who are we to argue?"

Her words are detached, adult, but her voice doesn't vibrate with an uncanny presence: It's all her. She shakes back her hood to display her bored defiance. That's when it starts to hurt, scraping on something so deep that the pain registers dull.

"There you go. I've had the conversation you were going to have. Decided."

Sage says, "But—"

"Shut up," Myri says, a girl annoyed by her brother. "It's boring. It's me."

She strolls back to the sofa and slumps. Teresa reaches for her, agony and resignation blurred on her face, but Myri shrugs her away and stares down at the tiles.

I try to register pain. This is *Myri*. She sang behind a locked door. She really is that trapped girl, imprisoned in her possessed body, in the fate she knew was coming.

But the bright calm reshapes the sadness into pride. She's doing this for us.

Eyes turn to Jonah. His are closed; he's deep inside himself, struggling. Myri sighs, exasperated, pulls herself up again, and whispers in his ear. His face crumples, then we feel the rush as the colored light and the droplets on the leaves eagerly swallow his pain. It echoes as Teresa gives up hers. A smile flickers across Myri's face, and the smile isn't hers.

Jonah's eyes open. Calm. "That's decided, then. Let's get to work."

CHAPTER TWENTY-THREE

SLEEPWALKERS

I SHOULD BE PANICKED, SICK WITH DREAD. AND THERE IS A CONSTANT PRESS-ing at the edges, insistence there's something I need to look at, *right there*.

But then I remember: I don't need to. What I feel doesn't matter. A process is happening, and I just have to give myself over to it. At that thought, peace sinks over me, and the fear transmutes into excitement.

I fling myself into preparations, helping Kiera double-check her trans-lations, organizing relics, making sure we have *plenty* of candles. The moment Jonah said, "Let's get to work," that's what we did; thinking's a luxury there's no time for.

Two nights before the brink, Myri makes the announcement, candlelit face twisting before she speaks, like she's going to cry. But she just says, "It is stirring; the time is coming to welcome it," and the cheers echo, and we collapse into hugs and kisses and celebrate until dawn starts to soften the sky.

I'm yawning and drooping into bed when I catch raised voices. A low, angry male tone and the lilt of an Italian accent. Coming from Myri's cabin.

I grab a cardigan to slip out and investigate, but Giulia's already on my doorstep, face thunderous. Her anger fascinates me; the rage must be hot and hard to burst out through all her softness.

She's exasperated. "Aoife, can you help? Maybe she'll listen to you."

The rush. I became a person people *turn* to. I follow her, cool air clearing my head.

I haven't been in Myri's cabin since my kidnapping, impossibly far away now. Just like I remember: beads, ribbons, glyph charms spinning. Myri's cross-legged on her bed, a packet of crisps—a rare outside-world treat—beside her. Sage is pacing, his father's habit.

"Aoife, *tell them*," Myri says. "Tell them, *please*, that I know what I'm doing."

"Myri knows what she's doing," I echo automatically.

"I know you do." Sage ignores me. "You are just *consistently refusing* to look me in the eye and tell me that you want to."

"And you"—Myri puts on a mocking voice—"are *consistently refusing* to tell me how you know what it's like to have a *fate*. It *sucks*, Sage! It actually sucks a lot! And what doesn't help is someone saying 'let me do this for you' when they can't! Stop!"

Sage looks at Giulia, his crooked *do you see this nonsense* smile overlaying wretchedness.

I swallow an ache. She is choosing this.

"I want to talk to Aoife." Myri stretches, exuding all the authority of a slightly bratty prophetess. "You two can go and be dramatic outside, please!"

Sage huffs and strides out. Giulia gives me a *please do something* look; I raise my eyebrows: *I'll do my best.*

"You okay?" I ask Myri. Stupid question.

"Nope." She shuffles up to make space for me. "I'm really scared and really sad. And bored of people trying to save me. Crisp?"

I take a crisp and try my best. "You . . . don't have to do this?"

"A new and original perspective!" Myri claps her hands. "I am *sick* of it. I've had seven years to deal with this. I got some extra life in exchange for *this;* I was only ever borrowed! But they keep throwing false hope at me like it will *help*."

I look around for some reply. Soon there might not be a Myri. The thought's hit me again and again, but bounced off the surface of that peaceful surrender.

"What happens to you?" I ask quietly.

"I don't know." Myri curls into her knees. I put an arm around her; the sharp bones of her shoulders move like half-formed wings. "I just know . . ." Her breath shudders. "You heard me screaming. I dream other paths. I see where they go. It's got to be me."

This is more than I can respond to. With Myri, it always is.

"Please," Myri says. "Trust me. I saw . . . I know . . . ." She's trying to find her way somewhere, but lets the thread go. "Tell me about Tallerton again? Tell me the *boring* stuff. I like how you . . . remember the world."

We stretch, sharing a pillow, staring up at the ribbons. They wave like seaweed. All I can give her is what she's asked for: a distraction. A taste of the world she'll never get back.

I dig into my memories. They feel unreal, or this place seems unreal next to them. I tell her about disastrous camping, the broken washing machine, underpasses, and corner shops. Was my world really so small? How did I not . . . suffocate?

Myri's breath evens out. Her eyes move behind closed lids, chasing other stories in her dreams. I should have pushed. But her sleeping face is stubborn; she's decided.

I lay her blanket over her before I leave.

Sage and Giulia are outside, sharing figs from the tree. Sage tosses me one grudgingly, and I sit, where I once whispered to someone I wanted to save.

"Any luck?" Sage asks.

I shake my head. "She isn't going to listen to any of us, is she?" I bite the fig, smear the paste across my tongue. Ana told me that the wasps that pollinate figs become trapped inside, break down and dissolve into the sweetness. What must it be like, the last thing you know being that cloying stickiness, drunk on nectar in a suffocating dark?

Sage's head drops into his hands. His voice is harsh. "Did you even *try?*"

"Sage," Giulia says softly.

"No, fuck this." Sage looks up. "You like knowing everything, don't you, Aoife? You like being *special*; that's why Dad's inviting you into the inner circle. Make the new girl feel important so she won't question the stuff she hasn't been blunted to yet."

I draw a sharp breath, the glow of pride dimming. Jonah wouldn't . . . .

"You want in on secrets? Okay. Want to know how Myri died?" Sage's eyes are so much like Jonah's, like Myri's. Glossy with the sunrise. "I killed her."

I'm so busy trying to uncrumple my pride that it takes a second for that to hit.

Sage holds out his story like a weapon. "When we were kids, we visited this place every summer. My Gran, Mum's mum, was raised on the island, she . . . had scraps of knowledge about the Unseen. Dad doesn't like telling that story, does he? It's all *his* discovery. But it was me that Gran taught glyphs and hymns. It was me that Gran told about the cave, saying something special and dangerous was in there. It was me she made promise to only go in there if something really bad happened.

"After she died, we kept coming here for holidays. One day the sea was wild, and Mum made us promise not to go out on the rocks, but I dared Myri. She got scared on the rocks and I called her a chicken and it turned into playfighting and she slipped, I slipped, I didn't mean to, she—she hit her head, the sea was rough, she . . . ."

Even when Sage falters, his eyes stay fixed on me, challenging.

"I jumped in after her but . . . you know. I couldn't find her because the ocean was all nightmares. When I made it out, she'd already washed up.

"She was cut all over, but she wasn't bleeding, and she was cold. Really cold."

Giulia puts a hand on his shoulder, but he doesn't react.

"I called Mum and Dad. They were screaming, and I didn't have a sister anymore. Mum went to get the boat to rush her to the village; Dad ran for blankets because he wasn't thinking right. I was alone with Myri, her body, and I saw the cave and remembered what my Gran said. I heard it whispering. I picked her up and ran inside.

"It was so dark. I guess it closed behind us. I thought the island had swallowed us, and I deserved it for killing my sister. Then I felt her heartbeat, and she started screaming, and somehow, we were on the beach. But I looked at her, and it wasn't just Myri. There was something in there with her."

He looks away at last.

"There. Now you're one of the special ones who knows. Feel good?"

"I'm"—I scuff my bare foot in the dust—"really sorry."

"But you get it, right?" Sage's sandal moves next to mine, digging deeper rifts. "It should be me. It's not fair."

The trees are bathed in pink, clouds lurid with light. I hate it, but it does feel good, knowing this. Another piece of the story in place.

"Maybe it shouldn't happen at all," Giulia says.

"What?" I look up sharply. She's studying the sky, face troubled.

"You ever see what Teresa does with the goats?" She gazes up. "She'll be so kind to one. Put it in a field with the best grazing, bring it treats, sing to it. Give it the best day of its little life before slitting its throat and gutting it. The meat's tastier if it was happy." She finally looks at me. "We don't *know* what the Unseen wants. It gives us bliss when it wants, but we don't know what else it's planning. Am I not allowed to even *think* that maybe releasing it would be bad?"

"We don't have a choice." I search for steady ground. "We made a vow—"

"Snap out of it!" Giulia shouts.

Wind tears through the trees, like the sky's protesting her words. Shock silences me.

"We're doing what we're *told* to." Giulia grits her teeth, but the words keep coming. "Someone killed Elise, and we don't *talk* about it, because we're fucking sleepwalking. And now, we're sleepwalking into killing Myri, and maybe killing the world, too."

"Don't." Sage's voice is sharp.

Giulia ignores him. "Look at me. Aoife. Tell me you, your actual self— not what *he* tells you to be—tell me *you* want this to happen."

Sharp eyes regard me in a snub-nosed face that can slip from soft to harsh in an instant. She warned me not to come here. She tried to push me out. She was afraid for me.

"I don't want anything to happen to Myri," I say cautiously.

Fury and frustration boil in her. "Then what would you do, to stop it?"

The answer's harsh, bathed in the light of the stories I was just telling Myri, fluorescent light, empty places, shame and smallness. And it hurts, but she was chosen for this, and she chose to embrace it. Who are we to stop her?

"Nothing. I want this."

I keep my eyes on Giulia's, so I see the rage and hope crumble, replaced with fear.

"Oh—" Her hands rise, like she's going to defend herself, then drop. Her eyes are wide. "Please, Aoife, don't tell anyone—"

"She's upset." Sage puts a hand on my shoulder. "Okay? She didn't mean that."

The first sunbeams cut across us. Giulia's breath is shallow; Sage's hand trembling.

I should say something. She's lost. Jonah can help her shed her doubts.

"Please." Giulia's voice cracks.

I squeeze her hand. Maybe I'm just a sucker for my friends. "I won't."

She blinks back tears. "Thank you. I . . . I want this too. I'm just scared sometimes."

Her words come out blurting, uneven.

"Look," Sage says, the reasonable voice for once. "We're tired, we're overwrought, we're not thinking right. Let's get some sleep?" He reads me. I offer him a hopeful smile, and he seems to take it. "Thanks, Aoife. For listening."

"No problem," I say.

His eyes linger on me, then he nods. "Night. Or morning."

Giulia glances back as she follows Sage, and I give her a thumbs-up. I call, "Just trust," and she smiles weakly before turning away.

Look how everything glitters. It speaks to me in patterns of light, soothing me with half-understood promises. If I stare long enough, I think I see something stirring in the filaments, closer every moment.

CHAPTER TWENTY-FOUR

ONE BODY, ONE BEING, PLUNGING

THE FINAL NIGHT IS COMING.

Tonight's feast is the grandest. The day's work is preparation; garlands of flowers to be hung, food to be cooked, bonfires to be built. Music pumps, excitement rising. Couples and triads slip away; people dance and drink as they work. Myri walks among us, whispering blessings and secrets.

I find Larissa on my bed, wrapped in a sarong and eating apricots, because Larissa. We get ready together, her mauve jumpsuit and jasmine garlands, my flower-print dress and gold body paint. Instead of asking her to hide her face, I enjoy the cool pressure of her eyes on my skin, the everyday intimacy of us.

The garden's full of life. Lights dance, glasses clink. The feast is luxuriant, cream pastries and goat stew, figs in honey, fiery spicy sauces.

We lift morsels to each other's mouths, little benedictions. Teeth and tongues brush fingertips. I nip at Frida as she slips an olive between my lips, and she squeals. We close our eyes to be surprised by each new mouthful. We are one being.

What are we nourishing? We're fueling each other's bodies for our great work, but what will a god do with our flesh and fat and marrow?

Just trust.

Enough wine, enough stars and swinging lanterns, enough rhythms from the improvised band, enough fingers stroking my face, and blissful excitement overwhelms the last traces of fear. I'm crying as I dance on the beach. They love me, and wherever we are going, we are going together. I've never known joy this pure.

The dancing becomes a cobbled-together ritual, chants and howls rising. We run in giddy clusters to our huts, snatch things from our old lives, and fling them into the bonfire. Letting the world go.

The chants subside, lips and bodies meet, clothes are tossed aside.

I'd usually withdraw, but tonight I want to plunge. I want to give myself over, be ripped apart and remade in a wash of pleasure and anticipation, lit by the burning remnants of our old lives as they become energy and color and ash.

Larissa appears, lipstick smeared from kisses with Giulia and Zina. My eyes say, *Go on,* and hers glimmer with all those secrets, and she gathers me in.

When me and Craig's bodies joined in a mash of sweat and sheets, it was just another way to be close to him. And there's still an awkward hesitation in me, a self-conscious disconnection. But Larissa's lips taste of sweet wine, and I find myself gasping when her hands move down my body, seeking places that will melt me. The heady bliss of this night has stirred something, the Unseen moving in my flesh.

She whispers, "Finally." I pull her closer, luxuriating in her soft expanses. Once I knew she was a gateway; now we resonate with the same essence.

We taste a god in each other's mouths.

Others join. Hands and mouths on my back, neck, thighs. My body's theirs and theirs mine.

I'm sweating and flushed, my dress hanging from a pine branch, by the time I look up and spot Kiera under a tree nearby, watching the ocean.

I fall back, exploring the small of Pietro's back with my lips, then pull myself out of the crush of bodies. The wind is cool on my naked skin, the stars wheeling above, my lips tingling. I wriggle back into my dress and run to Kiera.

I lower myself onto the log beside her. My head's spinning, a grin splitting my face. I can't believe I did that.

"I wonder if it'll all still be here," Kiera murmurs. It takes a second to readjust. "Do you think the Unseen will change everything right away? Do you think we'll still have, you know, matter? Senses we understand?" She twists her lips. "Do you think we'll miss it?"

We dig our feet into the cool sand, sharing the same sensation.

She looks at me sidelong. A sharp face, handsome in all its angles, switching between jabbering excitement and faltering nerves. Tonight, that's curiosity. She didn't drink, did she? She's hesitating on the brink.

I want her plunging with me. Larissa was a doorway. Kiera's a hand to hold as I explore the other side. "It's going to be beautiful."

"I think of it as a revolution," she says. "Overturning the rules, you know? Only not the human rules. All of them."

I nod. "A revolution against the laws of physics."

She stares out to sea again; something dark flashes across her face, and she winces. I brace myself, but she smirks. "Gravity's just a conspiracy to keep us *down*, man."

I groan and throw sand at her, and she cackles not at her joke but at my reaction, and I slap her shoulder but somehow miss and we tumble onto the sand, and I swear, total accident, honest, we land entangled, mouths meeting.

For a second time tonight, I taste lips I'd longed to taste. Kiera's tense, but lets out a quiet sound of delight and softens. Kissing Larissa was intoxication; this is comfort. Our heartbeats echo: *It'll be okay. We're together.*

We break apart, and Kiera laughs, rolling over and sprawling. "Oh, wow. We don't know what happens tomorrow and *now* we do that? I should just have been like, *You make me panic and I kind of can't stop thinking about kissing you,* instead of telling you fun facts about ancient languages." She catches her breath. "Fun facts are my love language."

I shrug. She said *love.* "Apparently the apocalypse is mine."

She laughs again. It feels like a present. Light passes across her face from somewhere. "Were you having fun? With the others?"

"Yeah? No more than I ever had hanging out with you, but it felt like tonight was the night for it." I don't add, *Might as well enjoy this body; who knows what the Unseen will do with it.* She's relaxing; I don't want to pull her tight again.

A flash of mischief, and she shrugs off her shirt. "Shall we?"

So, this is how I'll spend the old world's last night: utterly free and whole, between sand and stars, entangling my body with dozens of others.

Music throbs, my blood thunders, my gasps melt into the chorus. One body, one being, plunging toward another world.

I am so caught up that I don't know how to respond when rough hands pull me loose.

Cold air hits me; I stagger to my feet, feel fingers digging into my arms, see the face staring into mine, twisted with shock, grip painful, infinitely familiar—

"What the *fuck* are you doing?"

The world overturns and falls back fractured.

It takes a moment to gain control of my voice, choke Craig's name, and make it real.

CHAPTER TWENTY-FIVE
A TRICK PICTURE

I BARELY REGISTER THE YELLING AND PUSHING OVER THE SCREECHING SENSA-
tion of trying to force two worlds into one mind.

Craig. His fingers, with their chipped black nail polish and the calluses
from guitar strings. The lopsided curl of his mouth that's love in some
lights, fury in others. His hair's grown, has mine? What do I look like
to him? Short-haired, smeared with lipstick and body paint and sweat,
tanned, stronger, naked—

People are holding Craig and Larissa back as they square up. All I can
do is climb back into my dress, mind blank, body throbbing with pleasure
that doesn't belong in it now.

The world pinpoints on me and Craig, staring at each other in a
maelstrom.

Oscar's there, and Aksel and Kai, ha, he plays guitar, he and Craig can
be friends, and Darya and Ana, surrounding Craig, pulling him toward the
farmhouse. He's shouting my name, and these two worlds *do not fit in me.*

But at the sound of my name, in his voice, joy surges out of the confusion.

Craig. He's here, for *me.* He didn't—he still—

The joy clicks something, and my feet start moving, and I'm yelling to Oscar, "Stop! He's my friend!"

Eyes turn to me. Craig's are wide. His fury and fear are boiling up; it's my job to simmer them down. It always has been.

"Let me talk to him." I raise my hands. They wouldn't hurt him, but what do they see when they look at him? An invader, raging, strange. "I'll explain."

Oscar looks me over. He hasn't been throwing himself into the party, either, has he? He's been alert, watching us. That makes me feel safer. "Are you sure?"

I nod. My mind's clearing, now there's something to cling to: Talk to Craig, *explain*, before my two worlds rip into each other.

Oscar quirks a lip at Craig. "Sorry, mate. You're a bit unexpected."

Craig looks like he's about to rip himself free and punch Oscar, but he doesn't, and a few chaotic moments later we're inside the farmhouse. Craig's on the sofa, eyes wild, jaw twitching. Like he wants to kick off but knows he's outnumbered. Oscar nods again and the others file out, and it's me and Craig, alone.

Neither of us moves or speaks; we just stare.

We let out long, shaky breaths, then Craig leaps up. Three strides across the carpets, worn combat boots approaching my bare feet, and he's inches away, *him.*

I cringe away.

His arms circle my waist. His kiss tastes alien on lips still raw from other mouths, but then it's the best thing in the world. I was made to slot into these arms.

My blood sings. He didn't forget me.

He presses his forehead into mine. "What the hell, love? It was just a stupid fight. I've been so fucking scared for you. But I *really found you.*"

"You found me." I remember *where* he found me, what I was doing, and I'm laughing and I don't know how to stop.

"Hey, stop that." Craig digs his fingers into my waist. I'm more tender with him, like his touch can bruise me in a way nobody else's can. "You're freaking me out."

I swallow my laughter. I remember how he wants me to. "Sorry. How did you . . . ?"

"How did I find you?" Craig's fury rises so suddenly my throat closes up. "It was not a fucking picnic. You spent half our savings; I had to empty the account so you wouldn't hop on to Malaysia or something. And you didn't answer my calls. I had to look you up on missing people sites, a few people from this island were on them because of some girl a few months back, and one eventually recognized you. *I* had to take shifts at Leo's bar and borrow money, and I got here and these rude fuckers in the village were like"—he puts on a hick accent—"'If she's up there, she ain't coming back.'

"And all this time I'm thinking, 'Shit, Aoife's so innocent, what are they doing with her?' And I finally get a boat and get here and find you in the middle of an orgy?" Violence flares in his eyes, but I don't step away. Just trust. "What did they *do* to you, love?"

"I thought we were over." The words spill out of my mouth and into his, like he's devouring them. "It didn't mean anything—" Kiera's face flashes, and I still define *mean something* like I did in the old world, and with her, it did, but—

Craig mimes punching his head. "Fuck's sake, love. I don't give a shit."

The lie's buried in so much rage it almost doesn't register. "I want to know why you *disappeared and showed up half a continent away*."

The god that sleeps here sank its threads into my soul and knitted me into this place. That sounds ridiculous. Looking through his eyes is like looking at a trick picture, like my vision's flipped it into a different shape. It makes my head ache, and I want it to stop.

"What *is* this place? Some weird, hippy sex farm? Why would you leave your life for this?" His hands drop. His voice shakes. "Why would you leave *me*?"

Tears well; Craig blurs.

Don't lie. It hurts him, and then everybody hurts. "We're a community. We live together, we farm, we . . ." How to say it? "Commune. With . . . we call it the Unseen."

The quiet hovers. Craig stares. Then dark laughter bursts out. "Holy shit, this is gold. Aoife joined a cult. Aoife went nuts and joined a fucking cult."

Humiliation swells. It's dawn of the *last day*, and that seems impossible. The pieces don't fit. "It's real. I touched the Unseen. It's . . ."—*I believe this*—"beautiful."

"Go on, then." Craig reins in his laughter, but it dances in his eyes. "Show me. I'll convert straight up, promise."

I know that face. Go on, introduce me to these "friends." Go on, show me this art you've been "working" on when you had fucking housework.

I have to try. Show him the Unseen, let it paint the world in new colors for him. If Craig sees what I see, I won't feel like this anymore. Like I'm split down the middle, and neither half of me understands the other.

A god is in my bones. I can do this.

There's a fruit bowl on the table. A peach, soft-skinned and fresh. I grab it and lift it to Craig's mouth. Try to capture what Larissa had, that captivating intensity, that faith. "Try this. Take a bite of the peach and just . . . just give up the taste, okay?"

"Give it up?" His baffled look is a weapon.

"Imagine . . . no, don't imagine, feel it, there's something here. Something all around us, in the air and in our bodies, just waiting to take what you offer." Am I doing this right? Do I sound like I believe? My voice is shaking. "Just take a bite and let the taste go, and feel what happens."

Craig raises an eyebrow, but humors me, and bites down. I watch him chew, watch the fragile, sweet flesh come apart between his teeth. I wait for the revelation.

"It tastes like a peach, love." He's gentle. "Was something meant to happen?"

"Keep trying," I whisper, but I know where this is going, and he does too, and he swallows, and the hope slides away down his throat to burn up inside him.

I try to give up the confusion, beg, *Take this from me*, but it's wound through me and I can't let go, and nothing's there to take it, is there?

I crumble. I stagger, and sobs come over me in waves.

The other half of me, Craig's Aoife, takes hold, and my fantasy dissolves. I see a camp full of weirdos, who keep a girl locked up and never talk about the disappearance of another. I imagine drugs, brainwashing. *You made this too easy.*

I stand there choking on tears, not bothering to cover my face.

"Oh, love." Craig's arms fold around me. "It's okay. I'm here."

His chest smells like home. I try to breathe, but more tears come. Relief and despair and confusion crash together.

"Oh, now," Craig strokes my head. "They cut your beautiful hair off. What have they done to you?" He pulls back to look into my tear-stained face. "You've always been so trusting. Little bit naïve, maybe?" He grins reassuringly, and I manage a smile and hiccup. "Tell me who to kick in the balls for taking advantage of you."

"They're . . . good people. They never hurt me."

Craig shakes his head. "Love, you were naked, they were pawing you all over, and you've been seeing shit. They messed with your mind. But you're okay. You're just sick, and we need to get you home and get you better. Okay?"

Home. Blankets warmed by our bodies. Craig strumming his guitar as I fry bacon. Every fight followed by a reconciliation that just makes me love him more.

It seems . . . so small.

Why is it that now he's here, he doesn't feel like enough?

I've dissolved in the heart of the unknown. I've danced under wheeling stars. I've tasted a god in a girl's mouth. Even if it wasn't real, how can I go back to my life after that?

"I have to think." He reaches for me, but I dart to the door. "Oscar?"

"No! Come on, think straight." Craig's in my face, grasping my arm, that bruising touch. "This isn't you. You're my lovely, dozy Aoife. Don't let them in your head."

I can barely form the words; I've never said them to him before. "Let me go."

The door opens: Oscar was right there. "You want to let her go, mate," he says lightly. He takes my other arm, and I'm bridging them, caught between my two worlds.

I know exactly what to do.

"I'll come back for you." I tumble out into the sun, Craig's chipped nails leaving scratches. The door slams; there's a thud as he throws his body against it. "I promise!"

Oscar draws me away from the door, sharp with concern. Lights in the trees compete with the incandescent sky. "Are you okay? Did he hurt you?"

I shake my head. I want to spit out all the questions Craig's filled my mouth with, let Oscar toss them away. But there's only one way to fix this.

Just trust. I'm here for a reason. Craig must be, too.

"I'm okay." The lie comes out shaky. "I need to speak to Jonah."

It's nerve-wracking knocking on Jonah's bedroom door. My mind's swirling and keeps throwing up images like Jonah in pajamas and a nightcap. I want to laugh hysterically, which isn't a polite thing to do when waking a prophet at 6:00 a.m.

He isn't sleeping; the circles under his eyes are pronounced. I glimpse three figures on the bed. Final family time. I swallow; there isn't space for those feelings.

"Aoife." Jonah closes the door gently. "I hear you have . . . a guest."

"I wanted to ask—sorry, I'm interrupting." Why are these words so jerky and gushing? Is this how I used to talk? "I need to talk to you."

Jonah leads me to the library, a lavender-orange sunrise outside. He sinks into an armchair, hiding a yawn; the moments when he's human feel like a gift for me. "Tell me."

I can do this. Craig always saved me; now I can save *him.* I've become something here. I can use that.

"I know"—I'm rocking on my heels—"he doesn't understand things here, he wasn't invited, but . . . Craig's my partner, he came here for me, I love him."

"We won't hurt him," Jonah says gently. "Not unless he harms you. If he has . . . ."

"No!" Why does everyone think he'd harm me? "Look, I . . ." My fingers won't stop *moving*. "I want him here. With us. For what's coming." Because otherwise it's a choice between *this* and *him*, and whichever I choose will kill half of me.

Jonah's eyes are full of sympathy. "Aoife. There's no time to initiate him. The cave will not open for someone who isn't ready."

"But if . . ." It's not fully formed. If we ascend, claim our reward. If the Unseen turns its eons-old rage on those who never loved it. If. Who knows?

Jonah's quiet. I've never *persuaded* him of anything. Has anyone?

"Can't he just come to the ritual? All he has to do is chant and blow out a candle." I garble some unhinged joke about birthday parties. It falls flat.

That stare's cutting into me again. It can silence anyone.

My jaw clenches. I meet his eye. What does my own stare look like, these days? I've seen things, too. I'm changed. Maybe there can be subtle blades in my gaze, too.

"So you think it's chance, that he arrived now?" If I think about what I'm doing, I'll stumble, and it will fall apart. "You know the Unseen best. You know it doesn't make mistakes; you know there aren't coincidences. Would you risk having the rite fail because—" Oh god, Aoife, shut up. "—*you* ignored a sign that someone else saw?"

Jonah's inscrutable. We're contained in a drawn-out moment, my chin tilted but my face not daring defiance, sunrise light spilling over us.

Something like recognition flickers. A hint of a smile. *I see you.*

"You understand why I hesitate," he says. "One person missing might render the rite useless. Or one person too many. Or if too many are wracked by doubts . . . But"—a glimmer invites me in—"perhaps if *we* are united, we could carry someone without faith."

Hope leaps.

Jonah leans forward, intent. "Has anyone expressed doubts to you? Perhaps if we can smooth those out, there will be space for your friend."

This should feel like a devil deal. But this isn't a devil; it's Jonah, tired at the end of the road, afraid all he's built will crumble at the last moment. We're not fighting. I see it in that approving smile. We're allies.

I will see the world reborn, without pain. I will hold Craig's hand as it reforms in wonder. And it's not like I'm harming her. She needs help to find her way again.

Still, it takes effort to say it. "Giulia."

Jonah looks unsurprised, which makes me feel better. He waits.

"She asked me what I'd do to stop it." I remember that I *promised* her, and my guilt speaks for me, babbling. "But she didn't mean it, she was just worried for Myri—"

Jonah winces, then calms. "Thank you. I'll talk to her. And yes, bring your friend to the rite. Give him some of Teresa's tea, keep him compliant. All right?"

Relief's bright. I'm clinging to this thread, this one thing that can bind it all together, and I felt it so close to snapping, but now it's stronger and steadier. "Thank you."

Jonah takes my hands. "Tomorrow there will be no more questions. Do you trust?"

"I trust," I murmur, and the flood of doubts that hit me in Craig's arms ebbs away. Jonah kisses my forehead. It lingers on my skin long after he's gone.

CHAPTER TWENTY-SIX

RASPBERRY, GINGER, OTHER

I WAKE TO FIND THAT, IN A TYPICAL AOIFE MOVE, I'VE SLEPT THROUGH THE world's last day.

The second I left the farmhouse, relief drop-kicked me into exhaustion, and I slumped into a hammock and a sleep too deep for dreams. I wake to a low sun, lengthening shadows signaling urgency.

There isn't time to think. There's so much I won't have time for now. Still, the peace in me is back, without a ripple. Peace and purpose. So easy to let everything go, boil it down to what matters.

The wind dances my dress, everything simmering.

Teresa's at the kitchen table, head in hands. When she looks up, I see traces of flour and spices in her hair, and her smile's thin. The ripple around her is constant, a feeding frenzy, the Unseen drinking her pain as fast as it builds, and it just keeps building.

"Tea," she says. "Right? I've brewed some. Your friend isn't the only one who'll need help getting through tonight."

I want to ask if she's okay, but I don't know where the words are. But there's the peace, glowing. I put together a sandwich for Craig, while Teresa pours the tea.

"It's a soft one, but potent," she says. "Something to keep him calm, something for euphoria, something to loosen the grip of this reality. Want some?"

Her voice is buoyant, her smile stretching further each time I look at her.

"No, thank you." My own smile plays on my lips. "I want to be in it completely." There's no fear to soothe. It's all light and foam and colors in my core.

"You always were brave."

Quiet opens up where Myri's name should be, and it's starting to hurt when the garden door opens.

"Teresa!" Kiera's mussed. My chest contracts; she's beautiful like this. "Ana said you had something to make the fear go away—" She stops short, seeing me. "I mean. I'm not scared—" Her gaze drops.

"A little one," Teresa says. "You'll need your head clear."

Kiera nods, blushing miserably. "Aoife, I . . . ."

"I . . ." I want to tell her so much. I want to listen to her talk. I want to taste her lips again. "I have to go. Craig . . . ."

She nods. Resignation. "Craig. Okay."

Still, we stare at each other. Absorb every detail. The light on her face. The smears of lipstick on her skin. The missing button on her shirt. The spray of freckles.

Teresa hands Kiera her tea and unlocks the living room. I swallow the feelings down to dissolve in the peace inside me.

Craig's on the sofa, staring with a childish fear that becomes suspicious fury when I appear. I know that look. I've disappointed him.

"You said you'd come back." The tremble in his voice is buried.

This is what I do when I've disappointed him. I show him I'm sorry and I'll make it better. "I'm here now. Ta-da. Did they feed you?"

Craig snorts. "I'm not eating what they give me."

"I made this myself." I flash a playful look and bite the sandwich. "Safe. The tea too."

The steam curls. A sip won't hurt, just add gloss to this glow. It tastes of raspberry and ginger and honey.

Craig's stare doesn't soften, and fear cracks; what if it doesn't work? But he shrugs, tears into the sandwich, and swigs the tea. "Huh. You miraculously got good at cooking."

I laugh. Craig softens and laughs too. It's weird; that comment doesn't sting like his digs used to. People like my cooking here. He'll learn to like it. If cooking and food exist tomorrow.

I sit beside him and watch him eat, the movements of his mouth and throat. I love feeding him. My energy and creativity becoming food, the food fueling his. Harmony. It's twice as beautiful knowing the mischievous secret I'm slipping him.

Drink up, love, and come with me to a better world.

"Christ," Craig says, "stop staring. You've got *shiny eyes*. Gives me the fucking creeps."

I hold back a laugh. "I . . . I just never thought you'd come."

Craig's lip curls, then his face goes warm. You get used to his shifting weather. "Of course I did. We're a team, right?" He's hiding the fear, but his voice shakes. "How are we going to get you out of here, love?"

He fumbles with the cup, woozy. Teresa's right, it's potent.

No point in trying to convince him; he'll see for himself. The thread's clear; I follow it. "Tonight. They'll notice if I'm missing from the ritual this evening. So we play along, you say I've talked you round, come to the ritual, then we'll sneak off after, when they're drunk." I slip my hand into his. "This time tomorrow, we'll be free."

His fingers bite into my flesh. His face is calm, but the pain intensifies; my breath gets shallow.

"I love you, you fucking beautiful idiot," he murmurs, "but they've mashed up that brain cell of yours. So listen. If we don't get the hell out of here tonight, you go down with me. Get it?"

I lift his hand to my lips. I can handle him. It just hurts sometimes. "Trust me?"

"Not even a little bit." His voice tilts, fuzzy. We grin. His grip eases, and I lean in, breathing raspberry and ginger.

I kiss him long and soft, holding him close as delirium spreads through his veins.

At sunset, we gather on the beach.

We are beautiful in peachy light. Some gleam in sequins or silk; some improvise robes; many go naked, relishing the breeze. Myri, with a last flicker of humanity, wears jeans and a jumper, hood thrown back to show her face daubed with symbols.

We greet each other with kisses. Craig isn't the only one whose eyes are unfocused. Even Oscar's dizzied, red-eyed, the only time I've seen him let his guard down. Giulia's leaning on Pietro, silver dress askew, laughing too long and too high. People eye her; maybe I missed something while I slept. When she hugs me, I smell ginger and raspberry.

Fine. Intoxication's sacred; we're in dream states, sinking toward a new dream.

See how everything shivers. Even the trees and ocean know it. Something is coming.

I find Aksel and Maisie, and deliver them a bedraggled, shiny-eyed Craig. They can handle him. I kiss him and whisper reassurances; these are my friends, we'll have fun, I'll be right there. He nods, glazed, happy. I grin, thinking how much easier life would have been if I'd had Teresa's tea in our old kitchen.

There's Teresa, beside Myri, who reaches out to squeeze her hand. The air resonates as Teresa gives that sensation up to the Unseen. Myri pulls back, her god-self briefly smiling at the morsel, her human-self flinching with hurt.

I wince, then give away that wince, too. There is no space for suffering, only glory.

I take my place at Myri's shoulder with the others chosen to play parts in the rite. I'm dizzy with joy. A whole life led here. All of history led to us, me, here.

We sing wild, formless chants until we're drunk on our voices, energy swirling. We light candles, laughing when the wind blows them out. Sage is struggling; his candle keeps guttering, and Myri's human for a moment, giggling and yelling, "Sage, you're *failing* at fire!" She grabs her brother's lighter.

The shudder takes her suddenly.

She freezes. Stillness ripples out, the wind dying down. Her eyes close, and she lets out a wordless cry. My soul quivers.

When her eyes open, something else stares out, a blank page ready. There's a pang: Maybe her human-self is gone. I'd expected some good-bye. But it's a bittersweet and beautiful pain. This is her gift to us.

We are ready, feverish and blissful, and Myri leads us to the cave.

CHAPTER TWENTY-SEVEN

ONE BREATH, AND DARKNESS

I'd wondered how we'd reach the cavern through those drowning passageways. But the cave's open, its waters just a trickle. You'd think it was a quirk of the tides, unless you knew.

Before, I was here alone in suffocating darkness. Now I'm part of a procession, clutching a candle and the brass bell from the library. Something fragile and ancient, something Kiera and I smiled over as our fingers almost touched. Jonah gave it to me earlier, beaming like a grandfather. I was the omen; now, with this bell, I will ring in the new world.

The flames illuminate craggy walls, even more claustrophobic with the lack of exits visible. We came out of here once; doesn't mean we will again. Who knows the will of the thing we move inside?

I breathe away the nerves. Its will is holy. Soon everything will be wider than skies.

Kiera slides her hand into mine; there's a tremble in it. Her eyes are liquid with candlelight, pupils dilated, the book containing the ritual tucked under her arm.

A chant rings through the passageway, a hum that slips from harmony to discord and back. It grows more otherworldly; everything's a shell, about to crack.

Under it all, a thunderous heartbeat, pulling us into its inner chambers.

Deeper, and we emerge into the cavern, the Unseen's heart wrought in salt and rock.

The ceiling towers far above our candles' pale glimmers; darkness stretches ahead, the future lost in it, something intangible looming through the shadow. The stillness is stirred only by our movements and that heartbeat. We are beyond anything; we're at the very core of it. My body tingles, that blissful, awestruck terror.

Ankle-deep water reflects the candlelight, a glow under our steps. Everything keeps fracturing because I'm crying. How to describe this completeness?

Myri said the cave would provide, and she was right. A slab of rock, chest-high, a natural altar. I look at it, and my joy quivers, anticipating, aching.

The hum rises; we sing a single note, smiles wide, as Myri leads the ritual participants to the altar and a circle forms around us. I see Craig, gripping his candle like a toy, gently guided by Maisie. I offer him my most brilliant smile: *It's fine; we're together.*

A weird laugh echoes off the rocks. Giulia's laugh, off-key and off-kilter.

There are final hugs and kisses. I hesitate, knowing Craig is watching, but I kiss Larissa's cheek and taste happy tears, and squeeze Teresa's shoulder, and accept Jonah's kiss on my forehead, and stroke Kiera's hand before we all join Frida and Oscar and Pietro in the inner circle around the altar. Teresa presses her forehead against Sage's and takes both his hands, the first gesture of affection I've seen between them; when she steps away from him, though, she's shut down, everything buried and smoothed over.

Myri says nothing, just lies on the altar, arms wide. Open and ready.

Teresa and Jonah lean forward—Teresa expressionless and Jonah's mouth twisted with emotion—and kiss their daughter's blank face.

The chant dies down. The silence hangs in candlelight. Even the heartbeat slows. It's time, it's *time*. I say a final, quiet goodbye to the world I knew.

Jonah nods to Kiera; she nods back, shaky, and begins to read from the book. I don't understand what I'm seeing in her: It looks weirdly like loneliness, but we're all here with her, aren't we?

The words she reads are meaningless to me, but I still shiver as they echo over the water and into the dark. Her hesitant speech grows sonorous and powerful.

Frida binds Myri's wrists with a silk scarf.

Jonah traces saltwater on Myri's forehead, cheeks, throat. She convulses, and her movement sends out an invisible ripple.

My god, I *feel* it stirring, kicking in the shallows of the world's nightmares, rising.

Sage presses a knife to his fingertip and whispers, "I'm sorry," as he traces Myri's eyes and lips with the blood that wells up, black as oil in the candlelight.

Everything trembles, creaking under pressure.

Teresa coos as she opens her daughter's lips and places herbs on her tongue. Myri spasms and releases a moan, caught in a fever dream, so close to waking.

My heart's pounding. The Unseen moves inside me, too, straining. My flesh shudders, knowing its own vulnerability. I breathe deep, remember there's nothing worth holding on to.

Whatever I will become, it's written in me already, that moment already existing somewhere. We will tear our way out of our chrysalises. I will be a butterfly.

Myri's back arches, chest heaving, hands struggling against their bonds.

Everyone's chanting, rhythmic huffs of breath.

The candlelight's brighter, the spectrum of colors stranger, violet and indigo and mint in golden light on golden rocks.

Kiera's reading crescendos, and Jonah shouts a word I don't know but understand: It means doors opening, horizons beyond horizons, convulsive delirium.

Larissa slices Myri's bonds.

Her limbs splay—

Something surges out—

Peace seizes me, I ring the bell, notes echoing—

Lost under a scream.

Giulia breaks the circle, splashing through the water, face wild, yelling, finger tracing a symbol.

Everything stutters.

The candlelight flares out into darkness.

A thick, gagging stench fills the cave. An overwhelming swell of competing reeks: rotting fish, decaying seaweed, stagnant saltwater, the sea-bleached plastic and moldering food of a trash vortex; imagine the smell of a whalefall, of blubber fermenting in the depths. Something thick and slimy clots around my feet, stroking at my ankles.

A flicker as sudden as lightning; the great vaulted ceiling of the cavern flashes with countless points of light, a sickly blue-white glow. *Phosphorescence*, I have time to think, and I have time to think that it's beautiful before I see what it illuminates: smears of that same blighted rot across the pallid cave walls; the water at our feet is thick with blue-brown algae, a bubbling stew—

Deeper, this rot goes deeper; it's mingling and warping, sending a spasm through something impossibly powerful. I feel it because it's happening inside my bones—

Stone, I know, cannot rot. Cannot fragment when decay gets into its heart.

I know that that is true. But that doesn't make the screams any less harrowing as the cracks spread across the ceiling, splitting apart the phosphorescent trails.

Impossibility won't stop the cavern roof from caving in on us.

A rumble, a crumbling, a tremor, rollercoaster screams, Kiera's hand reaching for mine, a blast of something right through my core, and then dark.

In that dark, there is an opportunity.

In the dark, there is a choice.

I don't have time to understand, but it doesn't matter; in the dark, I make the choice. I say yes.

CHAPTER TWENTY-EIGHT

MEAT

SAND IS COOL UNDER MY BACK. STARS ABOVE, SMEARY. MY HEAD'S SPINNING, weight constricting my chest. Smells of salt and metal and pine.

Someone's screaming.

The world's solid, but my mind isn't. Every sensation is too much, but woozy, distant. Pain kicks in my head, an ache builds in my limbs, assuring me I still have a body. I'm alive. Everything came apart, and I'm still alive. But there's no relief in it.

Even my fuzzy brain gets it. This isn't a world remade, no transcendence, no respite from nightmares.

The ritual failed.

I struggle onto my elbows, battling through the fireworks behind my eyes and the weight of despair. Weight on my chest, too.

I'm on the beach; I see other prone bodies scattered. The cave must have expelled us as it collapsed, the Unseen tossing us unconscious onto the shore.

Which explains the weight: Someone's sprawled over me. My eyes are adjusting, flashing with static when I try to focus, but I make out muscular shoulders, red-tinged hair.

"Sage, wake up."

No response. Something's wrong, but I'm too disorientated. Everything's colder than I think it should be. My dress is wet. There's a smell, caught in my throat, nauseating; I think of the blight, spreading across the cavern, and wait for it to fade, but it doesn't.

I shake Sage, then stir strength to roll him over.

The metallic stench redoubles.

His chest and belly are ruptured.

He's split like a sack of grain, gobbets of him spilling, the *meat* of him, cold, pulverized—

My hands are black with blood.

His *face*. I can't tell which of those pale streaks are skin, and what's bone. One of his eyes is half out of the socket. The other, like the whole side of his head, is crushed.

He was surly and standoffish and cared for his sister fiercely; he was the first to enter the Unseen's heart; he was cold to me but shared a secret; he loved a girl who disappeared; he was always up early in the kitchen; now he's guts and juices soaking my dress.

A light stumbles toward me, capturing me in its beam.

Sage is all over me. Sage is a substance. I can't tell what my mouth and body are doing: screaming or laughing? They're a substance too, and everything dissolves eventually, doesn't it?

"Fuck. There you are!"

Why does Craig's voice sound so steady; didn't I drug him? Was that hours ago? Time is twisted. I want to throw up, but my body doesn't know how.

"Get the hell up." Craig ignores Sage's body, perhaps he can't see it, perhaps this is a special torment just for me. "We have to go."

"I can't walk," I explain, trying to be helpful. "Sage is broken."

"Fuck's sake. Don't come apart on me."

A hand yanks my arm, and I yell. I don't trust flesh; doesn't it rip off the bone like tender meat? It's like he's pulling me apart, a roast yielding to a fork, *come apart on me*. That fits; I laugh as I stagger, and there's Craig, a warm, safe place, except he's not holding my arm now, he's retching onto the sand.

I work hard on staying upright. It seems like something useful I can do.

Craig straightens; the shadows of his phone torch on his face are funny, he looks warped, my poor love, he's seen something you shouldn't. I try to stroke his face, but he jerks away—right, bloody hands, silly Aoife, messed up again, now he'll be sad—

The stars swirl in the wrong directions. Pain rips from my core to my skull and maybe I'm splitting open too. Consciousness fragments, and vanishes.

CHAPTER TWENTY-NINE

GONE

ANOTHER WAKING. I DON'T REMEMBER. THIS ONE'S GENTLER.

I'm cradled, pillow, blanket, sweaty in the heat. This isn't my hut, is it? I'm all the wrong directions.

All of me aches. I bury my face and moan in the hope that this will make sweet tea and food appear. Nothing happens.

I roll over. Pain spasms through my limbs and unleashes a screaming flood of memories. Giulia's face as she lurched forward—the rumble as the rocky ceiling came apart—*Sage*—

I'm up and stumbling toward a door I hope to god is a bathroom. My surroundings are flashes: a shuttered window, a painting of daisies. And then I'm over the toilet, innards convulsing as I vomit bile, wracked long after my stomach is empty.

All of me is empty.

We failed. We were meant to be in a new world. Instead, the cruel weight of the old one presses down, and it's missing at least one of us.

Jonah. Kiera. Larissa. Giulia. Myri. My mind superimposes their faces onto the fleshy morass that Sage became. They were right there. Which of them were caught in the rockfall, clenched and crushed in that stony fist?

I collapse against the cool, tiled wall. An ornamental duck statue on the windowsill doubles and quadruples as my vision blurs. I need to figure out where I am, but my head's spinning.

Did the collapse damage me, too, deep inside? I don't feel right.

My vision clears a little, centering on the bathroom mirror. The new Aoife, with her suntan and cropped hair and confidence, is peeling away. I'm ashy under my tan, circles under my eyes. My t-shirt is black, with the crumbling logo of a metal band. Not the aesthetic of Elise's clothes. More like Craig's.

Red stains in the shower. Rusty water, or did someone scrub the blood off me? I drag my body to the window and peer through the shutters. Light smarts. Vines, an alleyway onto a harbor, a stray cat washing itself. The village. I'm across the island, in the village.

How long since I was last . . . anywhere, other than the Farmstead? We never think about dates, calendars; time is the breath of the Unseen, an erratic rhythm sweeping us up. It was early summer when I arrived. Now the leaves are yellowing.

Sound filters in; voices, chairs shuffling on the balcony. I massage my temples like that will ease the ringing in my ears, but the voices are muffled. I shift closer.

". . . police aren't that helpful. You know how it is in small towns, someone's friendly with the landowner, money changes hands and suddenly it's someone else's problem." The voice is female, accented. "Best report it on the mainland. Something might get done."

"Something should be done *now*." Craig's voice. The one he gets when the world isn't going his way. "I want to get the fuck off this island, but I can't believe nobody's . . ."

"Well." Something clicks, a lighter? "It's always been off up there. They bring in money, and nobody wants trouble, but we'd be happy if action was taken."

Craig breathes through his nose. I know that sound. His patience is fraying. "You're talking like they're neighbors who don't tidy up their rubbish. They *kidnapped* and *brainwashed* my girlfriend. They *drugged me*. They were going to sacrifice a kid. And they killed a guy! I saw his body!" He's always been good at hiding fear under anger; I've always worked so hard to soothe it. "They gutted him, smashed his skull in—"

I didn't know I was moving, but I'm reeling in sunlight, terracotta tiles hot under my feet. "They didn't kill him!" The words come out rasping. "The ritual went wrong, and the cave collapsed—it was an accident, and they weren't sacrificing Myri—she offered *herself*—"

I quiet. Craig looks me up and down. "Well. If it isn't the consequences of your actions."

The woman is familiar—maroon hair, blue eyeliner; the waitress who drew me the map. She looks between me and Craig, like she's unsure who's more baffling. Her gaze settles on me with suspicion and solidarity. *What you said was utterly deranged, but he seems worse. Do you need me to punch him?*

People give me that look sometimes around him. They don't know what he's really like.

But it snaps something in him, like he suddenly sees me properly. His mouth opens, all compassion. "Oh, no, love, look at you." I'm wearing his T-shirt, legs bare from the thighs down, skin bruised. "Let's get you back inside."

He puts an arm around my shoulder, casting an *I'll handle this problem* look at the café owner. The door closes behind us.

***

Craig deposits me on the bed and slams the shutters. The electric light's weak after the brightness outside; the air's suffocating.

"Where . . ." I try to find my way around words. "How are we here?"

Craig sighs, frustrated sympathy. "I got you out, love. You were hysterical when you were conscious, basically had to drag you into the boat. But you're safe now, okay?"

Safe. Safe, away from them. Despair resurges, sickly. I sink my head between my knees. The pain kicks and writhes; I let it swallow me. It's easier than admitting the images flashing through my imagination.

Craig hands me a bottle of water. I gulp it desperately, although I don't trust my stomach to hold it. The plastic crunches between my fingers. In the hot, shadowy room, he's another shadow, my vision fraying him. "I feel weird."

Craig chuckles. "Love, you're having a comedown. Remember all the times I've had to babysit you because you went too hard? Those fuckers must have had you drugged up to the eyeballs to believe their bullshit. You're going to hurt like hell while your body works it out."

He strokes my head. His hand's damp with sweat. The comfort's not in the words, it's in his presence. It's *him.*

"I hope so," I manage.

Craig's hand moves down to the back of my neck. So sticky in this dark, muggy space. All the horizons were meant to be smashed open, but they've closed in tight enough to smother. "We'll get you to a hospital on the mainland, okay?"

Mainland. A wave of dizziness. "We're . . . going?"

"Yeah. We're taking the next ferry." Craig pulls my head to his chest. "I'm going to get you home, love."

I shake my head, face still pressed into his chest. "We have to go back." The image springs up, a flutter of hope; me and Craig, sailing back around the island, wind in our hair, a team, saving my home. The two sides of my life knitting together.

Craig shoves me. My worlds rip apart again. I tumble back, everything spinning.

"You want me to leave you here?" His voice is barbed. "I came all this way for *you*, and what did I get? You drugged me. I forgave you, I went through hell getting you out, and you want to go *back*? Well, I can piss off. You want that?"

I cringe. I'm fucking this up; he did this for me—

I need to tell him I'm sorry. But I can't. I can't breathe right in the grip of the room, and he's throwing me even more off balance. I'd forgotten how unpredictable he is, how to avoid the hidden traps in him. At the Farmstead, there was danger when you were reckless, but you could side-step it if you stayed in line, and forgiveness waited if you slipped up. With Craig, it's all pits and trip wires.

I'm quiet long enough that Craig swears under his breath and stands. My muscles tense, loosing another wave of pain. But he doesn't yell.

"Okay." He begins throwing clothes into his backpack. I remember another fight, stuffing my own backpack, crying while he watched, sneering, daring me. "If you want to stay here and fucking die, stay here and fucking die."

Pain pins me to the bed. The nightmares roiling under reality, dragging me down and absorbing me. It takes all my strength to sit up and say, "I'm sorry," then choke out the other words: "But they need me."

Craig snorts. "To do what? Collapse all over them? You're a fucking mess. You're a liability even when you *aren't* on a comedown."

I slump. He's brutal—he has to be—but he's right. I can't help them, can I?

The mattress creaks as Craig sits beside me, caressing my bare leg. "Oh, love. Of course I'm not going to leave you. Are you going to calm down and listen?"

I nod. The room presses in, keeping me flat on the bed, like I'm tied down. I'm greedy for forgiveness; I could gorge myself on it, and I'd just keep craving. But I'm not sure it's his forgiveness I want. I want Jonah's lips on my forehead, I want Teresa's arms, I want Larissa kissing my neck and calling me silly and not meaning it. I want Kiera.

His voice goes heavy. "You were out of it on that beach. I wasn't. It was bad, Aoife, okay? There were bodies everywhere."

The pain tears into me. It doesn't swallow the memories whole. It shreds them, leaves them toxic and bloody.

I already knew, didn't I?

I squeeze my eyes shut, like that might stifle all my senses. I want to be nothing.

"You know how places like that finish up, don't you?" Craig's hand moves on my skin. "What we saw on that beach, that was the endgame. That was what happens when brainwashed maniacs turn on each other. I won't let you get sucked down, okay?"

I stand, the suddenness of my movement surprising me as much as him. I want to launch myself at him. Scratch, bite, kick, and stamp, feral. I want to leave him bloodied and moaning, keep going until the moaning stops, then stare down at his broken remains and scream, *It was a fucking cave collapse. They're not monsters from a true-crime show. You will* respect *my* friends.

My hands convulse, like claws are yearning to burst out. My jaw clenches, bones grinding.

"I'm sorry, love," Craig says gently. "I'm sure some of them were good people."

It's the *were* that breaks me.

Craig gathers me into his arms, and whatever was swelling inside me bursts, and tears spill out. I sob into his shoulder and he rocks me and I keep sobbing.

I quiet the rush of violence. His smell overpowers me. I'll melt into him, become a new organ wrapped up in the hot and dark inside him. Safe.

Later, I'll feel the weight of everything I lost. For now, I'll focus on him.

"Okay," I say quietly.

Craig squeezes my knee. "You know I love you."

I surrender and let the pain be what I am now. Craig's fuckup girl-friend who joined a cult and nearly died along with them, but he saved her. That's my story. His.

"I love you, too." I can *feel* myself shrinking. Good. Less of me to miss them.

"Okay. I'm going to get my stuff together. Ferry should come soon."

I force myself to stand and open the shutters. The beauty of the vil-lage is a cruel kick in the throat, but at least I can breathe. On the balcony is a glass of fresh iced lemonade, left there for me.

CHAPTER THIRTY
SNAP OUT OF IT

I'M NOT FEELING ANY BETTER WHEN WE SET OFF. I LOOK RIDICULOUS, LIMP-ing, wincing at the sunlight, in Craig's baggy T-shirt, his jeans belted around my bony waist. The clothes feel like a marker: *This is mine.*

The harbor's gorgeous and hurts. The vivid pink of the bougainvillea conjures Larissa; I see Giulia in the subtle olive leaves, Kiera in a pile of used books, Myri in the orange fur and playful gaze of a stray cat. I will see them everywhere.

When it was a beginning, this village was beautiful. Now the palm trees and colorful shutters and fishing boats promise an ending. Soon everything will be concrete blocks and rain-washed shops and suffocation.

"How are you feeling?" Craig asks, solicitous, hand on my back.

I look back at him, doing my best to be grateful. "Like shit, to be hon-est." Empty words next to the crushing void inside me.

Craig grins and kisses my forehead. "Everyone loves a comedown. Let's keep moving, all right?"

I nod, then freeze.

Suddenly it comes clear, what I'd been staring at for a good minute, blunted by familiarity. A bright-painted wooden boat.

The Farmstead boat.

We didn't come here on that one, so—

Someone else got out.

Hope leaps; lights flicker in the void. Someone else is running, too—

Someone else got out, the colors of the boat say, and they might need you.

Craig's arm's heavy around my shoulder; he'll never let me look for them. But I imagine Myri small in my arms, Kiera clinging to me, or a ragged group of survivors pulling me in, and I will absolutely not let it go.

The Aoife I was before might. But I do things she never could.

I moan. "Oh, shit. It *hurts*." I bury my face in his T-shirt, becoming soft and broken, in need of saving. Everything he wants me to be. I look up, pleading. "Do you have painkillers?"

"Woman thinks I'm a pharmacy," Craig mutters indulgently, ruffling my hair.

"They have them in the shop." I wilt a bit more. "I don't . . . know if I can walk. Can you get me to a bench?"

Craig huffs but eases me onto the nearest bench. "I can't leave you, love. What if they come back for you?"

I'm so busy playing at confusion that I almost miss the inconsistency. But it sneaks in anyway, and begins chewing away, suspicion and hope grinding together. "You said they were dead."

"Not *all*. Fuck's sake, stop putting words in my mouth." Craig sighs. "You think I trust you on your own right now?"

I see that mistrust. That familiar, affectionate disdain. Silly Aoife, can't be left without supervision. How it's always bled from him into me. How it bleeds now, twisting the picture again, I'm having an *Aoife moment*, falling back into the brainwashing—

A shiver through my body. A flicker, light through palm leaves fluttering on the cobblestones. A jolt of energy, clearing my head, the pain easing.

I know what I'm fucking doing.

"You won't be able to trust me at all if I pass out, will you," I say drily, cute and sad and above everything, weak.

Craig sighs. "Fine. I'll get your bloody drugs."

I gaze up, pathetic, grateful, all his. "Thanks."

"Finally, she says it." Craig snorts, kisses my head, and disappears toward the shop.

I pull myself together, despite the ache and dizziness, and stand. I've won only moments, and I'll get hell for this. But I don't need to wonder where to look, because she's already running to me.

Mustard-yellow shirt, azure trousers, hot-pink scarf. Curls blowing in the wind. A bird of paradise.

"Larissa!" I forget the pain and fling myself into her arms. Warm, soft, *her*. She's *here*. Her breath on my neck, arms strong around my waist.

We pull back and examine each other. "You look like hell," she says, and I snort in an extremely undignified way. "You okay? Where's your boyfriend?"

I look at the shop, panic rising. How long does it take to buy painkillers in an unfamiliar language?

She reads my face. "Come on." A hand in mine, a shoulder to lean on, and we're hurrying up an alleyway shaded by grape vines, concealed between whitewashed walls. I sink onto a step, feeling like I could root in here and nothing could pull me away.

"What are you doing here?"

She slides down beside me and jostles my shoulder. "Looking for *you*, you noodle."

I wait for the wince of shame that comes whenever Craig says something like that. It doesn't come. It's suddenly clear, the difference between *aren't you silly for thinking I wouldn't love you* and *aren't you stupid for thinking anyone else would.*

"You got out!" A miracle. Her. "Come with us! We're taking the next ferry."

She shakes her head. "We have to go back."

I don't want to know. I have to. "What's happened? Is everyone . . . ."

Larissa sighs. We watch a grape leaf fall, spinning in the trapped breeze. "It's bad. Sage is dead."

That sentence shouldn't bring joy. But it does. *Sage* is dead. Not *everyone* is dead. Sage. One name.

"Everyone else is . . . alive." Look at all those sunbeams slicing through the leaves, look at me among them, smiling despite everything. "But it's horrible. Myri's . . . gone weird. Teresa's locked herself in the kitchen with Sage's body. And I've never seen Jonah like this, he's . . . . He blames Giulia." She swallows pain. "And . . . there's something else . . . ."

She struggles, like the words refuse to be spoken, then stops short as a shadow falls.

Craig's in the mouth of the alleyway. Frozen, furious. Outlined by the sun. And it can't be right that there's no leap of love, just panic.

"Get the hell away from her." Craig's voice shakes. "Aoife. Come here." Speaking slowly, like I'm a child he's coaxing down from a high ledge. I don't know why that makes me want to laugh.

Larissa stands. Her hands are raised, her face steady, and I see how tightly she's holding that calm. I know so little about her past, but she's been here before, hasn't she, facing down someone full of rage? "Hey. It's okay. I won't hurt her."

"No, you won't," Craig says. "You're going to fuck off. Now."

Larissa dares to break eye contact and looks down at me. "If you want to go with him, go. I'll tell the others you'd gone already when I arrived. If you *want*."

The pain redoubles, then recedes, fog clearing. It's like when I was between him and Oscar, stretched like a thread between two worlds, ready to snap.

This time, one of them offers security. The other offers only catastrophe, a spiral into something worse. Craig's warning echoes: *You know how places like that finish up.*

I look at him, really look. My rescuer.

I stand up.

"Don't you dare," Craig snaps. "Aoife. You know these people are just using you."

I don't think anyone expects me to burst out laughing.

I definitely didn't, but here we are. Larissa and Craig, as united as they will ever be in anything, stare at me blankly. Absurdity bubbles through me.

The lie I'd wrapped myself up in crumbles and comes out in waves of hilarity.

"Using me for what, Craig?" I say sweetly when the laughter subsides. "I'm a *liability*, right? Only good for, you know, paying your bills and cleaning your house? If I'm so useless without you, what do you think they want me for?"

Craig's face is contorted. That vicious curl of his lip; I never said anything, after his face did that. I didn't want to know what would happen.

Seeing it now, I don't fear what he'll do. I see the cruelty of what he already did.

"You lied." My voice is full of wonder, echoing my awe at the Unseen; sometimes your reality overturns, leaving you struck down, marveling. "You said they were dead. You knew what that would do to me."

Is that panic? His reality's sliding away, too, pitching him into a new one.

"Get out of my way," I tell him. "I'm going home."

Larissa's hand finds mine, warm. I don't need to see her face; I know it's glowing.

"Go on, then." His disgust doesn't ring true; there's a tremble there. "There won't be a pretty ending up there."

"I know"—and there's the weight of that, but there it is, bright and clear—"but I still choose that over you."

We emerge into the brightness of the harborside. Larissa helps me into the boat and fires up the engine, and I don't look back at him, not even once.

The boat powers out into the ocean, eager waves slapping. The wind's cool with a touch of evening.

I don't feel right, still, but it's not sickness. Something silky is sliding along my bones—a strange, sensual tingle. The dizziness has turned into a high. Something's wrong, but I've snapped cords I didn't even know were tying me down, and I'm bloated with bliss.

We round the headland, passing rugged cliffs, and Larissa cuts the engine, leaving us bobbing on the deep turquoise water. Everything's so bright, colors oversaturated.

"You sure?" Larissa asks. "He's an asshole. You were right to tell him where to go. But . . . it's not good. I won't judge if you leave while you can. I'm . . ." She grits her teeth and says it, impossible words from the bird-of-paradise girl who dances with danger, the girl so close to the Unseen it shimmers on her skin. "I'm scared."

She's right. This moment feels tenuous, like a final exit; if I don't take it, I'm bound into whatever happens. I *get sucked down with the rest of them.*

"I'm not running." I wrap my hands around hers.

Her kiss is luscious, startling. When we split apart, we smile. That glow in her eyes used to hint at secrets. Now it's bouncing back to me, conspiracy, even if the smile is lopsided and the secrets are darker.

Larissa ignites the engine again, and the rocking of the waves, the width of the sky, the tingling in my blood, feel like flying.

Despite everything, arriving at the Farmstead is a wash of sweetness. The sun turns the ocean gold, flaring light across the cliffs, the huts, the twisty trees and vines. Home, home, home. I thought I'd never see it again.

Larissa ties up the boat at the rickety wooden jetty, and I run onto the beach to fling myself down and kiss the sand. Then slow, panting, my joyful laughter choking into quiet.

There's no music, no smell of cooking; the voices echoing from the fields and groves are subdued. No laughter. But it's not just that.

I look at Larissa. She nods, confirming what her voice didn't dare form.

The exquisite energy that swirled through everything here. The way the soil and trees and sky thrummed and whispered and loved us. It's not there.

The high in my blood sours and crashes.

I can't feel the Unseen anymore. It's gone.

CHAPTER THIRTY-ONE

FORSAKEN

I STAND NAKED IN MY HUT. I'M NOT SURE HOW LONG I'VE BEEN HERE, JUST staring at Craig's clothes on my bed.

Part of me wants to burn them and dance, laughing in my new freedom. But most of me is empty, the high turned sickly and strange.

He was cruel. He was kind. He tried to save me. He tried to own me.

I dig through my new clothes. Elise's. Weird, I never knew her, but I wish she was here. I'd ask her stuff. Whether she ever made the choice I made, to tie herself to this place even if it destroyed her. I press my face into a striped sweater before throwing it on.

I'm home. That's something. That's everything.

But home is not the same.

Thorns bite into my bare feet; they never did before. The insect chirps—a lullaby before—grate, and when I brush my fingers along a branch, sap clings.

The farmhouse doors are closed; even the windows are shuttered.

I slip down the overgrown path to the garden, and there are barbs that I don't remember, snagging my sweater, which already feels too hot for the muggy evening.

I've never known this place so silent.

Singing rings behind the kitchen shutters. Teresa. I hold my breath, terrified I'll catch the scent of the raw meat that was a boy who was never my friend.

There's nobody in sight, but food's laid out in the garden: bread, cheese, cured meats, covered with foil to keep away the droning cloud of flies. There weren't flies before. Should there even be flies? The sky's darkening already, an evening chill setting in.

Still, now the sickness has abated, my stomach's squirming hungrily. I find myself grabbing handfuls of food, tearing and gulping like an animal. Even awareness of a corpse nearby, even the bloodstained memories of last night, don't hold back my appetite. My belly cramps urgently, demanding more, even once I've scoffed a whole plate of cheeses and flatbreads and figs. I'm hollow.

I want to give up the hunger, the emptiness, the fear, but there's nothing to take it.

My mouth's still crammed embarrassingly when someone finally approaches up the path. I swallow and wipe the crumbs away.

Oscar. My face brightens, then my smile falters.

Cold, flat eyes, his colorful shirts replaced with a black turtleneck, his lazy smile with a hard line.

"Hi—" My voice gives way.

"Come with me." Expressionless.

His hand on my arm is heavy. I don't resist, but he still physically tugs me into the farmhouse, bypassing the kitchen, through back areas of the house, along dusty corridors, up shadowy side stairs.

"What's happening?"

"Jonah wants to see you."

Fear and relief mingle. It's Jonah; he'll kiss me on the forehead and tell me secrets. It's Jonah; nobody knows his moods, and he has every reason to be furious.

"Up," Oscar says. "Solarium. Go."

Every step up those spiral stairs feels heavy. Oscar waits below, arms folded. He doesn't feel like a friend or guide now; his posture says guard, lieutenant.

Evening's shaded into twilight, muting the stained glass. The butterflies are stupefied by the gathering dark. Lamps buried among the leaves outline their veins starkly and cast confusing shadows.

I barely notice any of that.

I just see her.

Myri sits in a wicker chair among the foliage.

She wears a purple silk robe. She's loaded with flowers. Lilies and roses, hibiscus and jasmine and lavender, woven into a crown, wrapped around her arms, piled in her lap.

Her face is a window to nothing. Hollow eyes. Open mouth. She sits straight-backed, but there's no light in her.

Jonah's kneeling at her feet, forehead pressed into her hand, mumbling.

I can't speak. It's like stepping into a cathedral, a tomb long undisturbed. Like if I even cough, I'll disturb some holy balance.

It's Myri that disturbs it, a sudden spasming kick, a shout. "Let me out, let me out! Swans! I don't remember, the flowers were yellow, it went wrong—just one loud crack and it hurt—I'm all wrong—"

As she speaks, the flowers garlanding her wither and blacken.

Not just the flowers—oh god, is that her *skin*, shriveling on her flesh, mottled with mold, a mushroom swelling visibly on her lip—

And then she shivers and the flowers revive, and her skin is smooth and unblemished, and her eyes are empty again, stripped of self.

Something snaps in me. *Myri.*

Jonah turns very slowly. I almost buckle. He always looked tired, but now his dark circles are bruise-deep; his flyaway hair's flattened, like it's wilting too.

"When she was little, she collected insects in jars." His voice is strained; I expect it to echo, like we're in a wider, emptier space. "She got so upset if one of them escaped or died that Sage started researching them, made sure they were fed the right leaves, kept warm enough. They named them. Wood lice and beetles and snails. Then one day she let them all go because she was scared they were unhappy. She kept shouting 'I don't know if they like it!'" His impression of a child's voice is unnerving, a high-pitched twitter. "She's all goodness, all the way down. So was Sage. The two of them having adventures, finding insects under tree roots. Whole worlds to look forward to."

I can't respond. A butterfly alights on one of Myri's eyeballs; she doesn't blink. It flutters up into one of the lilies in her hair then takes off rapidly, realizing it's landed on something meaningless, a husk.

Jonah tears out the lily, tosses it away, and begins hunting through the plants.

"We're forsaken," he says.

Forsaken. The word settles, and the last of the euphoria of return dies.

I'm here, but nothing's the same; we're *forsaken*.

"The Unseen abandoned us. It emptied itself out of her and took her with it. The blight's in her, feeding on whatever scraps it left behind. I don't know if her body will last. I don't know if any of us will."

A stupid instinct, some vestige of the old world, wants to yell that she needs a hospital. I crush it down. There isn't a cure.

I don't know how I know it so certainly, but I'm looking at something beyond saving, a corpse moving on strange strings. It didn't even sound like her when she cried out. Every instinct screaming to save her comes from a place we're far beyond now, means no more than a child asking when a dead grandparent will come out of the box again.

I choke back a wave of tears. She clung so hard to herself, then offered it, for nothing. She's gone, for *nothing*.

Jonah snaps around, an orchid between his fingers, too tiny, fragile. "Say something!" he shouts, and the suddenness of it sends me reeling.

"I'm—" I choke. "I'm sorry?"

"Sorry?" He's silky, an unnerving shift. The leaf-sliced light casts craggy shadows on his face. "Why? What did you do?"

He hasn't asked me to sit or offered me tea; this is not his bright sanctuary, it's a dim-lit snare he's pulling me into, a spiderweb.

He steps forward; I step back, heart thumping, but *it's Jonah; Jonah always forgives*.

His tone drips venom. "Giulia leaves, claiming she will sell her family home and bring back money. She returns with a stranger. A stranger who does not *tell me* about Giulia's dissent until the *last minute*. A stranger who brings an outsider to our most sacred rite, a boy who arrived *coincidentally* the night before the brink. A stranger who is present when this *blight*, this corruption, is called into our rite, when my son is killed and my daughter emptied and our god abandons us. A stranger who flees in the aftermath."

I swallow as a pattern forms.

"I didn't run!" I blurt. What's that edge in my voice? That weird jolt, something crawling inside my bones. This is *unfair*. "Craig *took me*. It wasn't my choice!"

The words settle on Jonah like mist, with no effect.

Fear, sharp and cold. I don't even know what of yet. Lights reflect on the glass, windows turned to mirrors in the dark. Myri's eyes the same, unseeing.

Jonah tenderly weaves the orchid into Myri's hair. She shifts and looks up and murmurs, "My shirt was all wet. Kept looking for the sky, but there was no sky. Now I can't feel anything but wrong."

I jerk back as the flowers droop again; her eyes turn to me, two puff-balls of mold.

I cover my mouth to choke off the scream. She blinks, and her eyes are eyes again, soft green, blank.

"You're on the edge of a precipice," Jonah informs me, businesslike, another shift. "We all are, but you most of all."

He takes my hand. Strokes it. Examines it, as if assessing its value.

I swallow. I keep looking to Myri, like she might help. Everything's slipping, and when it's gone, it's gone forever, and then does it matter what happens to me? Twice, I've given everything for this place. I have nothing else. I want nothing else.

"Tell me what to do. Anything."

"Kneel to her," he orders. "Pray."

I sink to my knees in front of Myri and take her hand. It's limp, her pulse weak.

She won't look up. She doesn't feel it. When the fear's eased, that's going to hit me and leave a crack I'll never shore up.

I whisper a chant that Sage taught us, that I guess he learned from his grandmother or Kiera's books. Wordless sounds that used to shiver my bones. No shivers now, nothing to respond. I add murmurs of "Come back," as if one girl begging a living ghost could call back a lost god.

Something cold, hot breath, on the back of my neck.

Keep chanting. Instinct grips my throat. *Show him how strong you are.*

Chilly metal moves from the top of my spine to the tendons at the base of my skull.

It's the shears, isn't it? The ones he prunes the flowers with.

Blades parted, moving around my head as he breathes heavily. Settling around one of my ears, then the other. Pressing against my throat.

He's going to kill me he's going to kill me—

Just trust. Myri's hand is cool, like a bloodless creature. I keep chanting.

Blade parted, either side of my windpipe. They're sharpened. How many snaps will it take? How long will I be aware before my brain fizzles and dies? I keep chanting.

The blades withdraw.

"Stand up."

I stand, the chant dying away. My breaths are steady, but I'm shaking and shaking.

Jonah places down the blades and holds me by the chin, inspecting me like a specimen. He nods to himself and steps away to examine the chrysalises nearby. Fragile jade-green things, caught in strange shadows.

"Broken down," he whispers. "Melted to mulch. And reborn."

He snaps back to me, settled. Some decision made that I can't fathom.

"Giulia did this." A singsong rhythm. "Giulia killed my son. Giulia broke my daughter. Giulia took our god. And Giulia will not admit what she did. Giulia glares and cries and cowers. Giulia will not tell us why or how she did it. I need her to say it."

I nod. I don't know what else to do.

Myri moans, coughs up a tangle of fungi and worms, and falls still again. Jonah strokes her hair, but there's nothing to soothe there.

"Giulia is your friend," Jonah says, thoughtful. "She trusts you."

I grimace, picturing her fear when she admitted her doubts. "Not totally."

Jonah chews the inside of his cheek. "But if she thinks you're an outcast, too . . . ."

Part of me balks at the cruelty of that, but a glow sparks. He's talking like he might trust me. I showed him my devotion, didn't I? He's pleased.

"What you can learn from Giulia could save us all. Especially you, because you are still teetering. Are you willing?"

I look at Myri. Still as a mannequin. Beyond saving by any *human* power.

I feel the emptiness of a world without the Unseen.

I am so much more than I was. I've shown it twice today.

"I am," I say.

CHAPTER THIRTY-TWO
PRISONER

Oscar's silent as we descend, still sharp and cold. Like whatever cataclysm tore the playfulness and warmth out of Myri did the same to him, left him as an automaton. Nothing left in him but purpose.

I try not to let it chill me. We're all struggling.

Through the creaky door to the wine cellar, down rocky stairs in the light of a spiderwebbed bulb. I've been here before, retrieving home-brewed wine or whiskey from the mainland. A cool, damp space, rickety shelves lined with bottles.

What isn't usually here is Giulia.

She's curled against the rough-hewn stone wall, still in her silver ritual dress. Her hands rest on her knees, wrists tied to one of the cabinets with a blue plastic rope.

I wish her eyes were dull. They aren't. They're wide and bright with fear. She has a black eye; the indents of fingers bruise her neck and arms.

A pang of pain for her stirs a visceral awareness of what's waiting for me if I fail.

Oscar shoves me across the room. "If I come back in here and she's untied, you'll get the same treatment." Expressionless. Doing his job. "We'll decide what to do with you. Use the time to pray."

My act begins here. Why hold back? I've learned this side of me now.

I put on my shakiest voice. "Please, I—"

"You know what you did," Oscar snaps.

His footsteps echo up the stairs. There's a pause, like he's stopped to reconsider. Then the door thuds and the lock clicks.

Even though I chose this, the door slam wakes panic. I imagine calling out and getting no answer. I imagine ropes binding my hands. I'm inches away from where she is.

It swells over me. I'm alone and everything's wrong—

I can't fail. Myri needs me; surely if we fix this, she can find her way back before she rots out altogether. Kiera, Larissa, they need me. Everyone needs me.

Giulia says, "Hi," drily, and releases a laugh that's strung too tight.

I sink onto the dusty stone floor. My linen trousers are too thin for this close, cool air. The lightbulb flickers in its net of spiderwebs, and I have a sudden terror that it will go out. A darkness that grips you, and you never come back.

I manage a "Hi," back. Suspicion is taut in my nerves, I don't understand what she *did*, but it's Giulia. *Your friend. I hope.* She can't have meant this. Finding the truth could save her; she'll explain, and we'll both get out. If I play this right.

I reach out and link my hand with hers. Sun-browned fingers, calloused fingertips, stubby nails. A strained smile.

"Don't worry, I won't ask you to untie me. Not going to fuck with your loyalties." Giulia rests her head against the wall. "He's going to kill me either way."

My head swims. That's not right. Her hand's warm. I feel her pulse. She's a soft, bright thing in the world, alive. Jonah would never take that away.

I remember the cold of the shears at my throat. He's in a shadowy, broken place. But he's still the same: tests and games, teaching us who we are. He pushes us to the brink to see what we'll do. But he never pushes us over. He wouldn't. Even now.

"He's just trying to find out the truth," I assure her. "He needs to understand."

Giulia snorts. "I love you, but you don't see the Jonah that I see. He killed Elise. And now he will kill me." She sighs. "It's okay . . . I just need to . . . get my head around it." She looks down at the rope. The rope we use to tie up the boat, to hang nets to catch olives. To keep goats from struggling when we slaughter them. "Why are you here?"

I reshape the story as I tell it; me and Craig ran, Larissa brought me back, Jonah blamed me for Sage's death. No lies, just a coating of color. My voice falters when I can't tell what's embellishment and what's truth.

"Huh." There's strangled humor there. "Busy day."

It's my turn to snort.

"Drink?" Giulia says, voice still dry. "You'll have to serve yourself, but the good news is we have very, very much wine." She shrugs. "Better to die drunk, right?"

"Nothing's going to happen to you." *Just trust.* Still, the bottles look tempting. I choose a dusty one and take a cautious sip. Perfect: a thick, sweet white.

"Do you mind . . . ?" Giulia tilts her chin, gesturing to her bound hands. I lift the bottle to her lips, and she takes hungry gulps, like a baby sucking on a milk bottle. A droplet lingers on her lip. "Should hit fast. I haven't eaten. Pietro brought food, but I didn't eat. He was telling me we were over unless I confessed. Took off my wedding ring and threw it away. It's over there if you want it. Might be worth something if you get out of here." Her laugh's dark.

I ignore it and take another slug of wine. If I *get out of here*, I won't care about wedding rings or money or anything else.

"I'm sorry," she says. "I didn't mean to get you mixed up in this."

"What did you *do*?" It's my opening, I take it, but the confusion is real. "*Why?* We were going to end the nightmares. Free the world."

Giulia watches me with genuine pain. "You really believe that. Still."

"Of course." It *aches*, how close we were. I won't think about how it's her fault that we're not adventuring in a better world. If I get angry it will eat me alive, and there's too much I have to do. I've held back anger all my life; I can't let it in. I need to hold her hand and guide her back with me, calm and gentle.

"And our new world, that was worth Myri's life?" Giulia asks sharply.

I grit my teeth, remembering the empty body decked in flowers. Maybe they put her in the solarium because she used to like the butterflies and flowers and colored light. Maybe those struggling remnants of consciousness do like it; or maybe they're too lost, aware only of their own decomposition.

Not gone. Myri is with the Unseen. We will bring her back.

Giulia nods at the wine; I lift it. Despite myself, rage tingles. Unexpected pain lightning-flickers, like something biting at my bones. I push back the anger and smile at her, sad, a subtle agreement that I mean and don't mean.

She swallows and pushes the bottle away with her chin. "I didn't want this. We just wanted to help Myri." The shelves rattle as she tugs at her rope to get more comfortable. She sags when she realizes she can't.

Sadness for her surges, but there's a simmering pride, too. Pietro left her, Oscar locked her up, she was beaten, she said nothing. They couldn't crack her open. But I have.

A shiver runs through me, an oddly delicious sensation concentrating deep in my gut. A ripple of resignation and anguish and courage, half-familiar, half alien.

"We thought, if we disrupted things, there might be a chance for Sage to be the vessel. We thought maybe we could stop the ritual altogether." Giulia winces. "I didn't think the Unseen would *vanish*. I didn't think . . . I didn't think any of that would happen."

Something in her seems to curl up smaller, a hunching of her shoulders, widening of her eyes, like she's growing even more breakable. I should feel bad for her, but the anger's rising, hotter, surging.

I catch the crucial part almost too late. "Who's *we?*"

"Me and . . . Sage." She flinches; I know the images flashing through her mind. They're in mine, too. "You know how fascinated he was with the blight. He thought of it like a living creature, thought he had some connection with it. He . . . found a way to summon it. We talked about using it to disrupt the waking, and we agreed not to, but . . . ."

She focuses on me, and I wonder if she's suspicious; I swear there's blame there, although it's muted, sad more than angry.

"I guess Jonah knew I was questioning," she says. "Before the ritual he . . . he took me out onto the rocks and held me under. In the nightmares. I don't know how long for. I felt Myri's pain. I felt how scared and alone she was. I felt his, how much he didn't want us to know, I felt . . . everything, all of it, all the horrors in the Unseen, and I was drowning in it, and it wasn't like when we were all there together, it was just me, all of that just on me."

I shudder. It was the right thing to do, she had to see, she had to remember what it was for. But I remember how it felt in there among the nightmares. My body remembers, more vividly than ever. Another eager shiver passes through my nerves.

"He brought me back and made me drink that tea until everything was ginger and raspberry. He stood there watching while I dressed up pretty. Held my hand steady while I did my makeup. Everything was fuzzy, and I kept thinking I would . . . fall out of the world.

"But it did something, I think. I didn't really know who I was anymore, but during the rite my mind said, *Stop this*, and I remembered the summoning that . . . that Sage taught me so I . . . did it. Summoned the blight." Her nose scrunches; she sounds like she's about to cry. "I thought they'd see it as a warning and maybe stop the ritual. For Myri, for us. We're so caught up in our fantasies we never thought *what* we would unleash."

"You were scared." I don't disguise the disdain.

"Fear's smart."

"Yeah?" I thought I'd crushed my fury, but it's still there, clawing around my ribcage. "Look where your fear got us."

The door opens. Giulia winces, and sympathy twists through the anger a little. Seconds later, though, the door slams again. All is quiet.

"You know what?" Giulia says. "I hope whatever they're going to do to me, they get on with it." She attempts a smile, head lolling like the wine's hitting. "I really need to pee."

I annoy myself by snorting again; her smile looks a little less mangled, and we're halfway to laughing when the door opens again. Footsteps echo down the stairs.

Giulia reaches her bound hands for mine. I grip them, then think how that will look, and pull away.

The look on her face guts me, but I shove my hands defiantly into my sleeves. I will not let her take this place from me.

Oscar stands over us, pale in the flickery light, voice recorder in his hand. His eyebrow's raised as he taps a button.

Giulia's voice plays out of it, staticky. "... during the rite my mind said, *Stop this*, and I remembered the summoning that ... that Sage taught me so I ... did it. Summoned the blight."

Giulia stares. I swear I see something inside her crumble. I think she's going to shout, blame me, but she just looks at the ground, slumped.

Oscar yanks me to my feet, and my foot knocks the bottle. Wine glugs out over Giulia's bare feet and the hem of her dress. I don't know why that's when she starts to cry.

"Good job, Aoife," Oscar says. "Join the others on the beach."

I should probably look back as I scramble up the stairs. I should look her in the eye.

But I can't. The angry thing is still moving inside my chest, clawing out images of Myri's withered, mold-mottled face and the bloody mess that used to be Sage. I push it down, but what's left is burning pride that I proved myself. I don't want her to see that.

So I don't look.

Before Oscar closes the door and locks her in there alone, he switches off the light.

CHAPTER THIRTY-THREE
BROKEN DOWN

I WALK TO THE BEACH ALONE, SNUGGLED INSIDE MY JUMPER AGAINST AN unusually cold breeze that slips through the knitted holes.

I try to picture winter without the Unseen. Scraping food will be tougher; Jonah said Giulia went back to sell her house; are Oscar's funds running out? I imagine hunger, that emptiness lingering. A harsh blow after a blissful summer.

I imagine winter with people missing. Sage. Myri. Giulia?

A fig squelches under my toes, sticky and moldy. Stones and thorns bite into my feet; half-rotted olives adhere to my soles. I walked barefoot with no trouble, before. That aching hunger hasn't abated, the food I scarfed down sitting heavy in my stomach but offering no satisfaction.

I fight a sudden urge to kick at everything, scream into the knotted necks of the olive trees. It wasn't meant to *be* like this. I smash my fist into a low branch, searing pain through my knuckles but releasing none of the frustration.

I want to set myself loose on that tree. Snap the branches, tear the leaves with my teeth. I want to smash something. Dry flowers, a ribcage, a universe. I want to beat and scream until something is shards and even that won't be enough.

I don't have the strength, do I, to express this fury? The tree and the world are unchanged, unimpressed by the size of my rage. I'm just me. A scream builds in my throat.

Something surges through me, pins and needles from head to toe; my muscles tense like they could bulge, my skin twitches like it longs to rip open—I look down, and I could swear there's the softest trace of a phosphorescent glimmer under my fingernail—

No. Gone. This anger's fucking with my head.

I need to bury it. I always let feelings overtake me—what else do we have feelings *for*—but I never let anger own me. Whisper it calm. I'm Aoife, joy and boldness and awkwardness, but not anger. Over years with Craig, I learned. Softness over rage.

I divert my path to the beach. The wind's at my back and adrenaline rises against bleak images of dark times coming and I run, screaming wordlessly at the stars. There are so few, the Milky Way dimmed. The run ends too quickly; I'm at the end of the cove and none of the anger is gone.

I swallow it, bury it simmering in my core, and turn to the scene ahead of me.

A bonfire flickers at the base of the cliff, smaller and weaker than usual. Ana and Maisie struggling to feed it before it gutters. Everyone's gathered, wrapped in scarves and sweaters, or braving the chill naked.

A chant circles: *Adore, Unseen, surrender.* Familiar words from countless rituals, from infusing pastries or linen with a reminder that every moment was an offering.

Now they're torn from throats crying to the sky, mumbled through sobs. Some people sit cross-legged, but others are on their feet cursing the stars, or lie shouting into the sand.

The desolation is absolute. It stirs the same desolation in me. *Forsaken.*

I slip onto a blanket next to Larissa. And there's Kiera, folding me up in a brief hug, a reunion I needed so badly I almost choke on it. I feel a hitch in her breath, too. We share quick-fire smiles, *this is shit, glad you're here.* I want to tell them about Giulia, but when I think about her, my mind goes white. There's no chance, anyway: Frida's standing over me.

"Chant," she snaps. "We're not here to *chat.*"

I start chanting, but cold digs through my clothes and pinches, and the smoke's making me cough, and mosquitoes whine around my ears. Were there mosquitoes before?

A stirring's up in my body, all wrong. Kicks in my organs, churning in my bones. Pain and pleasure; if I wasn't busy chanting, I'd let out gasps. Out of the corner of my eye, it looks like my skin is glimmering, but when I look directly, it's gone.

What if the ritual messed me up? Memories of Sage's corpse stir nausea. I think of Giulia and how she might be empty and gone now, too.

And I think, *He wouldn't, he loves her,* but something twists, and I also think, *For what she took from us, I'd kill her myself.*

The fear unfurls into fury again, and the chant becomes a howl.

A shudder, a convulsion from toes to crown, and it feels like despair and desperation and it doesn't feel like mine. Beside me, Kiera lets out a long sigh.

I focus on the chant. Clear my head. Clear my head.

Adore. The rhythm takes over, and drowsiness rises. *Unseen.* Frida, Pietro, and João pace around, poking or kicking people whose heads are nodding. *Surrender.* Frida splashes people awake with saltwater. *Adore.* It's a relief when she trickles some onto me, stirring me into focus.

Unseen. I'm tempted to leap into the ocean, let the water spark me awake. *Surrender.* But Darya tried that, and she's curled up by the water-line, gasping as Kai works a sea urchin spine out of her foot. *Adore.* It's not nightmares in the ocean now, just hostility.

Unseen. The whole island feels hostile. *Surrender.* It doesn't want us anymore. *Adore.* We're the meddling invaders who drove away its god.

Unseen. Don't think. Relax. *Surrender.* Don't sleep. Focus. *Adore.* Let the rhythm take you. *Unseen.* Dissolve into the sound. *Surrender.* There's peace in it.

Adore. Breathe soft now. *Unseen.* Surrender. *Surrender.* Hush.

Sound blasts, shatteringly loud.

A generator judders into life and music erupts from speakers among the trees, abrasive, a combative bassline over drums that mimic a furious heartbeat. I jerk and cover my ears; several people scream.

Shouting. "Get up, everyone, move!"

We've been chanting and praying for hours; the noise is disorientating, panic blaring in the most primal part of my brain, *danger, danger.*

Larissa pulls me to my feet, and I reach for Kiera's hand as she looks around in confused terror. Oscar's voice rises over the cacophony: "Get to the farmhouse! It's time!"

We stumble across the sand, the music a warning siren as it bounces off the cliffs. It's too dark to see much apart from the farmhouse lights, bobbing with our steps. I'm trying to think, but I can't; it's like being dragged from the depths of a dream.

"What's happening?" Kiera asks, like we have answers.

Larissa shakes her head as if to clear it, curls bouncing. The fear's sharp on her face, but there's something behind it. A desperate hope.

A table's set up in front of the farmhouse, under two trees at the fringe of the beach. A massive copper tureen steams.

My eyes fix on it, and my nerves prickle; I can't place why. But the scent of thick, herby, meaty soup hits my nostrils, making my stomach rumble eagerly. Teresa's there, looking exhausted, her eyes bright and wild. She's still singing, the song half-lost under the muttering and shuffling of the gathering crowd.

Still, something good: *food*, a proper meal. I'm *ravenous*, like I haven't eaten in days. Bodies jostle into a queue as Teresa doles out portions in earthen mugs. She looks confused, like she's doing this from far away. My mug steams and sloshes, warm, like holding a still-beating heart.

Nothing feels real.

The smell of the soup is heady. I gulp, the hot liquid burning down my throat. Bone broth, flavored with rosemary and spices, rich and salty. It's good, chunks of meat crumbling between my teeth, although there's traces of something gritty. It settles in my belly, comforting, taking the edge of my hunger, even if I ache for something more.

Oscar and Aksel and Pietro pace around the crowd like guard dogs. A few people seem to be holding back. Ana asks if there's anything vegan, but Oscar shoves a cup into her hand and says, "Drink," so fiercely that she curls her nose and takes a sip anyway.

Kiera's eyes flicker toward the trees. Her cup sits between shaking hands; I don't think she's even tasted it.

I'm feeling more and more off. My senses are brighter and sharper, but distorted, a television tuned wrong. There's panic in it, the world growing insubstantial.

Larissa's arm is around my shoulder; her breath smells of broth. I'm not sure why Kiera's looking at us like we're alarms about to go off.

People are finishing their soup, and quiet's falling. Even with food in my stomach, the dizziness of the interrupted meditation makes the world spinny. Weird how a few days ago it was natural that we'd get a good meal, but it feels ominous now, like we've been fed to gain strength for something.

Static fizzes, and the music shuts off, and Myri emerges from the farmhouse.

Jonah and Oscar guide her. Her legs move mindlessly, like a windup doll. Brown petals scatter from flowers adorning her. A strange, broken bride.

Gasps shudder through the crowd. I guess most people hadn't seen her like this; even for me, that hollow face is a blow. When she was in the throes of the Unseen, there was still some strange life in her. Now, there's just void.

Even as I think that, she stirs, and the flowers droop again, her skin drooping too. She looks up and says, matter-of-factly, "I can't find my passport; do you know where it is?"

The last of the flesh sloughs away from one of her hands; a centipede crawls out from the hollow of a finger bone.

Before the screams die down, she shivers, returns to her blank self. Her voice crackles from the speaker. Prerecorded long ago, a frail mock-up of a prophecy.

"The Unseen never asked us not to be scared. It says let the fear come, but trust it. Just trust. Fear is a gift. Like awe and wonder.

"We don't know what the Unseen is or wants. We're right to be scared. But we can't throw that away, that gift. We should give it up, too, with the rest of ourselves. An insect doesn't know what it's doing when it weaves its cocoon. It doesn't know it'll be broken down and reborn wonderful. It trusts the process. We'll trust the process.

"We walk into the unknown. We're shaking but we keep going forward."

The words ring; the girl who spoke them, weeks or years ago, stands still, vacant.

"Fear, but trust," Jonah says, as the recorded message falls silent. He lowers his daughter into a chair. "Walk into the unknown. Our holy mission.

"We failed.

"We let this place become a happy holiday camp, clung to our humanity, when we were here to become more and less than human. We should have begun that transformation long ago. Shed ourselves truly. We might have succeeded."

Is his voice slurred? Or is that my hearing? The stars move funny when I crane my neck back, and everything's pressing in on me.

"Still. We have a shadow of hope. One last, desperate act."

"Oh god, what," Kiera whispers. There's no question in it, just dull dread.

"It has begun," and yes, that's a slur in his voice, distortion. "A few leaves and berries from our own garden, is all." He swallows the last of his soup, and toasts.

The world goes incoherent. Something might be bad, but I can't hear

258

it over the buzzing in my ears. Everyone's quiet like something's about to hit and hasn't yet, not quite. Kiera's pale; a little moan escapes her throat. Larissa's arms around my shoulders are stiff.

Jonah laughs into the terrified quiet, off-kilter. "Oh! To be clear, I meant just a few little intoxicants, to help us to do what we must!"

Gasps and laughs of relief. Kiera's face twists, close to tears; Larissa buries hers in my shoulder. Kai's cackling loudly, like he has so many times, holding to the one thing he knows. "You bastard! You had us there!"

"Kai," Jonah says. Across the crowd, laughter slides off Kai's face. Jonah's smile isn't right, but maybe that's my eyes reading the world in the wrong language. "Amusing, was it?" That smile widens. "I'm glad you're enjoying yourself. Have some more soup!"

Kai's angular face, the face that shaped into silly contortions while he strummed guitar, that was always popping up during parties, is pale. But he pushes his shoulders back and walks to the table. He doesn't have a choice.

Teresa ladles another portion into his mug, still distant. Kai looks around like there will be an explanation, but we're all silent, watching. I feel my gaze adding pressure, pushing him. Jonah gives an encouraging nod.

He downs it in one gulp, showman-like, and gives jazz hands, nervous under the weight of our stares. "Teresa. Masterful as ever."

His confident act falls flat. Teresa's eyes widen then narrow. She won't stop singing.

Jonah's smile has crawled from a place where nothing should be seen. "You like life here, Kai? The parties, the food, splashing in the shallows while the depths writhe in pain. I'm glad you enjoyed the soup. Why don't you say thank you?"

"Thank you?" Kai offers.

"Not to us." That's not exactly a smile now. He churns the ladle in the tureen, and I don't know what I'm dreading but dread rises, and turns to horror as I see what he's dug out and understand how far gone we are.

The world slides sideways.

It's a skull. A human skull.

Boiled down, although scraps of flesh and skin adhere to it, sauce sloshing out of its eye sockets, a nice, rich soup of bone and flesh and offal. Teresa wastes nothing.

"Say thank you to my son," Jonah says.

CHAPTER THIRTY-FOUR
BUTTERFLIES

PEOPLE ARE YELLING AND RETCHING. LARISSA GULPS BACK VOMIT; KIERA'S staring at her cup like she doesn't get how it connects to the situation. My belly cramps, a wave of repulsion as I understand what it contains.

It's the aftermath of a blast, everything breaking apart. We're in a place nobody should ever find their way to.

The image comes to me: Teresa in the kitchen, singing as she butchered her son's corpse and boiled his bones for stock. No wonder she looks like that. You don't recover from that. You don't get to be human again.

Did Jonah make her do it? Did she choose to, giving the last shreds of herself in desperate sacrifice? Or was she holding on to the only instinct she had left, that when meat comes to her kitchen, she cooks?

I can *taste* him I can fucking *taste* him—

Jonah said when Sage was little, he taught himself to care for insects to keep Myri happy. And now I taste the residue of him on my tongue—

"You feel this? This horror?" Jonah's words rise over the gags and sobs.

"This *revulsion?* That! That is Sage's final gift! That is what we shielded ourselves from when it was *what we needed!*"

Quiet settles.

"This was my mistake." Jonah's voice is soft, but we hear it.

Teresa stands, emptily curious. Myri sits among flowers, just empty.

"I let us stay human. Human bonds, human taboos. We wove our cocoons but did not break down. Of course we failed to release our god. We were human. Weak.

"To call it back, we must transcend that. Cross every line. Strip our bounds, our boundaries, our bonds. Feel him inside you: This is how it begins. From his death, we build strength. Grow our new forms as pure, devoted servants of the Unseen."

Kiera's muttering, "Oh god," and Larissa's clutching her belly and moaning a chant. I want to comfort them, but I can't, because our human bonds are crumbling, like he says. How can I kiss Kiera with lips smeared with the grease of her friend? How can I touch Larissa with the hands that lifted that cup to my mouth?

My mind keeps sealing over to protect me, but my body reminds me. A scrap of meat between my teeth, a busy rumble from my stomach. Heat's rising around my ears, cold at the back of my neck, my flesh knowing something's ruptured and I don't come back from here.

Is this what the insect feels in its cocoon, as dissolution begins?

Music blasts, jolting us. Just a few bars, to throw everything off. My head's not spinning, the world is.

"You did love your feasts and parties." Jonah tuts affectionately. "Turning our holy work into games. Well, here is a last party, my son's burial and wake. Eat up, and dance him into energy! Drink up, and begin the work of alchemy that will return our hidden one to us!"

Music bursts out again, burying the gulps and tears and rapid heartbeats.

We do as we're told.

We play pretend. A mockery of our parties, but we move our bodies, feet on the sand, hands to the stars, reality smearing.

A chant overlays the music, pulsing, familiar, now underlying everything, my new heartbeat: *Adore, Unseen, surrender.* The rhythm is a rope, I cling to it for sanity, and it wraps around me and pulls me deeper, and I chant it and I chant it as it drags me down.

More mugs filled with Sage are handed around. Pietro shoves a cup into my hands, and I think, *I am transforming, coming apart so I can grow into something; isn't that what I wanted?* I choke it down, I am so hungry. Sage washes down my gullet and it tastes good and that makes everything numb so I just dance.

Larissa finds me and her cheeks are wet and she presses her mouth against mine, hungry, and I taste Sage in her mouth. This is how we change. Isn't it? By diving this deep into what's unspeakable?

"Adore! Unseen! Surrender! Adore! Unseen! Surrender!"

She pours soup into my mouth, I swallow greedily, a miracle drug to take us to our paradise.

I can't see Kiera but I see faces, and they don't look right because we are in a cocoon and we are disintegrating, liquefying, and when we're done, we won't be human anymore.

Time skips and twists. Moans and shrieks echo. I'm alone. I'm lying under a pine tree staring up at clouds that hint at a deep blue dawn. My jumper's riding up. I'm staring in fascination at my own paunch.

Something's moving within me, sliding from skull to toes, spiky and silky all at once.

Adore, Unseen, surrender. The chant echoes through the hollows of my mind where there used to be clear thoughts. If I listen, it'll drown out what we did.

I swallowed a feeling, that fierce feeling I am not allowed because I'm too weak to bear it and it just means shame. Then I drank the remains of a boy; what alchemy happens when those things meet inside? It's like it's Sage that's so angry, prowling around inside my skin, yearning to kick and tear.

"Aoife?"

I blink. Kiera's approaching through the half-light.

She kneels; her voice breaks. "We have to go."

I sit up, and everything swirls.

"We can't," I say. "We're in a cocoon. We're melting." I don't know if it was what I meant to say; what I meant is that I want this to happen; it has to happen.

She pinches my cheek. "Look at me."

I look at her. Although it's the chilliest part of the night, she's wearing just a vest, she's discarded her fluffy white jumper somewhere. I like that jumper. I like burying my face between her shoulder blades when she's wearing it, getting fluff in my nose and making her squeal with surprise. I should tell her that seeing her in that jumper makes me happy. That seeing her makes me happy. I keep the thoughts that are light, let the chant drown the rest. Make it simple. Kiera makes me happy.

Then I think maybe she's going to be cold without her jumper. I clumsily wrap around her. "Hey, I can keep you warm."

"Aoife. I know you're not very together right now, but trust me, okay? Come on."

We're both kneeling, my arms around her shoulders. "Where?"

Her jaw tightens. "Jonah's snapped. He lost his kids and his god; he's broken and he's on a power trip and he isn't going to stop. You can't *just trust* someone who's out for revenge against his own followers. It's going to get worse—" She inhales. "—and we have to save the ones we can, and we will, but right now we're in the most danger, and we need to run."

I cling to the chant, and it pulls me down and pulls me down. Kiera's far away again.

"He's talking about *stripping* our *humanity*," she says. "He made us eat fucking *human flesh*. You see where this ends?"

I try to see. The chant pulls the thoughts down, and I settle somewhere safe, thinking how pretty her eyes are right now.

"Okay." She closes her eyes. "Let's try another way." She speaks slowly. "We're going for a walk. In the hills. You and me. Okay?"

Kiera. She's trying so hard. I plant a messy kiss on her lips; she shudders and pulls back. I'd forgotten. I choose to forget again, let the chant bury the memory.

"All right. Up." She climbs to her feet and helps me stagger to mine. "Quick."

My feet root into the ground. Stubbornness swells.

Her tone is getting desperate; she looks over her shoulder, toward the firelight, the dancing and yelling bodies. "Please, let's go?"

"I don't want to go." I'm talking to Kiera, but I'm talking to Craig and remembering that hot room where he stroked my hair and said my friends were dead. Dread hits me that this place will be gone when we get back. That if I'm not here for this strange spiral, my home will be lost.

"I'm home. We'll make it better. We'll be butterflies."

She pulls at my arm, but I stay rooted. Look at me! I'm a pine tree, I'm all those vines and flowers, dug into this soil. You can't pull me up.

"Aoife." She grips my hand. "Please. Just follow me."

I force my mind to quiet the chant, let the rope stop pulling me into the depths. I owe it to her, not to drown in this for just a moment. To be as lucid as I can as I speak.

"Kiera," I say quietly. "There's nowhere else. There's only here. I go where they all go. I'm not just high and stupid. I chose this."

She stops tugging. Something shuts down. A settling of her eyes, her lips.

"All right." Her voice is flat, and so tired. She leans against my shoulder, and her arm's all goose pimples; she must be so cold. "All right, Aoife. I'll stay here with you."

I feel her relax, something going out of her.

I try to rub her arms warm, and she goes still. Pietro and Frida are there. Pietro's arms are folded, face set; he looks like a mini-Oscar. Frida's drawn the circles sigil all over her arms and face; bits of bone are woven into her plaits.

"Kiera and Aoife, up a tree," Frida trills. "Doing what they shouldn't be! Come on, lovebirds, Jonah wants us on the beach!"

Pietro flinches at nothing. "Kiera, aren't you cold?"

Kiera laughs wildly. "Cold is good! Pain is good! We're changing, right? Yes! Not weak anymore!" Her voice hitches. "Let's go to the beach and be butterflies, Aoife?"

I smile and say, "Butterflies," and snuggle in to keep her warm as we follow them toward the crowd.

CHAPTER THIRTY-FIVE
SOME ITEMS, IN A BOX

THE CROWD. LARVAE SQUIRMING UNDER DAWN-BRUISED CLOUDS. THE world's the purple of a ripe fig, and we crawl through it like wasps, drunk on sweetness, dissolving, and when it's done, I won't feel this dizzy disconnection, this howling loss.

We're formless, eyes and hair and lips and limbs vague shadows, one body, one being, and that being absorbs me and Kiera. Breaths, music, giddiness, fingers in my hair, sticky bodies; it feels good to be a cell in this melting form. Kiera's holding my hand hard and it hurts, but she said pain was good.

Is that rhythm music, or my heart? Colors and darkness spike in my vision—that's the beat—our feet stamping to a rhythm. *Adore, Unseen, surrender*, rendered into a wordless pulse, pulling us down still further.

"Do you feel it?" Jonah, close, far away, distance dilates. "Feel him in your veins!"

Everyone roars.

I roar. Kiera roars, face screwed up like she's screaming from somewhere deep she can't get out of.

"His goodness, courage, anger, pain! Does it fuel you?"

A chant breaks out, and it might be "Sage" or "saved" and I join in
and it's so easy to ride this, to forget what that word might mean.

"Be his hands!" Jonah cries. "Be new homes for his spirit! He died
afraid in the dark! Be the instruments of his revenge!"

This roar is the loudest yet. Sage, yes, Sage is part of me now, and I
feel anger and pain and it must be his. Curled and curdled in my core, a
lifetime of rage, and it can't be mine, because I was never angry, I'm Aoife
and I smile and trust the universe, and it brings me gifts. It's Sage screaming rage from my throat, Sage punching the air with my fist, yearning to
pound the world to dust.

"You have walked far into the dark. You must walk a little further. The
Unseen is waiting for us to show that we are ready."

I'm ready. We're ready.

The music stops; when did the music come on? But our stamping
doesn't stop, we're shouting, "Sage," heads swimming and bodies stag-
gering and blood-dark clouds spinning. Sage courses through us as energy,
the fierce and furious joy of oneness.

My mind isn't clear, but our mind is. We will tear through metal, galaxies, flesh, to become what we have to, to reclaim our lost god. We will
be worthy. We will do anything.

That's when they bring Giulia out.

It's quiet as she arrives.

Oscar pulls her by the rope, its electric blue vivid; the house lights have been turned up bright, floodlights strung up, bleaching everything, flickering and stuttering. Pietro marches her by the shoulders. Her head's bowed, her dress filthy.

She's fragile. A dry leaf, a chrysalis, a vase, something that would be satisfying to smash.

Reality surges, then falls back. I'm Aoife, watching them lead my friend into the glare of the crowd's rage, and I'm part of this breathless, furious body, and the rage is mine.

The speaker crackles. "We thought maybe we could even stop the ritual altogether . . . so I . . . did it. Summoned the blight." A confession. I heard that before.

Murmurs spread, a half-understanding through blurred senses, stirring the energy. Someone yells, "Fucking traitor!" I don't know who, maybe it was me.

Giulia's tied to the tree. That must be uncomfortable, poor Giulia. Her eyes are closed; how dare she not look at us? We're her friends. We're her friends, she betrayed us, she *took* our *god* from *us*.

Fury pounds. Nobody moves.

"Maybe *we* could stop it," Jonah mimics Giulia's shaky voice. "Who's *we*, Giulia?" He looks to the crowd. "Rot! Spreads! Anyone want to tell us who *else* took part in this desecration? Or will you stand there with your bellies sucking up nutrients from my son's body, taking his gift, and lie to us?"

Eyes settle on me. I'd forgotten I was separate. I'm Aoife. Aoife, who came here with Giulia, brought a stranger to the ritual, then ran.

Those are snarls on those faces that smiled at me before; fists from the hands that stroked me and marked my body as theirs and theirs as mine.

The crowd, the body, moves. Muscles contracting. Moving me and Larissa and Kiera. Disgorging us under Jonah's eyes.

A little flash of clarity wonders why. Surely he knows that it was Sage who helped her? But we broke his trust, didn't we? Giulia was a thread that snapped; he must be eager to find other weak ones, unweave them from this fabric. And maybe I didn't prove myself enough. Maybe I'm a weak thread, in need of snipping out.

Clarity slips away again, and the thought goes with it. "She wouldn't." Larissa's syllables trip over each other. "Loves it like we do!" Are those her arms? They're warm, we're one, they won't hurt me, I am them.

A hand's gripping mine hard, and I have to look who it is, and when I do my lips break into an awkward smile despite everything. Because that's what I do when I see Kiera.

Jaw and lips moving, she's always struggling, Kiera, seeking a way. She looks like a child when a monster looms, the second before the scream.

But she doesn't scream. Her face smooths, she breathes deep, and she's looking at me and the light's moving in her eyes, all swimmy. She whispers, "Fuck this." A quick shrug. "Live, okay?"

I want to reply, but my tongue is somewhere else.

She drops my hand and turns, laughing, a laugh that's high-pitched and unhinged and bitter. "Everyone, look at me! I saved the world!"

The murmuring falls quiet. I don't know why I'm frozen.

"Giulia said we don't want to do this"—Kiera's words fragment, maybe laughter, maybe something else—"and I said, oh god, I'll help you, I said, let's summon the blight. I thought, clever, right? Rot saves the world!

"Because we didn't ask the world, did we? I said to Giulia, we didn't ask some guy in an office in Beijing or some lady in a field in Argentina, 'Hey, want us to wake a god that might wreck our reality?' We didn't have a right! There's a world out there; we didn't get to choose this for them! So I showed her how to summon it, right there into the cave." She looks at Jonah, and she's stopped laughing. "So fucking take it out on me, okay?"

We step away from Kiera. She was part of this body and fabric and now she isn't and she chose that and it hurts and it hurts, cutting off this limb, ripping out this thread.

What's unfurling in my chest, a hot pain I know well, the flare of rejection? Everything's jumbled. The sky's pretty. I want to snap something.

Kiera's looking around in panic. "It would have been my fault, I found the ritual, I could have killed the world," and Oscar and Pietro are pulling her away. She starts making this noise. It's weird. I don't like it.

Reality cracks, a final sundering. Oscar's binding her up to the tree, that's Jonah there, they're good, they know why Kiera needs to be tied to a tree. It must be okay, Kiera isn't fighting, just making that noise that might be laughing. Silly Kiera!

Jonah's hand is on her neck; that must hurt. He's saying, "Nobody else?" and Kiera's saying, "Nobody" in this strangled voice. He drops her, and she starts laughing again and twitching, maybe the tree is uncomfy.

"Them," Jonah says softly, but we hear him; we're quiet, something thrumming. "They killed my children. They took our god."

My breathing's slow, intense. Ripples move through us, one body again, violence rising. I know that those forms up there are Kiera and Giulia, and I am Aoife, and I love them. I know it, but the me that knows it is somewhere else, kicking against shadows.

"But hope is not gone. We can call our god back. If we dare to be more and less than human and walk into the dark together. Can we do that?"

I don't know what I'm agreeing to, but the roaring feels good, united fury, all of us wrapped up in it, we are a hurricane.

Frida has a box. Frida puts the box on the table. There are all sorts of things in the box. Bottles, knives, hammers, hacksaws. Some of the things glint. Some don't.

Giulia's eyes are squeezed shut. Kiera's quiet. I wish she was still laughing.

"Kill them," Jonah says.

CHAPTER THIRTY-SIX

STATIC

OUR BODY GOES STILL.

Kill them?

We look around, faces blurred in the hazy dawn. Painted with symbols and spirals, smeared makeup and sweat, marks of tears, desperate hope, despair. We hesitate.

This might be real.

"Nobody is to deliberately strike a final killing blow," Jonah says. "Not for cruelty or mercy. These deaths do not belong to you. They belong to Sage, and to the Unseen!"

He pauses like we'd cheer at that, but we're quiet. Zina's hands are on her mouth, and João's staring at his fists, and Maisie's leaning on Ana's shoulder, and Larissa's looking side to side, and I don't want to—

"Do it. For the Unseen!"

We stand, one body, one being, frozen and blinking.

That's disgust on Jonah's face. Shame burns, even though reality's wobbling again and I can only half-understand what he's disgusted at.

"Whining, self-indulgent children," he says. "No wonder our god abandoned us."

I'm so sorry, Jonah.

Myri sits on the house steps, staring blankly, twitching occasionally into a mutated, decomposing form, muttering things I can't hear over the roaring of the crowd, the roaring of my ears. Jonah gestures to her. "Take a good look. This is what your weakness has done. This is where your weakness will bring you."

He turns to Teresa beside him. Hands folded, she's still singing. She was in a cocoon, wasn't she? Behind a locked door, singing as she melted down. She's hatched now. Become what she's meant to be. Detached, at peace.

Jonah speaks softly. She nods, expression unchanged, and walks to the box on the table. A kitchen knife. Of course. Teresa the cook. She's going to chop salad, gut a fish. Everything's normal. The buzzing in my ears is back.

Teresa approaches Giulia. Giulia's eyes are still closed, and she's whispering something. Teresa kisses Giulia's forehead. Teresa strokes Giulia's cheek. I think it's a lullaby Teresa's singing, off-key, the only sound beside the waves and dawn birdsong. She does this with the goats and chickens.

Giulia raises her head, dares us to look her in the eye.

Adore, Unseen, surrender.

Still singing, Teresa drives the knife into Giulia's belly and slices neatly downward.

Giulia gasps. Something splinters. There's black on her dress.

Kiera screams, a hollow, howling shriek into the quiet. Her eyes are closed and she's screaming long and loud and the scream keeps going until it fragments because Oscar, with the same blank-faced calm, swings a hammer into her face.

Like some barrier's snapped, permission granted, the crowd surges.

The world dissolves into static.

Buzzing. Everything in flickers. A TV tuned wrong, picking up bits of expanding universe.

There are things I can't stand. I don't know what they are.

There's a moment when Kiera isn't screaming but looking at me, half-focused, face the wrong shapes. Voices chant my name. I always feel good when Kiera's there. She tries to choke out my name, too. Something in me likes being the last thing she will say.

I don't see the rest.

Buzz, buzz.

Larissa's sobbing, broken wine bottle in her hand.

Melting bits of light.

Adore, Unseen, surrender. Tearing as though we can rip open a door and our god will come through.

Frida has a hacksaw. She's laughing wildly.

Buzz, flicker, there and not there.

I'm laying something silky and warm on the grass as everyone howls.

I don't know what my hands do. They're everyone's. Everyone's are mine. Every blow and kick are mine. One being, frenzied, hungry.

Pain and terror and disorientation and despair sit inside my skin, alien enough to feel rich and good, like a shot of sweet wine.

We keep going long after they stop making any sound at all.

And it's funny: They don't look like people now, and we don't feel like people, either.

And we are standing winded and blood-soaked, and our god does not return.

CHAPTER THIRTY-SEVEN

DRIFTING

There is no way to exist after that.

—⊖—

I lie on the sand. Our body lies on the sand. My hands are black and sticky. We mumble chants, pressing our faces into each other's bloodied shirts, crying, kissing.

Stupor. But not sleep. Fragments of dozing end with sudden, stunned wakings. With each, it gets more real. Waves crashing, the blow more brutal every time.

—⊖—

I lie on Larissa's chest, Zina's head on my belly, my arm around a Dutch guy I've barely spoken to. Listen to our breaths. We're bonded, even more than we were.

I listen to Larissa's heartbeat, and I try not to think about what's fueling those beats, and I drift.

Somehow, I still exist.

I yawn. Everything's soft. My mind won't hold anything. Larissa mumbles; I feel this protective rush toward her body, the skin and muscle of her, like something might take them away and there wouldn't be a Larissa. I don't understand.

Two objects hang from the trees, reddened and hollowed.

On the grass below them, a sigil. A closed circle inside an open circle, one bisecting line. Sketched in bone and blood and limb, clumps of brown hair, loops of gut and tendon.

I sit cross-legged and stare. It's quiet here.

Behind my hut, I shower remnants of my friends off my skin. Usually, the solar panel can scrape up warm water on a chilly morning, but today the shower runs cold and spits. There's something black under my nails I can't get off.

I can't stand it. I can't stand anything.

Teresa was happy. At peace. I could be like that. I'll slide into it. The last of Aoife will dissolve, and something else can grow. This is how we transform. I'll be a butterfly.

There's chores. Food to be harvested, goats to be fed, laundry to be done. We've been slacking. So much to do!

I keep expecting to see Kiera. She'll be around, nose in a book, chewing on a peach and panicking at her sticky fingers. I slow outside Giulia's hut to say hi. Pietro's sweeping when there's no dust, whistling. I hurry on.

We don't avoid each other's eyes when we meet. We look and see our reflections. We don't look like ourselves there.

There are things we can't say, aren't there? I'm getting better at not even thinking them. There are flashes where I exist, but there are blissful moments too where I'm an automaton.

So when I join Kai gathering fruit, he doesn't say, *He's going to kill us all.* And I don't say, *Probably.* And he doesn't say, *Who do you think is next?*

When I pass Aksel on the path he doesn't say, *Frida scared me last night,* and I don't say, *You scared me,* and he doesn't say, *I scared myself.*

When I find Maisie in the kitchen she doesn't say, *I want to leave but there's nowhere to go,* and I don't say, *Even if there was, I couldn't.*

When I pass Zina and Darya and João smoking on the beach, I don't say, *I miss them already*, and they don't say, *We do too.*

I practice moving my mouth so it looks like I can smile. I hold it like that. It's not too hard.

The kitchen's clean. Anything of Sage that didn't make it into the soup has gone into the compost. I'm so hungry, but the thought of eating makes me nauseous.

Teresa's gathering herbs. I watch her fill her basket. I should learn her songs. I watch leaves and berries nod in the breeze.

Teresa waves cheerfully, eyes blank.

I watch until her poison garden is harvested down to naked stalks.

Kiera and Giulia are still there. So is the flesh sigil, gathering flies.

When I see that, I feel nothing. It goes wrong when I think of how Kiera held my gaze when she laughed and how Giulia closed her eyes to savor wine and how Sage's boots were always untied and that time Myri told me she loved cartoons because she didn't have to think about anything serious. That's when the world screams into fragments.

I'll carve a space where those thoughts can't rise. It will be nice and quiet.

So when I find Larissa outside her hut washing blood off her sweater, I don't say, *What have we done*, and she doesn't say, *We loved them and we killed them.*

I tease knots and gore out of her hair; she touches my wrist. I remember how she touched Giulia's in the restaurant, more love in that gesture than I'd ever known. The same hand drove a broken bottle into Giulia's face.

An observation drifts across my awareness like a scrap of cloud: If he tells me to kill Larissa, I'll do it. If he tells her to kill me, she will.

So when she kisses me, I understand that I'm going to die here.

We followed the Unseen when it left, chased it into the depths of its nightmare. We'll churn inside it for as long as we survive.

Jonah gathers a little group in the living room. The solarium's beautiful, and we don't get beauty now. Teacups steam, scenting the room with herbs, fresh biscuits piled beside them. We don't touch them, even though I'm so hungry it hurts.

Jonah claps his hands and says, "Well, look at this!"

Pietro's still whistling. Oscar keeps changing the music every few bars, then skipping back. Teresa's shiny. Larissa washed the blood out of her sweater, but it's still smearing her arms and neck.

"We showed our courage last night." Jonah's pacing, a spring in his step. "Our *devotion*. We are on the right path. Can you feel the transformation beginning? Try to find the threads of the weak thing you were. They're burning away. Can you feel what will grow in their place? Something pure. Something worthy. Something the Unseen will return for."

Frida gives the biggest, wildest smile and grabs a biscuit, taking an enthusiastic bite. Everything's discordant. Those are finger bones in her plaits.

Jonah shakes his head. "But we have so, so much more to do."

Larissa's hand clutches mine. Jonah gives us a sharp glance, and she drops it. It doesn't matter. We don't deserve comfort, and these soiled bodies have nothing to give.

The music skips, a blast of guitar followed by cheerful bubblegum pop. Oscar likes that; he lets it keep jangling into the broken quiet.

"I need your help." Jonah's twinkle is brighter, manic. "We must ensure that we are all on this path together. I need you to watch and tell me what you see and hear, and if what you see and hear threatens our work, I need you to stop it."

I am working at smiling. Jonah trusts me again. Will I enjoy what I do now? Maybe I will. It will help me become a butterfly. I imagine walking back to the beach, finding Zina slacking and smoking and mourning. I imagine whispering in her ear about being pure, and saving her. I imagine how tidily a knife would slip between her ribs. Is that something I like?

"Not everybody will survive these days of purification. Show me your strength, and perhaps you will."

Oscar's face is slack. He brings his fist down on the stereo, again and again, smashing the casing and wrenching out wires. The music fizzes and dies. Oscar's face stays slack.

"Very good," Jonah says. Oscar beams, childlike.

Teresa covers her face, for no obvious reason.

Jonah doesn't bother to dismiss us. He walks out humming, jaunty, hands shaking.

Frida's still eating the biscuits, giggling. The teas are growing cold. We sit in silence, quietly pupating, coming apart.

Larissa leaves. I sit, contemplating the broken pieces of the stereo. I imagine being broken like that. Stripped for parts. I'd be of use, wouldn't I? It would be a kind of love.

I remember that Larissa went outside so I say, "Well, good luck!" and follow her out.

Larissa's on the front steps staring at nothing. "I'm cold."

The sea's gray. Quicksilver with reflected cloud.

She speaks dully. "I don't like thinking about them in the cold."

If I look inland, I'll see them. I don't. It doesn't matter if I see them.

Larissa's voice tilts, queasy. "I want to take Giulia a blanket."

"Larissa." Unthinkable. Sheer, naked sacrilege.

"I'm going to take Giulia a blanket." She heads toward the grove, purpose in her step.

I follow. I have a job to do.

"She liked the one from Turkey. I find it scratchy. We had arguments when she was cozy and I was itching and this is not the fucking Unseen, it would not want us to do this." Her eyes are wide; she needs me to agree. "When I kissed her, it was an offering. When she made me laugh, that was holy. It doesn't want this."

My mind won't make full thoughts. That would pitch me over an edge.

"She took the Unseen from us." My voice is unsteady.

"I know the Unseen." Larissa's jaw's set. "It's not *keeping everyone in line*, it's not *purifying*. Fuck that. It loved her."

My mind's full of precipices. I do not have a knife. Larissa's stronger than me. If I go to Jonah, will he be pleased? I am meant to be transforming, we are meant to be transforming, and she is not, she is going to ruin *everything*.

We're inside her hut, and she's scrabbling in piles of multicolored clothing, digging out a woven blanket, clutching it like a toy.

"He'll kill you." That's not the right thing to say. I shouldn't be warning her. I should be stopping her. "He'll have us kill you."

She shrugs. "We died last night." Her face of beautiful secrets is pale and crumpled now, but something flashes. "He can do what he likes. I'll find her in the Unseen."

I look around. She grows plants in wine bottles. They're hard and heavy and it would be neat, wouldn't it? It would be tidy.

She reads me. Her face says, *Go on, then.*

That peaceful, agonized certainty. A thought muscles in before I can decide if it's safe: There might have been a world where I'd had enough time with Kiera to feel that. To defy everything for one gesture that she'd never know about.

She stayed for me—

There's a bottle in my hand. I don't know why.

I say, "Kiera took her jumper off."

And the pieces fall together. I wish they hadn't. Cups of soup surreptitiously poured away; maybe they stained her sleeve, left a mark she'd rushed to hide. She was the only one clear-headed as we spiraled down, and she knew exactly what was happening as we—

Larissa says, "*Shhh,*" although I don't know what sound I was making.

I'm tumbling into the abysses inside me.

I drop the bottle. We watch the water pool on the carpets, and neither of us do anything. I follow her out.

I remember last night only in fuzzy flashes, but in the clear evening light, it doesn't take me long to find Kiera's jumper, balled up and shoved into a bush.

My last memories of her are mangled; so's her body; there wasn't anything to hold until this, this stupid jumper, and now I'm falling and Kiera's not here and Kiera's not here.

This body helped kill her. It doesn't deserve tears. It doesn't know how to mourn.

Larissa lets me stand, my face buried in the fibers of the jumper. It smells of herby, meaty soup. Of soil and pine. Of Kiera.

"If all moments exist at once eternally," Larissa says softly, "if time's just something we make up to make it make sense, then those times we were with them are all still there somewhere. But that also means what we did to them is still there, it's forever, they're—"

I say, "*Shhh.*" She blinks like she doesn't know what she said.

She takes my hand. We walk to the trees by the farmhouse.

CHAPTER THIRTY-EIGHT

OFFERINGS

IT'S LATE AFTERNOON; THE SUN'S WATERY THROUGH THE CLOUDS, BUT THE bodies have been there since dawn. Flies drone. The smell of meat, slightly off. Iron and rot on the air.

I can't look this time. I look. Pieces. Disassembled.

Is that all a person is? Where's the way Giulia screwed up her nose, or how Kiera tapped her foot when she concentrated?

We're past the edges. There's no right thing to feel. Larissa's breathing's unsteady. But she rolls up the blanket, grays and browns and vivid reds, and maybe that's her and Giulia's colors, subtle and earthy against blazing and brilliant. She kneels, and places it beside the butchered remains of the girl she loved.

She doesn't speak. There's nothing she can say.

My neck prickles: I look back. Darya, João, and Zina are standing on the beach, staring. Ana's watching from the path. Kai's on the steps, head turned to us. My stomach churns. Who else is looking, hidden?

They will kill us tonight.

Everything buzzes, my vision blurry.

My head's a jumble, and I can't find my way. All instinct. I step forward too, Kiera isn't there, all I can do is stand in front of a mess of meat and mumble, "I should have gone with you," and lay down the jumper.

There's no release, I'm still falling, unraveling, pupating.

Larissa's eyes are downcast. She doesn't walk away. I don't, either. We stand with Giulia and Kiera and wait for the consequences.

Footsteps: Ana's approaching. I brace myself. She's strong, Ana. A lot of what she did last night she did with her bare hands.

She places down two roses from a nearby bush. She steps back and stands with us.

I don't know what this feeling is.

Kai appears, and places his ridiculous hat beside the roses, along with an old fantasy novel he lugs around. "It's really silly; you'll hate it," he mutters, his grin in tatters.

Darya and Zina follow. Darya unties friendship bracelets from her wrist, and Zina digs out a cigarette for Giulia and tears pages out of her favorite poetry book for Kiera. They stand beside us, too.

And then there are others, people who see what's happening and join. Maisie brings Giulia's sketchbook, the one I stole once, and one of Kiera's notebooks. João returns with fresh honeycomb. Aksel pulls out figurines he'd been whittling.

I recognize this. The rituals we invent on the fly, that bond us and shape our world. They're what we know. They're what we have to give.

Even Teresa, dazed, lays down bread and fruit. I don't know if she understands what she's joining. She takes my hand as we wait.

I take off my cardigan—*Elise's* cardigan, woolen, embroidered with dandelions. She'd have given a gift, too, right? I lay it beside Giulia. Strange to feel awkward here, now.

With each gift, something rolls through me, waves of emotion, like a new understanding. Teresa's confusion, Aksel's guilt, Darya's fury, so many textures. What happened to bond us so deeply that I feel what they feel?

And it doesn't heal us, and it won't save us and we don't deserve to be saved and we will pay a heavy price for this. But.

There are dozens of us, holding hands, standing quiet together, when Jonah's shadow appears in the farmhouse doorway.

My heart seizes. He steps out into the light. Those eyes dissolve me every time. I want to yell, "I wasn't part of this," fall at his feet. I want to shove a knife through Larissa's windpipe and be forgiven.

But nobody moves. He stares down at us, and we stare up at him. It isn't defiance: There isn't any defying him, and he's working so hard to return us to our paradise. It's a resonating awareness: We have to do this, and we will take what happens next.

Nobody says, *You told us yourself, even when the grub reforms into the butterfly, something remains of what it was before.*

Flat eyes, impassive lips. It's like watching a coin spinning. Heads or tails decides your life.

I'm deeply aware of my blood and flesh. I wasn't afraid of being next until this moment, but that guarded gaze makes promises about the thud and slice of improvised weapons, the deconstruction of my body. I remember how long Kiera kept screaming. Or will it be something else? What other ways of melting away our minds can he invent?

I'm going back to the Unseen, one way or another.

Something cracks on that face. Fury or despair leaks out, the hard lips fracturing apart. It's about to begin.

A movement in our body. Teresa steps forward, hand outstretched.

Anything might happen in that moment. But it's interrupted; Pietro bursts from the tree line, winded, red-faced.

"Boat," he gasps. "There's a boat coming."

CHAPTER THIRTY-NINE

OUTSIDERS

WHATEVER WAS HOVERING BETWEEN US CRASHES AND SPLINTERS.

Pietro catches his breath. "Heading toward us. Fifteen minutes away?"

"Fishing boat?" Jonah asks.

Pietro shakes his head. "Didn't look like one."

We exchange panicked glances. We're isolated with horrors—Jonah, unknown forces, ourselves—but the idea of outsiders discovering what we've done is worse, unspeakable. We turn to Jonah, fear or defiance evaporating.

"Aksel, Zina, cover—" He waves at Giulia and Kiera. "—that. The rest of you, gather *everyone, wash off the blood*, get weapons. Keep them concealed, or *yourself* concealed. Be ready."

A shared thrill; eyes lock together, hands twitch, part of us still ravenous for violence. A hopeful thrill; the beautiful, daring feeling of fighting for our home could wash the blood away. A fragile thrill; the kind that comes before disaster.

"Aoife." Even now, I flush with delight at Jonah's attention. "Oscar's in the library with Myri. Fetch him. Stay with her." The attention moves away from me, spreads over the group like a net. "If any of you think about betraying our *family*, you'll *beg* for the mercy we showed Kiera and Giulia. Go."

Everyone's moving, a hive startled into activity, with no time to grasp whatever strange unity gripped us in that improvised ritual. I run into the farmhouse, take the steps two at a time. The heavy quiet's confusing against the adrenaline.

Stepping into the library is a stab. Kiera should be looking up from a book, eyes wide like my existence is a happy surprise. But instead, it's Oscar, at *her* desk, reading *her* books, like it wasn't him who—

It was all of us. But he struck the first blow on her, and I'm sure he hadn't drunk as much soup as us. Clear-headed, doing his duty.

My fingers clench, something hot writhing under the skin—

The feeling passes. I choke a quick explanation—boat, danger, outsiders—and Oscar leaps up and is gone without a word.

The quiet holds me in his wake, stifling. Danger's coming, and I'm here alone, locked out of the beautiful fight. Jonah chose me for that.

Myri's by the window, mouth open, eyes glazed. The abysses in me yawn wider. I approach her, not daring to hope that she'll grin and say, "Got you," reveal another layer of surprises.

Her pulse is slow. Her skin's rice-paper thin, like even her body's fading out; whatever was left must have rotted away now. Still, I lift water to her lips, and she swallows a little. Instinctive, a body working without a self.

How does every loss have a different flavor? Kiera's is a scream, Giulia's a roaring emptiness, Sage's a surge of disgust. Myri's is a dull, suffocating ache, tempered by the awful hope and fear that there might be something left somewhere.

I'll fight for that, if these outsiders try to take her. She's Myri.

I cast around for a weapon. The idea of hitting an invading stranger with a book is so ridiculous that I swallow an inappropriate giggle. Then I think of heavy objects, a hammer to a face and my vision becomes white flashes—

It would be nice to slip back into quiet, drift away from those flavors of pain.

Focus. They need you.

I grab scissors, grip them hard. I measure moments in breaths and heartbeats.

I used to be an innocent chasing something unknown. Now here I am. Ragged and broken, surrounded by the presence of the girl I maybe loved and helped kill, her blood under my fingernails, the nutrients of a dead boy in my veins, blade in my hand to defend an empty girl. Giddy with hunger, cruel with loss. Something, someone, made me monstrous.

The nightmares that once infused the ocean have flooded our home now, but we stood together, our ritual. I'll fight to the last scrap for that. I'll be a monster for that.

"I know you."

I jump. Myri is standing, even though her body is half-decayed, tendons visible through flesh frilled with strange fungi, speaking with a tongue black and putrefying. The flowers adorning her are blackened, crawling with flies. She gazes at me with empty sockets, clotted at the edges with threads of mold.

I am too far gone now to feel the full horror of it.

"I know you," she says again, and there's confusion in her voice. "One night. You were there. White shirt. You didn't talk to anyone. Wine—"

I can't move. Emptiness gazes at me. That's not Myri talking.

"What . . . what are you?" Sickness in me, and yet I grasp it because it's a better and purer sickness than what I've felt all day: This horror came from somewhere other than me. It's better.

"I'm starting to understand." The voice is gulping, slurring, suddenly rapid, as if trying to desperately get out a thought that will vanish as soon as it appeared. "Figs. The wasps, they crawl in, and their wings are torn away, and they die in the dark and dissolve. What if they say *no*? What if they won't metabolize, if something holds on, a little nugget refusing, what does that do to the fruit?" A smile on lips bubbling with ooze. A cocked head. "I helped you break the window, didn't I? I want to help."

"Where's Myri?" I grip the scissors. No fear left. All I can feel is this desperate hope that I'm about to see a way to save her.

The empty eye sockets widen. What were once gums are now a residue of black on gritted teeth. "I don't want to keep hurting her, but she keeps struggling. There's not space, there's not space for both—"

The thing that was Myri shivers, and the rot falls away, and the flowers bloom again, and she's still, green eyes unblinking. I take a step toward her—

Three knocks. My heartbeat spikes.

"Aoife?" Darya. I open the door only a crack, like she might morph into someone else. Her hands are raw, washed over and over.

"Myri's not going anywhere." A fierceness I didn't know I was capable of. She could be saved. She might be saved.

Darya shakes her head. "Jonah's asking for *you*."

I blink, shaken out of the strangeness of confronting the blight, back into the cruel cold light of whatever's coming.

"I'll look after Myri. Go."

She doesn't say, *It's going to get bad,* and I don't say, *I hope you make it.* She always intimidated me with her acrobat's muscles and strident laugh, but I clutch her hand and our eyes meet for a long moment before I run.

The quiet house echoes the slap of bare feet. Into the afternoon light, past the sheets hung up to hide the bodies and laid over the flesh sigil, and I see them.

The waitress with the maroon-dyed hair and cigarette. And two uniformed men, guns at their hips.

Panic spikes.

Police. The bodies. One glimpse, and the final thread's tugged out, and it's over.

We were unraveling, wrapped up in the dark; we weren't going to make it out, but there was still home. There was us, and discovering that we wouldn't dissolve so easily.

But now? If they find the corpses?

Maybe we surrender. Trials, our faces circulating online, documentaries and podcasts dissecting our lives, *how did sweet people go so wrong?* Prison. Myri in a hospital or home, fallen prophetess fed soup by nurses, or succumbing to the blight, my strange encounter leading to nothing, a body rotted away from within.

Or.

My fingers twitch around the scissors in my pocket. The guests would take some of us down, but we'd buy time to end this on our terms.

It's calm for now. Oscar's offering the guests biscuits, Frida's tossing her plaits and smiling, Larissa's chatting. People watch, trying to look unthreatening. But we're a few bedsheets away from final disaster. One gust of wind blowing the smell of rotting meat in the wrong direction, and we're over.

One of the officers steps aside. I see the fourth figure, and it makes sickening sense.

Craig's eyes meet mine.

I see the subtle shifts I've learned to read. Relief painted on, righteous anger hiding a more twisted rage. And underneath, where only I can see, a flicker of smugness.

Weird; even when I last saw him, there was love. Even as I walked away, he was my Craig, who kissed my neck and wrote me songs and sat with me on a suburban rooftop, spinning fantasies of world tours.

Now it's like a veil's torn away. There he is, laid bare.

It would be him. It fucking *would be*. Here to take the last, precious shreds of another thing I loved. Because that's what he does.

"That's her." He speaks over the woman from the café, who's elbowing one of the officers and saying something in the local language. Craig's not running toward me, not calling my name, because this isn't a rescue: This is revenge.

"What's going on?" I have to keep their attention. If they're there for *me*, it's down to me to stop them. Who am I to do that? I'm so horribly small.

The waitress looks suspicious, of me and for me, weighing me up. "Your boyfriend reported you kidnapped."

"He's not my boyfriend," I snap. When have I *snapped* before? I feel it inside me, fire, rot. I swallow it back. "I chose to come back here, and that's not his business."

One of the policemen grumbles something she doesn't translate because it's obvious: *Oh great, another lovers' row.* He's older, uniform straining like he rarely bothers with it, moustache unkempt.

The younger officer examines me. "Are you okay? You look sick."

God, I can't imagine. Pale, disheveled, unhinged. "A bit. Might be to do with *someone* dragging me around the island in the middle of the night."

I want to look at the others, but one wrong move could send everything spiraling. One glance and they'll wonder, am I afraid, am I hiding how badly I want rescue? So I glare at Craig. He keeps the smugness buried, but it shines out of his eyes. *Gotcha.*

The waitress crushes her cigarette in the sand. I twitch like she's driven it into my flesh. I've seen plenty of Farmstead people do that, but this feels different, like deliberate pollution. "Would you like to talk to someone alone?"

Don't go near the house. "If you want. I just want to go back to my nap."

I dare to glance at Jonah, a little "sorry for all the stress" smile, the slightest eye roll. Part of me is laughing, delirious. I'm not acting exactly, but I am, and I *am* good at it. But I'm tightrope-walking, and if I fall, everything falls.

"This is bullshit." Craig's smugness falters. "She's drugged, *look* at her. You're not going to *search* the place? They *killed* a guy."

That weird stirring in me strikes up again, but it doesn't feel like sickness. It's pleasure, rippling like music on strings.

I'm on the brink. This feeling I always denied is all I have left.

"You told them a lot of things, didn't you?" I look Craig in the eye. "You'll tell them anything if it means you get to drag me home, won't you? Because when I'm not paying your bills and making your bed, you realize you can't look after yourself?" Even teetering above disaster, it feels good to say this. Something pounds in me, louder and louder. "Or because when I'm not around to tell you you're special, you realize you're not?"

Craig only snaps for a second. But in that second, he steps forward, fist raised, and that's what everybody sees.

The older policeman puts a hand on Craig's arm, sharing a look with Jonah, before chuckling something to the waitress.

Teresa translates, fixing a crooked smile on Craig. Her voice is dry, clarity born from desperation; you'd never guess the broken thing she'd been these past hours. "He says they're not a free service for getting your ex back."

The tension snaps. The waitress and the young policeman laugh, and Jonah and Frida laugh too. I shape my smile carefully to match theirs.

"I think it's okay," the young policeman says. "If you come back to the village soon so we can see you're safe?"

Hope gleams. They don't want trouble; Oscar's money, Teresa's relatives. And there's two officers, dozens of us. They don't *want* to find anything. "Of course. If you make sure he"—I jerk my head at Craig, smile apologetically—"leaves me alone."

The waitress's face is still suspicious, but there's warmth, too, solidarity. The young policeman eyes us all, earnest, but knows the deal. Out here, we're the law.

Only Craig doesn't accept it.

He gives me that look that comes before something I care about, a sketch, a gift, a friendship, is wrecked. He rips his arm away from the policeman and shouts, "Fuck this!"

And he's striding up the beach, crossing the short distance to the farmhouse, the hanging sheets.

"Not even going to *look*?" Craig shouts, as everyone moves to cut him off, hands moving to hidden weapons. "They told me the police here were lazy, but this is *something fucking else*."

"Stop!" I yell, and that's the wrong move, I've fucked it up, *again*, but it's too late now. "I'll come with you."

Craig's eyes find mine and flare with triumph. He's seen my gaze flash to the sheet. That's his goal now.

When I love something else, he breaks it.

I expect fists and knives, but Jonah's shaking his head. Show that we're hiding something, and it ends the same.

Jonah looks resigned. Jonah, *defeated*. There will be blood on the sand soon. There will be bodies and silence in the groves tonight.

The bubbling in my veins escalates, something stretching through my sinews. *No.*

Craig rips the sheets aside.

CHAPTER FORTY

UNFURL

THERE THEY ARE.

Two trees smeared with blood. Two bodies mangled beyond recognition. Half-concealed under a kicked-aside sheet, a sigil drawn in organ and bone. The words *what have we done* rendered in gore and gristle.

There's absolute stillness.

A calm comes over me. It's like my awareness is spread out. I see everything, feel everything.

The older policeman breathes a local swearword; the younger one's struggling not to throw up. The waitress swallows a moan of horror. My friends, family, exchange glances, seeing through strangers' eyes how monstrous we've become.

Craig, though? The shock hasn't hit him. Maybe there will be horror and disgust later, but right now his face sings with vindication.

He knows he shouldn't smile. He wouldn't get away with that.

Golden sunset through thin clouds, the trees stirring, not with the wind. Something thrumming in the soil, waves crashing with more urgency. Shock rippling out through the island, like it's seeing this for the first time, too.

Not shock. I know what's spilling and spreading. It's coming from me. It's rage.

I had something beautiful. I was quiet all those years, let the anger simmer deep, under layers of fragile daydreams. But then there *was* something better, something beautiful, and it was rotten and dangerous, and it unraveled brutally, but it was *mine* and I was happy. It is not theirs to take. It is ours, to destroy or to somehow save.

I never allowed myself rage. It wasn't for me. I didn't know how to hold it, just embarrassed myself with it. But now there's nothing else and a lifetime of fury rises.

It chimes with the stirring inside me.

The stirring of the thing that's lurked in my core, feeding on swallowed anger and pain, waiting to emerge.

The thing I misread as sickness, emotion, hunger. The thing that was perfectly disguised by the turmoil, hidden in plain sight.

It wakes up. It unfurls.

Once the universe was infinitesimally small. An expanse of fire and gas and light coiled up tiny. Think: We all contain universes, safe inside our skulls. Bend the rules and why couldn't you compress something vaster than galaxies and hide it inside a girl's body?

In the dark, as the cave collapsed, there was a door in me, and I chose to open it. I let it in. In the chaos, I snatched up something half-awakened and took it into myself for safekeeping.

Even now it's still newborn, hatching bloody out of my ribcage and belly and spreading its wings.

Sort of. Those aren't exactly wings, just like those aren't quite tendrils, eyes, or any of the things they see. It, I, it is me and I am it; it isn't something human senses can process. Their visions draw angels and monsters so that they can half-comprehend it. Me.

I'm as much the ground under their feet and the branches above them, the air in their lungs and blood, as I am the creature they perceive. I'm stretching, it's flexing, through everything. Spreading, finding its way through matter.

Reality flickers, struggling to adjust to something it wasn't made to contain.

All of this is me, all of this is mine. Mine to play with. To break.

Lives are bright, pulsing things, the panicked flutter of hearts, the dance of electricity inside cells, the glorious expanse of *minds*, wonderful constructions of energy. So many laid out in front of me. So much to toy with.

I am new and I am hungry. And I am so, so angry.

Angry enough to go slow.

Once there was a boy, and I was afraid of him; I thought that was what love was. But what is a boy, really? Muscle and organ and tattooed skin, neurons and nerves. What is a boy's body but a temporary arrangement of energy? Energy is neutral.

Energy is food.

I take the time to explore him first.

I swim through his veins, nestle in his lungs and guts, see the world through his eyes, feel the plunge of terror as the world reveals something he was never ready to see. Such a breakable, fascinating thing, a boy's body, a boy's mind.

Desire creeps through everything. This will be an intimate, indulgent death. The last beats of a heart I once slept with my ear to, seeking the sound of home.

I understand those jolts of energy, the rushes of emotions that weren't mine. The presence inside me was feeding, growing fat off grief and dread and desperation, growing greedy for more. I just take more this time. I take it all.

I whisper inside his skin, *Despite it all, I love you*, and I unravel him.

He howls as he comes apart, unspooling, and I draw him in with relish, waves of sound and light, dissolving him and delivering him into the air and soil, into my core. The stuff that made up Craig Bauer returns to the stuff that makes up the world, and I drink it, body and mind, an exquisite elixir.

So tenderly. *Shhh.* I bring him home.

His terror persists for a moment, then there is nothing. He pumps through me like a drug, and the groan of ecstasy rings through every-thing. I'm laughing and laughing beyond sound; look at this. Craig finally made me happy.

But this newborn thing is hungry, still.

More.

The burly policeman is on his knees, sobbing; he knows the legends. He whispers a name in an ancient tongue, and I say *yes*, and he surrenders his body. If Craig was hot and sharp and sour, this morsel is stolid and warm. Their tastes mingle, and everything shivers with pleasure.

The younger officer bolts for the boat, but poor thing, space expands and contracts at my will. His screams are gifts taken in gratefully; the rest of him goes with them.

I pulse, drunk on flesh and despair. The sea sighs, the wind moans.

I am half-seen, moving, there and not there, aglow. A human is a potent little thing, and inside me they are transmuted into power, shuddering and ready.

The waitress didn't bother to run, or believe, just shut down. I like her. Cynical and rude and tired, but not unkind. She brought me a lemonade when I was trapped. I desire her, too; I can make beautiful things of her matter, soak her up like sun on leaves and let her flower somewhere. But instead, I whisper Go, *tell them all to stay away*, and she runs.

I could keep going, gorge myself. But there's time. To savor the feast laid out before me, a feast shaped like a world.

For now, I am sated, and I know what to do with this thundering power.

I flow, find what I'm seeking, pour out the energy of three lives and get to work.

Bones knit together. Ruptured flesh solidifies, dried blood liquefies, feeding insects come apart and give back what they've taken. Skulls heal, eyes settle back into sockets, organs squirm into place and the fluids spilled from them rise from the hungry earth. Brains regrow their folds. Ribcages close back around lungs and hearts, and there, heartbeats, breath, life.

What is a girl's body but cells and atoms? So easy to rebuild.

And there are two girls under the trees now, a snub-nosed girl staring with huge eyes, a freckled girl screaming, stunned, whole, alive.

Not everything can be undone. Sage is dissipated through dozens of bodies, burned away as energy. Where or what Myri is now, I don't yet understand.

But I return two lives, the first of my gifts.

And now my own body is my focus, singing an unfamiliar pleasure as the thing that hid inside me slides back in, neat as a hand into a pocket, and flesh heals up around it.

Hello, I say to my new self, as it snuggles back into the hidden spaces in my depths, delivering the nutrients of its feast into my blood. I feel it, throbbing, electric.

I look up.

My whole family is on their knees, faces pressed into the sand, or arms flung to the sky, shining eyes, eyes that dare to stare at me, or don't dare, averted, dripping tears.

They're chanting, exultant, crying: *Adore, Unseen, surrender.*

My consciousness disintegrates, and I fall onto the sand.

PART THREE

SURRENDER

CHAPTER FORTY-ONE
VESSEL

I WAKE AMONG FLOWERS WITH THUNDER IN MY BONES AND LIGHTNING IN MY nerves.

I do not know who or what I am.

I lie on sand. The flowers are monstrously huge: roses and frangipani the size of my head, fist-sized jasmine. Hideous, vast hibiscus and lilies pile over my belly and breasts.

Things move among them. Insects, snakes, weirder things. I feel them as though the petals are my skin. My shiver is confused pleasure, gathering in the hot flesh at the core.

Stars spread like pollen. More than before.

All is thrumming potential, dreamlike and soporific. My smile is wider than a smile should be.

I savor a strange tenderness, pliability, in my body. My perception spreads into the sand and trees and air. I could mold them too, like putty.

There are screams, intimately close. Resounding in the hollows and passageways between my collarbone and pelvis, from the flowers and stars.

Distressed and disintegrating, lost in a labyrinth. My body is a labyrinth. My body is soil and sea and flowers and starlight, and they are a labyrinth. The energy that was people is rich; its struggles to remember itself feel like a luscious caress. The labyrinth giggles and stretches in bliss.

I could name those teasing flutters in my flesh. Two were men who tried to enforce human order, bless them, against the universe's unknowns. One was a boy who adored making someone small in his shadow. One was a girl who was small in his shadow but she stepped into the light and—

My mind coalesces. I open the labyrinth's mouth and shriek.

The flowers scream. The ocean screams. The stars scream.

I jolt up, and I'm yelling, "Craig!" and there's no answer; no, worse, there's an answer, pleading shudders through my flesh and flickers among the trees, he isn't gone, he's *in me*, the screams are light and the shaking ground, and my mouth, oh god, opens wider than a mouth can and I still can't scream loudly enough—

The scream dies. The remnants of Craig and my other meals fall still.

In the stillness, an alien euphoria rises. My mind's terror; my body's bliss. The contrast screeches, broken.

Pleasure eases in the understanding.

The Unseen.

The Unseen is in me, and the petals rustle, the weird pain of something feeding on a stem. Stars dance on my skin *and the Unseen is awake and free.*

The ritual worked.

The Unseen was released, and sought a place to hide from the tumult, and I welcomed it into me. It waited dormant, tangled up with my buried fury. When that fury burst, it woke.

Awe. Horror. Joy. I want to run and run, building energy like a storm, the beauty of this is so much vaster than I will ever grasp and I'm scared, oh god, I'm *scared*.

How to hold something this vast? I'm so small. I fuck up everything, I—

A force raises my hands; is it me? My fingers stretch, spindly. Shadows move under my skin, my flesh growing translucent.

I gasp in revulsion, and my hands return to normal, easy as molding clay. And through my parted fingers, I see that I'm not alone.

Distressed and intoxicated by the new workings of my body, I hadn't seen Jonah. But now I'm viscerally aware of him, in new ways.

I'm knitted into him. I'm the air slipping through the membranes of his lungs, the blood caught in the satisfying thud of flesh in his heart. I crackle through his brain; that electric shudder is his thoughts.

A disgusting, overwhelming, fascinating communion.

Jonah's afraid, too. It's written in the throbbing of his body.

He's cross-legged on a rock, staring. When I look at him, panic spasms; he bows his head, like suddenly it's dangerous to behold me.

"Jonah." My voice is thunder and subtle music. It's too much. We both wince.

He raises his head. Fear on Jonah's face; fear of *me*. Unimaginable.

Something opens and draws some of that fear inside. The greater, stranger me wriggles happily. Terror's a special little delicacy.

He shivers, then calms and looks at the stars.

"There are more now," he says. "Aren't there?" He stares up, hunting some peace. I taste it: He thinks this might be an ending. "I hope I've pleased you."

I could say, *No.* I could wrack him with visions, of his wife butchering their son, of whipping his followers into a murderous frenzy. I could descend in vengeful fury, drink the enticing energy of him, turn that trembling flesh into power.

The most terrifying thing is that I want to.

I speak in my own voice, thin and high. "Jonah, help."

I shocked him; I feel the jolt.

He tries to measure what he's seeing in me: the god he gave his life to, and the girl he gave as an offering. Neither. Both.

He kneels among the flowers, a worshipper. I am the altar.

He dares to touch my forehead; his eyes widen with childlike wonder. How to square that with a man who almost killed us? Just like he can't square messy Aoife with the god inside me.

His hand's slick with sweat.

"Faceless one." His eyes shine with tears. "Thank you for returning. Thank you for taking this girl's body and walking among us."

A helpless "You're welcome," a reflex. Jonah doesn't notice. A new horror: being the shell holding the thing he communes with.

"Whatever you ask," Jonah whispers, "I am yours."

Irritation and hunger stir in my depths. I taste his hot blood and marrow as I move through it. I want it. And that want can't be mine, it crawled into my mind, parasitic. I brace like I'll be punished for my disgust, and the tears start.

"Help," I repeat. "It's me, I can't—"

That's how he knows I'm me. The words *I can't.* That's Aoife.

He pulls back, examining me, and the balance shifts. He's still full of fear and wonder, but seeing Aoife, rather than what's inside. Relief suffuses the scent of the flowers. There's a fascination in his face, something almost like a doubt, like he's reshaping some awareness, adjusting to some shock I can't read.

A cautious smile at last. "Extraordinary. You look like you. Well . . . your eyes are different."

The petals flex. I rein in my tears. "How?"

He angles his head. "They keep changing. Voids. Infernos. Mirrors."

"Do they ever look like mine?" My voice is small. I feel adrift.

Jonah embraces me, gentle. His body responds to the thrum and boom in me, adoring, even as he holds human me and breathes, "Hush."

"It's not like it was for Myri." I try to feel the comfort of his arms, not that disturbing interweaving through his body. "For me, it's all the time and it's restless, hungry, and . . ." I search for the word. "Volatile."

Jonah pulls back. Sound waves move matter, caressing. "What is it going to do?"

Branches shift; lights flicker. The insect song grows melodious, a sweet chord.

"Grow," I whisper. The lights pulse agreement.

The Unseen's shiver escapes my mouth as a gasp. The stars flare. Anticipation.

The longing's clear in Jonah. "My . . . my children?"

I don't know if it's me or the Unseen that offers him the kind lie, but it's spoken from the flowers and stars. *Beloved always in my core.*

Agony moves through Jonah and settles deep. He sits back and marvels at the lights.

I can't switch this off. The world moving at my whims. When he places a hand on mine the lights turn a richer gold; that's what comfort looks like. "A girl with a god in her skin. You're right to be afraid, but you should find joy in it. You were always brave."

Lights dance along the veins of leaves. Jonah watches with innocent delight. He doesn't understand that the light is me struggling to find courage, feeling it slip away.

"The others," he says. "They can't know. That you have your own mind."

The flowers pulse like they, too, are startled.

"They did terrible things, approached a brink, they need to know they're saved. They need to believe in your power. They need the Unseen to be inscrutable. All the unknown things blooming inside you."

Imagine being a god, and feeling the sting of a strange rejection, at being told you, as yourself, will not be enough. What stings more is that he's right.

Their unspeakable, beloved god, returned from its nightmares to save them from theirs. What will they do, when it speaks with the voice of Aoife, the klutzy new girl? Saying, *Uh, hi, surprise?*

That makes me laugh, surprising us both. The soil and saltwater laugh with me.

Jonah stares at the laughing god-girl and forges ahead. "It would be best if you hid your human face and allowed me to mediate."

I remember how he enjoyed playing us like instruments in that brutal dawn, taking us apart to seek relief from his own pain. But we were all broken, weren't we? He's Jonah, and he loves us; look at the hope in him. He became monstrous when he suffered something unbearable, but we all did, and he's himself again. What he did is undone, and we need him more than ever.

I can't guide them when I'm in the dark too. I can only imagine standing before them with armfuls of stars and flowers, having no idea what to say as wonder dies in their eyes.

What a relief to have this terror out of my hands. He's always guided us.

"A god and its priest," I say. A little of the weight lifts.

"Good," Jonah says. "I sent them to meditate, I didn't know . . . what you would do." He pats my hand, almost businesslike. "It's time you appeared to them."

I search for the courage to learn this. To contain a tempestuous unknown. To move the world as I move my body, shape and color it around myself.

Every step I take along the shoreline, my surroundings respond. Light bends, misshapen; sound swells and booms. I'm learning it like an infant learning its limbs, a terrifying process, like I might botch it and break it all.

But it gets easier; there's a weird pleasure in shaping matter, painful and satisfying, like pulling off a scab. I practice blending my flesh into my surroundings, melty-twisty limbs appearing as melty-twisty branches.

I am at the edge of the grove, in front of them, and they don't see me.

They feel me, though. Hair rising, an ache like coming home, breaths that won't catch. There are crusted tears on cheeks; I taste that salt. I taste it all.

Frida's sobbing, mad with ecstasy. João and Zina chant between kisses. Oscar's on his back, staring at the stars. Larissa's touching everything around her, feeling me in it. Myri sits empty on the sand, Teresa singing hymns to her. All lost in worship, the bliss of reunion, dread and anticipation.

Dread thickens in me, too. If I think about where this is going—

They look up as Jonah approaches. Breaths held, tensed.

"There are things I must tell you," he says, solemn.

The size of this silence.

"We have lost Aoife."

Pain ripples. All that shock and sadness and love—that's for *me*. I taste it in their flesh. Larissa's actually sinking into Darya's shoulder and weeping.

I drink it in instinctively as they give it up to me. The veins in my body and the veins in the leaves pulse, bloated with their grief.

"There's no shame in mourning her." There's subtle pressure on the words, inspiring shifting glances. Giulia and Kiera are locked away, but our offerings to them still lie by the trees, uncomfortable reminders.

"She gave her last moments fighting for us. She gave her life to our faceless one without question. Have no doubt that she is one with it, that she persists in rapture."

He's not wrong. Another dizzy laugh, rippling in the insect song.

It's disorientating, being mourned. Like I'm actually gone. But so beautiful and strange, to understand now how much they love me.

Jonah gives them a moment before his face splits into that wonderful smile he unleashes only occasionally, boyishness on an old man's lips, a smile you'd follow anywhere.

That's my cue, isn't it?

So stupid, to freeze up. Like I could get this wrong.

So stupid that a memory surges up. Two years after my mother laughed and said, "Good fucking luck" when I called after running away with Craig. A wedding invite from my brother's fiancée, plans for a surprise reconciliation. Weathering Craig's rage to spend a week's pay on a dress, the thrill as I waited for my reveal. How they ignored me. How my brother spotted me and snorted into his prosecco. The shouting, the broken bottle, the security guard who chuckled as he escorted me out. The last time I saw my family.

I have always fucked everything up—

I look to Jonah; I look *into* Jonah, taste desperation and machination and hope and triumph. Stronger, I taste faith. The Unseen cannot get anything *wrong*. His lip twitches, acknowledgment. *Just trust.*

I trust the Unseen. I trust him.

The unknown is not void, it is rich and resonant as it spills out of me.

The wind swirls into a gale, the waves rise in glassy chaos, exultant, scented with jasmine, salt, and iron. Carrying discordant music, resonating not in sound but in emotion.

The stars flare into harsh brilliance, bright as daylight.

I emerge from myself.

None of the crudeness of its first emergence, when it smashed bloody from a ribcage and gut. I open, fractal, each layer a subtle infinity of possibility. Nothing recognizable as eyes or wings or limbs.

I appear as Aoife, clothed in stars, mirrors in my eyes.

I appear as reflections of other dimensions, untouchable, horrifying, beautiful. Shapes without name, colors perceived by other senses.

I am monstrous and beautiful, and I cringe at myself in terror and awe.

Jonah had tamed his panic, but it grips him again as fervor. "Our god has awoken!"

They're mesmerized. There's no screams, no chanting, no giddy dancing. Just gazing, voices and minds lost to holy terror.

I'm lost to it too, paralyzed in the light and gale that I myself summoned.

"It will—" Jonah falters. His eyes try to turn from me, but they can't: I am all around him. Enfolding them all in my terrible glory. He perseveres. "Sustain us. Protect us. And give us gifts even our darkest dreams could not contain."

They dare to cheer, hesitant, awestruck. The Unseen shows me what to do. It moves my feet, my fingers, my newer, stranger limbs that are windows and echoes and waves.

I place tastes on their tongues, stir pleasure in their nerves, subtle tendrils massaging their lips, lungs, bones, learning the secrets of their bodies. They grow loose and limp, high on me, surrendering, as the maelstrom swirls around them.

Love suffuses them. Love and fear, indistinguishable.

The sadness that gripped them over my death is dust, blown away.

But the deepest love I could imagine—a song written in my name, the touch of a wrist in a café, the words *I'll stay here with you*—that's thin gruel, next to this feast of devotion.

Frida's zealous glow and Larissa's luxuriant surrender and Teresa's confused relief and Kai's terrified excitement and Oscar's fierce, panicked loyalty. They're mine; I am their world. My offerings, giving themselves every moment. To *me*.

Adoration, washing away the fear, a heady brew I drink until I'm swollen.

I speak the Unseen's words in light and insect song and heartbeats. *I have given you this and still I am just a fragment; hold fast and I will bring you universes.*

CHAPTER FORTY-TWO

MIRACLES

They celebrate long into the night. I don't think they'll need sleep now. I won't.

I can't adjust, yet, to not needing rest. Returning to my hut seems absurd, so I settle in the solarium. The butterflies aren't exactly butterflies now; I've been playing with them.

Ridiculously, I worry that Jonah will be annoyed about me claiming his office. Silly. This was built in my name; it's my cathedral. *Mine*. Will I ever get used to that?

The sunrise has new colors, indigo and green among the pinks and oranges, scarring the sky with a new texture. I lie in a hammock and explore my new, extended body, breathing light through the leaves of a monstera, fracturing my vision through a butterfly's eyes. Nectar! Here I am, learning how nectar tastes.

It's all magical, overwhelming; my fear is all that holds me back from drowning in it.

I don't know how much of what happens now is my choice. But there's something I need to do.

Calling someone is easy. My awareness finds Oscar in his room, on his knees, praying as he disassembles his clock with a spanner. "It's broken," he mutters between prayers, "broken, keeps saying the time wrong."

A mischievous smile flickers; it isn't the clock that's broken. The smile isn't mine. Or it is. It's hard to detangle.

I tug at Oscar, seeping through the intricacies of him. He stands, trancelike. I'm thrilled despite myself. What else could I make people do?

He enters the solarium cautiously, gaze pinned to the tiles. How should I feel, being too much to behold? If he saw the way the light splinters around me, what would he do?

I watch, surrendering to fascination. At the disparate pieces of him. How those sparks and chemicals form a desperate urge to hold things together, to *control*, when he is just a powerless scrap of matter and mind. Even helpless before me, I feel his mind whirring, like he's still trying to mold the situation around him.

I tell him, "*Bring me the girls I returned from the void.*"

And he does. He goes to obey my order. I'm left blinking at that. Somehow being *listened to* is more dizzying than playing with starlight or summoning gales.

The Unseen simmers, enjoying the afterglow of Oscar's feelings, and I wait until Giulia and Kiera appear.

—⊙—

Unblemished. They were bones and innards. Now they're whole. My miracles.

Oscar's pinned Kiera's arms behind her back; he's enlisted help, Pietro marching Giulia with a heavy hand on her shoulder, expressionless. Kiera's shaking, trying to form words but choking on sobs. She manages a few scraps of a prayer, then repeats "wasn't so bad," over and over until the words come apart. Giulia's bowed, tight-lipped, tight-wound.

I grin, a grin of my own for the first time since the Unseen woke. I can't wait to surprise them.

"*Leave us*," I tell Oscar and Pietro. The door clicks behind them, and there's that rush where I remember locks can't stop me now. They know that, too. That lock isn't for me.

Kiera sinks to her knees, swallowing tears. Giulia stares at the floor. Butterflies flit around them, curious in the strangely curving sunbeams.

"*Look at me*," I say, grin wide. I'm not sure how wide it's meant to be, actually.

Giulia covers Kiera's eyes, like she's protecting a child. Her voice trembles. "No."

My grin falters. The leaves rustle. That's not a cloud passing over the sun, is it?

"No," Giulia repeats. "You gave my life back, but I still have myself, and I can still choose. I choose not to see."

A strange wrench. Darkness slipping across the sky, leaves curling, betrayal livid, and next to it a bright burst of human love. Everyone said I was brave. But look at Giulia. Look at *that* courage.

"Giulia," I say, my voice. "It's me."

I feel the shock through their bodies, but they stay resolute, not looking. Again, it's like they don't hear me. Like I'm my ghost, far away. And it hurts. It would be so easy to sink into my new self. So easy.

I approach them. Leaves brush my arms, their new luminescence more vivid now that the sunlight is burnished.

"Please." I could tear this room down, rend their cells, reduce the butterflies to flecks of ash. I'm begging. "Please see me."

Kiera lifts Giulia's hand away from her eyes. Curious eyes. Kiera's, tearful and hopeful. "Aoife?"

"It's fucking with us," Giulia hisses. "It's not her."

Kiera stands. I wonder what she sees in my eyes. Voids? Lightning?

She must see something, because she reaches for me.

I step into her arms, and she's warm, alive; I saw that face beaten to a slurry of meat, and now it's pressed into my shoulder and we're trembling together. I did both those things.

"I'm sorry," I gasp, my human self, like the ringing glass and the sudden too-bright blast of sunlight are someone else's problem. "I'm sorry, I—"

"No, I don't want to think about it, I—"

"You—"

"No."

It isn't forgiveness, this; I know that. It's a twisted, poisonous bond, friendship and something close to love, mingled with the intimate union between murderer and victim. There's no closeness like this, and there's no gulf like this, either.

All those sparks in her brain and nerves. The Unseen can't guide me when it's me and her and we're trying to surface together from crushing depths.

"Well, fuck," Giulia says. "You are still you."

I detach from Kiera a little. Giulia's looking at me now, nothing soft in her stare. I reach for her, but she recoils. Her terror hasn't eased; I feel it spiking.

"It'll be fun." Her words are icy. "To be killed by a god with our friend's face."

Kiera tenses, arms around my waist taut like that's a determined act of faith.

"I won't hurt you." The glass shifts to hues human eyes have never seen. "I won't let *them* hurt you." A plaintive note. How can I still be getting things wrong, when I'm carrying a living universe? "I brought you back, didn't I?"

"And *that thing* in you." Giulia swallows, and what she's swallowing is her reverence, so that she can load the words *that thing* with disdain, pronounce her god a monster. "Can you control it?"

It shifts inside me; are those my feelings? They aren't human feelings at all.

My silence translates into sad satisfaction on her face. "I didn't think so."

"I wouldn't—"

"You . . ." Giulia's face twists. "In the basement. The last time I reached for anyone. The last contact I had with anyone who wasn't tormenting me. I just wanted a bit of comfort before I was nothing, and you pulled away like I was a disease. You did that to please them, didn't you? If it tells you to harm us, if *he* tells you to, you'll do it."

A familiar feeling, newly free, screams through me, amplifying the Unseen's thundering. "You think I'm weak. Don't you? You think I'm still stupid, pathetic Aoife."

Kiera leaps away as my body triples like an overexposed photograph, smears of void and twisted matter in the spaces between. Darkness like knives, light curved like claws.

"I am not weak." My voice thuds though the tiles under Giulia's feet.

Giulia cringes but doesn't look away. Her jaw sets. She's seen and felt things no human should. She can stare down a god.

I hate it. Is this burning rejection, or something alien? "You're fucking welcome for your life back, by the way."

"Do I have your permission to leave, Unholy One?" Her sarcasm stutters, doing its best. "May I return to my prison?"

Kiera stares between us, silent.

"You're free." My anger subsides, my body returning to its own shape. The lock evaporates in a mist of silver. "Leave, if you want. Take the boat."

She softens, too. The tiniest, saddest smile. "Bit late for that."

She turns anyway. She glances back at Kiera, then she's gone, leaving us alone among shuddering tropical leaves.

I disappear into the leaves and the pulsating of Kiera's flesh, letting the last of the fury burn off. The less human feelings persist like a strange taste in my mouth. I try to parse them, but they slip away.

Kiera doesn't speak. She's still shaking.

"Do you want to go, too?" Dread of her answer thickens in my mouth.

She shakes her head, then nods. She bites her lip, and the small pain releases the words. "I'll stay."

Her heart convulses, a fist gripping the fragment of my awareness in its chambers. I could hide here forever, feeling the thud and rush of her every moment.

"I'm scared, too." Sometimes, I say the right thing. "She's right, I can't contain it. I just . . . ."

"Love it." Confidence erupts in Kiera, that burst she gets when words overflow. "And fear it. And we always felt that, but there was something abstract about it, but now it's *real*, and it's like those feelings have immediate consequences—"

"Exactly," I say, "only it's also like, I don't know where it ends and I begin."

"That's"—Kiera lets out a surprising laugh—"horrible and wonderful. Is it like, a spectrum? Do you have thoughts and not know whose they are? You sound like you but—"

We stop, beginnings of grins on our faces, realizing we're back to our normal state, babbling, trying to work out rules when there are none. As soon as we notice, it collapses.

Kiera inhales and cautiously touches my cheek, her face all tumult.

"I'm touching a god." There's joy, but the words buckle under pain, too. I'm her god and murderer. There will never be a moment again when we're just two people testing possibilities.

"Revolution, right?" I try for a smile that might look human.

The Kiera I know would joke awkwardly about making the laws of physics our bitch. This Kiera lets out a nervous half-laugh, a sound of loss.

I have to show her.

I touch her cheek. I draw sunlight into me, let it flow through my fingertips, warming her, until she glows, her eyes and parted lips releasing waves of light.

I can play the world like an instrument. I want to fill her with music.

"We're out past everything"—I draw on the power inside me, instilling my words with unimaginable confidence—"together."

I kiss her, sunlight meeting sunlight. She stiffens, shocked, then eases into it. I can name what blooms in her mind: boldness.

We're bright and liquid. I was hesitant, but it's a revelation, feeling every sensation in her body mirrored in mine. I'm her hungry gasp; I dance in her fingers gripping my waist.

She is mine, my gift to the world, my first sign, my unlocker of secrets.

Foliage thickens, swaddling us. I'm silk on her skin, nectar in her mouth. We're incandescent; I've never given anyone anything like this.

I will fill her to the brim and further we will be one.

There's fear in her; I know it in the shivers and palpitations, but it just piques her bliss and mine, stirring formless, urgent desires. I sip at her terror and pleasure, courage and fascination, relish them, want more, more.

She is mine, most adored, I will melt her into a drug to intoxicate the world drink her every drop she will flow through me always burning, my brightest fuel—

The blissful stupor snaps. Leaves furl into themselves as I pull away, panicked.

She steps back too, gasping, flushed, caught in my flash of horror.

"What?" The last of the sunlight I infused into her escapes her lips with the word.

"I don't know, it . . . went weird." I shiver.

Kiera traces the petals of an orchid, like she's trying to distract herself. She asks anyway. "Was that you? That kiss. Was it you, or it?"

"Both?" I shake my head like I could shake off the turmoil. "I . . . *I* wanted to, but . . . ." I calm, breath steadying. That couldn't have happened. I translated it wrong.

"I don't know either." Kiera's voice is small. "If that was you, or it, that I . . ." We're floundering. Kiera sighs, frustration, wonder. "I can't think. I was dead yesterday."

She rips a scrap off the orchid. A jagged tear left behind.

The sun's coming back. That's probably good. I reach for her hand.

She flinches; the fragment of petal falls. "No!" She snaps, raising her hands, leaping away like I'm red-hot.

The word catches in the foliage and colored light, echoing like a bell: *No.*

"I'm sorry." Her words flood out. "I look at you and it's okay, it's *you,* then it's not you, it's *it* and I feel afraid and I feel love and I can't tell if it's for you or the Unseen, and then it's you, only you last night, coming at me, that *look* you had, you didn't understand what you were doing but I see *that* and I see *it,* and I'm trying to see just you but—"

The guilt is so wide. It could engulf me. She looks wretched.

"Hey," I attempt, lightening. "You said *love.*"

"I did." Quiet, miserable. "Don't know what that means."

There isn't any meaning; you will learn the absolute end of every concept, the stones that construct your prison falling one by one.

"I killed my ex," I say, surprising myself. "Craig. I drank him like lemonade. He made my life hell, made me *small,* and now he's just screams echoing somewhere in me, and it feels good. And I love him and what's left of him loves me."

Kiera takes it in. Broken miracle, hair mussed, eyes downcast away from her god.

The twisty patterns of the stained glass swim, distorting plants, butterflies, colors, thoughts, us. There's nowhere to go from here.

She doesn't ask permission to leave. I don't give it. She walks away.

I am a god moving through my temple, matter distending at my will. I'm a scared girl running through a home that isn't home, guilt and panic surging. I demand the worship I'm due. I yearn for a promise that it will be all right.

Yesterday, the poison garden was stripped. Today it's flourishing, but those leaves and berries are warped by iridescence or crackling with shadow, promising stranger things than death. I bloom in the jasmine, too, the wildflowers and the lavender. They grow wild and monstrous, expanding in a sudden burst and turning the garden into a labyrinth as Teresa and Jonah look up in shock.

I want us to be hidden for this.

Greenery whispers as it parts for me. Teresa's eyes are closed in prayer. Jonah's are fixed on me, alight with worship and calculation. They turn to my hands: human hands, shaking. He knows, from that, what he's speaking to.

"You can speak freely in front of Teresa." Jonah smiles indulgently, speaking to Aoife even as he kneels to the god in me. "Can't she, love?"

Teresa murmurs. She's serene, but the turmoil below is too agonizing to bear.

"I'm . . . ." I don't know how to describe what happened upstairs. I try to shape it, and the sky flexes into rainbows. "It's restless. Hungry. Kiera—I nearly—"

Jonah raises an eyebrow. He's going to make me say it. I taste his wonder that he can *make* me do something, when I'm the force that's making the earth ripple. I taste him exploring all the implications of that.

"I was drinking her feelings"—I try not to let my voice crack—"and it would have . . . kept going. Until there was nothing."

Jonah stands. My human self remembers that I'm naked, and my god-self clothes me in shadow. "Why did you not? Perhaps that is why it brought her back, no?"

Branches and blossoms crack like whips; the air thunders. Jonah flinches.
"No. I will not."

Jonah sighs and reaches for my hands. "My clever, fierce daughter. You cannot *refuse* the Unseen. It *is* you, more than you are." A sideways smile of pity. "Perhaps you'd truly feel the majesty of this, if you abandoned the idea that these choices are yours. What is our holiest word?"

"Trust." As the word forms, a weight eases, only to redouble as I remember what I nearly did. Trust came easily when I was trusting in mystery.

"I see doubt." Jonah sighs. "Where's that girl who gave herself unflinchingly? Where's that girl who chased a call into the night? Where is that girl who flung herself into its nightmare? What happened to her, hmm?"

I am here. I grit my teeth, draw up every scrap of faith. *Trust.*

There's some relief in knowing that there is no fighting. My hands are moved by a force greater than me. The terrible things they do won't belong to me.

"Perhaps it will help to remember what trust looks like," Jonah says softly. "Teresa, look up for me, love?"

Teresa looks up, obedient. God, all that roils behind that placid gaze. I sip, gentle as a hummingbird at a flower, and taste agony, confusion, absence as wide as the world. Guilt, the wretched tang of hope. Inside me there's a cramp, an appetite piqued.

"Do what you always do," Jonah whispers to his wife, kissing her on the head. "Give it all up. The Unseen is here to take all burdens from you."

Teresa beams up at me and offers up all that she feels.

It rushes into me like a drug, rich and heady. Thick with glimpses,

Sage under her knife, Myri's blank stare. Older memories, of kneeling in the groves every evening, taking her love for her children, the most precious part of her, and handing it over to the Unseen. All she has offered up, to her husband and her god and her home, the years of quiet hollowing out. As fast as feelings arose, she'd give them over to become the smiling shell he needed her to be. Utter trust. Utter devotion.

The sky flickers, my wider body twitching with bliss.

I don't take all of her. The sheer scope of her agony leaves me quenched, if not sated. But she knows I could and remains kneeling anyway, gazing up at me in glory.

I take all that hurts from her and leave the relief. See how she smiles, at peace?

This is the Unseen's work, not mine. I have never trusted myself. But I can trust the thing that moves me.

"Believe in it," Jonah says. "Believe in me, too. Let me guide you."

I am a god before my priest, bloated with the stuff of a sacrifice. Still, in a human reflex, I bow my head and murmur, "I'll try."

And Jonah says, "Good," takes his wife's hand, and leads her inside.

CHAPTER FORTY-THREE

ROT

My followers know a divinity walks in the groves. They steer clear or kneel as I pass. I walk naked. I used to feel awkward and exposed like this, but now all it exposes are shadows that hint at wings, tendrils, stranger possibilities.

I walk to the cliffs, trees and sand mutating around me. The sky's smoked glass and lava, an apricot sunset glowing at midday. The Unseen still thrums with pleasure at the scraps of Teresa's pain. I'm trying to trust, even if all I see is how Kiera looked at me.

I ask the presence in me, *how*? How am I human enough to fuck up, yet too far beyond human for the bonds that make fucking up bearable?

It gives me no answer. I sit at the edge of the cliff. The sea heaves, reflecting greens and purples that don't match the sky.

Kiera. We broke her. She stayed for *me*, and we—ripping, chopping, bludgeoning—something in her's *gone*—I did that—

The island quakes. The sky flashes incandescent.

No wonder I'm wracked with doubts. How can I trust myself, *anything*, after that?

I'm home; I want to go home. I want to lie with my head on Larissa's chest. I want to dance on the beach. I want to drink coffee with Kiera as she dissects myths at two hundred miles an hour to avoid saying the things she wants to. I want to fix us.

Spears of sun stab through roiling marmalade clouds.

Maybe I still can.

The words *Cut out the rot* come, and I don't know if they're mine or the Unseen's, but I almost smile at how perfect they are. There is a rot here, the beauty of our little world turned sour and putrid. And it's taken a form, one I don't understand, but one I urgently need to. Perhaps now I can.

I reach; my mind rolls through the warm air and the trails of bees (well, what were once bees; things are a little different now), into Larissa's hut. She's open to me, sitting in meditation, chanting with tears pouring down her cheeks. She opens her eyes as she feels my presence and lets out a gasp. The sheer, fervent devotion in her makes my breath shudder.

"Bring me Myri."

I settle down to wait, examining the bees; I'm quite pleased with what they're becoming. The warmth on my skin no longer radiates from the sun, but from something inside me. Time stretches and slips, and then they're there, Larissa supporting Myri in her mindless steps up the hillside.

Larissa kneels, eyes averted. I wonder if I should say *hi*. I wonder if I should kiss her. I wonder if I should confess everything. But look at her, look at the bliss she trembles with.

"You may go, most beloved."

Another gasp, and she's scrambling up and fleeing. Even from here I feel the stretch of her mouth, the sheer width of her smile, the tears of joy concentrating in her throat. I don't know why it hurts.

I turn my eyes to Myri. She stands, obedient, empty. Strange shadow. Somewhere in that chaos as the cave collapsed, both of us opened doors within us, didn't we? A god entered through mine, and made me divine and glorious. What uncanny blight entered through hers and made its home inside her?

I place my hands, human hands, on her shoulders, human shoulders. I stare into the blank green eyes. Once, a long time ago, not so long ago, we sang a stupid show tune at each other through a closed window.

My awareness sinks into her.

From the outside, she seems so placid. Below the skin is a battleground, a strangling, an imprisonment. Filaments of rot, sticky mires, strangling vines, squirming insects, wrapping around a trapped, screaming self.

The entity—yes, Kiera and Sage were right, this is a *thing*, a being— that holds her tight within pulses and surges, warping around the boundary between real and unreal, gripping her taut, sometimes getting enough of a foothold to emerge fully. It is suffering, it has been suffering so much, but it is determination to the core. It has found flesh and bone to nestle in again, and it clings to it even as it submits it to decay.

I fall back from her, and I am looking again at the blighted creature, all rotting meat and stringy mold in the smoky, amber light.

"I know you," it says again, through a mouth now half decomposed away.

A thing that was meant to die in the dark and dissolve, it called itself; a thing that refused. A wasp in a fig that would not break down, poisoning the fruit. A thing that tried to help as much as it tried to hurt, a splinter of life persisting, haunting. A ghost doesn't have to look like a ghost. Confused and lost and decomposing all these months, amid flashes of lucidity, of distress, of agony, but refusing to slip away, determined to leave a stain on the place that tried to forget her. What a deliciously petty thing to do.

Rotting a window for me to open. Blooming where Sage walked, and retracting at his touch. Coming at Giulia's call, at the sound of her friend's voice, unleashing cataclysm simply because she did not understand what she was doing. A presence. A dead thing that rotted, but refused to be gone.

"I know you too," I say. Aoife's voice. Because I owe her that. "Hi, Elise."

She looks back at me through empty eye sockets, understanding and not understanding.

I know what to do.

I will give them another miracle.

⊖

I stand naked on the cliffside. My body's Aoife's, but my skin's translucent, revealing hints of swirling cloud and flame. I like playing with ways of being hideous and magnificent.

The sky's wine-deep purple. The moon's rising, markings palpitating in rhythm with the movements below my skin.

My followers approach chanting, shivering with anticipation. The anticipation's mine. I've called them, and here they are. Will I ever get tired of calling, and having people *there*? Being impossible to ignore?

Part of me still quails. I am the force that placed new lights in that sky.

But I'm also Aoife, awkward, only half-daring to acknowledge forbidden things, to risk upsetting a delicate order. But I trust; I have to trust.

I say, *"There is a person you were afraid to speak of."*

Tonight my voice is insect song, bee-buzz, goat bells, the bubbling of a stew pot. The sounds of home.

Their hearts thud. Guilt, panic. Jonah watches, arms folded; he's seeing Aoife, not the Unseen, and he's hiding his concern, but I taste it. I can't name the feelings it stirs. Giulia's eyes are wide, hand clenched around Larissa's, her need for comfort bigger than her anger. One person seizes with fear, and I notice that.

If I trust and plunge, this feels good.

"What happens, when a person's name is buried, when their memory is strangled? They persist. They stay, and they rot, and they rot."

"She's—" Giulia. Vulnerability in a voice that challenged a god just hours ago. ". . . dead?"

Eyes turn to her. They know she's forgiven. They're still suspicious.

"What is dead?" I ask. *"We are dealing with bigger and bolder things than life and death."* I like that line. I wonder if it's mine, or the Unseen's. *"Elise is not alive, but not gone. Do you want to see her?"*

Myri stands beside me, unmoving, blank. I see how that unnerves Jonah, having his daughter so close to my grip, and I can't resist a little inward smile at that: Just trust, right, Jonah?

I touch her shoulder and call up the blight, the decomposed shadow of Elise, and feel the flesh under my fingers soften and wither away. The empty eye sockets, bone visible now, survey the crowd.

"You buried her name, and she rotted. Here she is. Your blight. Your Elise."

The gasps are pain and regret now.

"*I am here to heal broken things and break what is whole.*" I smile, and the smile feels real; I'm starting to trust, the Unseen bolstering my courage, my body and voice moved on two strings, human and divine. "*I am here to cut away the rot and free you from monsters.*"

Still. Now it reaches that moment, a part of me quails. This rotten thing, she knows and doesn't know that she was once a girl who watched black swans and was adrift in a strange country and kissed a redheaded farmer boy and sent her old boss cookies out of spite. She holds the concepts, then they slip away.

Which is to say: She both understands and doesn't understand what's about to happen to her.

Which is not to say that she is not afraid.

Scraps of Elise persist; they half-remember laughing with Sage, flicking cherry pips at Myri, drinking and dancing herself giddy in a foreign city, early-morning cigarettes in a dull commuter town. They don't want to stop being. Without eyes, with a throat clogged with rot, from another girl's body, she says, *Please*, and she says, *I won't go. I won't.*

The Unseen shifts. Yielding, excited. Hungry little rifts opening within me.

There are cruel choices to be made, in being a god. There are things that must be destroyed, aren't there? Cutting out the rot is not a gentle process.

The Unseen unfurls. The earth and sky shudder at the sight of me. My followers cover their eyes or stare, tiny in their awe. Look at what I've become.

The blight that is Elise is woven deep into Myri now, into her flesh and mind. But I can unweave it. I unthread it, draw it out, and hear a single cry of desperate refusal, feel a sweet kick of resistance, as Elise dissolves into me at last.

She is far from a person now, echoes and fragments and corruption, nothing that could truly satisfy. Still, she's lightness bubbling through me, a bright life, all those bright memories. I learn her; I learn all of her, all that happiness and tenacity. Terror, too, but in me it's transmuted into something that feels like joy, and I spill it out to the others: "*See? She is one with me.*"

They kneel and weep.

And beside me, louder yells, yells of actual sound, ringing across the cliffs as Myri falls forward onto her knees, shrieking as she regains control of her body. Which is fair: This must be a hell of a thing to wake up to.

Myri the oracle, twice resurrected, now Myri the girl, swallowing her scream and looking around.

"What?" she says.

Jonah and Teresa sweep her up, suffocating her with kisses and tears. Joy replaces the crowd's shock. I am a good god, aren't I? I have given her back to the world. I've given her back the world.

"I don't understand," Myri's laughing as much as she's panicking.

Look. I saved the girl in the cabin.

This would be so perfect, the sweetness of one life restored and another brought to peace, even unwillingly. I'd be a happy god, a laughing god, gifting bliss to my family. But.

With a final screech and sob, the last of Elise unravels in me, and releases the rupture at her core, the memory of a death.

I learn what happened to the lost girl I followed here, and triumph gives way to rage.

This is my *home*. Before it broke, it was pure, all I'd been promised and denied. The rot was new. The rot wasn't in *us*.

The last of Elise comes apart, and I know that's a lie. The rot was here, always.

Fury boils through the Unseen; waves tower, clouds and grass thrash, strange scents stir on the wind. A maelstrom. I ride it, and I don't crumble. A god in my bones, awash with a dead girl's mind, the sky screaming my feelings, I'm powerful enough to unleash this anger, not cringe from it.

As suddenly as the storm whipped up, it calms. All is still. Even the ocean, even the sky, frozen. A pall of peace.

I return to a human shape, as close to Aoife as can be. Within me, though, subtler things are warm, open, eager. I know what to do. I can't feel the Unseen guiding me, but it must be, because I am so certain.

The air whispers, *"Oscar, come forward."*

Oscar's pale in the rich purple light. He was the first person to be kind to me here. He let me win at backgammon. He switched the light off so Giulia would spend her last hours in the dark. Did he enjoy that?

I kiss his forehead, spiraling pleasure and pain into his nerves. *"Tell them what happened to Elise."*

Jonah's mouth opens, perhaps to order me to stop. He can't. I'm sorry, I know this isn't what he wants, I know I'll regret it. But this is mine, this justice for the girl who transformed my life.

Oscar's lips form a word; I think it's *mercy*. I think my eyes are voids. His shoulders sag. "I spied on Elise."

My tendrils squeeze inside him. Playing him like an instrument.

"I spy on all of you. To keep the peace." He gulps air. "Recording devices. Drunk conversations. I try . . . to make sure all is well."

My tendrils clench. *"Keep going."*

"I spied on Elise and Myri. Elise saw a side of Myri that most didn't, and wanted to help her. She offered to be the oracle so Myri could live a normal life. I heard them planning."

His voice is a whisper but carries on the warm air. Not warm like a summer evening, but warm like the inside of a living thing.

"They were going to try a ritual to pass the Unseen to Elise. I waited by the cave. I was just going to warn them." Pleading now.

The misery on his face. I try to feel bad for him, but there's a hollow where that should be. Something moves in it. "*Tell them. Not me.*"

He turns, heavy, and looks into the eyes of the people he's laughed with and manipulated and spied on. "I had the shotgun. Just to scare her. But she refused to listen to reason. She . . . the sacrilege, I. I had no choice. She was entering the cave, shouting for Myri to follow her, and I just——"

"*Say it.*"

"I shot her."

Larissa lets out an audible "No," Giulia's face screws up, Jonah winces, Teresa covers her eyes.

"*She fell into the cave.*" I pick up his thread. "*I closed around her. She bled out into my nightmares, and my dreams trapped her between life and death. She resisted, would not fade away. She rotted, and the rot spread.*"

I speak from deep inside Oscar and say, "*Look at me.*" I feel how it's a relief to look at a god's void eyes rather than the accusing faces of his friends.

I say, "*Shhh,*" and stroke his face. I'm sinking into the reality of what I'm about to do, growing more certain that I can do it. That I *want to.*

He is so warm, and I am so hungry. Elise was shards of a person, but he is whole, alive. There are tears in his eyes. He knows.

A last question. "*Did you enjoy it?*"

Oscar stiffens. "I—no! Of course not!"

"*Then why?*"

Desperation, in a man under a strange sky, a man who will not be a man much longer. "For you!" He falls to his knees. "She was breaking the rules, blaspheming! I had to!"

I tilt up his chin. Where is this coming from? I move with confidence, doing all this exactly right, riding the rush. I press my lips to his forehead, and he sobs, briefly absolved.

"*Imagine,*" I say, so softly, but they all hear it. "*Standing on the edge of the absolute unknown, and thinking about* rules."

Again, blissfully, I unfurl, wide open and magnificent and strange.

"Please," he whispers, unable to look away.

Once Oscar reassured me when I was sure I was too small and weak to belong here.

Tonight my power spans the sky, and I understand *how* that power will grow.

I relish the heat and the silken textures of him, unravel them all, and consume him with exquisite slowness.

I enjoy every scream and every drop.

CHAPTER FORTY-FOUR

PORTENTS

THIS IS HOW MY POWER GROWS.

I feed.

How can something as small as a person give me such nourishment? I don't fully understand. Something about how tiny sparks flare into fires that swallow forests.

Oscar crackles through me with electric brilliance, making me shudder. Somewhere he wrestles—resisting, poor thing—his transformation into something greater.

He called himself a maverick, a freethinker. He approached the brink of the sublime. But he refused to accept that what he saw there was terror, and stumbled back to the things he knew. Monitoring. Manipulating. Control.

Never mind, Oscar, you will blossom into something new in me. You will change, and change the world.

I heave with paroxysms of pleasure and growth, bulbous with power.

My followers grip each other in shock and ecstasy. Some scream. Zina, who was one of Oscar's lovers, is on her knees, horror and joy; *it took him, it chose him.* João sobs into Ana's chest. Giulia's fists are curled, but her face is pale. Frida's begging: "Take me too!"

Amid the tumult, quiet resonates between me and Jonah. But I look away from him; this moment belongs to me and Oscar.

It belongs to our friendship. To everything that interweaving of devotion and betrayal will birth.

Oscar boils out across my limbs. The sea and sky groan and I *expand.*

I take what was Oscar and Elise, killer and victim, the rot and what the rot wrought, and I turn them into threads, and wind through a planet. I taste the depths of the Mariana Trench, the tang of pollution above Shanghai, scars through forests, lava rumbling, a burst of laughter from a bar in Mombasa.

I taste the world. I do more than taste.

Tonight is a night of portents.

Oscar and Elise are vines bursting through the skin of a highway in Riyadh, tropical plants alien to a desert city, crushing cars and scenting the hot night with flowers.

Oscar is inspiration gripping an artist in Istanbul. She screams as she sketches. This picture will go viral, and all who see it will be seized by holy fervor.

Elise is a Himalayan town where the lights go out, revealing low-hanging stars, turquoise and toxic green and magenta. Close enough to touch, if you climb onto a rooftop, which the children do, and curious adults, too. One touch reveals disturbing secrets.

Oscar and Elise are strange creatures, human and fish, both and neither, that wash up on a Korean beach. Elise is a street in Mexico City where the graffiti writhes, alive. Oscar is a café in Stockholm where the patrons cackle and dance and rub their naked bodies against the whitewashed walls.

Oscar and Elise are the promise the Unseen sends into the world. *I am coming.*

I see it all. I see a world rocked with glimpses of the uncanny, haunted by signs. But the revelation of what is truly coming is just for me.

The flare of violence is as brutal and dazzling as a nuclear detonation.

What I'm seeing isn't real. Not yet. But as it luxuriates in the aftermath of its meal, as it weaves signs through the world, the god in my body dreams of what's to come.

It dreams of destruction.

It dreams of atoms ripped apart, stars flaring and exploding.

I dream of screaming through matter, beautiful calamity. I bear down on human bodies and minds, taking monstrous forms at their scale to relish the majesty of teeth and despair and hearts falling still on my tongue. I burst from ribcages, leaving bloodied shells. I wrack minds with transcendent visions.

I swallow cities. I inhale mountains. Beyond it, in the expanses, I do stranger and vaster things. Black holes and nebulae melt in my mouth.

In this dream, I am beyond Aoife; I am a force of sheer destruction, beyond name or self. Still, somewhere in that force a fragment of Aoife remembers smashing a vase, imagines crushing a chrysalis. She's free. A wild, cathartic release of something that's been coiled so tight in her that she didn't know it was there. Snap, bounds gone, it's out.

She's laughing, it's delirious, delicious; she's bathed in blood and stardust.

The Unseen dreams of the feast to come. Of reality, all its facets, disappearing between my jaws.

I dream that when it is gone into me, the nightmares end. There's peace. My belly bloats with the broken universe. I rest, sated, and my vast body works, transmuting it. I swell pregnant with a different reality.

What I birth will be without pain, without fear, clamorous, unbound, and glorious.

CHAPTER FORTY-FIVE

ALONE

The Farmstead celebrates.

Too late for a feast, but dry bread offers tastes that no human tongue knew before. My followers gather rotten peaches and find them fresh and ripe in their hands. They get drunk on seawater that tastes of nectar.

I ate reality.

They celebrate my presence, Myri's resurrection, Elise's release.

They dance to music from the sky, in the ocean's aurora glow. I pepper the night with wonders. I used to sketch with biros, hide my creations in my underwear drawer; Craig would laugh. Now the world is my canvas and miracles are my art.

I hear the screams. I hear the silence after.

They're desperate in their wildness, grins stretched, dances delirious. This is bliss, their faces say, grimly determined; we saw a friend dissolved and devoured; that was holy; *this is bliss.*

Some can't hide their tears or trembling. Oscar was cruel, but loved.

Elise was long gone, but they feel her absence all over again.

The aftertaste of galaxies and minds in my mouth.

I go to them as shadow and whispers. They tense like I will punish them. I say, "*Shhh, they suffered and suffer still, but they are something wonderful now.*"

They watch in awe. I'm alone.

Perhaps soon I'll have the power to make them forget for a while what I am, so we can be human together.

I don't want to think about how I will get that power. Oscar and Elise flow through me, fresh and piquant with pain, and nothing in me regrets that feast. They softened the Unseen's yearnings for now, but the question of who next is a sickening weight and thrill.

But for tonight, our paradise is rekindled, and I move through it, alone.

All this will be gone. The sea, the stars already so strange, these dancing bodies, recycled into something new within me.

I try to think about it; it comes apart. Most terrifying is the fear that if I look at it directly, I will see acceptance. Or *desire*.

I run my hands over my chest and belly; god, this sensation of *containing*. Promises of what I'll feel when I contain it all. A universe, its potential, its souls and stories, ends with me; ends *in* me. It's my shadow that will fall across them in their last moments.

I watch Frida and Zina turn cartwheels, scattering sparks, laughing hysterically.

I don't want to.

A familiar laugh bubbles in my blood. A human voice.

Going to stop the collapse of reality, love? Fight a being that can melt you into mist? Nice, look forward to seeing that.

I wince. He's gone, he's fragments seething through my body. But the sky and ocean are laughing at me, and my quiet "no" stands against a cacophony that's degrading and distorting the fabric of everything.

I find Kiera in a familiar spot, though it's distorted and degraded, too. The driftwood log she loved to sit on undulates, sand ripples when she digs in her toes, she's bathed in late-night sunlight. Matter knows and celebrates: She is precious to me.

She's wrapped around herself, shaking.

I creep closer, hidden in shifts of light, my power oiled by the flush of energy from the feast.

She senses my presence; light flares; she leaps up, setting the air vibrating.

I'll say, *It's still me*. I'll say, *I had a vision, I have to warn someone, I'm scared.* I will say, *How do I fight something that feels this good?*

I'll say, *But I have to fight, so you'll stop shaking and look me in the eye.*

But she runs, leaving me alone with disturbed flecks of light and sound in her wake.

I return to the solarium in a maroon and crimson dawn. This night was too long and too short. Time's recoiling, startled.

The plants have changed; too much time around me. The orchids have swollen, bleeding glowing, neon-amethyst sap. Leaves pulse visibly. The patterns on the butterflies' wings form messages; their bodies are ten-eyed, arm-sized.

Amid the sugar-sickly air, the bioluminescent glow, there's Jonah.

How long has he been waiting? Sleepless and disheveled in the lurid light. Despite it all, there's a sudden twist of fear in me; he's come to confront me, hasn't he? I let him down. I let him down again.

He's pacing, but stops, drops to his knees, and sobs.

"Thank you." His words are mutated too, by distress and joy. "Oh god, oh my terrible, monstrous, beloved god, fuck, *thank you*."

He presses thin lips to my feet. Saliva and tears smear my skin.

"Twice," he chokes. "You gave her back to me and I, your gift . . . I didn't . . . you brought her back. Never, never again . . . . My Myri. Everything, I . . . ."

I surprise myself with my human voice. "How's she doing?"

He wraps his arms around my ankles and curls up sniffling, moaning holy words. He doesn't answer my question. It's not me he's seeing.

I wasn't prepared for this. I forget sometimes that all this began with his love for her.

"I'm yours," he whispers, "in eternal gratitude, I am yours in Myri's name."

I let him sit, kissing my feet and mumbling prayers, as the clouds lighten, turning moss-green in the bloodred sky.

He relents, and straightens, eyes resonating with something different.

"Aoife. I'd like to talk to *you*. If you're here."

"I'm here." I am his terrible, monstrous, beloved god; still, I cringe. When Jonah looks like that, alarms blare.

"I want to know"—he locks his arms behind his back—"why you took Oscar, not me."

The orchids pulse with shock.

"You weren't subtle. You give back my daughter, do the thing, the one thing, I yearned to do. Then kill my friend in front of me. I'm not a fool; I know what you're trying to say. That I'm no longer in charge."

Was that something I intended? *Cut out the rot.* But I can't see Jonah that way. He's the heart of this place, light and rot all at once. I need him.

Everything's too big. I want him to take my hands and tell me it will be all right. I want him to stop looking at me like we're eyeing each other over a game board.

He smiles. "You won't take me that way. You know they need me. They live for you. But they look to me for the answers that you are too vast, inscrutable, to give. They need a human hand. And there's not much left in you that's human, is there?"

A windowpane smashes. It echoes far away, a punch thrown in a Phnom Penh street, a dam cracking in a Turkish valley.

I examine my hand. Does it look like flesh, *me*, or a costume? Shadows move under the skin, lights bloom under the nails. It looks thin-stretched, too small for what's inside.

"You see yourself growing in awesome power," Jonah continues, gentle, "but I see a remnant clinging to a body that isn't hers. A residue, playing pretend as she transforms." He takes my hand, studies it. "It's a beautiful, holy process. Don't mar it with human games."

He kneels again and brings his hands to my belly. There is a bulge to it, straining with sheer eagerness. He presses his lips to the swelling, like a proud father with an unborn child. He shows no shame, kissing my naked skin; it's not my skin, and my body isn't my body.

"Jonah." I have to dare. "Help me. I saw what it wants. It's . . . it's so angry, it's just angry and hungry, it's . . . the world, the whole universe . . . it's going to . . . destroy everything."

I wait, like the Unseen will snatch me out of existence for speaking the words. Nothing happens; it's beyond that, responses stranger than vengeful anger.

I wait, like Jonah will react in shock, reach out to help me. But his smile closes over what I've said, not a ripple.

"I serve you alone," Jonah murmurs to the swirling inside me. "If you are here to destroy, then I will revel in my own destruction."

Outside the window, side by side, like a photograph exposed wrong, two suns are rising.

CHAPTER FORTY-SIX

HUMAN

THERE'S SCREAMING AND PANIC IN THE WORLD. I FEEL ITS RESONANCE.

Not everybody sees or believes; but plenty speak of a second sun, multiplying stars, patterns in the portents. The echoes say, *Mass hysteria, end of days.*

But that's far away. Here, I stand in splintered sunlight, trying to fit around the fear and beauty. Distress floats, disturbing the butterflies, making eddies of cold air.

I'm tempted by distraction, lured toward things I could be for a while: a sandstorm, an oil pipeline, a cancer cell. I've barely begun to plumb the depths that opened in me when I absorbed Oscar and Elise. I don't need to be Aoife right now; I can be clouds, industrial accidents, a sunbeam splitting into rainbows.

Outside the window, two suns hover over the mountain, heavy with dawn. A mirrored pane reflects my face.

The reflected girl looks almost like a person. My eyes are wrong. My skin looks thin. Were my arms always that long, my mouth always that wide? My belly and chest bulge, distended. Jonah was right: I look like I'm pretending to be a human, unconvincingly.

I play. I stretch, I contract; my bones crack painlessly as my flesh reshapes itself, into something like a storybook monster, into something angelic, into something more real than reality, something more and less than human. I gaze in fascination and excitement, then lapse back into terror.

I contain a god; I am a god; where are the boundaries? Perhaps Jonah's right. Perhaps I'm already gone.

Are you here? I ask the Unseen, reaching into my mind and flesh, seeking words. *Speak to me. I gave you my body. You owe me that.*

The only answer I receive is a delicious shiver that begins in my core and surges out across thousands of miles, rippling crops and sand dunes and the skin of strangers. Inside me all stays quiet, though I wait and listen for a long, long time.

⊖

I move through the house as myself, or as close as I can get. I slip into Teresa's room and steal a faded flower-print dress, the first time I've bothered with clothes since I became . . . this. It's baggy on my distorted frame, too short for my limbs, but it'll do.

I savor the awkwardness about stealing someone's clothes. It's human.

It's human to run my fingers along the walls, even if they trail sparks. Human to stretch, even if my limbs extend like putty. Human to seek a friend.

I find her in the kitchen, helping Teresa attempt to cook. Food puffs colorful molds; seeds sprout inside spice jars. Water boils in glasses. The bread Teresa is kneading moves, like living flesh.

Doesn't matter. We're nourished by other things now.

When I enter, Teresa presses her hands against her eyes, murmuring another prayer. She loves me, trusts me. But she also remembers, viscerally, seeing her friend unravel into blood and guts and cells and vanish into me.

Myri doesn't cover her eyes.

Her heartbeat's steady. Green eyes regard me under that messy ginger fringe.

"*Myri.*" I have to let it echo through the stones and shiver the growths, don't I? Not sure if I'm a god playing at humanity or a human playing god. "*Come.*"

Face in her palms, Teresa doesn't see the reassuring glance that Myri shoots her before following me into the living room. The light in here's doubly bright, dancing.

Myri looks up at the god that returned her twice from death and cocks her head. "Want to watch something? A cartoon?"

A typhoon whips up in the South China Sea; in Prague, every bird takes wing at once; a bottomless pit rips open in a garden in Devonshire.

I burst into tears.

She spoke to me like a person. A goddamn person. And now she's standing, no caution when she puts her arms around me and lets me sob onto her shoulder. She must feel the power shuddering in me, the way my senses twine into her cells. She must not care.

"Sucks, doesn't it," she says; I giggle through my tears.

We slump onto the sofa, a shared movement, and exchange lopsided grins. The Unseen still roils in my bones, but it's not as overwhelming as it was. She's grounding me.

"It's so lonely." I wipe my eyes. "I'm scared, I could just . . . disappear into it, so easily, and I will, and I . . . ."

"I know." Myri puts an arm around my shoulder. "I was lonely too."

Light moves eerily across plains somewhere, an unexpected gentleness comes over people in squares and offices and markets.

"You're okay?" I ask her. "You're . . . ."

"I should be screaming broken, right?" Myri shakes her head. "Like, I was in a dark place struggling to wake up for *days*, and I come back and . . . this?" She shrugs, playing with her ponytail. "I've been weirder places when it was sleeping in me. Nightmares for days, impulses, senses going all twisty. I wasn't even totally dead this time!"

I laugh. There's a heaviness to her, but her words skip across its surface, light. She doesn't mention Sage. She must know he's gone, but I hope she doesn't know what happened to his body. I try not to notice that a tiny part of me is delighted at knowing something Myri doesn't.

"And I woke up and . . . it's not there. I'm still full of empty places, but it's not in them anymore. I'm Myri. I like rom-coms, and sometimes I write fanfiction. I pretend to like my mum's cooking more than I miss junk food. I might get a crush on someone one day, or maybe I'll just have friends. I might do a job and have a name tag and someone'll say, 'Myri's a weird name,' and I'll say it's short for the Latin word for *nutmeg* because nutmeg's sweet but dangerous, and they'll laugh and I'll snack in a park after work." She looks up at me; those eyes are very big, now. "Thanks. For giving me that."

I swallow. Does she know those things won't happen? Is this a comforting fantasy? I could read her for faith and fear. But I want that fantasy, too. I can't tell her.

"Thank you for thanking me. And not getting creepy and rubbing my belly like I'm going to pop the Unseen out *Alien*-style." Look. A human joke.

Myri groans. "He did that?"

I remember me. I'm pretending, maybe just a glimpse of myself, but it feels right. "He *really* hates that I have some of myself left. He kept accusing me of trying to . . . take over from him, when that's so *small*, compared with what's really happening." It surprises me, to hear those words from myself. I can't imagine Jonah ever thinking in small terms; surely there's more to it than this.

Myri nods slowly. "He's like that. He loves me. But sometimes he stopped seeing me and just saw *it*. He didn't like when I wanted to be a person, kept thinking I'd undermine him. Why do you think I was locked in the cabin?" She puts on a Jonah voice. "*It's dangerous for you to interact with people, my love.*"

The walls convulse sympathy.

"You wouldn't believe how stage-managed it was, when *it* spoke through me. I'd have a vision, and I'd tell him and have to put on the Possessed Myri Show. I hated it. But I had to." She chews the end of her ponytail. "I didn't know what he'd do."

My jaw clenches. Part of me, suddenly, yearns to make Jonah suffer in my core. Most of me is shocked at that thought. He's *Jonah*. Without him, what are any of us?

"But he's my dad," Myri says. "We're in this dark place together. We need each other."

"I won't hurt him," I promise, blinking away tears. My vision is prisms. Maybe the world is prisms right now, the light changing in sync with my senses. "I need him, too."

Myri continues to chew on her hair. "I'm sorry. It was meant to be me. The vessel."

"Sorry?" That laugh must be too high. "It's scary, it's baffling, but . . . it's wonderful. It's an *honor*. I've never been important. I only made tiny marks on the world, and they were cleared away. Now everything reshapes just for me. I *exist*. Like nobody else ever did."

I smile to show her I mean it. The teeth are wrong, the lips cracked, something moving behind them. But I smile anyway. It's our language: crafting illusions, fantasies neither of us believe in, wrapping them around each other's eyes.

Myri's eyes are clear. "I mean, it *should* have been me. I saw this, okay? You heard me scream. You know why I offered myself for the ritual. If it wasn't me, things were going to spiral. I saw the two suns. I saw the fracturing that's coming. I saw the hole in the world, I felt . . . what happens . . . to me. It wasn't like a normal pain."

I grit my teeth. She knew. She spun images of future Myri, free, as another daydream. And now she's dropping the fantasy, but I can't; the idea that I might have to fills my voice with heat. "I won't let anything happen. Not to you."

Myri lets her hand fall into her lap, staring down at it. A small hand, cells and energy. "It's okay. It's too late. So I have to be okay about it."

Something grips me, sour enough to be anger but softer, an urge to reassure. How much is it mine? The words that emerge from the air aren't, I don't think. "*You are precious to me; you will be protected and rise as something extraordinary.*" I fill the room with swirls of light and color, promises of unformed euphoria.

Myri's eyes widen. Her face hardens.

All the fantasies are unraveling; I grip my own self again but all my own voice has to offer is desperation. "Can we watch something? Talk about buses or swans or whatever?"

She doesn't reply. She's shut down, face blank now, but in the air around her, I taste a sad resignation. She saw me as human before we talked. She doesn't see me as that anymore.

I nod and leave.

My followers shy away as I move along the beach. With two suns and other lights cascading around them, the day's uncannily bright. Washed out by brilliance, like it might dissolve. I am brighter still, hurting their eyes if they dare look.

The sea's a lazy white-gold mirror, moving like molten metal.

I made all this.

Quicksilver whispers in the garden.

Larissa and Giulia are on the swing, kissing furiously. I've seen their rhythm since Giulia returned; fierce, furious, unforgiving fights, *you betrayed us* against *your hands helped to kill me*, followed by agonized, desperate, unforgiving embraces, *it's us, we're still together, we're still both here.* Cycling over and over, one just leading to the next.

I slip closer, invisible in the brilliance as they break apart and fall back into their argument.

". . . relax and see how beautiful it is." Larissa gestures to the blossoms, how they writhe in the uncanny light. "We dreamed about this! It's among us, doing its work."

"And you're"—Giulia lets out an angry sigh—"okay with whatever *its work* is. Yes, Oscar deserved what he got. Maybe Elise gets peace. But don't tell me it wasn't the most fucked-up thing you ever saw. Those people *coming apart* and *sucked into it.* Don't tell me that's not going to be in your nightmares, imagining that happening to you—"

"Then my nightmares will be holy," Larissa snaps.

Good girl. A smile, intangible, maybe not mine.

Larissa softens. "Please don't talk like this. I . . . what if it hurts you?" She brings her lips to Giulia's neck. Their tenderness always made me ache. "I just got you back. Can't you be grateful?"

Giulia leans into the kiss briefly, then stands, looking down at her shaking hands. "Back from where? Who sent me there?" Her tone's thick and bitter. "I *still feel it*, do you *get* that? My body remembers dying. Every blow. I was still awake, I *felt it*, hands, inside, *pulling.* That feeling *lives* in me now, every fucking second."

I try to feel her pain, my guilt, but it's very far away.

Larissa. Unkempt and gorgeous and hurting, in the unearthly glow. "Lia, I—"

"Don't." Giulia raises a hand. "I love you, but fuck's sake, Larissa, do not ask me to forgive you. And do *not* ask me to worship the thing you killed me for." She turns in a circle, like she's trying to leave but can't, some tether holding them together.

"It brought you back," Larissa repeats, voice shaky as she tries to hold on to it.

"And now everything's fine," Giulia sneers, sarcastic. "I get to watch it stroll around in Aoife's corpse, melting us down one by one for its nightmare world." She sets her chin. "All I've got left is that tiny hope that I can salvage something before we spiral into hell. And if you have a problem with my blasphemy there, just murder me. You already did once."

This time she finds the strength to walk away.

It's startling, being so lost in other people that you forget that you exist.

355

Aoife's corpse. Larissa flinched, a deep hurt, when Giulia mentioned me; she didn't tell her I'm still here. Keeping my secret. Or she doesn't believe I'm still me at all.

Larissa's stricken, blinking back tears. My bird of paradise, trying so hard not to be broken.

I'm going to tell her.

I coalesce. Gawky limbs, mess of cropped hair, naked on the lawn.

She catches her breath and looks straight at me, bold as ever. My pulse pounds through the lavender and the poison garden.

I say, simply, stupidly, wonderfully, "Hello."

Her lips widen into a smile of delight, and she dares to approach me. I am the world, and I surround her. She's Larissa who I worshipped once, and I'm dancing in her cells.

"Please," she says. "I'm all yours. I love you. But please don't punish Giulia. She's so lost. Please, let her find her way back to you."

I place a hand on her cheek. She closes her eyes, pure bliss and amazement. *Don't fear for Giulia,* I want to say. *Because I'm still Aoife, and she's my friend.* But the words that come out are, "*She is my beloved child, too.*"

Peace and relief sweep across her face. Her eyes open; she gazes at me, enraptured.

It's intoxicating, how she looks at me. She loved Aoife like a friend, a pet, a student in her way of multicolored living. The Unseen, she adores with her whole soul, and I soak that up like drinking sunlight. I yearned to have her look at me like this.

I can't say it.

Instead, I send my power out; she rises from the ground, bubble-light, laughing in surprise. I rise, too, and we hover, breezes whipping around us. Look at her joy, as innocent as it's deep and holy.

I gather her in.

A long, slow kiss. I reward her with whole new flavors of pleasure. The heat of her blood is an offering. Her shivers are prayers.

Aoife could never have given her this. I taste in her mouth everything that I can be, if I allow it.

Over the Arctic Circle, the sky flickers out like a switch has been flipped, and fireworks burst brilliant out of the stars. In an industrial town in Thailand, factory walls melt into the same sparks, and the breeze carries enchanting whispers into the workers' ears.

We hang there, a god and her acolyte wrapped in each other. And when we sink to the ground, she stands flushed and astonished and overflowing with love. And despite everything, as I walk away, my smile's so wide it could split the sky.

When I touch the grasses, they flame. When I touch the rocks, they melt to water.

It's giddy, it's beautiful, I'm feverish.

I'm hungry.

I'm laughing among the treetops, my laugh bouncing off the washed-out sky; imagine, just a few hours ago, I wanted to stay human. I am changed, blissfully changed.

Look what I can do.

I find Jonah at the lip of the sea, letting the waters lap at his toes. There are not nightmares in the ocean, now. It is not exactly an ocean, now. Bioluminescence blooms in it in extraordinary colors, visible because Jonah stands in darkness, despite it being the middle of a painfully brilliant day. It's just a little rift in light or time, nothing to worry about.

I tell him, "*Hello*," in a voice that's both Aoife's and the Unseen's, because who *cares*, really, where that line is now?

He's hesitant, wrong-footed, looking up in his shard of night to see tendrils of light surrounding me. Still on a high from Larissa's touch, from her worship, I can barely contain my glow. I might just erupt supernova any moment.

"You were right," I say, and my *god*, the confidence I speak with now, the delightful recklessness of it. "We need you. I need you, Jonah. I need you to lead them, and I need you to help me hold back from devouring it all. Because I will. I am going to hold back. I'm not going to destroy this world. I'm going to make it a paradise."

He closes his eyes and savors the light I pour on his cheeks.

"*But please. Let Myri have her freedom. Give me that, if you love me as your god. I do not know what my hands will shape this world into, but she will not be a prisoner again, you will not ask her to playact oracle again, and she will walk free in it.*"

See what I can do? Myri might shrink from me, but I can still liberate her. I can be a good god, a wonderful god. I can shape the luminescence in the sea into a whole aurora. I can speak truths I would have stifled, before. See where it begins?

He opens his eyes, and the fear settles, replaced by something even I'm not sure I can read. A resolve, I think. "For you, unknown one, anything. You will see what I can give."

He kneels, and kisses my feet, and I close that shard of dark, bathing us in the light of a mutated sky, at peace. I ignore the muffled weeping in my veins and cells and promise him and myself, "*Then it will all be beautiful.*"

CHAPTER FORTY-SEVEN
TO MOLD INTO
SOMETHING GLORIOUS

Moving so fast, it speaks the language of momentum; I'm roaring traffic, a spinning wind turbine, a waterfall, a gust sending a seagull off course over the rooftops of Valparaiso. *Faster spiraling irresistible, toward ever greater glory.*

Moments are cramping and dilating. This day has lasted days. It's lasted seconds.

I hang above the ocean, clothed in twists of light, a light that corrodes and dissolves, turning memories soft and strange if anyone gazes into them too long. I know I'm doing this right because I am not submitting to the hunger starting to yawn inside me again. I'm distracting that emptiness. Jonah's helping. Look: He's gathered them. They kneel in the agonizing light and chant, following his lead. *Adore, Unseen, surrender.* The words touch my skin, physical.

Look how they love me.

One by one, Jonah guides them to the water. They place flowers on the sun-bleached surface. They kiss my feet and make their true offering.

I look into their eyes and see minds edging toward breaking completely. Some already have. Frida's thoughts are wrenched apart by more joy than she can hold. I gulp Kai's denial, so fierce he can't comprehend his own senses. João's insistence that Oscar is talking to him is sweet in my mouth.

It's okay. They love me. I'll make everything wonderful for them.

Teresa comes to me, so, so little of her left, but I take her offerings greedily. Larissa scatters jasmine, and I drink deep from that well of devotion, and still there's more. Giulia wades through the shallows, dull-eyed and reticent, scattering poison berries. I take nothing from Giulia.

This will not satisfy me, but worship sings through me like a drug.

Jonah comes to me with hothouse flowers, twisting in his hands. I take nothing from him, either; my little peace offering. I am being a good girl, a good god, letting my priest guide the way. We will work together, I remind him, in the breath of hot wind on his cheeks. We will work together and make everything beautiful.

Kiera brings me origami flowers. She folded them herself, scrawled on them, and a little of me smiles because even now I struggle to read her handwriting. She kisses my feet, stares up through the fierce light, and unlike the others, chooses what to give me.

She offers memories of a wide, golden landscape, clouds chasing their shadows, a rickety wooden church under a rickety wooden cross. Of the girl she kissed there the day she learned consequences. Of a thumb out to traffic, nowhere to go. Of a city and what it did to her. Of second chances and piles of books, dying houseplants and *please, I can't fuck this up*, caffeinated and shaking in a lecture theater. She offers me the story of Kiera, that she never dared tell me.

All this she gives up without resistance, and I reach deeper, out of kindness, out of love, to take her fear from her.

She grips it like a lifeline. She *refuses*. The trauma of her death, the terror of what's to come, she clings to, ferocious. She says, "Please."

I let her keep it. I'm a gracious god.

Waves of offerings keep coming, gifts I grow drunk on, the stuff of their selves.

This won't satisfy me.

I take only what they offer, but it stirs my appetite, and my body cramps with its cravings. Think of the miracles I have wrought already, just from a few bodies and minds. Imagine. Imagine how much more I could be, nourished by my adoring congregation; imagine growing vaster and vaster until it's easy to drink down a universe and recycle it within into something perfect. Simpler than reshaping this one, no?

But I am a good god, so I hold fast to my humanity, and I let the scraps they give me be enough.

⊖

Somewhere in the Atlantic, I'm tossing a cargo ship on vast waves. I'm stirring riots in Bukhara and Barcelona. Here, I am a girl who is not a girl, in an ill-fitting body, moving through corridors that ripple at my presence.

The patterns of the carpets turn fractal. I'm hungry.

I pause outside the library doors, examining the stained glass. It's pretty. I take those colors and expand them, let them cover the sky for a while, turning sunlight to smoked crimson and rich azure. I giggle at the beauty and become stained-glass colors myself, and pass through the light and the colors into the library.

Kiera's been curled up in a corner, but at the skin-tingling sense of my presence, she leaps to her feet. She winces in my light, and raises her hand to cover her eyes, but still, she approaches me. With curiosity, with grim determination.

I let the light simmer down, though it still flickers like static. I try to remember me. I shape my body; I won't get it right, but I try. Sharp cheekbones, knobby knees, hot mess of an impulse haircut. All the things that never fit me right. All the things Kiera liked anyway.

I know I'm getting it wrong because she can safely look at me now, but she still can't hide the revulsion. I know she just sees a monster pretending to be her friend. But is that worse than standing here as the girl who killed her?

The jolt at that thought makes the walls spasm like flesh, sending books scattering across the floor. I soothe it. There won't be pain anymore. I won't let there be.

"Is it . . ." Kiera breathes deep. "Still you?"

"I think so," I say. "Me and it, all at once." I smile, and all things feel my smile.

I've made my art of every corner of the Farmstead; my vaster self is doing the same to the world, softening it to mold into something glorious. Only the library stands unchanged. Perhaps eerily, dust motes unmoving and shadows at the wrong angles. But I left her sanctuary untouched.

She's staring at me, hostile suspicion.

"It's okay," I tell her, and I try to lean against the sofa, like a person would, and I make extra effort to make sure it stays a sofa, that it doesn't immolate or transform at my touch. "I'm . . . I think I'm starting to see everything that's possible, and it's . . . it's amazing, Kiera, it's so fucking amazing." I shake my head. I sound like me, I think. "We were right; we were really right. Waking it, waking me, letting it free . . . we can make the world into a paradise." I hope my grin's playful rather than hungry. "Make the laws of physics our bitch."

I gather light in my hands and toss it to her; she flinches, and it flickers out.

I try to keep the smile wide, the normal width. "I'm going to need your help."

". . . Help," she says doubtfully, and it sounds like a plea more than anything.

"Help." I stand up and lope around on the midnight-blue rug, and it almost doesn't ripple under my feet. "I don't . . . ." Is something faltering? My confidence stutters for a second; I grip it. "I need ways to help to contain it, to contain myself, to make sure I . . . I keep all this under control, so I don't. You know." *I'm hungry. I can taste your heartbeat. I can taste the heartbeats of a whole world, and I yearn to feel them pulsing in the back of my throat. To feel you there, for a moment.*

"*Contain* it?" She runs a hand through her hair. Disheveled, disheveled Kiera, a pale thing crawled free from death. It hangs around her, still, though, an invisible fog.

"Your books, right?" How odd, to be trying to talk someone into something. I could force her. "All your little rituals and secrets. There must be something."

Kiera shakes her head, crackling with nervous energy. "I don't think anyone ever tried to figure out how to *contain* it, because everyone who knew it could wake were like"—she jerks her head—"them, happy to be swallowed if they got to playact as chosen ones on the way down, and oh fuck, I just remembered what I'm talking to—"

"Me, Kiera," I say. "You're talking to me."

She closes her eyes again. "You don't look right."

"I'm trying my best." How is my voice so small?

The world spirals on, stranger and stranger, at the edge of my awareness. The Unseen plays in viruses and fungi, tides and wires.

"If." I feel Kiera's courage falter. She's thinking how one wrong step will be her ending. She's remembering how Oscar screamed. She's trying to see Aoife but sees a mockery. "If I say anything, god, I already—will it—"

I shake my head. "I don't think it . . . punishes, like that. There's love in the hunger. It takes what it wants, I take what I want, but . . . but it's, I'm, not going to annihilate you because you speak your mind."

She nods miserably, trying to trust. "I don't know. I don't know if there's anything out there that can contain something that can double the sun."

We look out of the window. A long midday, pale as opal, over hills that waver in shades of jade.

"Looks like it's fading," she says dully. "The world. Only it's not that peaceful, is it? It'll tear it apart before it feasts. Before you feast."

I look at her sharply.

"I know." She swallows again. "Jonah kept records of Myri's prophecies. He never shared them; I had to dig. But she saw what's coming, didn't she? You'll destroy everything. Devour it all to make space for your paradise. He knew this might be how this ended. He knew, and we . . . closed our eyes and followed him."

I try to find anger at that. I can't. He trusted. He was *right* to trust.

"It won't happen," I insist. "I'm still here, I'm still me. I won't do it. I'll channel it, I'll find ways, I'll make everything beautiful." My voice strains, trying to hold the scale of that promise.

We stand shoulder to shoulder. She stares at the light-bleached land-scape, fighting something somewhere inside.

"So help me," I say, at the same moment she says, "I'll help you."

Our eyes meet, and we grin at that timing, and then we're laughing, a joyless, scared laugh. It's almost bonding, but there's a gulf it doesn't cross. We're laughing, but we're not laughing together.

I say it, the thing I've been trying to warp reality to crush and can't. "Fuck, it's so beautiful, and I'm so scared."

And then her arms are around me, and mine are around her, and we're clinging and clinging. I taste her resolve, I hear her whisper, "I've got you." I killed her. I'm the god she was killed for. She's terrified. And she clings to me anyway, digs her fingers into my skin, seeking safety, offering comfort, taking refuge in the arms of the very thing she fears.

I scream to yawn open and draw her in, think what power she could give me, but I focus on what human sensations I can find, her, ragged breathing in time with mine.

My limbs shift, my features soften, and for the first time since I woke with a god in my skin, I feel my body take a familiar form, settling into the contours of my human self.

"I've chanted *surrender* so many times," she muses, face still pressed against my shoulder. "It's hard not to. Part of me still trusts, you know? It feels easier. To let go and believe there's something after the end."

"It does," I say, and, "there will be," and that tempts me, too, or tempts the Unseen in me, or maybe both.

"Fuck it," Kiera whispers into my skin. "No. This is my world. It's shit and brutal and bloody weird and it suffocates and it's *ours*. I died for it. I'll tear this library to shreds and get torn to shreds myself if there's *anything* to find, *anything* we can do. To do what you want to, right? To make this world better, rather than obliterating and replacing it. We can do that."

We breathe together, excited and terrified, and that's what glory would look like, isn't it? All the thrill and wonder at the world that we feel when we're together, all my power and her enthusiasm and our curiosity, working together. Imagine the universe that would birth.

I wonder, distantly, why this doesn't feel right. Why it doesn't feel like *enough*.

She pulls back, and we share tired, wan grins, and I say, "Yes?" and she says, "Okay." And I see in her the fear, and I know it's not of the Unseen this time, but of *me*, of her killer. Still, hope is there too, just as vivid in those gold-brown eyes.

Chanting swells in the distance, floating in through the open window.

A rhythmic wash of voices. The presence inside and around me shivers deliciously. A summoning.

My beloved ones, calling me. Joy surges. I'll stand before them and soak in more love than I ever imagined. I'll know their devotion when the best that human Aoife ever had was half-hearted acceptance. I'll take all they give, and they will give me more, and I will fill past the brim.

"Aoife." A warning note. "Don't go, okay? Let's . . . let's take a minute, look for things we can do, to make sure you keep control. They'll still be there after."

She puts a hand on my arm.

My arm, that isn't my arm, that is an emanation of an endless, ravening thing. My skin that's inhuman under her fingers, all jolts and embers and oil slicks.

She recoils.

And I hear them calling, and desire stabs through me.

I follow my worshippers' call.

CHAPTER FORTY-EIGHT
GIVEN FREELY IN LOVE

TIME'S UTTERLY SCREWED. WE WERE IN THE LIBRARY FOR MINUTES, TWIN suns still high. But hours have passed out here—hours of work, the groves decked in lights and fabrics and torches and flowers.

It looks like a wedding. White-linen, candlelit romance, undisturbed for now by the primal strangeness spinning in every atom.

The Farmstead is gathered, in their wildest ritual gear, animal masks and fairy lights and leaf crowns, body paint and formal dress. Jonah in robes, Myri defiantly ordinary in her hoodie. The music from the speakers is distorted, but sweet and strange and solemn.

I feel it in their bodies. Something's happened. A decision's been made.

Feel that despair and excitement. Taste it in the complex salt crystals in their tears. That sensation of approaching a brink, that we've felt together so many times. So strange to stand outside it. So strange to be the brink.

There's just one sun now, dipping below the horizon.

I cling to my human body. I know what to do now. I'll take their love, I'll relish it, but I will not take the world from them.

My breath shakes. I like that. Mine, even if those aren't really lungs now.

The chanting quiets as I approach. Light palpitates. The sand under my feet melts to glass and cracks. I hear Kiera yelling protests as the crowd absorbs her, holding her back.

Jonah bows deeply. I stand before him, not unfurling, just me.

A tense part of me notices that someone isn't here. Dread widens in my stomach.

Jonah's calm; a prophet again, intoning. "Our hidden one emerged into light. Our creature of nightmares released. Our gratitude and love are as wide as the sky."

I wait for the payoff, nerves dissonant against the anticipation.

"We offer you a symbol of our utter surrender, to bolster your power."

Myri shakes her head urgently. I catch her eye, to nod and say *no*.

But then I see the one person who was missing.

Larissa's always beautiful. Beauty that left me breathless, especially when it was effortless. Larissa disheveled as we ran for the ferry. Larissa with sleep-dust in her eyes and sheet rumples on her face, yawning with smeared makeup, sweat-soaked in the fields.

Tonight, emerging from the trees, she's more than beautiful. She's radiant. A bride.

She walks naked, daubed with paint, glyphs scrawled in lipstick. Jasmine in her hair. Colorful beads line her neck, wrists, ankles. Silver rings glint.

I recognize other people's jewelry. I imagine them giving it to her. Parting gifts.

Her smile's broad, so happy it almost disguises the desperate pounding of her heart, the tears slipping from her eyes. Terror and joyful completion overflow; I feel them in every pulse of her warm flesh.

A hole opens in me, filled with revulsion, at what they're doing, what *he's* doing, and at the delight that it stirs. What a gift. I can't wait to unwrap and tear into it.

Of course Larissa would be the one to open the sky, bloat me to span the universe.

No.

"Larissa was all yours from the first moment," Jonah says. You have to listen carefully to hear the smugness. You have to know how well that can hide. "You shine from her eyes; she has lived her every moment in your name. We give her freely in love, to nourish your glory."

I remember his calm when I confronted him and told him to leave Myri alone, his double-edged promise: *You'll see what I can give.* This is nothing holy. This is a human move. This is familiar. This is punishment.

The arrogance of it, to try to punish a god. The hubris. I should turn on him. But I can't; I'm captivated by Larissa, her every emotion, every tremble in each of her nerves.

Giulia's shouting, "Stop, *no.*" Pietro holds her back, deer mask blank and implacable. "Larissa, look at me." Her voice cracks.

Larissa looks at her, her smile loving and sad, and shakes her head.

Giulia grows quieter, so only I will feel the words. "Aoife, please."

I want to say I won't.

But a vaster desire paralyzes me. Frenzy's rising inside me, hunger convulsing, and next to it I am nothing. I grit my teeth, gripping what's left of my body, straining to contain the ravenous thing inside.

And she's in front of me, Jonah beside us in the fiery sunset, a mockery of a marriage. She looks me in the eyes. What does she see? Starlight? Void?

I feel the warmth of her, taste her blood, the adrenaline, the dread in her belly, the interlocking parts of her, the majesty of her body, the brilliant width of her mind, the sheer love and adventure and recklessness of her. Spaces yawn wide to enfold it all. What power she'll become, with such a whirling, multicolored world inside her.

She says, "Beloved faceless one," and falters, briefly too scared to speak; my heart cracks. Then her face settles. "No, not faceless. You look like Aoife, a little."

Jonah watches. Giulia's yells are muffled, Kiera's and Myri's, too. The chanting is far away. The world's grown gentler, distant; we're the only thing that's real.

I won't. It's *her*.

"I *am* Aoife." I whisper. "I'm me."

The wonder in her dissolves.

Her glow of worship disintegrates as something human and fallible speaks from the mouth of her god. There's shock there. Consternation. *Disappointment.*

It's the briefest instant, then her tearful smile returns. "No. You're so much more than that."

She leans in, all courage, and meets my lips.

That kiss undoes me.

Fingers on a fresh bruise. Her *disappointment* that I'm alive and here. She's not kissing Aoife, she's kissing the Unseen; what am I, against the expanse of what she worships?

The hot rage of rejection crumbles my resolve.

Hitching breath, sweat and jasmine, warm skin, stirring an alien greed.

The tenderness of this. I spiral into her and know every cell and know she chose this over me. I know fear in Larissa, the girl with confidence as wide as the sky. Not all my instincts are hunger. One is to soothe her terror with my body.

But my body isn't my body. It's yawning jaws, a hole in the universe.

She lets out the softest sound of pleasure and terror, love and regret, surrenders herself and dissolves into me like sugar on a tongue.

The pieces of her whirl away through me, sweetest nectar, screaming; she's gone too fast to comprehend it.

Stop—come *back*—

The horror's unending. I fall into it and keep falling.

I *feel* Larissa in me, fragmented, luxuriating, struggling. I reach inside in panic, to undo what I've done, but with every touch she comes apart more, breaking down into pure energy, irretrievable.

Oh, the luscious glow of her transmuting. A high like no other. Any moment now—

But in the moment before that moment, there's Giulia.

She bursts out of Pietro's arms, fierce and fearless and broken and running at me. Hair blowing on the wind, freckled face screwed up with fury.

They let her. Why would they care what I do to her?

She flings herself at a god. So quiet, but there was always something feral in her that the strictures of ritual and the mysteries of the unknown couldn't hold.

I expect her to pound at my thinning skin with her fists, vent her fury on the body containing her lover. But she pulls up short, twisting her face into a defiant sneer.

She said all she had was a scrap of hope she could salvage something. She knows that's gone now. All she has left is to go down fighting.

That's how I understand, too, that it's too late to stop any of this.

She knows what will happen. She says it anyway.

"I knew you were fucking weak."

Rage surges.

The elixir that was Larissa flows into it, instant alchemy. I erupt, anger transforming the last of her into sheer power.

Giulia is living and livid and her fury and pain are rich and good. I come down on her in a fever of delighted greed and rip her out of the world.

The explosion of power redoubles as she bursts through me, hot and bitter.

My senses are fireworks. New senses, showing me new things.

The fiery cores of stars. Black holes suffocating light. The freezing void. Planets spin out of their orbits; time goes punch-drunk, distances crumble.

Giulia and Larissa gave me galaxies.

Cracks emerge. Reality forgets its arrangements. There are openings, tunnels, walls. There's a clutch of people, grabbing each other as fever quakes wash through all existence.

I sprawl through the endless universe, briefly sated.

Follow those tendrils and there's a body that doesn't look human. The fragile thing I'm rooted into curls up and cries, feeling their disorientation and pain coursing through her, caressing her. She's thinking about two bags at the foot of a tree.

She's remembering how she left hers there, so it would look like she wasn't alone.

⊖

There's a time. A moment. A century. I'm looking at Jonah, and he's looking at me, and there's nothing and nobody else.

I see him. A petty, power-drunk man, punishing a god by breaking me utterly. He's won. I didn't know this was a game, I trusted, and I lost.

A universe quakes with unquenchable rage.

He looks away from me, to Myri, brushes her hair behind her ears as she stares and trembles. "Don't be afraid. You know it's just what she— it—does to the things it loves."

⊖

Space and time fracture.

I'm not sure how I got here.

The kitchen's full of people, dancing, laughing, delirious. Music's pumping, food cooking, Darya spinning in circles, Pietro sobbing on the floor.

I blink. The kitchen's empty. The table's stained with blood.

My mind's clear.

Jonah. Jonah made me do this.

I turn. The living room is full of ocean. Waves crash with a force that could fell cities, maelstroms swirl. The horizon stretches too far; there's no end to that violence.

He gave me what I couldn't resist. He wanted to show me that I couldn't resist its will, that its will is his, that he can manipulate even a god. He won.

I stumble through a door, and somehow, it leads to Larissa's hut.

It's always soaked in color. Crystals, clothes, rugs. Now the colors have warped. Radioactive neon; colors that shouldn't exist, that rot something in your soul. I love her so much and she isn't totally gone and I scream it in colors gone horribly wrong.

It still smells like lying in her arms.

I can hate him now. I can say it: He is the rot. She's gone, worse than gone, because of Jonah. I will kill him.

I look in the mirror, like I might see her there, dark eyes snapping. Instead, I see myself. My skin's translucent; my innards squirm, inhuman anatomy. New passageways, new hollows, to work something finer and stranger. Perhaps this shattering of space extends to my body. Step into my throat and maybe you'd tumble into the core of the sun.

Was it him, though?

The glass shatters, refusing to reflect me.

It wasn't just him. I'm weak and angry, a toxic mix. Who made me this, the perfect vessel for all this furious hunger?

Through the door, and I tumble into a familiar town, a concrete monstrosity of a high street. The doors and walls of Tallerton have become living things. Fluids pool in the gutters. The buildings thrash, and I listen to the screams within. A desperate face at a jewelers' window; I admire the gemstones glittering in rows. What secrets are hidden in their facets? Maybe that this was just a town, that it was something else that stifled me all those years.

Craig molded you into this, perfect for the Unseen to nest inside.

I scream, too, an agonized howl from almost-human lungs, a howl from my own twisted husk of a body, and it rings out through the undulating streets. But there's no release in it, no relief, because the rage isn't in my body, but suffusing all of reality. Coiling in the earth's core, erupting in stars, fragmenting time and space into shards.

Peace comes over the streets, the screams falling quiet. I'm starting to understand.

It wasn't just Craig. It was a whole world. A world that sneered at me for yearning to be more than just a dutiful daughter and girlfriend and employee, a body, a tool. A world that tenderized me and thrust me into the grip of people like Jonah and Craig, so they could shape me into this.

Through the nearest door, and I'm in the solarium. It's drowning in flowers, stained glass darkening a red glow from outside to bruise-purple. My temple.

A chrysalis hangs from a branch. A life inside, transforming, keeping its memories as it breaks down. My fingers, almost like human fingers, stroke the silky, papery skin.

I can stand in my rage now, in my strange infinite body. The last thing this reality will know, as my jaws engulf it, is how wrong it was to underestimate me.

Snip. All the illusions fall away.

All of this needed to happen, to make me what I am: the end of this reality, the start of a new one. I see that now. There's peace in it.

The rage seething through every atom becomes giddy and bright. Nothing will ever matter. I'm free, and I choose to break this world between my teeth.

The light's brighter now, splintering between the leaves.

I squeeze, and the chrysalis splits, life thick and slimy on my fingers.

CHAPTER FORTY-NINE

IN THE FINAL HOURS

I DON'T KNOW WHERE I FIND JONAH. THE GROVES, THE SOLARIUM, THE kitchen. Maybe we're inside the chambers of one of our hearts, or in a black hole. Wherever we are, reality's forgotten what it's meant to be.

Darkness moves like cards shuffling. Scents hint: lavender, pine, ocean, blood. Rotting rubbish, petrol, antiseptic.

The only light is on us, side by side. We got here moments ago; we've always been here. I've been explaining to him what is to come. That all this is the death spasms of reality. That when he gave me Larissa, he killed the world. That of our family here, some will persist in the new world I birth, and others will be swallowed up as the final spark that begins the end.

He's not surprised. He knew where his games might lead. He just didn't care, focused on the next maneuver, perhaps believing that the consequences would come later and be for others. I'm trying to understand that. I never will.

The light on Jonah keeps changing. Blazing, swimmy. It doesn't want to touch us.

"Who will it be?" He's calm, curious. Not asking *directly* what will happen to him. Humble Jonah, always serving his god.

Not you. Even now, something in me loves and needs you. But I can't say that.

"Whoever chooses to give themselves." The words don't sound like mine. The hunger behind them is, now, I think. "They're willing."

I squeeze his hand. Those aren't fingers. His shiver of revulsion is so lovely.

"That they are. Larissa went so easily, didn't she? All I had to say was that the Unseen loved her best of all and chose to unite with her." I can't tell if this is cruelty or comfort. In him, they're intertwined. "She cried. She didn't want to go but couldn't say it. But she was brave."

She squirms in me, tingling, half-remembering. Her remnants miss life.

I can't turn back from this pain. It's not a presence, it's a process. A one-way road.

"I would love," I whisper, "to tear you nerve from nerve and atom from atom. Not even to consume you. Just to watch you feel it. The only reason I don't is because I promised Myri. She *wants* me to spare you, even after everything you did to her—"

I'm surprised by the violence in Jonah's voice. "I'm *doing this* for Myri!"

The darkness echoes my stunned laugh.

He sighs, anger dissipating. "This reality killed her. I want her to have a world without suffering. All this was for her, and I only understood that when I'd already lost her."

I shake my head in wonder. "You were going to let her be the vessel. You locked her away; you made her your puppet—"

He looks at me sidelong. We read it in each other: We both know what it is to be so dazzled by your own power that everything you wanted it for is lost in its glare.

I admire his angles: loving father, zealous prophet, little despot. He's all three dimensions, a prism slicing her—all of us—into strands of light too fragile to last alone.

That's why he and I sit together, unwilling allies. We've both discovered or decided that to love is to break.

"I don't care about the new world." I lean back and find cold metal. The door of a cabin, or a cheap flat. "I just want this one to burn."

Reality's fragmented, tenderized for the feast. My worshippers are scattered through the scraps.

Some are in the remaining pieces of the Farmstead. Pietro stares at the bedsheets he's feeding into a bonfire, Teresa's harvesting glass baubles from the trees, Darya's turning cartwheels on the ocean. Myri's in her cabin; the ceiling opens to a dizzying drop down the cliffside.

Others are trapped in fragments of memories. Ana in a jail cell. João sheltering from punches in an alley. Kai cringing on a sports field as other boys sneer and shove. Aksel dialing an ambulance as Frida lies unresponsive. Maisie hearing a key click and knowing her husband's home. Zina drawing on a napkin under a table, hungry but knowing better than to ask for food.

I spread through my tendrils and find them.

The time for words is over.

I show them how it will feel when I swallow up the reality that gave us our doubts and shames and bruises. I show them the quiet after the nightmares end, a new world growing.

I wait for joy.

Through all the broken angles, they sink to their knees and thank me and love me. But their hands tremble, their voices choke, tears spill. The joy doesn't come.

So, I show them the cost, and savor instead their holy terror.

Space folds over itself.

"Did you make this?" Kiera asks.

We're on the library balcony. That was always our place. Sun, our legs propped against wrought iron spirals, geraniums, awkward smiles over coffee.

It's not *right*. The dream logic of our guttering reality can't grasp it. The iron spirals twist, the geraniums unfurl like optical tricks. The sea reflects a night sky, but the sky glows red, a fleshy writhing, sunlight filtered through muscle like torchlight through a hand.

"I think so. Space and time are fucked; I don't know how much I'm controlling it."

All moments exist forever. We've always been here. We just arrived.

"I don't like it," she says.

"It's still home. It's just forgotten."

She says, "I'm so fucking scared." I reach for her, and she looks at what my hand looks like and flinches away.

The flesh of the sky convulses. We lapse into quiet.

"Is there *any* of you left?" Kiera asks. "Larissa, Giulia, you . . . killed them."

"It's transmuting, not killing." I almost believe it. "They'll persist in me forever."

"Jesus." Kiera stares at me in wonder. "You're so far gone you actually think that's comforting, don't you?" She closes her eyes. I become muffled sunlight on her eyelids. "Does it hurt them?"

I want to tell her there's pleasure in it, tell her about the delicious intimacy and sublime glory of it, but I just say, "Yes."

She opens her eyes. "Thank you. For not lying."

A thrill grips me as I realize what she's doing: choosing her fate. Explore the new world I birth or burn in me to build it.

"In this new world"—her voice cracks—"will I still watch my death over and over? Will this still feel like some fucked-up epilogue?"

Sun breaks through a slice in the muscular sky; the celestial flesh and skin part, a patch of daylight moves across the sea, and in it everything looks normal. It passes over us, and for a second, it's us.

It's her and me and even here, human, I have no idea how to respond to what she said. It's still like every word could shatter something precious.

We never figured out how to fit our fractured selves together, did we?

She stares at the world, at me, not knowing where one ends and the other begins. "How did we get . . . here?" She waves her hand at reality in its last gasp. "Why did it have to choose *you?* It could have . . . we could have been . . . ugh. Maybe wherever I end up, I'll find Aoife, and she'll know."

I shake my head. How can I describe it? It's so clear. Once I smashed vases, snatched a sketchbook, now existence itself lies at my mercy. I always lived with destruction curled in my ribcage and belly, waiting.

"This is what I always was. It didn't *choose me*. I chose it."

The flesh of the sky closes over. The light on her face fades. Something gone, irretrievable.

"Fine," she says, with a hardness I've never heard from her. "Fine. Then I have something for you. Bon fucking appétit, faceless one."

And she opens to me, and makes an offering.

I open to her, and I take it.

I inhale an image of a girl at the edge of the sea, hair newly shorn, unfamiliar clothes loose, staring in playful wonder at a pebble between her fingers. An instant liking of that awkwardness, that love of the world. A sense of stumbling, being unable to get anything right, up against that girl's bold curiosity, willed ignorance and occasional surprising cleverness. Of a throat growing tight at the sight of slender, muscular arms growing tanned, bright eyes flashing with enthusiasm, a jutting hip and a pierced belly button when her t-shirt rides up. Of a giddiness, *Why is she looking at me like that*, of shared laughter like bubbles bursting. Of admiration, *She ran right into the cave for Myri. She's good, isn't she? She's brave.*

Of a desperate urge to reshape herself into something that could fit around this girl's sharp edges. Of finding comfort pressed against an unfamiliar body, of that body growing familiar, of an ecstatic kiss on a beach at the lip of disaster. Of shock at her realization that she'd follow her into darkness, into her own destruction, just for the brilliant way their minds sparked together. Of realizing, *You are my courage.*

And then a *despite. You are you and I am me*, despite. Desperate hope, despite. The taste of her on her lips, despite. A search for comfort in those arms, despite. A cycle: *You're what I fear, and you're my courage; I can't face my fear of you without you to tell me it's okay.*

Kiera takes all she feels for me, the bold, beautiful, clever thing I am in her eyes, and she gives it up irretrievably, and I swallow it whole, and it's gone.

She watches me enjoying it, face steady, and she's harder now, bitter and brave.

"Thanks for that whole resurrection thing, by the way," she adds. It's sarcastic, but sincere, too, like she's saying a thing she has to, to clear it away.

"Finally, she says it," I say drily.

Kiera wasn't here. I'm alone.

The sky spasms with bursts of pleasure. I feel vividly, hungrily alive.

⊖

At the brink, we dance.

Time and space grow a distortion of the groves. Bioluminescence dances. Music echoes, changing, thudding drums, clanging guitars, the ringing of goat bells, askew.

My coils wrap around arms, waists, necks, enjoying sweet, pulsing bodies. But loosely, they're free to move, because at the brink we dance.

The coils hide the sky and sea, which is good. I don't think they want to see what those things look like now.

People are crying anyway.

But at the brink we dance. I remember that giddy night before the ritual. I want them to have that again.

So I tell them, *Dance*. They dance; they want to please me.

There's Frida, arms above her head, hips swinging. She's chosen; now every moment is precious because they're dwindling and what waits after is all she yearns for. There's Aksel, hands on her waist, knowing her moments are dwindling and he isn't following her.

There's Zina and João, dancing a hammed-up samba inside a curl of tendrils. There's Darya turning circles to make the luminescence whirl. There's Maisie in Ana's arms, making a weepy joke about how sixty-eight is too young to be devoured by a god, but they dance as they cry. There's Pietro, staring blankly at his wedding ring as his limbs go through the motions of happiness.

They're grinning. The grins are rictus.

Kai finds Kiera, curled among my coils, whoops, and pulls her up. She screams, animal panic, seeing her murderer lunging at her again. But the Unseen said, *Dance*, so their fight becomes a dance.

They all look to me, again and again: *Are we doing this right?* Trembling, sobbing, fraying, holding to one thing: The Unseen wants us to dance.

And this isn't right; I want a night of bliss and glory, a bittersweet goodbye. So, I reach inside them, to tease out pleasure and calm and euphoria.

And those things flow, in moans and giggles and cheers, but I just paint a veneer over the terror, sending minds spiraling as they struggle to contain things that don't fit together.

João screams as Zina kisses his neck. Darya's lost in the lights, pupils dilated, spinning. Ana and Maisie cackle, poking at my tendrils like they're a cute joke. Kai holds Kiera's flailing limbs, "It's okay, it's me," and she's wild-eyed with panic, dissonant with the honey taste on her tongue. She clutches that fear like it will keep her alive.

Jonah and Teresa dance with their daughter. She tries to push them away, but they tighten their grip. She glares, refusing to cry.

This is all wrong. I'm giving them a *new world*. And all they have is fear and helpless hope that they're doing enough to satisfy me.

It hurts. They're suffering. They're not making me happy at all.

I let it end.

CHAPTER FIFTY

TORN APART

A PERFECT DAWN.

Wisps of cloud reflect the bronze-gold sunrise. Foam bubbles trap light. Mist hangs in hollows. Blossom's peachy.

The island remembers itself, a final pure moment as everything draws its breath.

Through my spreading tendrils, I find quiet perfection, a rich sunset over the Philippines, a swarm of stars over the Atacama Desert, luscious sunshine in the Pamir Mountains. The mindless processes of the universe resume, galaxies coalescing. Reprise.

Nobody's reassured. The precision's eerie. It feels like goodbye.

Here, too, that perfection tells them that it's time.

The quiet is paralysis. They stand bedraggled in broken masks, torn suits, sweat-stained dresses. Eyes don't meet. Nothing will give comfort now.

I quail, too. I'm the end of *everything*.

Then it passes; I smile. I'm equal to this. This reality was made to disappear into me.

They don't try to hide the fear. Tears fall. Lips murmur desperate prayers to the thing about to consume their world. My poor children, they've wandered so far in the dark, and their fate's come to claim them.

They see Aoife, my body returning to itself. I feel like me, breeze on my skin, lemon and honey in my mouth. But just like this sinister peace, my human form reads as a threat. I'm a thing wearing their dead friend's face. However deep the love, the terror's fathomless.

But what's fear except self-preservation? No self, no fear. And they gave over their selves long ago.

They look to Jonah.

He doesn't speak as a prophet, no proclamation of glory. He just says, "It will be all right," with practiced ease, as though he truly believes it.

I feel in the workings of their bodies how that warms them. The irrelevance of their selves suffocates the fear. They'll go to a new world. They'll be butterflies. I'm grateful to him, briefly; he was right, he can give them the comfort I can't.

Jonah says, "Kneel."

They move like music to a conductor. They trust. They kneel.

I look to see if Giulia is refusing to kneel. But no; she's sunlight over the Indian Ocean, a whirl of gases in a nebula, a tasty twitch in my tendons.

Among the living, there's no resistance. Even Myri sinks to her knees. Even Kiera. This end is easy. All they have to do is follow.

Jonah kneels last. "It's time." A tremble of victory and reverence. "If you will give yourself, stand."

My excitement ripples galaxies. Among those tender, beloved bodies, those minds unhinged by stifled terror, are the ones who will surge through me, so soon.

Of course, Frida stands; most zealous, cheeks flushed under the eyes of her god; she's laughing, deranged by love and dread. I feel her heart leap and thunder. Once I teased her about her ring, now; now. She'll be exquisite.

Others stir, made bold.

Aksel stands, a *fuck it* shrug. He looks at Frida, a sad twitch to his smile; she beams. Pietro stands, sigh final. Maisie strokes the sand, then rises. Zina hugs Darya and whispers, "This isn't goodbye; it'll build somewhere beautiful from me, and you can go there," and I shiver thinking how her creativity and poise will taste.

Kiera tenses; pain and desire crack through me, but she stays still.

Myri stands.

Jonah freezes.

Something says, *No*, far away.

Small, fierce, hood thrown back, red hair spilling. How quickly those hollows in her filled, her humanity resurging even as the world disintegrated around her.

It's not submission in her eyes; it's defiance. It's not me she's looking at, it's Jonah.

I drink in his utter despair.

"Glorious, right?" Her lip quirks.

Jonah can't answer. He can't move. He kneels, open-mouthed, silenced by his own story as it prepares to swallow the last person who is still a person to him. He kneels, open-mouthed, as I win.

Myri steps forward, relishing her final rebellion. The other offerings steel themselves and follow, hands intertwined. I burst with love for them and watch them with a god's detached gaze and a god's infinite greed.

Even the breeze stills. A chant spreads: *Adore, Unseen, surrender.* Its resonance stretches something open.

Warm, frightened bodies kneel and brace themselves. Eyes downcast, or taking a last look at the world. The offerings exchange glances and turn to me, a silent agreement to look death in the eye.

They see there how very much I love them.

I speak to them in sunlight and thunder. *"You are so loved, my children. Now, we emerge from our chrysalis."*

The Unseen unfolds luxuriantly, its presence in my body spilling into its presence in the universe, ready to break out of both and break them in the process.

They see me, an echo of a girl at the heart of something indescribable. They see me and grip that chant, each other's hands, looking to their prophet, the hand that shaped them and brought them here. *Just trust, trust, just—*

The offerings cling to each other, sobbing panic and joy.

Myri stares forward. This is what she saw when she screamed. She offered herself as a vessel to stop it. Now she offers herself again, to have one thing on her own terms.

Her lip trembles, but her gaze is steady as my jaws open.

There is no moment except this one. This will be the last one.

Except it isn't; it's lost under a scream.

Jonah staggers forward, mouth open in an animal wail.

He stumbles, unbalanced, eyes wild, scream formless. He runs to Myri but can't form her name.

Robes askew, hair flying, a comically pathetic mockery of Giulia at the ritual.

I pause, maw wide, but taking nothing yet; a deliciously petty part of me wants to watch what will happen.

My followers, too, watch their prophet snap and collapse. He isn't a leader now, not a voice of judgment, not the first offering, not a gaze that pins them. Just a man, flailing and yelling. Just a man reaching for his daughter, refusing to lose her for a final time.

"No"—finally forming words—"Myri, don't—"

What blasphemy.

I feel it in them, the wrench I know, the reality before their eyes and the reality in their minds screeching apart.

A high-pitched laugh echoes. Kiera's cackling, head thrown back.

"Oh, god," she chokes. "You fucking idiot. You killed the world, this is so fucking funny, you wanted to control us so much you killed the damn *world* and we're going to *die*, and you can't even stand up straight." She looks around at all the blank faces. "It's so hilarious."

Others join, confused laughter, cruel laughter. The last threads of their story have snapped and sent them tumbling, and they make noises that might not be laughter at all.

There are things human minds can't process. Some knowledge is forbidden, because it would break us. They say things like me, unknowable, tear minds apart. That's wrong. The things that break us are the ones we know, the people so intimately woven into us that when they fall, we fall.

Jonah slows, realizing what he's done, looking at Myri, and Myri watches in frozen shock as the laughter makes them bold and they descend on him.

It's Teresa first, standing and reaching for her husband.

That strange smile as she comes to him, gentle. That off-key look as she takes his hand, head cocked curiously, and snaps his wrist.

I don't know if she means to. She's swirling down through a dark place. They all are.

Look, he's howling in shocked pain, confidence and wisdom gone. He's nothing, he's a man, look, he can feel.

That's why it's slow, at first, blankly interested people coming to discover the fragility of the man they gave themselves to. To learn that a kick to the stomach can wind him, that a slap makes him flinch, that he'll screech again when his finger snaps. That he's human. Meat. As flawed—breakable—as anyone.

In minds fragmented by terror, that discovery awakens rage.

They don't need drugs or pounding music or a bellyful of rendered corpse. Jonah achieved what he'd wanted, with that. They're stripped down, fragile as butterflies. There's nothing to stop them from kicking and tearing, burying their terror and loss in violence.

Jonah's cries become screams so fast.

They take a lot longer to go quiet.

I feel every rupture, every crack. I ride with him to the brink of death. Feel his despair, his understanding that every manipulation, every rush of power, brought him here, and he's over.

The last thing he's aware of is me smiling inside his every cell.

The wave engulfs Jonah and falls back, and all is still.

I stare down at my prophet. Meat, seeping onto the sand. He will go into me with the rest of his reality, mulch.

The triumph is sublime.

I soak in it. Admire all the clever, reckless ways he's broken.

The quiet is aftermath, reality folding in as minds catch up to what bodies have done.

Kai's screaming at his bloodied hands; Frida sobs; Zina's shaking Darya and shouting, "What did you *do?*" as if her knuckles aren't torn from punching; Ana stares at the jagged fence spike she drove into Jonah's gut, bemused.

Myri kneels on the sand, her father's blood soaking her jeans, pressing her hands against his chest, his spilled-open belly, yelling.

She looks up at me, pleading: *Bring him back.*

I could. Life's easy to play with. I could knit those bones, fill those lungs, mold that brain into the shapes that made him Jonah. Say, *I forgive you.*

I look to Teresa.

Her eyes are clear. Clearer even than before Sage's death. They're bright with violence, but behind that is the sharp mind and fierce love she spent years blunting to please her husband. Her flowered dress is blood-ied. Her smile's broad.

I know that smile. I return it.

No. I will not bring this man back.

I let his remains wisp away. Just molecules. Like with Craig, it astounds me: How did a construction of crude matter have such power over us?

They watch, baffled and distressed. He's gone. They did this, and they're alone beyond the brink.

I don't want them to hurt. I love them so much.

"*Just a man,*" I say in the fading of Jonah's colors. Words they've read in his bones and entrails. "*He served his purpose, brought you to me, our infinite love, our final union.*"

They fall quiet and turn to me, a vast formation of space and color and warped matter, Aoife's shadow at its core, its jaws starting to loom open.

Jonah stood between them and me, smoked glass over the sun. Now they're exposed before me.

They were stripped away, piece by piece, in kind whispers, in violence. They're empty, pinned butterflies. There's nothing left for them, *of* them.

Only me.

I know and they know what they'll do.

Ana throws down the bloodstained spike, Kai wipes his hands, Zina releases Darya's shoulders, Teresa pushes her hair back, indifferent to the blood she's smeared through it. Myri puts her arm around her mother's shoulder. As one, they kneel before my maw.

Take this from us, their movements say, *this us. We gave it away and got it back shattered and we don't know what to do with the pieces. Take those pieces. Make something beautiful.*

Perfect; bittersweet joy. They became my family, now they'll bloat my power. All those universes in their skulls and skins will flare inside me, fuel and spark.

This is what we're here for. We understand now.

Only one person holds back. Only one will persist and see what comes after.

The seed of my new world's pressed against an olive tree, throat too tight to pray, manic laughter extinguished. She can't look. The seed of my new world is fear, fear that says, *Let something of me survive.* Yes. I knew Kiera was worthy.

The others reach for each other, fingers twining, final kisses on bloodied faces, gore-smeared fingers wiping tears. Whispers.

They're killers, hollowed out and at their ends. But before, those gestures and murmurs were Jonah's, part of the world he wove. Now, they're their own.

I feel the life in them, electricity fizzing in their cells, the spiral, fractal brilliance of their minds, the utter fucking miracle that atoms came together to make this. That hideous appetite peaks, and I cannot resist.

Existence trembles before me, recognizing its end.

This excitement is familiar; I felt it in an airport, once. Leaving behind everything, heading into a new world.

I open wide. A rip, jaws dripping raw desire. A doorway to where the old reality will digest and the new one gestate.

They stare into that place and quiver and adore me ever more deeply. Look at those faces. I recognize that expression.

I can't remember what the fight was about.

It was Craig; we always fought. I said we had one of those fiery relationships where we argued for the sweetness of making up. Yes, he started those fights, but I provoked him. I was high-maintenance. Dramatic. Messy.

The kitchen, Craig in my face shouting, my cheeks flushed. Back then, I fought back. Things got broken. I'd sweep away the remnants.

But this time it was too much, and I crumpled next to the shards and cried. And Craig crouched and stroked my hair. "Oh, hey. Are you seriously upset? Oh, love. Come on."

I felt so safe, under his hands and lips. I cried, and he smoothed away the pain he'd created. Softening me to shape me, wet clay ready to mold in his fingers.

Reflected in a darkened window, I saw the look on my face.

The look I see again on the sacrifices below me. Jonah succeeded, or I did; they're butterflies.

Seeing that look, suddenly, I know: I refuse to be him. I won't be either of them.

There's no time to think.

I turn inward, toward that tear in reality, that throat stretching to engulf a universe. I gather all that's Aoife, and I gather the Unseen in me, and like a snake swallowing its tail I disappear inside.

CHAPTER FIFTY-ONE

BEYOND THE BEGINNING AND END

ALL MOMENTS EXIST ALL AT ONCE, BUNCHED UP AND FOREVER.

All moments exist all at once, and beyond the beginning and end, I see them all.

An infinity of them, wrapped around each other, existence warped around itself, and beyond it the howling, writhing void and the indescribable energies that swirl there, catching me in their gale.

I am a scrap of consciousness out of time and place, tumbling end-over-end through tempests huger than universes, clinging to that coil of moments that is our reality, but wrenched out of it.

All moments exist at once. Somewhere in there is the birth of a universe, and the death of that universe, in slow entropy or a vicious blast or an enfolding throat.

All moments exist at once. It's too much for me to begin to perceive, even as this, even beyond. I'm drawn instead to a smaller scale, one I can half-comprehend, peering into the reality I have been exiled from.

Before and after are incoherent. I see Sage kissing Elise, Oscar buying Larissa drinks in a beach bar, a young Teresa smiling shyly at a charismatic, bearded man at an office party, Jonah attaching locks to a newly built cabin. I see Aoife, waiting outside a station for Craig, whispering, "I'm running away with him," devastated by the romance of it. I see Kiera dressing carefully to hide her scars for her first day of classes. I taste those places, feel breeze and wood splinters and rain. Pressed against me, beyond my reach.

Future is a hazy concept. But I glimpse what comes after what Aoife did. I see what it looks like when that coil of moments becomes twisted, cracked at the edges.

A world fractured. Cities folded over themselves, towns in time loops, farmland rent with gaps in reality, the people that fall into them.

The survivors call what I did "the cataclysm." Like Kiera said, disaster always befell whatever stood in that cave; but those were mere flickers before the great eruption.

I see Ana pulling vegetables that melt into water. João skipping stones on a calm sea under hurricane clouds. Myri with an improvised radio, hearing screams in the static.

Teresa and Pietro sit by a fire flaring turquoise, among radioactive flowers. Frida and Kai swim in an ocean alive with planets and comets, solar winds stroking their bare legs. Kiera looks down through the floor at the stars and spills salt in glyphs there, screaming, "Come back! You come back and *fix it!*"

Aksel opens the kitchen door and tumbles into a void. Vines sprout from Maisie's skin and unmake her. Zina shrieks as Darya crystalizes abruptly into shards, translucent as sugar, and scatters.

I see before and after pressed against each other like living, feral things, whispering to each other, forming intricate structures, cycling and spiraling, a pattern I can't fully read.

Still, I see a story.

Once there was a god in a cave, bound by nightmares.

It sent whispers into the world. People came to know it. Monks worshipped it in secret. Locals warned against it, but the most desperate turned to it for aid.

Once a god sought to escape. It awoke a dead girl and moved in her. It bid her father to bring it offerings, and he warped into something cruel.

Through chance, through a playful theft, it came to a bored, sad girl behind a bar. It lured her with honey in her mouth and sun on her skin. And when disaster ruptured its plans, she was there, and she opened a door and let it into her body, and her rage awoke it. It wore her skin and mind and made her monstrous, and through her it drew its worshippers to the brink. But in the last moment she resisted.

This is the story we told ourselves.

Now I see it laid out before me and understand that it was a lie.

Instead, I see a cave. Inside the cave I see a thinning of reality's skin, a rip where power and energy from outside that endless coil of moments seeped in and began to work away at the fabric of things.

I see people over centuries witnessing those distortions, and seeking as people do to explain them with stories. Why did the sea seethe with visions of horror? Why was the earth so bountiful; why could the dead walk alive through those rocky passageways or be transmuted into something darker and odder? What gripped minds with incomprehensible urges; what sucked the emotions and sensations from their bodies?

A god, of course. It had to be the work of a god.

They dreamed it to be one, so it became one.

We molded that seeping energy into something we called divine. And I took it into my body and let it swell there, and never thought to truly wonder why the supposed god in my skin never spoke to me, appeared only as power and shapeless urges.

I see a mutated, hungering Aoife, moving through her reality as it degrades, feeding, yearning for more, destruction in her fingertips. She was not shaped by the god inside her; *she* shaped *it*.

Those urges did not belong to that dreamed-up, half-formed god. Those urges belonged to me.

My rage fractured reality. My greed for love consumed my friends. I looked at the world that stifled me, and I and only I decided to smash and devour it.

It was a god because we let it be. It was a cataclysm because I made it one.

And it is done now. I see it all laid out before me, a crystalized artwork, a billion stories settled into inevitable shapes, a billion threads all ending with me, and those few that continue frayed and shredded. It is finished.

The story is just this: disdainful hands shaped a girl into something as crude and cruel as they, she molded her god into the form they made her, and a universe paid the price.

Fuck that.

That will not be what this story is.

Because you know what? *No.*

My rage takes a new form, hard and bright and brilliant and all mine: refusal.

Fuck gods, and leaders and prophets and guides, fuck inevitability, fuck every rule of reality, fuck the laws of physics, fuck everything that made me small, fuck what being small made me, fuck the consequences, fuck anyone who thought they could own or mold anyone else, fuck the thing that Craig and Jonah made me. They do not get to set the shape of all those moments. *I still get to choose.*

I tear my way back in.

And as I do, that eternity of moments shatters into infinite shards of possibility.

CHAPTER FIFTY-TWO

HOME

OXYGEN, LIGHT, SOUND, FLESH, COLORS. THEY OVERWHELM.

Pink, beige, gray, and nauseous green swirl; sound waves swell. The colors form a person. The sounds form a voice, saying, "Gin and tonic and a white wine, please."

The man has a shapeless office jacket, arm around a woman with a pinstriped shirt and perm and a face that says, *Help me.* It's coalescing as I tighten my grip on this moment, body, universe. Sticky tiles, windows open to a spring street, traffic, cement. Around the corner, there's the river, with swans. Men in suits are downing pints, imagining what's under my shirt.

It's gross. It's real.

Look. I did it. Back to when the world was unblemished. A little grub, crawling out of its chrysalis, to before any of this happened.

The customer waves in my face. "Away with the fairies, love?"

It takes a second to remember how to move, three dimensions, time moving in one direction, neurons and tendons and bones oh my, but here I am, laughing.

I say, "Not exactly fairies," and laugh so long it hurts. I moved between universes, through time and space, to a bar in a soulless town, where I cackle as two customers back away.

I toss my hair. My long hair. I didn't cut it off yet. I didn't do any of it yet.

"You know what?" I open the fridge. Cool condensation. Sensations, life. I came back. "White wine. Whole bottle. On the house. Bye!"

I touch the woman's wrist, the subtlest brush, as I hand the bottle over. I'm still laughing at their blank faces as I rip off my apron and walk out into the sun.

⊙

Home, ha; this place was never that. Cramped, lit by watery sun through grimy windows. I hate it. The hate's delicious: It's real.

I keep touching everything, wondering at solidity.

The instants and centuries beyond our reality are fading, my mind unable to hold them. They happened; they never happened. Too many paradoxes. I won't try.

Later, memories will snatch me into sleeplessness and screams, but those will be memories of this universe. They will be a haunting. The scale of other realities is nothing next to the nightmares we inflicted on each other.

That face in the mirror, that's mine, Aoife's.

The cushions puff dust when I flump onto the sofa. I crack open my battered laptop, inherited from Craig after I bought him a new one (he needed it for his music). It whirs, and in the spaces for glitches I try to readjust. Every sensation's a crescendo.

I search online for names; Oscar Morrow. Jonah Nathaniel. Sage Nathaniel. Kiera LaRoux. Larissa Quinn. Giulia Rossi.

An abandoned LinkedIn page, latest position "seeking the unknown." An old interview in a financial magazine. More recent things: Oscar updated our social media for us during his village runs, to avoid awkward questions. I remember thinking that was normal.

A YouTube channel with a single video, "Survival With Sage," foraging in the hills, Elise laughing behind the camera. A Twitter account where the only activity's an argument about translation of some runes. An Instagram account updated yesterday with a selfie in a beachside bar, a little misdirection. A Facebook post: "My beautiful off-grid life continues! I will be back to visit soon, missing you all."

I curl over to protect the frazzled keyboard from the tears. They're alive. This is their world before I crashed into it.

Right now, Giulia and Larissa are kissing on the beach. Sage and Elise are helping Teresa in the kitchen, grinning over mugs of tea. Kiera's in the library, massaging her temples between bursts of typing. People are working the fields and sunning themselves. Lives untouched by the hurricane that was me.

Maybe I should leave them alone.

But no. Right now, Myri's locked in her cabin, dreaming; right now, they're under Oscar's watchful eyes, following Jonah toward a brink.

Time for a reckoning.

I'm singing softly, one of Teresa's songs. This time I'll do it right.

The flight confirmation email's just pinged when I hear a key in the lock. Instinct tightens my muscles; I cast around, heart leaping, for anything he might seize on. Mess, an unfinished drawing, a snack wrapper. *Couldn't clean up? Wasting your time on this shit? Want to get fat?*

Then I relax. I'm so happy he's home.

"The fuck are you doing here?" Craig dumps a bag of beers and crisps. "Aren't you working?"

I grin; there he is. That face I searched for depths and meaning. Messy hair, eyes that jump from cruelty to kindness so fast. I love him so much.

"I quit," I say cheerfully.

Craig freezes. Fury rises in the twitch of his jaw. Behind it, I recognize the anticipation of breaking something.

"I have a wonderful surprise for you." My smile stretches wide.

Wider.

Craig stares, brain refusing what his eyes see. He steps back.

As if it matters.

"It's okay." The curtains ripple. "You know I love you exactly like you love me."

It doesn't take long. I luxuriate for a while after, then pack, body singing with contentment.

I cut off my hair at 3:00 a.m. in an airport bathroom.

What's in the mirror looks like a person. Pale, skinny, with flower tattoos spilling over my shoulders. I don't look like someone who hesitates.

Fluorescent light flickers off the blades. I snip off my plait.

It coils into the sink and sits there, hairs unspooling like worms. I cut, and I keep cutting, and what's left is messy and incoherent and bright at the edges and all me.

I'm gathering the offcuts in my hands when the door opens. "You all right?"

The same woman as before. Well. Before. The same woman who I met in a reality that will never have happened and has always happened. Cleaning uniform, too much mascara, look of concern.

"Oh, you know." I give her a big, bright grin. "I just broke reality and I'm trying to make a new one. You know how it is." My laugh comes out all frayed and untethered.

The cleaner reaches for her walkie-talkie, face flat, then pauses. Sketched-on eyebrows draw down. "Have we met?"

The light thrums. Cracks, thin as filaments, spread across the mirrors, then heal. I grab her hand. "Probably! Somewhere!"

She doesn't pull away. She stares, baffled and wondering, as the stuff of a reality outside ours spills out of my skin and into hers, and swells there.

She sees the shape of my grin, and doesn't pull away, but doesn't dare to trust either. Good girl.

I wink at her, then gather up the remnants of myself from the sink and dump them in the nearest bin, and walk toward the departure gates.

The city's laid out, all pastel and gold and palm shadows, mine to explore. I walk through the streets as a harbinger, smiling broadly at everyone, fresh-cropped hair itching on my neck. I snack on local food, though it'll be days before I'm hungry after my last meal. I drink wine, watch stars through smog, dance with strangers.

Perhaps they see how the lights brighten around me, colors oversaturated. How stars multiply, waves swell, trees dance. How matter learns to be moved by fear and wonder.

I touch hands, wrists; I leave traces on empty wine glasses; I pass little gifts in eye contact. Spreading a strange virus, a secret benediction.

At dawn, I set out.

The rising sun hovers as the ferry powers out into the ocean. I sit alone on the deck, just me and a sky a thousand miles too wide. That sky knows me. The heaving sea knows me. They know I returned from another place and brought something with me.

Maybe my being here, half girl and half something more, will inscribe horrors on the future. I'm not the broken hungry god-thing I was, but I'm not anything *right*, either. I don't see the end. Or I saw it, fractured into infinite possible forms.

But under the olive trees of the path into the village, I couldn't care less.

I stir the scent of grass and pine. Everything caught in my well of gravity.

I pause at a turning to a rocky path. Through vineyards and forest, along cliffs, to groves and a farmhouse and a place where reality's skin is thin, where human imaginations placed a god.

I've returned to show them they do not need that god. Or its priest.

The stuff of the realm beyond reality churns under my skin. Inexhaustible, ready to slip into a kiss, a tea, a whisper, a pastry, a touch on the wrist. A glorious infection to spread from body to body, slide down throats and take root. Not enough to rend reality, but enough to bend and shape it.

They will not need that god, because I will make us all gods.

I run my tongue over my teeth. Jonah and so many like him are about to learn what real power looks like. Who knows? Maybe we'll spare them.

Breeze whispers, scented with honey and lemon.

I loop my hands through my bag straps, and turn onto the path.

ACKNOWLEDGMENTS

Books, luckily, don't happen on their own, and despite all the hours sitting alone at a keyboard, writing this one has been one of the biggest exercises in finding a community that I've ever had the luck to experience. So there are a ton of thanks to give, and probably a ton that won't even make it in here; if you so much as knew me in the past five years, you share some responsibility for this monstrosity. Sorry.

First up, this book wouldn't exist without hours down rabbit holes about cults. One thing that stayed under my skin is that they don't really look like the Farmstead anymore; you're maybe more likely to find them on a hashtag than on a remote island; but the urge to be part of a community and something that feels meaningful is probably more relevant now than ever. That aside, to the journalists and academics and, above all, the survivors who have unearthed and analyzed the history and psychology of these groups, endless gratitude.

The island, and indeed the country, where Aoife's story takes place is fully invented. However, most of the natural and architectural (and food!) aspects of the setting are drawn from places I've traveled and worked, and I owe a huge debt to the people in those places who let me into their worlds. I hope I was at least a half-decent guest and didn't accidentally leave any hideous old gods wandering around your towns.

The writing process, meanwhile—that's what I'm talking about when I say finding a community, because I have been stunned by the power of the friendships I've found while working on this book. I think the secret to making a book happen is to have a constellation of writing groups with names of varying absurdity levels, and the Wenches, the Wine Wraiths, the Goattes, the Islanders, and the Bob Mob got me through this with a thousand evenings of sprinting and snippet-sharing and hand-holding through querying and sub. Special thanks go to regular shrimp allies, critique partners, and beta readers: SJ, Charlotte, Sarah, Steph, Brooke, Melody, CJ, Hailey, Shannon, Leta, Amalie, Megan, Chloe, Julie, Therese, Gina, the other CJ, Anei, Goob, Nathalie, Makana, MR, Laura, Michelle, Mel, Ezra, Abby, and anyone else who's taken the time to read my words, prop up my ego, and call me out on my bullshit. I'm seeing some of you absolutely soar with your writing, and I know it's coming for the rest of you too.

That was what got me through writing and querying—what got me through the next part was having an absolute rock star of an agent. I would trust Lauren to wrestle a bear for me (although I promise I'd never ask her to), and I am incredibly lucky to have her wits and determination and patience and humor on my side. I owe thanks too to the many agents who rejected me but took the time to give me the feedback that shaped this book into its final form. But most of all to Lauren, for taking a chance on me.

The other person I've been wildly blessed to have in my corner is my hero editor, Alexandra, whose passion for this book made me believe in it again too, and who has helped whip it into shape while giving me freedom to be ridiculous. Her vision and imagination and willingness to say *but what if* have been a huge source of inspiration. Page Street has been the perfect home for this book, and everyone there has been brilliant to work with.

For my book's design, incredible thanks to Rosie G. Stewart, and to Peter Strain, the absolute dream cover artist. My copyeditor, Olivia, is a total star and our working on this together is a wonderful coincidence. Thank you all for all your work to unleash this on the world!

I suppose there are also real people I know in the world . . . thanks to my parents for incubating my love of reading and writing while also banning me from horror as a child, allowing me to do what I love and annoy them at the same time. My mum's always been my first critique partner, and I know how lucky I am in that (sorry for all the blood and the occasional naked bits, Mum; I'll write a lighthearted comedy some time, I promise).

I've written this book over the course of five years of bouncing between homes in London and abroad, and a lot of people have put up with my chaos in the process. To Nathan, Sky, Maria, J, Ellen, Kay, Sophie, Elliot, the Sydney Road lockdown chaos housemates, and anyone else who's shared a roof with me; to Alex (and Craig, Wini, and Monty), Jen, Cemre, Simge (and Lily Su), Courtney (and Jon and Ada, and Bonnie and Pablo of course), Mathilde, Quinn and Ezra, Trevor, Charlotte, Daniel, and others who have given me places to stay when I've needed to run away and type madly; and to Tom, Marek and Marx, Cat, Bernard, David, Raisah, Sharona, Liam, the other Jen, Hunter, Darran, Lorenzo, and all the other friends who've listened to me rot about this project or offered me escape and support, a million thanks.

And finally, this book was fueled 90 percent by caffeine, so to countless cafe employees and providers of coffee, a million thanks to you too.

ABOUT THE AUTHOR

As a teenager, Hester Steel got a crush and responded by dropping out of school and flying to the other side of the world. She's managed to finish school by now, and even stayed in one place long enough to get a master's in global sociology, but she's still notorious for making unwise life choices and being in unlikely places. She's currently based in London, where she works as a magazine subeditor, tries to remember to go swimming regularly, and often pretends to be a gnome for fun. She has never summoned an eldritch god, but has tried on several occasions.